A FALLEN SON

A.P. WATSON

A FALLEN SON

THE *CONCILIUM* SERIES

A.P. WATSON

A FALLEN SON

THE *CONCILIUM* SERIES

A. P. WATSON

A Fallen Son

Ebook ISBN: 978-0-9888019-5-0
Paperback ISBN: 978-0-9888019-6-7

Edited by Tamara Beard of Wrapped Up Writing
Proofread by Judy Zwiefel of Judy's Proofreading
Cover design and photography by Regina Wamba
Formatted by A.P. Watson

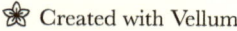

For Tiffany,

Because you were cheering for me to write this series when no one else knew it existed.

PROLOGUE

Tears dripped from my chin as Aden dragged me away from the abandoned warehouse where Conrad's body lay, growing colder by the second. Life as I knew it had come to an end. The last of my sworn protectors had fallen, and I was in the clutches of a man whose depravity had no bounds. What did fate have in store for me now?

Watching the man I love die for a second time shattered the remnants of my heart. Aden had murdered my entire family in cold blood, all for the sake of reclaiming his hold on me. The fleeting freedom I'd enjoyed for the last few centuries had been snuffed out as if it were no more than a flickering flame. As hard as I've tried to outrun my past, the task has proved impossible. I took my first breaths in the Garden of Eden, and as the original woman, perhaps my destiny will always be intertwined with the man I was created for.

Adam and Eve.

Aden and Evey.

No matter what names we use, the sins of our past remain. My hand in the Fall of Man gave birth to Aden's vile nature. The Tree of Knowledge blessed us with the wisdom of both good and evil, and even though I have strived to live in the light, my former husband has descended into the depths of darkness.

I

LOST

Throwing off the covers, I scooted away from Aden until my hands found the edge of the mattress. There was nowhere else to go, but I yearned for escape. As I pulled myself farther away from him, I fell to the ground, my arm thrashing against a small table. Fear overwhelmed my senses, coursing through my veins like a jolt of electricity. How could I be here? Why were the eyes boring into mine darker than the deepest abyss? Aden rounded the bed and made his way toward me, his expression unreadable. Panic consumed my thoughts and my body trembled uncontrollably in response.

The last time I rejected this man, he sent me to an early grave. Now, he stood before me and claimed he needed me back, but in order to accomplish his goals, he had stolen away the ones I loved most. My instincts told me not to believe his lies as he was no doubt hungry for more carnage. I knew the depths of love and this twisted version wasn't even close to the word.

As he advanced toward me, I scrambled across the cold wooden floor. I was nothing more than a caged animal. When Aden bent down in front of me, I fought the urge to scream. My eyes clasped shut. The thought of staring into his dark gaze sickened me. The moment he grabbed my wrist, a shudder slithered down my spine. His touch was like ice, stinging my skin with the pressure of his fingers.

"If you're going to kill me, just get it over with," I spat defiantly. Fighting against my instincts, I opened my eyes and watched as his hand jerked away.

"I'm not going to hurt you," he whispered. Pain harshened the lines of his face. "You're bleeding." He pointed at my arm that had bashed against the table. A small drop of blood trickled over the inside of my wrist. Taking my hand in his, he delicately kissed the spot where I'd been cut, cleaning the blood away with the bottom of his shirt. He then picked me up in his arms and set me on the bed, handling me like I was a crystal vase and the slightest disturbance would cause me to burst into a million tiny shards of glass. As Aden sat at the end of the bed, all I could do was stare at him in bewilderment. "There's no need for you to be afraid of me," he reassured me in a soft voice.

His gentle answer fueled my anger. "Isn't there?" I questioned, not even attempting to suppress the malice in my tone. "You murdered everyone I care for." I knew my eyes were filled with all the venom I felt in my heart. I didn't care if my salvation lay in his love for me. The life he offered wasn't worth the price.

"I did what I had to do in order to have you in my life again."

Confusion began to replace my anger. I was sure he wanted me to suffer. The only reason he'd been so eager to find me was to hurt me again. Why was he being so gentle, tender even? "I don't understand. I thought you hated me."

"I've tried to hate you so many times, and no matter what I do, I'm incapable of harboring even a minute shred of ill will toward you."

"So, you aren't going to kill me?" I understood the influence I had over people, how they were innately drawn to me, but his sincerity seemed unfathomable considering the depths of his cruelty I'd experienced firsthand.

4

"In this moment, all I want is to hold you and know that you're mine, just like we were always meant to be since the beginning of time."

2

REVIVAL

I sucked in a deep breath of air that burned my lungs like acid. Every part of my body ached, my muscles serving as a frank reminder that I was alive.

"Evey," I croaked. I tried to sit up, but a hand on my shoulder kept me down. It pressed me into the cold ground. My eyes opened slowly. Light flooded into view from all around me, stinging my eyes. Muffled voices were just discernible through the incessant ringing presiding over my ears. "Evey?" I repeated.

"Oh, thank God! Conrad, can you hear me?" Disappointment consumed the coherent part of my brain as I realized the voice didn't belong to Evey, but to her best friend. "Conrad, it's Caroline. Can you hear me?"

After another minute, the scene around me came into focus. "Yeah, I hear you." Caroline and Noah hovered over me, and while the expression on Caroline's face was frantic, Noah's was downright livid. Black sludge from the bodies of dead souls coated the ground, mixing with the crimson rivers left by fallen secundae. The memories of the events in the abandoned warehouse suddenly dawned on me. "Wait, how am I back? Evey—"

"She wasn't killed," Caroline answered in a soft voice. "But Aden has her."

Shit. I knew he would take her the moment I drew my last breath, but I didn't want to accept that she was now in the possession of that sick bastard. "How long have they been gone?" Hatred swelled just beneath the surface of my skin, devouring my consciousness from the inside out.

"You need to rest for a bit," she answered, trying her best to soothe me.

"I'll never be able to rest as long as he has her," I seethed. By sheer will, I managed to push myself up from the floor. "How did I let this happen?" Grabbing a piece of scrap wood, I hurled it across the room. The wood crashed into a concrete post, splintering upon impact.

Caroline approached me with caution. "This isn't your fault."

"I was supposed to protect her." My legs trembled beneath my weight. I had to get Evey back at any cost. I wouldn't lose her to Aden's wrath again.

"You did protect her," Noah said. "There was no way to know Aden would have an army of souls waiting for us in the middle of the city."

"We have to find her. We have to hunt him down." If Aden had Evey, I had to get to her as soon as possible. I wouldn't allow history to repeat itself. My legs shuddered uncontrollably. Coming back from the dead always took a toll on my body. Noah was at my side before I could crash back into the cement. He flung my arm around his neck to support my body with his.

"You need to rest," Caroline whispered with a shaky voice. "You . . . Conrad, you were . . ."

"Dead?" I looked at her as I uttered the word she couldn't. The rims of her eyes were red—it was obvious she'd been crying. "It wouldn't be the first time," I joked. I was trying to comfort her, but instead, I only made things worse.

She scowled at me. "That isn't funny!"

"You're right. I'm sorry." Moving to my free side, she wrapped her arm around my back to help Noah hold me upright. The three of us gradually shuffled to the steps that led to a landing above us. I set my hands on either rail, bracing myself as I collapsed on the bottom stair. The aged wood bent beneath my weight. A dim haze covered the room. The main source of light filtered in from an outdoor lamppost through the thick plastic sheeting that covered the windows. Death hung in the air, filling up my lungs as I sucked in another deep breath. I was exhausted just from walking to the stairs. Noah and Caroline stood a few feet from one another. A cold chill lingered between the two of them. "If she isn't dead, then why am I breathing?" I glanced at Noah, expecting an answer, but it was Caroline who spoke first.

"I made him bring you back," she answered, staring at the floor.

"But why?" My gaze fixed on Noah as I prayed he wasn't that much of an idiot. "Noah, you know I can't be brought back without the Concilium's approval. It's forbidden."

"Oh, screw them and their rules. You're the only person who can save Evey and you know it. Noah agrees with me. But he won't say so because he's still mad I knocked him out during all the fighting and hid him in the closet."

"You did what?" Her revelation stunned me. However, Caroline simply threw her blonde hair over her shoulder in triumph.

"What she did was keep me from helping everyone. I could've saved you, Milton, and Marie. I could have kept you from dying," Noah yelled.

"Aden would have taken you and would probably be eating your heart as we speak," she spat back at him. "I'm sorry, but I wasn't about to let that happen."

He glared at her. "You don't get to make those decisions. You aren't a secundae or consiliarius."

I could tell by her expression that his words stung. "Noah, she was right to do it. She prevented Aden from getting a consiliarius and she made you bring me back. That's something I won't argue with."

"I only did it to keep you from getting hurt," Caroline whispered.

"I know," Noah responded, though he still refused to meet her gaze.

To my right, a dirty tarp covered a mound on the floor. "Is that Milton?"

"Yeah. Aden took Evey and Helen with him. Marie is over there." Noah pointed to the other side of the room where a soiled sheet had been placed over her body. A red puddle soaked through the light cloth and stained the concrete floor around it. The empty warehouse had been transformed into a graveyard within a matter of hours.

"May they wait in peace until they can be returned to this earth," I whispered. I should've beaten Aden. I'd done it before; I was the better fighter. And yet, he wasn't the one left bleeding out on the floor. Shame seeped into the marrow of my bones as I realized I wasn't able to protect Evey again. I was her only secundae left, and when she needed me more than ever, I failed.

"You mean you won't be bringing either of them back?" Caroline asked.

"No," Noah replied. "We can't bring them back, Caroline. I could be stripped of my powers just for bringing Conrad back before the appointed time."

"Why can't you? Who makes these rules?"

"The laws were passed down from God to Thea and then to the rest of the Concilium. We can't just bring people back whenever we feel like it. There are rules about that sort of thing for a reason," Noah explained in an irritated tone. "God created these laws to keep us from abusing our powers. If we went around raising the dead at will, there would be serious repercussions."

"I may not be a consiliarius or a secundae, but I don't think God would want Aden to rip out your heart and fry it up for dinner like Hannibal Lecter."

"She does have a point," I said.

"I still could've done something," he said.

"You did," I stated. "I'm back, aren't I? Plus, now, I have the opportunity to track Aden down again and dispose of him . . . violently." While I suspected Aden wouldn't kill her, I couldn't shake the feeling he had a reason other than obsession for taking Evey. He had been a king for longer than I'd been alive, and during his reign, he'd engaged in countless wars, winning several of them. He was an expert in the art of strategy and a formidable opponent.

"Well, I'll help you," Caroline announced. "You can have Aden and I'll take Donovan. He's the one that lured all of us here by dragging Marie around like a rag doll. Someone needs to wipe that damn smirk from his ugly face."

"I hope the two of you aren't planning on doing this without me," Noah said with annoyance.

Taking the hand he offered, I pulled myself up. "Wouldn't dream of it."

"What do we do with the bodies?" Caroline stepped in Noah's direction, her hands rubbing her arms in an attempt to instill some warmth in them.

"We take them with us for now," he answered as he placed his suit jacket on her shoulders. "We'll bury them somewhere close to Everest's home. We have to make sure we can get back to their bodies when it's time for them to be reborn."

"Do you always have to be next to the body when you bring it back?"

"When we bring back the secundae, we reanimate their bodies. They aren't reborn as children like the primums. Instead, we heal their bodies and return their souls to them."

"This is all so much to take in, it almost feels like my head is spinning," she replied.

I nodded, understanding exactly how she felt. "Eventually, it gets easier to absorb."

We left the warehouse and the desecrated scene within it behind us. The air was cool, chilling our bones as we made our way down the empty street toward the caput's apartment. The three of us only passed one other person as we walked; the majority of the city's inhabitants were locked within the safety of their homes and resting in the warmth of their beds. Here and there, a single window would glow with light, but for the most part, we encountered no signs of life.

"What are we going to tell Everest?" Caroline was the first to speak, breaking the silence that hovered around us like a cloud of thick smoke. "Since he's the head of the Concilium, will he know you brought Conrad back?"

"No, we'll tell him about everything else that happened, but he can't know Conrad died. Also, the only way Everest would be able to tell I brought Conrad back is by examining his chest. When a consiliarius heals another, their handprint is left on that person's body for a couple of hours after the revival."

"So, Conrad has a handprint on his chest?" Tugging my shirt to the side, I showed her the red handprint embedded into my skin. "This is insanity," she whispered, her eyes widening.

"Noah, you should probably be the one to explain what happened," I added. "Otherwise, Everest will kill me and you'll have to revive me a second time."

"Leave it to me," he replied.

"We'll get her back, right?" Despite the darkness surrounding us, the tears streaking Caroline's cheeks were still visible. She wasn't as accustomed to loss as we were. Death wasn't something you could grow accustomed to, but it was an inevitable part of life as a secundae. The knowledge one could be brought back only lessened the blow of losing the people you loved most—it never eliminated it.

Nothing could eliminate it.

"I swear to you, as long as I'm breathing, I'll never stop looking for her." I took Caroline's hand in mine and gave it a reassuring squeeze.

"Good," she said.

We reached the garage of Everest's apartment building within a matter of minutes and climbed into the black SUV. The only signs of color in the otherwise white and gray garage were from the parked cars and the yellow paint marking the parking spaces. Like everything else in the surrounding area, it was vacant. Pulling out of the garage, we navigated the streets in the direction of the abandoned warehouse. Noah backed the car up to the door we had entered through and then we wrapped Milton's body before sliding it into the trunk. Marie followed behind him. My heart filled with guilt as I felt the weight of her lifeless form in my arms. These were people I cared about, people I'd known for centuries, but I was loading their corpses into the car as if they were nothing more than luggage. We'd spent so many years fighting side by side in order to protect Evey. I should have been with Marie, Milton, Guy, Mickey, and Kit right now. I failed them and the person I loved the most. Truthfully, I didn't deserve to be alive, but there was no way I was going to waste this chance. One day soon, I'd look down on Aden's lifeless corpse and smile.

One day soon, I'd tear him limb from limb again.

It took nearly an hour for the three of us to clean up the remnants of our battle against Aden. Even in New York City, we couldn't just leave puddles of blood in an empty warehouse. The vastness of this metropolis may add a layer of anonymity, but advancements in science and technology forced us to become more adept at covering our tracks. Discarding the rags saturated with blood and grime, we watched in silence as they burned to ash. Any evidence linking us to this place was now up in smoke.

My shoes seemed like they were made of lead as we finally rode the elevator back up to the caput's apartment. We were all past the point of exhaustion, but more work needed to be done to lay Milton and Marie to rest. I was already pissed off, and I had no doubts that the ass chewing I was going to receive from Everest would send me over the edge. My attention dropped to the hole in my shirt where Aden's blade had sliced through my flesh. The faint outline of Noah's handprint was still visible on my chest. I buttoned my jacket to hide the evidence of my death and Noah's subsequent help. I closed my eyes to collect myself, but every time I did so since waking up, I felt the sharp point of Aden's knife as it carved through muscle and bone. Pain overwhelmed my senses. Balling my hands into tight fists, I tried to steady a slight tremor. The pain quickly dissipated and was replaced with anxiety as Everest flung the door open before Noah even had a chance to knock. He stood in the doorway, his eyes drilling through the three of us.

"Where the hell have all of you been? I turn around for ten seconds and the six of you disappear without a trace." He didn't yell, but it wasn't difficult to pick up on the edge in his voice.

"Well, do you want us to tell you out here or can we come in and sit down?" I didn't care if he was the caput or not; after everything that happened tonight, I was past pleasantries.

"Where is Evey?" In an instant, his irritated tone was saturated with terror.

I exhaled slowly. Recounting my failure as a secundae was the last thing I wanted to do this evening.

"Aden has her," Noah answered.

His hands gripped the doorway with so much force his knuckles blanched. "Conrad, you let him get her?" he asked, his voice dripping with rage. "You let that monster take her away from us again?"

"I did everything I could to protect her!" I spat.

"Forgive me if I find that hard to believe since she always seems to be kidnapped or killed on your watch!" For a fleeting moment, I wished my heart wasn't still beating.

"I know better than anyone what my duties are. Don't forget who you sent to take care of him after he poisoned her in France," I shouted. I glared at him, daring him to speak against me. Blood boiled beneath the flesh of my face. I closed my eyes in an attempt to calm myself. If I allowed my temper to flare out of control, the result would be devastating for everyone. "Aden used Marie to lure us away from your party to an abandoned building a few blocks up the street. When we got there, we were ambushed by a swarm of souls."

The color faded from Everest's cheeks. "I want all of you inside. Now!" We stepped through the threshold of the apartment. The tables and chairs from earlier were gone, replaced by the normal furnishings from the day before. Caroline, Noah, and I all sat side by side on the couch as Everest occupied the chair across from us. Tension coiled in the slope of his shoulders, and he clasped his hands together. "Start at the beginning, Noah," he ordered.

"Donovan and Marie were here at your fundraiser. He played against Evey's emotions and used Marie to trick her to leave the safety of the apartment," Noah explained.

"Why didn't you call for help? Terrick, Warrin, and I were here. Our presence could've ensured victory over Aden." His words were spoken through clenched teeth, and even though Noah was doing the majority of the talking, Everest's steel gray gaze was fixated on me. He despised me as much as I did him. He'd never forgive me for being the reason Aden killed Evey all those years ago. But in all honesty, I couldn't blame him.

Probably because I've never managed to forgive myself.

"We had five people to protect her, and we thought it would be as simple as defeating Donovan and rescuing Marie. None of us expected there to be so many souls," Noah answered.

Everest cradled his head in his hands. "I can't believe this is happening again."

"Helen was the one who led Aden here," Caroline piped up. "She'd been feeding him information about Evey's location. He would've gotten her again no matter what steps we took to prevent it."

Shock dominated the features of Everest's face. "She did? But why?"

"Aden promised her no harm would come to Conrad if she could lead him to Evey," she answered.

"You!" In a flash, he was standing over me, breathing down my neck. "You will be the death of her again!"

My fists balled as I stood to meet his glare. "If you think for one second that I had anything to do with Helen's plan, then you're more of an idiot than I thought." I needed him to take a swing at me, anything that would give me a reason to bash his face in.

"Fighting won't solve anything." Caroline jumped to her feet and wedged herself between the two of us. Her hands pressed against our chests as she pushed us away from one another. Turning toward Everest, she met his icy glare with one of her own. "You know Conrad would never agree to any plan that would hand Evey over to Aden. He loves her more than anyone else on this earth, so stop being such an asshole!" Shock spread throughout the room at her words.

"Excuse me?"

"You heard what I said. You may be the caput, but since I'm neither a secundae nor a consiliarius, your title doesn't really mean a damn thing to me. Besides, if anyone can get her back, it's Conrad, and you know it."

Everest stepped away from her, looking bewildered. He collapsed in his seat, sadness evident in his features. "You're right," he admitted.

"Of course I am," she announced with complete confidence.

"Bourdet, I apologize for my comments. They were made out of anger. I know how you feel about Evey and that you would never do anything to hurt her."

"Piss off," I muttered under my breath as I nodded politely. Caroline and I resumed our seats by Noah. "Thanks," I whispered in her ear, to which she gave my arm a slight squeeze in reply.

"Well, where is Helen now?" Everest questioned.

"Aden took her and Evey," I answered. "Milton and Marie didn't make it."

"Our numbers are decreasing with each passing day," he replied, sighing wearily. "I own some land around the airstrip where your plane landed when you arrived in New York. I will accompany you there and we'll give them a proper burial."

"Thanks," I whispered. I couldn't believe how the last several hours had escalated. One minute, I was dancing with Evey, and the next, I was dying in her arms. Her beautiful face had been burned into every image passing through my mind. She'd been taken away from me too many times and I wouldn't allow it to happen again. There was no sacrifice I wouldn't make in order to get her back.

"I don't know if it helps, but there is one good thing that came out of this evening."

Noah and I turned to stare at Caroline as she spoke. "And what might that be?" he asked.

Her arm extended in front of her and she opened her palm upward.

I inhaled at the sight of three brown seeds dotting her skin.

She took a second to meet each of our eyes before answering Noah's question. "At least we know Aden won't be able to get the seeds."

3

PRECONCEIVED
IMPRESSIONS

"I don't understand," I stated, shaking my head. "You don't want to hurt me?" Aden had repeated his sentiment at least five times, but his words didn't seem fathomable.

"No, my love. I have no wish to cause you any harm." He rose from the bed and began pacing about the room. As I watched him, I took a second to gather my surroundings. The bedroom was decorated in nothing but white. The walls, bedspread, and even the vase holding a bouquet of white roses were all the color of freshly fallen snow. Every object was pristine. Floral paintings hung inside thick gilded frames, creating the ambience of a beautiful cathedral, not a bedroom. I couldn't find a single thing about it I didn't love, and the thought instantly dawned on me. He decorated this room as he thought I would have done it myself.

The only thing to clash with the serenity of the room was Aden. He stood before me as a pillar of shadows, masking the purity of our surroundings. His dark features were intensified by his black T-shirt and shorts. The thin fabric of his shirt stretched over his broad shoulders. Glancing down, I realized I was dressed in a nightgown. White satin hugged my body like a second skin, and left the majority of my flesh on display for Aden's viewing. When I returned my focus to Aden, he'd ceased his pacing in order to stare at me.

"Please don't look at me like that."

"Why not?" His playful tone set my teeth on edge. A dark curl tumbled across his forehead as he set his hands on the bed next to me. Scooting away from him, my back met the headboard. I tried to put as much space between us as possible, but even a thousand miles would still feel too close.

"Because it makes me feel uncomfortable."

"I'm sorry. I don't mean to make you uncomfortable," he replied with a smirk. I was nothing more than a slab of meat dangling before a bloodthirsty predator. Fear closed around my throat, making it hard to breathe. Slowly, he placed his knees on the bed one at a time. My hands started to tremble the moment I felt his weight counter my own.

I swallowed hard as I tried my best to keep from panicking. "Yes, you do." I was alone with a man who had been my husband for thousands of years, and nothing about his demeanor made me think he was seeking my forgiveness or approval.

"Can you really blame a man who has just been reunited with his wife after four hundred years of searching for her?" His gaze locked on to mine as he crawled across the bed toward me.

"I don't think you can still call me your wife after you poisoned my unborn child and me."

"Is it so hard to believe I can be genuinely sorry for all of the pain I've caused you in the past? We've spent thousands of years by one another's side. And I've made many mistakes, but I'm not the only one."

"Aden, please don't do this." Heat from his hands spread through the thin fabric of my nightgown, his face nearing mine with each breath I took.

"I could just take you if I wanted to," he whispered. He grabbed my hips, jerking me down until he was hovering over me. My hands slammed against his chest in an attempt to protect myself. "Do you remember when I used to chase you through the trees in the Garden of Eden?" His lips ghosted along the side of my neck so briefly that I almost thought I imagined it.

I shook my head. "No."

"We used to lie on the grass together and you would give yourself to me." My chest heaved beneath his weight as the rate of my breathing increased. I fought to remain calm as his mouth discovered the curve of my jaw.

"That was then and this is now," I replied, looking straight into his shaded eyes.

"I can still overpower you. You aren't as strong as I am."

"I don't think you will."

"And why's that?" His breath warmed my lips as he gazed down at me.

"Because you want this to be real. You want to believe I can love you again, but I can't. I'm in love with Conrad and nothing will ever change that."

I braced myself for his rage and the repercussions of mentioning Conrad, but he laughed instead. "You are in love with him—for now."

"You say that as if you expect me to change my mind."

"That's because I do." He bent forward, but I turned my head to prevent the kiss I was sure he wanted to place upon my lips. If he wanted me, then he'd have to take me by force, because there was no way I was going to submit without a fight.

Just as he was about to kiss my neck, the sound of shattering glass startled us. Sitting up, he glanced in the direction of the sound.

"Helen must be awake now."

Staring at him in disbelief, I asked, "Helen is here?"

"Yes, she turned out to be such the little helper, so I brought her here. I believe she'll be quite useful in the future." A scream echoed through the wall that separated my room from hers.

"What are you doing to her?" Jumping off the bed, I rounded on him as I spoke.

"I'm not doing anything to her. She's probably remembering what happened last night."

"Conrad," I whispered. His attention shifted in my direction at the mention of Conrad's name. The silence hovering between us was obliterated by more breaking glass. "May I go to her?"

He surveyed me with an incredulous expression. "Why?"

"Because she's hurting and I know how that feels. I was responsible for Conrad's death once. Something you no doubt remember." The overwhelming sound of her grief pierced like a knife to the gut.

"You do remember she's the reason you're here right now."

"I do. But I can't stand by and do nothing while she's in pain, especially considering I feel the same way." He scrutinized every line of my face with a newfound intensity.

"And what will you do?"

"Try to comfort her."

"I believe God broke the mold when he made you," he replied, kissing my hand.

"Considering the fact that you were the mold, that doesn't mean much," I spat. After I broke free from his grasp, I raced for the door. In the hallway, Donovan acted as an impregnable barrier, preventing me from entering Helen's room. "Move aside. I'm going in there." His lip curled upward in a snarl as he ignored my command. "I said move!"

"Donovan, you heard her." Aden loomed just behind me. With a quick bow, Donovan moved out of my way.

Slowly, I opened the door and stepped inside. The entire room was a wreck. Water dripped down the yellow walls and flowed to the floor, while shards of glass covered everything in sight. Paintings had been ripped from their frames and tossed aside like trash. Helen's crumpled form lay in the center of the floor. As I approached, I noticed blood oozing from her shredded knuckles.

I bent to my knees in front of her. "Helen? It's Evey."

"Leave me alone!"

"Helen, I'm so sorry."

"You're sorry?" Raising her head, she met my gaze. Dark streaks of black marred her cheeks. "If anyone should be sorry, it should be me. I tried so hard to protect him from you. I just knew you'd be the reason he died, but it was me. I killed him!"

Tears poured from my eyes as I recalled the image of Conrad's broken body drenched in blood. His eyes resembled opaque glass, the bright crisp blue turning cloudy as his life faded away. "What you did was wrong, but I know you did it with the best intentions." It took all my strength to keep my voice steady. The temptation to break down and surrender to hate was almost overwhelming. I wanted to cry. Hell, I wanted to blame her, but for some reason, I couldn't.

"How can you even look at me right now? I'm the reason the man we both love is dead. Conrad's blood is on my hands. If only I hadn't been so jealous of you, if only I'd done things differently, he would still be alive right now."

As much as I wanted her to feel responsible for Conrad's death, it was impossible to subject her to that fate. I understood how she felt better than anyone—the grief, the guilt, all of it. I had been the reason Conrad had paid the ultimate price once before. Part of me wanted to seek pleasure in her pain, but what good would that do? "Sometimes, we like to punish ourselves by thinking there was something we could've changed, that we could've made a difference, but it's not always true." I hesitated for a moment, but finally reached out to touch her shoulder. She flinched at the contact. "I'm not going to hurt you."

"You should," she sobbed. "I deserve to feel like this."

"Conrad wouldn't want you to suffer like this. He wouldn't want you to blame yourself for what happened." I stood and retrieved a damp towel from the bathroom connected to her room. "Here, let me see." Raising her head, she placed her hands in mine. I dabbed the towel over her knuckles with great care, cleaning away all traces of blood and glass. "Let's get you off the floor and into bed."

"Okay." After I helped her to her feet, we walked to the bed. The blue comforter had been thrown back, so I straightened it out as I tucked her beneath the covers. "Why are you being so kind to me? I've never been nice to you."

"I'm not being kind because I expect the same in return. Demonstrating kindness is the right thing to do, and the world is filled with more than enough hate," I replied as I perched on the bed next to her. "Besides, I understand the pain you're experiencing and I want to help you."

She considered my reply for a second before bursting into a fit of heaving sobs again. "I don't deserve any kindness. I don't deserve anything."

As I watched her cry, I realized all the hurtful things she said about Conrad and me didn't matter anymore. She was falling apart at the seams. I wanted to do the same, to lose myself in my own despair. However, there was no way I'd be able to help her if I did. And for some unexplained reason, I needed to help her. Before I knew what I was doing, my arms wrapped around her as I held her body to mine. She didn't fight against me like I assumed she would. Instead, she relaxed into the embrace. Combing my fingers through her hair, tears formed in my eyes as I sang my mother's favorite lullaby.

Eventually, her breathing slowed. I sang the tune over and over as I waited for Helen to drift off to sleep. Out of the corner of my eye, I saw Aden watching us from the doorway. The expression he wore was one of curiosity—as if he didn't believe what he was witnessing. I thought he was going to interrupt me, but he continued his role as a silent audience. Every word from his lips, every touch was an orchestrated move in his grand scheme. He may still love me and want to rebuild our marriage, but to what end?

Once I was sure she was sound asleep, I slid a pillow beneath her head and turned the lights out. She was still curled up beneath the blankets as I reached the door. Aden was already waiting for me in the hallway. When I tried to return to my room, he stood in front of me, blocking my path.

"What do you want now, Aden?"

"What I always want." His tone was light and playful like he was openly trying to flirt with me.

"Well, what might that be?" I stared at him in exasperation. He was eating up the little patience I had left.

"You," he answered, grinning.

"Sorry, but you can't have me. So, please, let me go back to my room."

He took a step in my direction. "I still want you."

"And I want Conrad. Can you bring him back for me?" Squaring my shoulders, I met his gaze head-on. "Because I don't want you or anything you have to offer; I just want him."

"It would be counterproductive for me to do that, my love."

Anger pumped through my veins as he gave me a sly smile. If I couldn't have what I wanted, then neither could he. My hand collided with his cheek with as much force as I could muster. The skin on my palm stung like someone had pricked me with thousands of tiny needles. "It's also counterproductive for you to try to make a move when I'm clearly not interested." His hands grabbed my wrists, preventing me from landing another hit. "Are you going to keep me prisoner here in the hopes that I may be your wife again one day?"

"That's the general idea," he answered, tightening his grasp.

"I hope you're prepared to wait indefinitely, because that day will never come."

He released my wrists and trailed his fingers up my arms until he reached the base of my neck. "I know you don't remember all the time we spent together. You might be surprised at your memories. You used to love me as much as I love you now." I shuddered as his face neared mine. "And memories like that can be very persuasive."

"When I met Conrad, I had no idea who he was. My memory had been erased completely, but the first time we touched, I had a flash. I began remembering things from my past. Almost every time I touched him, I was able to relive one of my memories," I countered in a harsh tone. "But you, on the other hand, have touched me at least a dozen times and I haven't remembered a single thing. Why do you think that is?"

"I—"

"I think my body and mind don't want to remember you at all. I have no flashes of you or the thousands of years we spent together. It's almost as if my lives with you never existed."

"You may not remember anything about me now, but you will."

"Perhaps," I said. "You can kill Conrad and the Concilium can wipe away my memory of him, but no matter what, I'll always want him over you." I turned away to prevent his lips from meeting with mine. He kissed my forehead before stepping aside to allow me to pass. My feet sprinted away from him, but as I reached for the door to my room, his voice stopped me.

"I'll bring some breakfast to your room in a little while. If you look around, you'll find everything you need is already in there. I took the liberty of getting you some new clothes and shoes."

When I tried to reply, no sound poured from my mouth. Instead, I nodded and continued into the safety of my room. Once inside, I made my way to the massive bathroom and turned on the shower. Not bothering to undress, I stepped beneath the scalding stream of water. My knees trembled beneath my weight and I collapsed on the tile. What started as a few tears transformed into heaving sobs. Water surrounded me at every turn. It flowed in long rivulets over my face and down my back. Perhaps if I sat under the current long enough, it would pool around me and I'd get lost beneath its smooth sinuous surface. It might be impossible for me to run away, but that didn't mean I couldn't escape in another way. I instantly thrust that thought from my mind. Conrad would be so disappointed if I allowed myself to think like that. He trained me to fight, to survive, and I'd be damned if I was going to let him down.

Sucking in a deep breath, I tried to still my nerves, but the task proved impossible. Would I ever feel the warmth of Conrad's touch again? It's strange how many things I grew to love about him in the brief time we were together and from the few memories I could remember. Like how joyful he sounded whenever he laughed or the way his gaze always softened as it landed on me or even the way he could draw me in with his presence and make me forget that we weren't the only two souls in existence.

How could I ever feel anything more than hatred for the man who took Conrad from me? Aden made sure there were no misconceptions about his intentions. For the time being, he was displaying patience. But how long would that last? How long would Aden wait before taking matters into his own hands? The thought of him overpowering me in order to take what he wanted made my skin crawl.

My only hope was that Caroline and Noah might try to find me. However, it would be impossible for them to locate Aden. If I desired freedom, then I would have to devise a means of escape on my own. Technically speaking, Helen was still an ally, but she was in no condition to do anything at the moment.

No matter what, I had to stop Aden from leading me down his path of death and devastation.

4

A SLIVER OF
HOPE

The image of Marie's and Milton's corpses smothered by freshly packed dirt haunted me as I washed the grime from my body. Each mound of mud and muck we piled on top of their lifeless forms weighed on me. It felt like I was leaving them to suffocate beneath the earth, like I was the one who'd stolen the very breath from their lungs. The simple tombstones marking their graves were remnants of the burial ground for Everest's secundae. Chunks of concrete were missing from the markers, no doubt worn away by decades of wind and rain.

By the time we drove back to our hotel from the airstrip, dawn began to break. For some reason, I hadn't expected Everest to help us bury them, but he did. He labored against the earth as we dug a pit large enough to house two bodies. After Marie and Milton had been laid to rest, I was ready to start working on a plan to get Evey back, but everyone else was exhausted and in dire need of sleep. Caroline moved in to our hotel room because she refused to stay by herself. Honestly, I didn't blame her. None of us wanted to be alone with our thoughts right now. It wasn't just that we'd lost Evey. We also felt the sting of losing Marie, Milton, and Helen. When I agreed to be one of Evey's secundae, I had known that death and pain would be a permanent fixture in my life, but knowing the suffering you will undoubtedly face never makes the reality of it any easier.

Once I was out of the shower, I made my way to the only empty bed in the room. Noah and Caroline were already fast asleep. His arm was draped over her side as he held on to her. It seemed, for the time being, Noah's anger had subsided. Perhaps he was too tired to hold a grudge. But my gut led me to believe that exhaustion had nothing to do with it. He was beginning to care for Caroline the same way I cared for Evey.

Despite being spent, my mind wouldn't shut down. Since the first time I laid eyes on her, she presided over the majority of my thoughts. Rolling over, I buried my face in the pillow. Why was it that no matter what I did or what sacrifices I made, some force was hell-bent on keeping us apart? Hadn't we suffered enough in the past five hundred years?

I'd never known pain until the day I watched Evey die. But she wasn't the only one I lost. Our son had been stolen away too. Aden could torture me as much as he liked, but I'd made a vow that he would never harm Evey again. I would be more than happy to forfeit my life if it meant she would be spared. Images of her face raced through my mind. The last thought I had before the sluggish wave of sleep swept over me was the sweet floral smell of her hair and the soft gray color of her eyes that reminded me of smoke swirling in the wind.

"Conrad, it's time to wake up." Caroline's voice cut through the fog of sleep as she shook my shoulder.

"What time is it?" The bones in my shoulder gritted against one another, compressing painfully as I sat upright. I massaged the area in an attempt to alleviate the stiffness.

"It's just before noon. We have to go and meet with Everest today."

Rubbing my eyes, I asked, "Where is Noah?"

"I don't know," she answered, her voice cracking on the last word. "I'm worried though. He woke me up really early and said there was something he needed to get. He didn't say where he was going, but I thought he'd be back by now. I didn't know what else to do."

"Have you tried calling him?"

"It went straight to voicemail, and he didn't answer my text either." Her tone informed me that she was on the verge of tears. Any moment now, she was bound to break down, and that was something I wasn't capable of handling. Disemboweling a sanguis demon was something I could do in my sleep, but comforting a crying woman was an entirely different matter.

What was it about crying women that made men feel useless?

"Let me get dressed and then we'll look for him." Jumping up from the bed, I grabbed my bag before running to the bathroom. I threw on a pair of jeans and a T-shirt. Then I pulled on a pair of socks and found my boots. Within two minutes, I was dressed and ready to go. As I stepped back into the room, I noticed Caroline sitting on the edge of the bed. Her attention was focused on the apple seeds resting in her palm. Her hand shook as she held it out in front of her.

"You wouldn't think something so tiny would be so significant."

"What is more significant is the fact that we have them and Aden doesn't," I replied. "I'm ready to go if you are." She nodded her head and tightened her fingers around the seeds. Walking over to her, I handed her a small knife. Her eyebrow rose in inquiry as she studied the blade. "There's no such thing as being too prepared." After I slid a larger knife into the back waistband of my jeans, I covered it with my jacket. As I reached for the door, it swung open. Shoving Caroline behind me, I brandished the knife in my right hand. A bewildered Noah stepped inside, staring at Caroline and then me.

"Did I miss the call to be on high alert?" he asked. "I mean, you could at least wait until I've walked completely inside the room before you slit my throat."

"It's not funny," Caroline scolded. "You left early this morning and didn't say where you were going, and after everything that happened last night, I was really worried about you."

"I'm sorry, but I had to get something we needed."

I returned the knife to my jeans and sat on the bed. "And what might that be?"

"This," Noah answered, removing a silver bracelet from a small blue box.

"A bracelet from Tiffany's? Does this mean we're going steady?"

"It's not for you, dumbass. It's for her," he snapped, offering the bracelet to Caroline.

"You woke up early this morning and didn't tell me where you were going and scared me half to death just to get me a bracelet?"

"It's not just any bracelet. Watch this." We both leaned in close and watched as he pointed out a small charm in the shape of a lock. Once he knew he had our undivided attention, he turned a pin in the key hole and opened the lock, revealing an empty square. Instantly, Caroline poured the seeds into the open cavity and shut the charm with a snap. "I thought it'd be smart to conceal the seeds in here. That way, we have easy access to them, but no one else knows where they are. Caroline mentioned Evey did the same thing with her necklace. That's what gave me the idea." I nodded in agreement and watched as he fastened the bracelet around Caroline's wrist. "I also know how much you like Tiffany's."

"Armani clothes, jewelry from Tiffany's . . . This feels a bit like bribery, doesn't it?"

"I'll be honest, I was upset with you, but you also saved my life," he replied as he kissed her hand. "And I wanted to show my gratitude."

"In that case, can I have your private plane too?"

Noah coughed in response to her question while I erupted in a fit of laughter. It was a good thing Caroline's father was a cop. I could only imagine the kind of trouble she and Evey found themselves in growing up.

"Geez, I was only kidding! You'd think someone your age would be able to take a joke."

Noah may have had centuries of experience under his belt, but Caroline was giving him a run for his money.

"All joking aside, there are some pressing matters we need to take care of immediately," he replied.

I tossed an extra knife to Noah and we filed out of the room. The drive back to Everest's passed by in a blur. It wasn't long until the red door to his apartment materialized before us. Today, the corridor seemed to be cast in shadows. The darkness served as an ominous warning for the dreaded situation awaiting us. It's ironic how the last place on earth I wanted to be was the one place I needed to be. Noah's knock was greeted by the appearance of the twins. Their shoulders sagged, a stark contrast from their usual arrogant nature. It seemed Caroline, Noah, and I weren't the only ones affected by the absence of those we lost last night. Despite our differences, being a part of the Concilium or being a secundae meant we were irreversibly bound to one another. Suffering and pain were inescapable fixtures for us, but those things weren't what mattered. We were chosen to be a part of something sacred and that duty was more important than the things we had to endure because of it. Terrick and Warrin followed us to the sitting room just as Everest appeared from his office. The six of us seated ourselves before devising a plan that would return Evey to us.

Looking to each set of eyes surrounding me, I inhaled before opening my mouth to speak. "Okay, I believe we're all in agreement that we need to kill Aden, but how can we kill him and destroy Thea's powers he still possesses?"

"Thea's powers aren't what have made him almost impossible to kill. Sure, it's allowed him to live continually without needing to be reborn, but his powers as a primum are what instill his true immortality," Everest answered. "We knew when you killed him the first time he would come back one day. It's the way the primums are designed."

"What?" I questioned.

"Thea believed we'd be able to bring him back and control him; she thought she could change him, but he'd already been polluted past the point of no return."

"I thought the purpose of the Concilium was to bring Evey and Aden back. If they are truly immortal, then why are you needed?" Caroline asked.

"The Concilium helps facilitate their return. The primums are always born naturally; they aren't reanimated like secundae are. It's the responsibility of a consiliarius to implant the primums into the right mothers at the right times so they can be born."

"Oh," she replied.

"All of this is explained in greater detail in the Book of Adam and Eve, but since Thea died before she could impart all of her knowledge about the book to me, there is still a lot we don't know."

"So, you're saying you have no idea how to kill him?"

"No, Bourdet, that isn't what I said." Everest's gray eyes were as empty as a bottomless pit as he
scanned my face.

"Well, it seems very impractical to keep information like that a secret from everyone," Caroline said.

"It was, but you have to understand that after living in peace with the primums for thousands of years, we never thought Aden would kill her," he stated, rubbing his hand along his chin. "In actuality, Thea wasn't supposed to pass along her knowledge of the primums to anyone else, but she did so because she believed another consiliarius should possess all the information she did."

"Why wasn't I or any other members of the Concilium aware of this?" Noah demanded.

"Because we didn't want the information to be available to everyone, especially the primums themselves. Since they were reincarnated over and over as prominent kings and queens, we knew there would always be the possibility of corruption."

"I'm sorry," Caroline interjected, "but I'm not really following what you're saying."

"Any time you give a person great amounts of power, there is always a chance they will abuse it and use that power for their own selfish purposes. And when you combine that power with the immortality of the primums, the next logical step would be for them to believe they are gods."

"Which is what Aden started to believe," I added.

"There is a way to kill him, though, right?" Caroline, Noah, and I turned in surprise to stare at Terrick. Both he and Warrin had been so quiet since we entered the apartment I'd almost forgotten they were there.

"There is, but no one has seen the Book of Adam and Eve since Thea died. I may not know everything she did, but I do know Aden can be killed. From what Thea told me, it was a failsafe plan of sorts."

"I've killed him before."

"Yes, but he can't be eliminated with just any weapon. In order to wipe him from existence, he must be killed with one weapon in particular," Everest said.

"And what might that be?" Noah asked.

"Aden must be killed with the sickle of Cain."

"Cain? Like the story of Cain and Abel?" Caroline asked.

Everest turned to look at Caroline. "Yes, I'm referring to Adam and Eve's first sons."

"How would Cain's sickle be able to kill Aden?"

"Because Cain was a cultivator of the land, he was familiar with several farming tools of the time. The sickle and scythe were among many of the tools that he used. In the Bible, the story says Cain murdered Abel because the Lord chose Abel's offering over Cain's. So, in a fit of jealousy, he took the sickle that he used to harvest crops and cut down his brother with it."

"That makes sense, but I don't see what that has to do with Aden," I interjected.

Everest let out a deep breath before continuing his story. "Cain didn't murder Abel simply because of jealousy. He murdered his own brother because he was poisoned by the evil his father had consumed from the apple in the Garden of Eden."

"So, with the Fall of Man, evil was brought with Evey and Aden and spread throughout the
world?" I asked.

Everest nodded in reply. "Yes."

"Then man turned on each other and spawned the first murder of this
world," I said.

"The fact that man has knowledge of evil is a constant reminder of the penance Aden and Evey are supposed to be paying," he added.

"Because Aden absorbed Thea's powers and knows he can gain more by consuming the heart of another consiliarius to fulfill the *Comedere Cor*, should we believe he's aware the sickle of Cain can kill him?"

"Since Thea was in love with him, I'd be willing to bet my life on it," Everest answered.

"Well, where can we get this sickle? Not that I'm not enjoying the history lesson, but I'm ready to get my best friend back and I would like to graduate high school before I'm forty." Caroline stood from the sofa and placed her hands on her hips as she stared at Everest.

"I'm with her," I said, joining Caroline. Noah stood up as well and I could see Terrick and Warrin grinning at Caroline as she spoke. It was apparent that, like the rest of us, they weren't used to anyone speaking to Everest the way she did.

Instead of countering Caroline's defiant nature, a look of despair altered Everest's features. Burying his face in his hands, he muttered, "The sickle is with Iola."

"What?" Noah asked, shouting his question.

"You left the sickle of Cain in the hands of Iola? Are you insane?"

"Of course not," Everest snapped at me. "After what happened to Thea, I thought the best place to keep the sickle was in her care."

"Yes, but she is crazy," Noah replied, collapsing on the sofa behind him.

Everest's glare fixated on Noah. "She also happens to be your sister."

"Wait, what?" Caroline's gaze darted from Noah to Everest to the twins and back to me several times before she continued. "Iola is who?"

"Iola is a consiliarius," Warrin supplied. "And while she has always been devout in her duties to the Concilium, she possesses a fragile mind."

"I thought we agreed she wasn't supposed to be as active in the

Concilium anymore. Especially after what happened to Thea," Noah yelled. His green eyes glowed with hatred. Noah was pissed and I didn't blame him. If Cecily had been placed in a similar situation when she was still alive, I would've been livid.

"No one would ever suspect Iola to be looking after something so important! That is why the sickle is safest with her."

"You promised me," Noah said, stomping toward Everest. Noah's voice was low, his composure teetering on the edge of rage. Iola was more than a sore subject to him—she was the only family he had left.

"And you made a promise of your own to the Concilium. Or have you forgotten about that?" The men glared at one another, neither wanting to back down. "Have you forgotten I chose you and Iola to serve the Concilium? That I deemed the two of you worthy to join our cause?"

"I forget nothing," Noah answered.

"Then perhaps you should put more faith in me and the decisions I make as your caput."

"Thea was the chosen caput," Noah muttered under his breath.

"And look what happened to her!" Everest shouted. "You think I don't worry about the safety of each member of the Concilium? You think I haven't experienced the sting of loss? Because trust me, I have. The choices I make are for the benefit of everyone. We must be committed to protecting one another."

The muscles in Noah's jaw clenched painfully. "I know," he spat through gritted teeth.

If someone didn't intervene, a fight was sure to ensue. And that was the last thing I wanted to mess with. Usually, I was the brash one and Noah was more well-mannered, but right now, one of us needed to maintain some levelheadedness if we were ever going to get through this—and it didn't seem like it would be him.

"I think after everything that has happened in the last twenty-four hours, it's normal for our emotions to get the better of us, but we still have a few issues we need to focus on," I said, stepping between Noah and Everest. "Noah, Everest is very careful in his decisions. You know he would only choose the option with the best outcome for everyone.

He was right to leave the sickle in her care." I waited for him to answer me, but he remained silent. "I know that you're worried about Iola. I'm worried about Evey, but the only way to protect either of them is to kill Aden. And this time, we make sure it lasts."

"You're right," he replied, his eyes still focused on Everest's. "Has she been moved?"

"No, she remains in her home still."

"Then we should leave now. I won't waste any more time talking."

"The three of us will retrieve the sickle and then return here to plan our next move," I said to Everest. He nodded, but his attention remained focused on Noah. Caroline moved to grab Noah's hand but, seeing his expression, decided against it. I set my hand against her back and ushered her toward the door. "Come on, we should get going." We turned to wait for Noah. As he moved to leave, Everest caught his arm at the last second.

"I wouldn't leave her vulnerable. I made sure she was well protected. You know I could never do anything to harm her."

"I believe you," Noah answered.

"Noah, you know how I—"

"I know," he said with finality. Stepping away from Everest, he ran past us and flung open the door of the apartment. He was already waiting at the elevator by the time Caroline and I closed the door to Everest's apartment behind us.

"What the . . . ?" I questioned under my breath.

Caroline leaned forward. "What is it?"

"I was just wondering what all that was about," I whispered.

"Isn't it obvious?"

"Maybe you can speak in code, but I have no idea what just happened between Noah and Everest."

"Everest is in love with Iola," she replied. "Also, he chose to turn her into a consiliarius and that has to be why. He was in love with her."

I stared at her in disbelief. "Everest and Iola? No, there's no way."

"Say what you want, but I bet you anything I'm right. Besides, did you see the look on Everest's face when he told us the sickle was with her? It was the same one you had when we told you Aden had Evey."

Just as I was about to answer her, we reached Noah at the elevator and the double doors sprang open, permitting our entrance. His hand repeatedly punched the button for the lobby, and once the doors closed, silence permeated the space around us.

"I can drive for the first half of the trip. It'll take us two days to get there, but we can drive in shifts. I won't risk us stopping anywhere overnight."

"We'll make it to her, Noah. We won't let anything happen to her," I said.

"Thanks," Noah answered in a stiff voice. He stood with his back to Caroline and me. The tension residing in his shoulders was almost palpable.

"Noah," Caroline whispered.

"I'm fine, Caroline," he snapped. His voice startled both of us, and we stared at each other in surprise. This time, she didn't hesitate—she stepped in front of him and took his head in her hands. "I said I was fine."

"I know you're fine, but you aren't alone in this." She wrapped her arms around his neck and kissed him. I could see the stiffness in his back melt away as his arms pulled her to him. Not a second later, the doors to the elevator opened and we made our way back through the lobby to the garage.

"Let's pack up everything from the hotel room and get on the road as soon as possible."

"Sounds like a plan," Noah answered.

The three of us moved about the room frantically as we packed up our things to leave. I crammed a handful of knives and shirts into my bag and threw on my leather jacket. I sat beside Noah as we waited for Caroline to finish packing.

"Conrad?"

"Yeah? What's up?"

"I thought you might want to hold on to this," she said, holding out Evey's bag to me.

I swallowed hard and took the bag out of her hands. "Thanks." My fingers were immediately drawn to the zipper and I tugged on it. Her smell flooded my nose as I pulled out a camisole covered with flowers. The fabric was soft to the touch and I couldn't help but remember the last time she'd worn it. I planned for the two of us to have a simple picnic on the rooftop terrace, but what that time with her had actually been was a second of peace in the midst of a never-ending war.

"I guess we should get going," Caroline said in a soft voice.

"Yeah, you're right." I placed the camisole back inside the bag. Shaking myself out of the daze I'd been in, I sprang to my feet. "Let's not waste any more time," I added, throwing my and Evey's bags over my shoulder and opening the door. Noah stepped out first and then Caroline. I was the last to leave, and I couldn't help but take in a deep breath as I left the hotel room behind and started forward with the only two people who could help me get Evey back.

5

FALLING

The once-blistering water now felt like ice falling in shards upon my skin. Slowly, I lifted myself off the tile and pulled a towel over my shoulders. I gazed at my ghostlike reflection in the mirror as I brushed my hair, but I quickly turned away, unable to look at my vacant eyes any longer. I didn't feel like myself. I was a captive locked within the confines of an inescapable purgatory. Grabbing a long flowing dress from the closet, I jerked it over my head. The lavender-colored cotton was soft against my skin, and no sooner than I had put it on, a knock sounded from the other side of my door.

"Come in," I replied with uncertainty.

Aden opened the door and stepped inside my room. He had an oversized tray balanced on top of his arm and it was laden with an assortment of food.

"I brought you some breakfast." He walked over to where I was standing and held out the tray to me. "Can you hold this while I make your bed?" I accepted the tray from his hands, watching as he stepped to the bed and pulled the sheets and comforter up to the headboard. Once he had finished, he took the tray from my hands and set it down. "Please come and eat," he said with a slight smile.

The smell of warm croissants and honey filled the air, forcing me to realize how famished I was.

"Okay," I whispered. I stepped hesitantly toward the bed and sat, while Aden positioned himself across from me. He plucked a white daisy from the tray and offered it to me.

"These are still your favorite, right?"

"They are."

"Allow me," he said, taking back the flower. He leaned over the tray, his hands trembling as he tucked the flower behind my ear. The skin on his fingertips barely skidded across the surface of my cheek as he leaned back. "I'm sorry. I won't touch you unless you want me to."

"I appreciate you saying that, because I don't want you to," I replied. "And you appeared to have no qualms whatsoever about touching me this morning in this bed." My heart hammered inside my chest—not out of desire, but fear. My life, like many things at the moment, was at Aden's disposal, and the uncertainty of my situation grated at my composure. However, I couldn't let him see my weaknesses. I had to be the strong, capable queen Conrad had fallen in love with.

"I know. Believe me, I understand I'm the last person you would ever want, but I couldn't help myself earlier. I've thought of nothing but you for the last four hundred years and I was unable to resist your pull."

"My pull?"

"I was alone in the world until you came along. I had no one to spend my days with. But one day, I went to sleep under a tree in the Garden, and when I woke up, you were smiling down at me. You have no idea what a relief it was to not be alone," he said, taking a drink from the glass of juice in front of him. "One look into your eyes and I was done for. All it took was one look and I was in love with you."

"I don't remember any of that," I replied. "I'm sorry, but the only memories I have of you are the atrocities I've seen you commit throughout the years. You aren't the man you were when we first met."

"What if I could be that man again?"

"Aden—"

"Please, Evey," he begged.

"I love Conrad and that won't change."

"I know what you must think of me, but you have to know I don't want to hurt you. I've done horrible and unspeakable things to get you back, but I'm trying to create a new life for us. I'm trying to make it so that we can go where no one will find us and we can start over together. You're the only one who can save me from turning into a monster. You took that apple not really realizing what would happen when we ate from it, but you have to understand that I never wanted to be like this. I just took a bite from an apple and it's cost me everything I love. Please, you have to help me," he pleaded.

"I can't," I said, choking back tears. He was right. I had encouraged him to eat from the apple that stole away his good nature. I was to blame for him changing. I never thought about my role in his fall from grace, but his fall was my fault.

"Try to imagine what it would be like to watch Conrad fall out of love with you. It would be worse than dying, would it not?"

I tried to fathom how it would feel to watch Conrad draw away from me. I thought about how I would feel if he replaced me with another. When I saw Helen and Conrad locked in an embrace that night at Noah's apartment, it felt as if my heart were being ripped from my body. It would tear me apart to watch him love someone else the way I loved him. A swell of sympathy filled my chest. Was that what Aden had to do when I fell in love with Conrad? "Is that what you did?"

"Watch you fall out of love with me?"

I nodded. My mouth was too dry to try to speak. His dark eyes locked on me, but they didn't look the same as last night. Rays of light filtered in through the curtains, warming the brown irises. Were these the eyes that saw me for the first time in the Garden of Eden?

"I know you'll never be able to forgive me for taking Conrad from you, but I did it to save my soul. I'm a man that has been torn into two different halves for so long and I seek to change my fate. You're the only one who can make me good again."

"I'm truly sorry for the hurt I've caused you, but I could never sacrifice another person for myself."

"I don't pretend to believe I'm a good person, but I do believe I can redeem myself. If I ever have to leave this world, I'll pay for the things I've done. Can't you help me undo some of those things in order to save my soul?"

"If you really want to undo what you've done, then start by bringing Conrad back," I ordered.

"*That* I cannot do."

I shook my head, knowing that would be his answer. "Then you don't really want to change."

"I do want to change, but watching you love another is something I won't do. I believe there is a chance you could love me again and that is the one thing I would sacrifice my soul for."

"That's the difference between you and Conrad."

"What is?"

"He would watch me love another if it meant I would be happy. He would sacrifice anything for my happiness."

"He also has never had to watch you love someone else before. He has faults . . . He isn't as perfect as you think."

"That doesn't change the fact that he would endure anything in order to make me happy. He's a better man than you."

"I know he is a better man than me. Why else would I have to kill him? I stand a chance at getting you back with him out of the picture, but if he is alive, I know I can't compete with him." He reached forward, setting a hand on top of my own. He was trying so hard to be like Conrad, but it wasn't the same.

"Dead or alive, it doesn't matter," I replied. "I'm not a competition and that's something Conrad understood." My hands slipped from beneath his. No amount of talking or explaining would change Aden. He'd do anything to get what he wanted, and the thought sickened me. As I stood and walked over to the door, my hand reached for the handle. I paused for a second to glance at Aden.

"I don't think you're a competition."

"Do you understand why I love Conrad so much?"

"Because he is good and I'm not."

"No, that has nothing to do with it. From the first moment I met him, he loved me. He loved me and never asked me to love him in return. He loves without seeking something in return for it," I answered, taking a deep breath before continuing. "But you love me and expect that I love you in return. You require my love as payment for your own." I waited for him to try and refute my claims, but Aden remained silent. He knew I spoke the truth. Plucking the flower from my hair, I set it on the nightstand before crossing the threshold. "I'm going for a walk, and I know Donovan will have to follow me. I would never stay here of my own volition." I avoided meeting his warm brown eyes and continued down the hallway to the staircase. How could I have ever loved someone so devoid of human compassion? I descended the stairs to the lower level of the house and headed straight for the front door. Donovan shifted in front of me, standing before it. His tall frame almost covered the entirety of the entryway. The white linen of his shirt gave way to his wide arms, almost appearing like it would rip along the seams at any second. I stared at him but was unable to see anything but his scar. Every time I saw it, a shudder slid down my spine. "Don't worry, as much as I'd like to leave, I can't. I don't even know where I am," I said. "Besides, with you watching over me, how far could I possibly get?"

"If you so much as *try* anything, I'll drag you back to your room by your hair," he snarled.

"Why do you despise me so much?"

"In my first life, you were the embodiment of everything I could never have."

"I don't see how that's my fault." My body shook before him. His light brown hair was slicked back, fully showcasing his disfigured face. Something about the welt carved into his chin haunted me, forcing me to avert my attention.

He leaned toward me. "You cost me everything once."

"I'm sorry, but I have no memory of who you are," I whispered.

A smile spread over his face, distorting his scar. "Perhaps one day I should refresh your memory." He turned and unlocked the dead bolt on the door. A black mark on the back of his shoulder showed through his shirt, catching my attention. It was in the exact place where Conrad's tree had been. Except what covered Donovan's skin looked nothing like a tree. It could have been at one time, but it was no longer lush or full of leaves. Now, his mark was gnarled and forever mutilated, just as his face was. He stood aside and allowed me to exit the house. What could have inspired the Concilium to make Donovan a secundae?

"Is your love for cruelty why Aden had you made into one of his secundae?"

"Aden has a propensity for collecting broken things," he answered. "Just ask Helen."

I considered questioning him further but decided against it. The air outside had a faint chill to it. The sun was still overhead, though it was partially hidden by dark clouds, and I guessed it had to be sometime in the afternoon. I studied the house behind me. It was large and made of brick with a white awning above the door. The house was nestled into a clearing of trees and the land around it appeared deserted. I knew better than to hope Aden would take me to a place where help would be available. Another person wouldn't be around for miles, and without knowing exactly where I was, there was no point in trying to run away. Meandering around the side of the house, I made my way to the backyard with Donovan in tow. He loomed behind me, stalking my every move. And he wasn't the only one. To my right, I noticed Aden's silhouette in one of the windows upstairs. I didn't have to look at him to know that his gaze was following me—it always did. My hand enclosed around the ruby pendant hanging from my neck. The stone dug into my flesh as I held it. This necklace was the only tangible thing tying me to Conrad and the life I was determined to fight for.

6

SALVATION

Everything within my sight lay hidden beneath a blanket of ice. The wind picked up speed as daylight relinquished its reign to the darkness of night. I brushed a layer of snow from my shoulders and stepped inside the cottage. The only light came from a roaring fire. Crossing the creaking floors, I tried to position myself as close to the flames as possible. In the corner on the left side of the room, two beds were shoved together, and on the right sat a table and three chairs. It was the only piece of furniture in the kitchen, and the only scrap of food in the entire place was a molded bit of bread sitting upon its wooden surface. It wasn't much —it wasn't anything really—but it was the only place I had to call home.

"Conrad?"

I heard my mother calling for me from one of the beds. She and Cecily had been ill for almost a fortnight and I was worried I would lose them both to the fever. I'd spent all day patching up holes in the walls and ceiling, but the freezing air still filtered in through the cracks. This winter was going to be worse than the previous one, and I could only hope the three of us would survive it. When my father had died, I made a vow that I would do anything to take care of them, and that's exactly what I'd done. "It's me," I answered, shedding my thin cloak and hanging it by the fire to dry. I set a fresh loaf of bread on the table and added another log to bolster the flames.

"Were you able to bring any food?"

"I managed to get a single loaf of bread. The number of people waiting more than doubled this time. There was barely enough to hand out to everyone." I made my way to her and sat beside Cecily. She was fast asleep as I tucked the blankets in around her.

"At least you brought back something," she said with a smile. The dark circles clinging to her eyes were growing larger by the day.

"I also brought back something even better." I pulled the coin purse from my pocket. "I collected on some of the debts that were still owed to Father, and I've gathered enough to comfortably last us through the winter. We won't have to go to sleep hungry every night."

A small tear trickled out of the corner of her eye, and just as she opened her mouth to speak, a knock sounded from the door. The sound shocked me, causing a wave of panic to seep into my bones. "Who could that be?"

I ignored my mother's question because I already knew the answer. It was the owner of the purse. I braced myself for whatever form of punishment I was to endure for my crime. Walking over to the door, I opened it and peered out into the darkness. A figure stepped forward, and in an instant, I recognized the dark green cloak. "Please come in," I said. I sucked in a deep breath as they stepped past me and into the house. Closing the door quickly, I spun around to face my fate. The figure stood next to the fire and I fell to my knees before them. "I know what you have come for and I will return it to you. I was wrong to steal from you, but I took it to help my family," I pleaded. "You may suffer me to any punishment you see fit, but I beg you to show my mother and sister mercy. They are innocent."

The figure said nothing but threw back the hood of the cloak. To my astonishment, the figure standing before me was the queen.

She removed the cloak from her shoulders and hung it beside mine. My eyes took their time absorbing every detail of her appearance. Dark red curls hung around her face, causing her fair skin to glow in the firelight. A small crown made of gold and pearls circled her head like an angel's halo. She was more beautiful than anything I had ever seen in my life. Suddenly, she dropped in front of me and cradled my face in her hands. "Please don't worry," she replied as she kissed my forehead. "I'm not going to hurt you."

"But why?" I stared into her gray eyes, unable to believe the warmth they possessed as she gazed at me.

Her fingers rubbed my cheek, prompting a rush of heat to overtake my body. "What reason do I have to hurt you?"

"I stole from you. That would be reason enough to sentence me to death." And because she was the queen, I could suffer a fate worse than death. She could punish my family and me any way she desired.

"I could never condemn you to such a fate," she whispered. "And after seeing the state of your home, I gladly give you the coins. So, as you can see, no crime has been committed." I couldn't believe the words flowing from her lips. "What is your name?"

"Conrad," I stammered. "Conrad Bourdet." The most affluent woman in the country knelt at my feet, gazing at me as if her very life was dependent upon my own. For a moment, I believed I was dreaming. This wasn't possible—peasants didn't find their way into the arms of a queen. And yet, she wasn't a dream, she was my salvation.

"Well, Conrad, I can't help but notice what quick and clever hands you have. I had that coin purse tied to my waist and you removed it without me so much as noticing. The only reason you were caught is because one of my guards saw you take it and he followed you here."

"My father was a blacksmith. He taught me to be good with my hands."

"May I ask you to do something for me?"

"Whatever you ask of me, I shall do it, my lady."

Her lips spread into a smile at my answer. "Will you become one

45

of my personal guards? You would be paid well, and of course, a room and food would be provided for you at the castle."

I glanced at my mother and Cecily, noticing that they were intently watching the exchange occurring between the queen and me. "My mother and sister are quite ill. They've been sick for some time now, and if I left, there would be no one to care for them." The queen said nothing but stood from where we were kneeling and walked over to my mother and Cecily. Gently, she touched a hand to each of their faces.

"How long have they had the fever?"

"Almost a fortnight."

"My belly hurts," Cecily whined.

"And what is your name?"

"Cecily."

"That's a beautiful name. Now, tell me, Cecily, are you hungry?"

Cecily nodded her head. "We've only had bread to eat the last few days."

"Would you like to have some hot stew for dinner?"

"Yes. I'd like that very much."

"Well, I should get to work, then." The queen walked back toward me and picked up my mother's apron. She wrapped the apron around her waist and held out the ends. "Conrad, could you tie this for me?" Standing behind her, I tied the apron. The fragrant scent of freshly picked wildflowers wafted from her, and I fought the desire to entwine my fingers into the long strands of hair flowing down her back. When she turned to face me, a smile hung from her lips. "Thank you." I watched as she moved to the door, unable to look at anything else. I'd seen her at the wedding celebration that had been held for her and the king, but even then, I couldn't keep my eyes off her. Every part of her drew me in, making me long to know her in every way possible. Slowly, she opened the door. "Guy, would you please come in?"

A sturdy-looking man with graying hair and a matching beard stepped inside. "Your Grace?"

"Would you go to the butcher and bring me his best cut of

46

meat? Tell him that I shall pay him for it tomorrow, and while you are out, whatever vegetables you can find will suffice."

"I shall go immediately. Will that be all?"

"After you have brought me the food, I want you to return to the castle. Please have Marie prepare two rooms near your quarters. Tell her to be expecting the guests to arrive tomorrow and that the three of them will be staying indefinitely. I'm going to stay here tonight and care for Conrad's sister and mother. They are sick with a fever."

"Of course, Your Grace," he said with a bow.

"Thank you." To my surprise, she returned his bow with one of her own. "Also, please send the carriage for the four of us tomorrow morning." He nodded his assent and swept out of the room.

"Are we going to live in the castle with you?" Cecily asked.

"Only if that is what you want to do, Cecily."

"Oh, please, Mama. Can we?" Cecily shifted her focus upward, waiting for our mother to answer her.

I watched my mother intently as she contemplated her answer. "Let's let your brother make that decision."

"Conrad?" the queen questioned.

"Are you being earnest?"

"Of course. Why wouldn't I be? The three of you will live in the castle, and, Conrad, you'll become one of my personal guards. That is, if you accept my offer."

"I think I'd have to be a fool not to."

"Good," she replied, smiling. She grabbed my hand and led me to a chair close to the fire. "Your hands are freezing." She held my hands to her chest, using the heat from her body to warm mine. "Come and warm yourself. You look exhausted." The flames warmed me, and I watched as she hung a large pot from the hook over the hearth and poured water into it. As the water boiled, she went outside and filled a large bowl with fresh snow. "Do you have any spare bits of cloth I can use?"

"I'm afraid not. Why?"

"We need to cover your mother and Cecily in cool cloths to help draw the fever out of them. Once we have drawn out the fever, they will start to feel better."

"All we have are the blankets on the beds and the clothes we're wearing. Everything else was sold," I replied.

"Hand me that knife," she ordered. I obeyed her request just as she took her cloak from beside the fireplace.

"You don't have to ruin your cloak on our account. You can use mine." I rose to my feet and placed my hand on top of hers, causing her to stop. "Mine is practically a rag. There's nothing to ruin."

"It's just a cloak," she whispered, raising her chin to meet my gaze. "I have so many already I won't miss it. If I use your cloak, what will you wear in the carriage tomorrow?"

"What will you wear? Your dress isn't thick enough to wear without a cloak, especially not in this harsh of a winter."

She freed one of her hands from my grasp and lightly touched the fabric of my shirt. "But it's so much thicker than your shirt."

"I'll be fine, my lady."

"So will I." Despite my protests, she tore the knife through the fabric of her cloak, ripping it into strips. She then soaked the green material in the bowl of melting snow before placing them on Cecily and my mother. She made them rest with the cold cloths layered on top of them until Guy returned with an armful of food. Both of their fevers started to break as she made stew.

"Thank you," I said as I watched her stir the pot over the fire. "I don't know how I'll ever be able to repay you for your kindness."

"No payment is needed."

"You've saved their lives." I glanced at my mother and Cecily. "You've done for them what I couldn't."

"And how do you know you won't do the same for me?"

"I believe I'd do anything you ask of me." She stepped away from the fire to occupy the seat next to mine. I moved over, helping her position her chair closer to the warmth of the flames.

She gave a slight laugh. "You only say that because I'm your queen."

"I say it because of what you've done for my mother and sister, not because of the title you carry."

Grabbing my hand, she stroked my skin with an unexpected tenderness. "You don't have to struggle to live anymore, Conrad."

My eyes closed, and I savored the feel of her touch. "It's been so hard," I replied, lowering my voice. "I feel like I've failed them."

"How can you think that? You're doing everything within your power to help them. You have been willing to risk life and limb just to provide your mother and sister with enough food to eat."

"But it still hasn't been enough."

"It is now. I'll help you care for them. I promise."

I moved to kneel at her feet. "Thank you. You have my sincerest gratitude."

"You're more than welcome." Suddenly, the tips of her fingers slid down the side of my neck, pulling the linen shirt away from my shoulder. "Who has done this to you?" Her eyes examined the bruises covering my skin.

"Sometimes I fight to earn extra money for my family. It's nothing."

"Please . . . show me all your injuries."

"It's just a couple bruises. That's all."

"Show me."

When I lifted my shirt, her hands traced each mark with a gentle touch. Bruises blanketed the flesh along my ribs and back. "Are you in any pain?"

"Like I said, these are nothing."

"How often do you fight?"

"Three fights per night, but I only do that a couple times a week," I answered. "Unfortunately for my family, I'm a better fighter than I am a blacksmith."

"Do you always make light of the injuries you sustain?"

"Only when my injuries seem to upset you."

"So much pain has been inflicted upon your body." The sadness lacing her voice made my chest tighten. "Please don't fight like this anymore."

"If that is your wish."

"It is."

"Then, I won't, my lady."

"Thank you. That puts my mind at ease." My breath hitched in my throat as I watched her lean toward me, her face mere breaths from mine. "Would you really do anything I asked of you?"

"Give voice to your request and I shall see it done."

"What I need more than anything is a companion."

Her request startled me, and it took me a moment to think of a reply. "Surely someone like you, a queen, is surrounded with friends."

Her lips curved into a solemn smile. "You'd be surprised how lonely it can be." She glanced away from me, focusing her attention on the bubbling stew over the hearth instead. Despair dwelled beneath the breathtaking features of her face. How could someone so beautiful be so sad? Even if we'd only just met, I realized I would do anything within my power to keep her from feeling that way. My thoughts weren't made out of pity, but rather sympathy. I understood how empty and lonely she felt, because I felt the same way.

"I'm a simple peasant though. Why me?"

"Because you feel as lonely as I do."

Now, it was me staring at the queen as if my very existence was dependent upon hers. I barely knew her, and yet, it was as if she knew me better than anyone. Without thinking, I took her hand, drawing it close to my mouth. "You never need to feel lonely again. I'd be honored to be your companion," I said, kissing her flesh. "And as I've said before, whatever you need of me, I shall gladly give to you."

"Conrad." A voice that wasn't hers sounded from somewhere in the distance. "Conrad, are you awake?"

"I am now," I yawned, rubbing my eyes. Sitting up straight, I remembered I was in the back seat of the SUV. Caroline was in the driver's seat and Noah slept in the passenger seat with his back to Caroline.

"Were you dreaming of Evey?"

"Yeah. How did you—"

"You kept mumbling 'my lady' in your sleep."

"Oh, sorry. I was dreaming about the first time I ever met her."

"What was she like back then?"

"She was unbelievably kind to the point where she would do anything to help someone in need," I replied. "And beautiful in a way that's almost overwhelming. But at the same time, you can't stop staring."

"It's incredible to hear the way you talk about her." She looked at me through the rearview mirror. "I only hope I find that kind of love one day."

"It sounds selfish, but I want more time with her. A week wasn't long enough after spending over eighty years apart."

"You'll get to see her again. We should be at Iola's house within the hour."

"Good. Do you need to rest? I can drive for a while if you need me to."

"Nah, I'm good. The roads are pretty deserted. I have to say I'm impressed with the time we're making. We've made the trip from New York to Bandon in less than forty hours. We basically drove from one coast to the other. I mean, we're in Oregon now. That's at least something to be proud of," she said.

"I suppose so."

"Can I ask you something?"

"Sure."

"What are those?" she asked, pointing at Noah's back.

Leaning over the middle console, my attention followed her finger. Noah was sound asleep, but his shirt had slid up to reveal his lower back. I'd only seen his scars one other time, but I knew I would never be able to forget them. The very sight of them made me want to look away. I'd seen my fair share of death and gore over the years, but seeing markings like those on someone you cared about was unbearable. Raised welts covered every inch of his back, and even though they'd been lashed into his flesh centuries ago, the scars still looked painful. I couldn't imagine the agony he had endured to sustain such scars. "I'm not sure I'm the one to tell you."

Her hand reached forward to touch him, but she stopped herself. "What do you mean?"

"I was foolish enough to ask him about them one day after a sparring session. I walked in while he was changing his shirt and saw

51

the scars. Before I knew what I was doing, I questioned him about them. He didn't say a single word to me for three weeks, so when he finally did start speaking to me again, I never brought them up."

"Oh."

"You can ask, but you should be prepared for him to react badly."

"Who could do something like that to another person? And how many times do you have to be whipped for the scars to look like that?"

"The whip had jagged rocks tied to the end of it, which makes it easier to rip through flesh. As for the other part of your question, I'm not sure how many times he was whipped or who did it. All I know is that he was tied down and whipped for hours on end."

"That's barbaric."

"The world wasn't always a kind place."

"It's amazing he didn't die. Shouldn't something like that have killed him?" Her voice wavered as she spoke, and I knew her tears were inevitable.

"You would think. I'm sure part of him probably wishes it did."

"Is that also when he lost everyone but Iola?" she asked.

"How did you know?"

She shrugged. "I just figured something happened to the people he loved most. I mean, everyone has family, right? It's part of life."

"I'd have to agree with you on that."

"How do you get over a loss like that? How can you live through being tortured that badly and still be okay?"

"To tell you the truth, I don't think he has ever gotten over it. He never talks about what happened, and he can't seem to move on. He's had centuries to heal—I just don't think he knows how. I've never really seen him with anyone but you." Her hand covered her mouth, suppressing a sob. "If I had to guess, I'd say he's never allowed himself to be with anyone else because he's scared the past will repeat itself."

"Oh, Noah," she whispered. Tears flowed down her cheeks as the car came to a sudden stop. "I think I need you to drive after all." She hopped out of the driver's seat and walked around the front of the car to Noah's door. I got out of the back seat and positioned myself behind the steering wheel. Caroline opened the passenger door and climbed up into the seat with him.

Noah awoke with a start. "What's wrong? Why did we stop?"

"I haven't been able to stop thinking about everything that's happened in the past few days and it made me upset and I didn't want to drive anymore. Would it be okay for me to sit with you?" Her arms were around him before he could even answer and she squeezed him tight.

He shifted in the seat to make more room for her and she rested her head against his shoulder. "Of course. You don't even have to ask." Her right arm rested across his lap, and Noah twisted the silver bracelet he'd given her.

"I'll never take it off," she whispered.

Turning the keys, I thrust the car into drive and pulled back onto the interstate. We still hadn't made it to Iola's, but I knew the three of us would feel a sense of relief when we finally arrived.

"How long has it been since you've seen Iola?" My focus stayed glued to the road as I waited for Noah to answer my question.

"Longer than I care to admit."

"But she's your sister. Why wouldn't you go to see her?" Caroline asked.

"Well, for a long time, no members of the Concilium saw each other because we thought it wouldn't be safe after Aden murdered Thea and went into hiding. We thought it best to separate ourselves from one another so we would be better protected."

My thoughts turned to Cecily. Noah's sister was alive and within reach, but my own was long gone. I'd never get to see her grow and have a family of her own. There wasn't even a grave I could visit and leave flowers on. All I had were memories of our childhood. I didn't pretend to understand the things keeping Noah from visiting Iola, but if Cecily were somewhere where I could see her, nothing would keep me away. That was one of the pitfalls of being a secundae. There were people I loved who could never be brought back. I loved Evey more than anything else in this world, but I longed to see my mother's and Cecily's faces just one more time.

"I'm sure she'll be glad to see you," she replied.

"I'll be glad to see her too," he answered. "Also, you have to understand that not everyone has a blatant disregard for the orders of the Concilium as Conrad does. I wanted to see Iola, but I thought I was doing her a favor by distancing myself."

"I wouldn't say it's a blatant disregard," I retorted. "I listen to and can understand their orders. I simply choose not to follow them."

"I'm starting to think you might be right though," he said.

"How so?"

"Look at everything that's happened. Aden has Evey and he could be on his way to Iola. Besides Everest and me, she's the only other member of the Concilium on this continent. Who knows how much Helen has told him. Even if Helen only knows Iola is in Oregon, he won't stop until he finds her. And if he isn't there, he'll be searching for another consiliarius. He will hunt us like animals until he gets what he wants. I just keep thinking that maybe if we'd banded together as you originally suggested all those years ago, instead of hiding ourselves away, we could've stopped him."

"You can't think like that," I answered. "None of us expected him to kill Thea and take her powers. She was the caput and losing her changed everything. Maybe Everest did the right thing by splitting everyone up and putting them into hiding. It's kept everyone safe."

"I know. I'm just anxious to see Iola. I don't want anything to happen to her."

"Why don't you just call her?" Caroline asked.

"I don't know what her number is."

"You've got to be kidding me!"

"The last time I saw her was before telephones were invented."

"It's like you people thrive on living in the dark ages."

"We aren't that bad," Noah defended. "But Everest is the only one who is able to contact all the other members of the Concilium."

"So . . . how long have Everest and Iola been in love with each other?"

Out of the corner of my eye, I saw Noah's bewildered expression. "How did you know?"

"Oh, come on, it wasn't that hard to pick up on. You and Conrad just have no perceptive skills. I could tell by the way Everest looked when he admitted to hiding the sickle with her. He fell in love with her and that's why he made her into a consiliarius, isn't it?"

"Yes."

"But doesn't that seem like he was using his powers and position to his advantage?"

"It wasn't like that; Iola was going to be made into a consiliarius regardless of whatever feelings she and Everest had for one another," he answered. "Also, you have to realize that secundae and consiliarius live much longer than everyone else. We don't fall in love with normal people because we would have to live for an eternity without them and there aren't many people who would bear the weight of that sacrifice."

"I see," she replied stiffly, turning away from Noah and fixing her gaze on the dark sky outside her window. It was obvious his words had stung.

"Evey made that sacrifice for me. She knew I wasn't a secundae or a consiliarius, and yet, she still fell in love with me," I added.

"Yes, but everyone else isn't like Evey," Noah answered.

I glanced over at the two of them and met Caroline's eyes for a second. "She still did it." Her slight smile informed me that my words hit their mark, and I shifted my attention back to the road. The white lines disappeared as I turned off of the interstate and continued down a deserted highway. Anxiety coursed through my veins. In a few more minutes, we would reach our destination.

"Turn left up here," Noah ordered.

I followed his instructions and turned down a secluded driveway. Trees lined both sides of the gravel road, bending together to form an organic archway. In the distance, a house was just visible beneath a shroud of leaves and limbs. Beams of light shot out from the headlights of the car, illuminating the faded blue paint of the house's exterior. I scanned my surroundings, but there was nothing else around the house for a few miles. Throwing the car in park, I jumped out and immediately noticed the sound of the ocean crashing against the shore in the distance. Noah and Caroline followed my lead as I walked around to the back of the house. A small patio lined with potted plants and benches lay before us. We made our way to the door, and as we neared it, two figures emerged from the shadows.

"Noah? Conrad?"

"It's us," Noah answered. "Farine?"

"We've been expecting you," she answered.

"Good. Is she inside?"

"Follow us. We'll take you to her." We trailed behind the two people into the house. They led us into a small room littered with parlor chairs, bookcases, and antique glass lamps. Piles of books seemed to cover every open inch of floor space and Caroline tripped over a stack as we stepped forward. Noah and I both flung out our hands to steady her as we walked to the center of the room. "Iola wanted us to bring you in here while we get your rooms prepared. It's good to see you again, Noah, and same to you, Conrad," Farine said, extending her hand to each of us.

"Thank you," Noah replied. "Christopher, it's good to see you as well. This is Caroline." He gestured to her. "She is a close friend of ours."

"Nice to meet you," Caroline answered. Farine and Christopher nodded at her in unison. Farine's dark hair was cut close to her head, and when she stood beside Christopher, she was the same height as him and the more formidable-looking of the two. Christopher's light brown hair hung to his shoulders and his pale skin contrasted with Farine's olive complexion.

"We'll get Iola for you. I'm sure you're anxious to see her," Christopher said.

"Thank you," I replied. Christopher and Farine shut the door to the study behind them, but they hadn't even been gone a minute before the door opened and Iola swept into the room.

"Noah!" She ran to him, yards of blue fabric from her dress

flowing behind her. "Oh, how I've missed you!" she cried, wrapping her arms around his neck.

"And I've missed you." He squeezed her tight. Iola's strawberry-blonde hair hung well past her waist and he grabbed on to it as their embrace continued.

When the two of them finally parted, Iola turned her attention to me. "Conrad!" Her arms fastened around my neck as she hugged me.

"It's good to see you. It's been too long," I replied, patting her shoulders.

Leaning back, her hands cupped my cheeks as she stared at me. "Oh, Conrad," she whispered. "You'll see her again, please don't despair."

"I—"

"I can see how much you miss her in your eyes," she replied. "She thinks of you often."

"How do you know?"

"Because when we are separated from those we love, what else could possibly occupy our minds?" As I scrutinized her features, I wondered what Caroline must think of the siblings' appearances—Iola's eyes were the same shade of green as Noah's, but unlike him, every inch of her skin was covered in freckles. She smiled and kissed me on the cheek before stepping away. "And you must be Caroline." Iola tossed a long curl behind her shoulder as her attention fixated on Caroline.

"I am. It's very nice to meet you," Caroline said.

Iola moved to stand next to Caroline. "You're very beautiful. I can see why he likes you so much." Iola combed her fingers through Caroline's hair as Caroline glanced in surprise at Noah, who rolled his eyes dramatically. "Your impertinence today is as tiresome as it was when we were children, brother."

Noah's cheeks reddened at his sister's words.

"You just became my new favorite person," Caroline stated.

"I knew you would be upset I haven't come to see you in a long time."

"I'm not mad at you," she replied, her focus still on Caroline.

"Don't be worried if he tries to pull away from you. He tends to distance himself from things he treasures."

"Iola! That's enough," Noah spat.

"What do you mean?" Caroline glanced back and forth from Noah to Iola.

"Two hundred years is such a long time to go without seeing you." Iola walked over to Noah and hugged him again. "I thought you were still angry with me."

"I never was."

"You haven't seen your sister in two hundred years?"

"As I said earlier, I was protecting her," Noah replied.

"I can understand that, considering I was an older brother once too. But nothing would keep me away from Cecily. If you knew you'd never see your sister again, I'm sure you would feel the same way."

"Oh, Conrad, you're as compassionate and devoted as the first day I met you," Iola whispered. "You were always the better man for Evey. That's why he sent you to her."

"You mean God?" I looked at Noah in inquiry, but he shrugged. Apparently, he had no idea what she was talking about either.

"You sound surprised," she replied with a laugh.

"I've never thought about it in those terms before."

"You appeared in her life when she was desperate for love and companionship. It wasn't a coincidence—it was fate." Noah, Caroline, and I were stunned by her revelation. "Well, you've been traveling a long way. Let's all sit down." She ushered Noah and me to sit in two armchairs while she joined Caroline on a small couch.

"Iola, Everest sent us here because he hid something important in your house and we need to get it," I said. "It's very important because it can help us defeat Aden."

"I know," she said as she petted Caroline's hair. "He hid it in my room."

"How do you know that?"

"Like all husbands, Everest thinks he can keep secrets."

"Husband? Did you say *husband*?" Noah raised his voice as he uttered the last word of his question.

"Yes, Everest is my husband. He has been for over a century now."

"And didn't you think that's something you should have informed your only brother about?"

"Perhaps you would already know if you ever came to visit," she replied with a shrug. "Men can be so dense, can't they, Caroline?"

"Definitely."

"Okay, everyone focus on the task at hand," I ordered. "Iola, do you know what's hidden in your room?"

"No, I only know that Everest put something in the floor beneath the bed," she answered. "It's been there for ages though. I didn't see him hide it, but I heard the floor squeak when I was getting in bed one night."

"Do you mind if I go and retrieve what's hidden?" I asked.

"Please help yourself to anything you need. When you go up the stairs, it's the first door on the right."

I jumped from my seat and bolted for the door. Noah was right behind me as we headed up the stairs. My heart pounded like a drum as I neared her door. Turning the brass knob, I stepped inside her room. I took a moment to get my bearings before I grabbed the foot of her bed and slid it sideways over the old wooden floor. As soon as the bed was out of the way, Noah and I dropped to our knees, shoving boxes and books out of the way. Our hands picked over the grooves in the floor with great care as we searched for the loose floorboard. The tips of my fingers scurried around a slat of wood, popping it up. A cloud of dust billowed into the air as I moved the board out of the way. Reaching my hand into the dark space, I grasped a metal handle.

"What is it?" Noah asked.

"It's a box of some kind. Step back for a second while I pull it out."

I set the dark wooden box on the floor beside Noah and blew off a layer of grime that coated the lid. The box was made of cedar and about the size of a small suitcase. A tree had been carved into the top of the box, and I recognized the image without fail.

It was the same tree marking my flesh.

"This has to be it," Noah said. "The tree looks just like yours."

I carefully lifted the top of the box. The inside was draped with red velvet, and I unfolded the material to reveal what lay beneath. A metal sickle sat on top of the soft fabric in front of me. The stone hilt was black, and a crimson stain had been embedded into the curved steel of the blade. I picked it up and turned it over in my hand, noticing an engraving on the inner handle of the blade.

"It's been branded with a mark," I said, showing it to Noah.

"That's the Hebrew symbol for the number seven. God set a mark upon Cain to protect him from being murdered by another. He was branded with this symbol on his forehead to serve as a warning. Anything done to Cain would be reversed onto the doer sevenfold." I set the sickle back into its box, careful not to touch the jagged outer edge of the blade or its pointed end. Both edges were sharp, and I began to wonder how this object had ever been considered anything but a deadly weapon. It was difficult to imagine that any weapon would be able to really eliminate Aden once and for all, but if it was possible, the sickle was the best weapon for the job. It was almost poetic that Aden would die by a weapon corrupted by his own evil nature. "Along with the seeds, I guess this is another good thing we're in possession of."

"It won't be good until we get to use it on him," I replied.

"I have a feeling that isn't too far off. But we should get back to Caroline. There's no telling what Iola has told her."

"You know you hurt Caroline's feelings in the car earlier, right?" The words were out of my mouth before I could stop myself. I wasn't the type to meddle in other people's business, but I felt protective of Caroline. For some unexplainable reason, she reminded me of Cecily.

"I know. I didn't intend for it to come out so harsh, but what I said wasn't untrue."

"That may be true, but let me give you a piece of advice that Evey once gave me when we were married. How you say something is almost as important as what you say."

"How did you know you were supposed to be with Evey?"

"Because the thought of being with any other woman wasn't an option for me after I met her. I only wanted Evey. It's one of those things you just know."

"I guess it is."

We replaced the missing floorboard and returned Iola's bed to its original state before heading back downstairs to the parlor. As I opened the door, Iola and Caroline were still sitting next to one another on the couch and Iola was twisting Caroline's hair into an intricate braid. I met Caroline's gaze, my eyebrows furrowing.

"Iola felt like playing with my hair," she explained with a smile. "Is that the sickle?" Upon seeing the box in my hand, she leaned forward in anticipation.

"Yeah. Here, I'll show you." Stepping around a stack of books, I stood in front of Caroline and opened the box, presenting the sickle to her.

"Is that blood?" Caroline asked with a grimace.

"I believe so. It doesn't look like it's been used since Cain had it."

"What is that for?" Iola stood to get a better view.

"It's the sickle Cain used to murder Abel. It's the only weapon that can kill Aden."

"Stabbed by his brother, murdered without cause just like she was," she cried. "She was stabbed in the heart, killed by him—by Aden." Her body trembled, and she rocked back and forth to still the shaking. "I saw. I saw everything."

"Shh, it's all right," Noah coaxed as he pulled her to him. "He isn't here."

"I heard them screaming, and then I saw blood everywhere." Tears poured down Iola's cheeks as Noah tried to comfort her, but the tighter he held her, the harder she seemed to cry. "I watched her die."

Caroline nudged Noah out of the way to take his place. "Iola," Caroline whispered in a soothing voice. "Come finish my hair. There are still a few loose strands and you're doing such a lovely job."

Iola's crying ceased and she began to smile as she fell into some kind of daze, her mind now preoccupied with Caroline's task. "Yes,

I forgot about your hair. I was fixing it so we could show Noah. Isn't she beautiful, brother?"

We all turned in unison to look at Noah. "Very beautiful," he answered, giving Iola a kiss on the cheek.

Noah and I watched as Iola braided the rest of Caroline's hair. Her hands moved skillfully through the long blonde locks. When Iola finished, she pulled Caroline up from the gold-colored couch and they headed for the door hand in hand. "I'll have her back in just a minute," Iola announced with a smile.

Shifting in the chair, I set the sickle in my lap. "We can head back to New York tomorrow night after we get some rest."

"That'll be good," Noah replied. "Everest will be glad to know we have the sickle, and I'd like to ask him why he forgot to mention that he is my brother-in-law."

"You really had no idea they were married?"

He let out a deep breath, sinking into his chair. "They've been together for thousands of years. I knew it was just a matter of time, but Everest has always been so discreet. Also, it's not like they're the only members of the Concilium connected to one another. Palma and Balen have pretty much been together since Palma joined the Concilium."

"I suppose it does make sense to be with someone who can live as long as you can, but at the same time, it doesn't always happen that way."

"I'm realizing that," he confessed. "I do care for Caroline, but at the same time, the way I feel about her brings up all the things I've tried to forget."

I stole a sideways glance at him and could see that he was resting his head in his left hand. I wanted to ask him what he meant. Noah wasn't the type of person who freely shared any information about his past, and I wondered if what he was talking about had any direct relation to the wounds marring his skin and soul. "You should put more trust in yourself. Your feelings for her aren't one-sided, and how long has it been since you've felt this way for someone?"

Before Noah could answer, Iola burst back into the parlor with Caroline in tow. Caroline had changed out of her clothes and was now wearing a pink dress almost identical in style to the one Iola wore. Noah's gaze fixed on Caroline. "Too long," he answered.

"I feel like I just stepped out of a book on Greek mythology."

"You look lovely," Noah said, standing up from his chair.

"I spoke with Farine and she informed me that both of your rooms are ready," Iola chimed in. "If all of you would follow me, I'll show them to you." We followed Iola out of the parlor and up the staircase to the second floor. We passed by her door on the right and continued down a narrow hallway covered in paintings from floor to ceiling. A few canvases depicting landscapes seemed to take up half the wall while much smaller portraits were tucked into the remaining cracks of space. The four of us came to a stop at the first door on the left side of the hall. "Conrad, this is your room."

"Thank you," I replied, placing my hand on the doorknob.

"Wait, Conrad gets a room to himself?" Noah questioned.

"Brother, am I to understand you're unwilling to share a room with a woman as beautiful as Caroline?"

"Well, I—"

"I only have two spare rooms and I very much doubt Conrad wants to sleep in the same bed as you."

"Fine," he mumbled.

A victorious smile crept across Iola's face. "Noah and Caroline, your room is this door on the right. Christopher already brought up your things from the car. If there is anything else you need, please let me know. I'll leave you to rest now." Iola winked at me and kissed both Caroline and Noah on the cheek before returning to her room.

"Wake me when it's time to leave."

"We will," Caroline answered.

"Good night."

7

DROWNING

I'd just returned from my walk with Donovan and something that was intended to calm my nerves, only exacerbated them. I couldn't stand my white prison any longer. The room Aden had decorated so beautifully was sure to become my tomb. I'd never be able to submit to his desires. How long would it be until his anger consumed us both? Grabbing a pillow, I slammed it into the lamp on the bedside table. The lamp fell to the ground, shattering upon impact with the floor as the end of the pillowcase ripped, releasing hundreds of white feathers into the air. They drifted to and fro like flakes of snow and pulled at a memory embedded in the dark crevices of my mind.

"Here, let me fasten that for you," I said, closing the front of my winter cloak around Cecily. "This is the warmest one I own, so it'll be perfect for you to wear."

"And then we'll go play in the snow?" Her bright eyes, so much like her brother's, stared up at me through a ring of brown fur.

I kissed her cheek and smiled. "Of course." I rushed to fasten the last button and took her hand in mine. We ran out of my room and through the halls of the castle until we burst through the doors, leaving nothing but a trail of laughter behind us. I made my way through the ankle-deep snow toward the apple orchard on the other side of the castle grounds. Suddenly, a ball of snow slammed into my back. When I turned around, Cecily was already picking up another handful of snow. "Oh no you don't!" I yelled as I ran toward her. My hands grabbed her waist as I pulled her to the ground with me. We rolled over, covering ourselves in a layer of fine white dust. The sounds of our laughter rang out as we continued to play. Flakes of snow fell through the air, adding to the pile covering the ground.

"Cecily?" I didn't have to see him to know Conrad was the one calling out for his sister.

"Conrad!" At the sound of his voice, she stood and ran to him. "Come play in the snow with us!"

"Come play with you?"

"Yes!" I watched as she flung her arms around his neck and he spun her around in circles, letting her feet fly off the ground. My heart filled with joy as I watched the two of them. After a while, I made my way over to them. "Now spin her!"

Conrad's gaze locked on mine. "I don't think the queen wants me to spin her," he replied hesitantly.

"And how would you know that?" I took a step closer to him, brushing snow from my gray cloak. "You haven't asked me, after all," I teased.

"Spin her! Spin her!" Cecily demanded.

"Yes, Conrad, spin me."

"If you insist." A smile tugged at my lips as he closed the distance between us and placed his hands on my waist. Wrapping my arms around his shoulders, I buried my face against the side of his neck. "You better hold on tight," he whispered. My grasp tightened as we began to spin. With each rotation, he increased our speed and my feet soared through the air behind me. When he started to lose his balance, I couldn't help but scream. Conrad plummeted to the ground with me landing on top of him. "Did I hurt you?"

"No. As always, you've done your duty and protected me from the perilous snow!" I laughed.

"Laugh all you want, but protecting you is something I take very seriously."

"You can't protect me from everything," I replied.

"Maybe not, but I would gladly die trying," he whispered.

"Don't say that." My fingers found refuge on the curve of his cheek.

"Why not?"

"Just don't." As I moved to stand, Conrad helped guide me to my feet. "The king will be looking for me. I should get back inside. Goodbye, Cecily," I said, dusting off my hands. "Conrad," I added with a nod. He bowed to me in response, his attention never shifting from my face. Grabbing the front of my dress, I took off in the direction of the castle and didn't stop until I reached my room. Why was it that every time I saw him, the pace of my heart quickened? I wasn't free to feel this way. I belonged to another, but that didn't change the fact that I wanted more. I longed to be saved from my fate of being Adam's wife for eternity. After I removed my heavy winter clothes, I pulled a thin chemise over my head. Someone knocked at my door, but I sent them away without finding out who it was or what they needed. It wasn't dark outside yet, but I was too tired to do anything but sleep. I buried myself under a pile of thick blankets and closed my eyes to welcome the familiar draw of slumber.

When I awoke, the entire castle was silent. Everyone had retired to their rooms to escape the bitter cold of a winter's night. Throwing a shawl over my shoulders, I crept into the hall, silently making my way through the castle. My subconscious knew where to lead me because there was only one place I wanted to go. Even though the stone floors felt like ice as I continued through the corridor, stopping wasn't an option. Elation warmed my flesh as I finally reached a small oak door. I snuck inside and closed the door behind me, trying to be as quiet as possible.

My eyes fell upon his slumped form lying in front of the fireplace.

"Conrad, why are you sleeping by the fire? Are your accommodations not to your liking?" The sound of my voice woke him, and he pushed himself from the floor to face me. I dropped to my knees, unable to resist the impulse to be near him.

"I assure you everything is perfect, but old habits are hard to break, my lady."

"You need not sleep on the floor anymore." My hand reached for his face. "You've lived here for a few months now. Surely, you must know this isn't going to be taken away from you." His body froze beneath my touch.

"Do you need something from me?"

"No, why do you ask?"

"I was just wondering why you would come to my room in the middle of the night."

"I hardly know myself." I shivered, the chill from the cold stone floors of the corridor spreading through my body.

"You're cold. Come and use some of this blanket to warm yourself." A large blanket was draped over his shoulders, and he held out an end for me to cover myself with. As I sat next to him, his shoulder brushed mine underneath the blanket. It was as if his body called out to mine, begging me to come closer. "May I ask you something personal, my lady?"

"What would you like to know?" I stared into his eyes, admiring the bright color.

"Why don't you stay in the king's room?" His question was blunt, and for a brief moment, I was startled by his frankness.

"Like many things in this life, the decision of marrying the king was one that was made for me. Choosing who you spend your life with is a luxury few have."

He nodded, his expression turning solemn. "And what about love?"

"It too is a luxury we all wish for but few ever have."

"You do not love the king?" Even though he posed the question, we both knew that he already knew my answer. He had been by my side for the past few months and could see I wasn't in love with my husband.

"I do not," I answered. I leaned toward him so that only a small sliver of space existed between us. My hair tumbled over my shoulders, barely touching the surface of his hand.

"And do you wish for it? For love?"

"Every day," I whispered. "Every day, I pray my fate will change. That I'll fall in love and start to feel again." A lone tear slid down my cheek as I met his gaze. How many years had I spent hoping, praying against all odds that I could be free to live my own life? The answer was a simple one: too many. I'd spent too much time longing for a change instead of acting on one.

He brushed the tear from my face. "Please don't cry." I stretched out my hand and placed my fingertips on his lips. I wanted nothing more than to discover what they felt like when pressed against mine. "Tell me what I can do for you."

"Would you wrap your arms around me and hold me for a little while?" I asked, my voice faltering.

Grabbing my waist, he pulled me into his lap. His bare chest was warm against my back, and I relaxed into him. "I'll hold you for as long as you need."

"Thank you." His arms tightened around me, forcing our bodies closer together. His presence brought me more comfort than my husband's had in years. I could've spent an eternity in Conrad's arms, and as he held me, I allowed myself to dream of a life where such a thing was possible.

"You shouldn't worry," he whispered, adjusting the blanket to fit around us. "You are very kind and place the well-being of others before your own; you won't be without love for long."

"I appreciate your kind words, but I doubt they will ever come to fruition."

"You may be married, but the king doesn't own your heart or your mind. Those are yours to give to whomever you choose. Any man alive would gladly give you whatever you desire."

I turned to face him, and his hands clasped behind my waist, maintaining our close proximity. "Any man?"

"Any."

"And what about you?" I asked. "Who do you want to give your heart and mind to?"

"A woman I'm not forced to marry." My fingertips found his face once again as I appraised his features. "My parents arranged a marriage for me."

"An arranged marriage?" Shock trickled down the hairs along my neck. The man I'd come to need in my life would soon be ripped from it.

"Yes," he answered with a nod.

"When will you be leaving?" I tried to pull from his embrace, but his arms prevented me.

"My lady—"

"When?" I questioned, urgency creeping into my voice.

"Never. You saved my family. That is a kindness I won't soon forget."

"If you want to leave the castle and get married, you have my blessing. You are free to leave at any time."

"I was supposed to get married, but I put an end to the arrangement. I never plan to leave your side. This is where I want to be."

"You don't owe me anything."

"You're right," he said as he released his hold on my waist, trailing the tips of his fingers down my sides all the way to my thighs. The gesture elicited a surge of contentment to fill my chest, and I sighed in response. "I owe you everything."

"Conrad?"

"Yes?"

I traced the edge of his bottom lip as I continued to look at him. "Do you think I'm beautiful?"

His brow crinkled into a look of confusion. "You're thought to be very beautiful by everyone in your kingdom."

"I don't care what everyone else thinks. I care what you think."

"But I'm just a guard."

"You are so much more than the title you carry."

"As are you," he whispered, wrapping a piece of my hair around his finger. "In all my life, I've never set eyes upon anything as beautiful as you. When I first saw you, I couldn't believe you were real—I thought you were a dream. And then, when you followed me home, I wanted to know you, talk to you. No one has ever treated me with as much respect as you do."

"That night we first met and I knelt in front of you," I said, leaning in to him so our faces were only a breath apart. "The moment I touched you . . ."

"What did you feel when you touched me?" He set his palm against my cheek and I placed my hand over it so he couldn't pull away.

"I felt like I wasn't drowning anymore." Sucking in a deep breath, I savored the relief provided by his touch. "When you look at me like that, it makes me think you can save me from all this."

"What do you need me to save you from?" Both of his hands were on my cheeks, tenderly cradling my face. In that moment, I knew he would do anything, risk anything for me, and in the back of my mind, a small voice told me I'd do the same for him.

"Centuries of emptiness."

"Centuries?"

It took me a moment to realize what I'd confessed. Conrad didn't know who I really was. He didn't understand why my identity had to be kept secret from everyone. I'd begged for a way to change my life and here it sat before me. Conrad would save me from it all, but the price he was willing to pay to do so frightened me. The thought of losing him was inconceivable, especially after I'd just found him. I longed to reveal my secret, and it wasn't the first time I'd wanted to either. He waited for me to answer his question, but I couldn't. The words I wanted to say dissolved in my mouth. "I'm so sorry. I didn't mean to be an intrusion. Good night," I said as I stepped out of the warmth of the blanket and hurried to the door of his room.

"Good night, my lady." I met his gaze one last time before leaving.

My memory-filled daze ended just as Aden entered my room. My moments with Conrad were replaced with the thought that he was the cause of all my pain and heartache.

"What now?" The distaste and hatred was apparent in my voice as I spoke. He had destroyed everything he set his hands on. Life seemed to disintegrate beneath his touch. It was only a matter of time before I was reduced to ash as well.

"I just wanted to see how you were doing."

"Why?"

"Because I want to see you happy," he replied.

"Brutally murdering everyone I've ever loved is the wrong way of going about that." He took another step toward me, but I held up my hands to stop him. "Please don't come any closer."

"Evey—"

"I said don't," I shouted. Tears welled in my eyes. Crying was something that was becoming all too familiar to me. It made me feel even more helpless, and while I wished I could be strong like Conrad would have wanted, I was locked in a room with no escape. I trembled all over as I realized there was no way out. My knees buckled, causing me to crash to the floor. Aden flung his arms around me. I tried to push him away, but his hold was firm. "Leave me alone."

"I never meant to cause you any harm." His warm arms reminded me so much of Conrad's. I looked up at Aden, but his face wasn't the one I longed to see. My eyes closed as the tips of my fingers slowly cascaded over the sides of his face. "What are you doing?"

"Imagining you're someone else."

His fingers combed through my hair. "Sometimes I imagine that I can be like him, that I can be the man you used to love."

"Do you think you can be him again?"

"I think you can make me him again."

"And why is that?"

"Because you're you," he answered. "You're the embodiment of everything good."

"I'm not all that good."

"You don't realize how easy it is to fall in love with you. That's why I can't completely hold a grudge against Conrad. You're the easiest person to love, Evey."

"That's amusing, because you have to be the hardest."

His hands slid down my arms and took hold of my wrists. "I've made it difficult for anyone to love me," he replied. "Can I show you something?" Pulling me to my feet, he led me to the door. His hand squeezed mine as if to ask for permission before escorting me any further.

"I'll go with you."

I followed him to the end of the hall. His fingers interlaced with mine as we approached a pair of double doors. They swung open when he pushed against the white wood, and my mouth dropped open as we stepped inside. "This is my room."

His room was twice as large as mine and covered in beautiful paintings. They hung on every inch of wall space and a few were even leaning against a desk—the only piece of furniture in his room other than his bed. However, what really caught my attention was that every painting was a depiction of me. He had dozens of portraits and even a few of the two of us together. I studied them, absorbing all the immediate details. The last painting I noticed was the largest one in the whole room. It hung just above Aden's bed and it was a picture of us as Adam and Eve. Our hands were inter-twined just as they were now, and we were surrounded by bright flowers while tree branches loomed over our heads. My hair hung over my chest and Aden's arm stretched across my hips in order to preserve my modesty. His hands touched me in fairly intimate places, and I couldn't ignore my expression of pure happiness. "Is that what it really looked like?" I let go of him so I could take a closer look at the painting.

"The Garden?"

"Yeah."

"It was very similar, but I'll tell you something else about it."

"And what might that be?"

"The day you appeared in the Garden of Eden, it became more beautiful."

My fingertips skidded across the painting's surface. I couldn't fathom how the man in the painting and the man standing beside me were one in the same. The differences between the two were like day and night. I saw Aden as he used to be—as Adam—a man living in the glory of light, and as he was now, one succumbing to the darkness that filled his soul. "And how could that be?"

"You gave me a reason to appreciate everything I'd overlooked. I felt as if I'd been blind for ages. But then everything around me was suddenly illuminated and I could see for the first time. The sun became warmer, the leaves greener, and flowers smelled more fragrant. I was able to admire the beauty of our surroundings because I had someone to love."

"Aden, I don't know what to say."

"You don't have to say anything. I just want you to know how I feel," he said. I sat on his bed and picked up a drawing lying on his pillow. A lump of melted gold rested on top of the parchment in my hand. "Your wedding ring."

"My wedding ring?"

"It's the one you threw in the fire when you were preparing to run away with Conrad. I waited until you were out of your room and searched through the embers in your fireplace to find it," he answered as he sat beside me. "I've had it with me ever since that day."

"Why?"

He picked up the ring as if it were the most precious thing he owned. "To remind myself of what I lost that day."

"And what did you lose?"

"Everything . . . I lost you, myself, and everything we stood for. I had nothing left."

"I'm sorry." I sighed. "I'm sorry I cost you so much. I never meant to cause anyone any harm, but in all my lives, I never had the opportunity to choose anything for myself. For once, I wanted to be able to choose who I could be with." My feelings for Conrad were beyond my control. I lived thousands of years, gazed upon thousands of faces, and never once did I fall in love with another person . . . until I met him. He was the one exception in an unending span of time.

"And you chose him."

"I may have been given to you, but I chose Conrad. I still choose him." My grasp tightened on the parchment in my hand. My own image stared back at me from the thick paper.

"It doesn't matter what I sit down to draw because I always end up drawing you. I've sat in front of sunsets, oceans, and mountains, but no matter what I do, no matter where I am, you're always looking up at me from the paper." He leaned closer, his shoulder brushing against mine. "I want you to have this," he whispered, setting the golden lump in my palm. As soon as it touched my skin, my whole body shuddered and my consciousness was transported into the past.

I stood in the shade of a massive oak tree. Light filtered through the leaves, illuminating dozens of birds perched on its branches. Their voices chimed in unison, creating a soft melody that filled my heart and soul with joy. Blades of grass padded the soles of my feet and the fragrant smell of roses surrounded me. A varying spectrum of colors materialized before my eyes. Green, blue, yellow, red, and purple decorated the world around me. Closing my eyes, I took a deep breath. Everything about this place was wonderful and I savored in its beauty. Muffled footsteps echoed in the trees behind me. Glancing over my shoulder, I watched a herd of deer grazing next to a row of trees. They wove in and out of the brown trunks with an easy grace, searching for food. As I rounded the oak to get a better view, I stumbled over a pair of legs. Before me, a man who appeared to have been sleeping, suddenly stirred. Kneeling beside him, I leaned forward to brush a stray curl out of his eyes.

His brown gaze scanned my face with curiosity. "Who are you?"

"I'm Eve," I replied with a smile. "What's your name?"

"Adam." He pushed himself up from the ground to sit beside me. He stared at me as if I would melt away into nothingness at any second. "I've never seen anyone else. I've always been alone." His hand caressed my cheek as his face neared mine. "I feared I was doomed to live in solitude, but here you are."

"You aren't alone anymore." My fingers swept away another curl.

"Good," he replied. Our mouths pressed together as his hands slid down my back. I pulled him closer, my lips still locked with his.

74

After a while, we finally separated, and my fingertips trailed down his chest. He flinched in response to the touch.

"What's wrong?"

"I don't know. It hurt when you touched me just now."

A large wound marred the flesh just above his heart. "You've been hurt." When I pressed my hand to the wound, a white light radiated from the connection and appeared to be healing him. The wound shrank until his skin fused together and only a faded white line remained above his heart. "Why did that happen?"

"Because you belong to me and I belong to you," he answered. Taking my hands in his, he kissed both of my palms. "You're mine now."

"Why do you think I'm yours?"

"Why else would you have been sent here?" He tilted my chin upward so he could join our lips again.

The warmth of his mouth was still present upon mine as the memory faded away. My grasp tightened on the ring, the metal biting into my skin.

"You remembered something, didn't you?" Aden asked, his voice teeming with hope. Instead of answering him, my attention fell to his chest and I undid the buttons of his gray shirt. I needed to see his scar for myself; I had to know if what I saw was true. At one point in time, I had loved the man sitting before me, but even after what I'd witnessed, it was impossible to fathom. "What are you doing?"

"I have to see your scar for myself." Spreading his shirt open, my eyes widened with shock. A thin white line marked the area just above his heart. The tips of my fingers traced over the scar in utter disbelief.

"It's been there since the first day I saw you."

"But why were you cut there?"

"You were made from me . . . We are made of the same flesh."

"The same flesh?"

"Made of and for each other," he replied.

"But we have been reborn as infants many times, so how can you still have a scar from your first life?"

75

"My scar is as much a part of me as my hair or my eyes. It's always been there, just above my heart. I believe it to be a sign."

"Of what?"

"That we belong together. I can be the man you used to love if you just give me a chance."

"I saw it." Words evaporated in my mouth as I willed myself to continue speaking. "I remembered the first time I ever saw you." Lifting my hand from his chest, I tucked a stray piece of hair behind my ear.

"And what did you think?"

"Honestly, I don't know what to think," I answered. "I've remembered things about you as my husband, but until now, I've only witnessed your cruel nature. I haven't wanted to think about how I used to be in love with you."

"But you did love me."

"And that was a long time ago," I countered. I didn't want to think about these things. I didn't want to remember what it felt like to be in love with him or how kind and gentle he used to be. I was responsible for destroying that man, and the more I thought about our past together, the guiltier I felt. "Can I go back to my room now?"

"Despite what you think, you aren't a prisoner here."

"Aren't I, though?" I set the drawing back on his pillow and stood. "I mean, it's not like you'll ever let me leave you."

"I—" he began but quickly stopped. My hand closed around the melted ring as I walked over to the door. "I'd like for you to stay."

"And I would like to go back to my room."

"Then I won't keep you any longer." He stepped to the door and opened it for me. "May I join you for dinner in your room tonight?"

"Aden, do whatever you'd like. It's what you always do anyway," I answered in exasperation. Hurrying past him, I saw Donovan perched at the top of the stairs. My only exit was blocked by someone I despised almost as much as I despised Aden. And to think, my former husband wanted me to believe I wasn't a prisoner. I may have technically been a teenager, but I wasn't stupid. As I approached my room, I remembered I hadn't checked on Helen since before breakfast.

"Can I have the key to Helen's room?" I loathed the thought of asking Donovan for anything, but I wanted to make sure Helen was still okay.

"No," he mumbled, too distracted by the newspaper he was reading to acknowledge my presence.

"I'd like to have the key to her room, please. I want to check on her."

He folded up his newspaper and laid it across his lap. "Perhaps I wasn't clear enough the first time," he spat with an intimidating glare. "No."

"It's fine if you don't want to give me the key. I'll just go ask Aden for it," I said. "Although, I'm sure he'll be most displeased with your treatment of me." I stared back at him, returning his glare with one of my own. Reluctantly, he stood from his chair and unlocked Helen's door. I smiled in triumph. "Thank you." I tapped on Helen's door before stepping inside. "Helen, may I come in?" Her door closed behind me and I flicked on the lights. The space had been cleaned since this morning. There were no more shards of glass littering the floor and the furniture had been rearranged.

"Evey?"

"Yeah. May I sit with you?"

She shrugged her shoulders. "If you want."

Sitting beside her, I noticed her knees had red blisters on them from being burned by a soul the night before. "I just wanted to check on you. How are your hands?"

"They're better thanks to you." She held her hands out in front of her. Several small cuts covered her knuckles. A basket of gauze and antibiotic ointment sat on the shelf beside her bed. I grabbed the basket and removed the ointment.

"May I put some of this on your hands and knees?"

"Sure."

"I'm sorry I didn't look at your knees earlier. I guess I was more focused on your hands. You had quite a bit of blood on them." I dabbed a little ointment on her hands before applying some to her knees. Then I took some gauze and wrapped it around each knee, ensuring that her burns were covered. "How is that?"

"Much better," she answered, smiling slightly. "Thank you."

"Have you had something to eat today?"

She nodded and tucked her legs underneath her. "Aden brought me some food when he came to clean my room earlier."

"Aden cleaned your room?"

"Yeah. He's very easy to hate, but he can also be kind. I'd like to say I hate him, but it's much more complicated than that."

"How so?"

"Well, I hate him for what he took from us, but he's also the reason I'm even alive today." She brushed away the tears rolling down her cheeks.

"Donovan told me Aden has a propensity for collecting broken things," I said. "I asked him what he meant, but he told me to ask you."

She shivered. Her T-shirt and shorts seemed too thin to provide any sort of warmth, so I grabbed a blanket from the foot of the bed and wrapped it around her shoulders.

"I was one of Aden's secundae before I served Noah. And I only left Aden after what he did to Thea."

"If you don't want to talk about it, you don't have to." Her voice was saturated with despair. She carried the pain of numerous wounds, and the last thing I wanted to do was add fuel to the fire.

"No, I want you to know this. After Aden executed Conrad, I tried my best to be there for his mother and sister, but his death was so hard on us—all of us," she added as she glanced in my direction. "Not long after he died, his mother followed him to the grave. Her health had been poor for such a long time and losing him was more than her body could take." She used a corner of the blanket to dab her cheeks, and I placed my hand on top of hers. "You and I cared for Cecily. I tried to be strong for her, but it was hard. I didn't know what else to do; it seemed like there would never be an end to the pain. My grief became too overwhelming, and I sought to free myself from it. So, two years after we buried Conrad, I climbed up to the bell tower of the church and jumped."

My hand slapped over my face in horror. "You killed yourself?"

"It was too much for me to bear," she sobbed. "I loved Conrad so much and I hated you when I discovered why he'd been killed. I blamed you for his death. I wanted him to love me, but he didn't. He only ever loved you."

"I'm so sorry." The tears pouring from my eyes mirrored hers. "I never wanted him to get hurt because of me. I tried to make him leave with me, but he wouldn't."

"I know. Cecily told me. She told me about all the kind things you did for her and her mother—that you cared for both of them when they were sick and always made sure they had enough food."

"I should've tried harder."

"You tried to help me right after he died, but I was too proud to accept your kindness. I wanted nothing to do with you, but I saw something that changed my opinion of you."

"And what was that?" I accepted the corner of the blanket she offered and wiped away my tears.

"On the first anniversary of Conrad's death, I woke up before dawn to leave a bundle of flowers on his grave. You had him buried at the edge of an apple orchard, right in the shade of one of the trees. As I neared the tree, I saw Guy standing at the perimeter of the orchard, which I thought seemed rather strange until I saw you sleeping on top of Conrad's grave." She grabbed my hand, demanding my attention. "Guy told me that you slept there every night and you only came inside when he or Mickey carried you back to the castle against your will."

"I didn't know. I mean, I don't remember doing that and Conrad never told me about it."

"That was the day I realized you loved him as much as, if not more than, I did. You helped his family and cared for Cecily when he was gone. I've tried to hate you all these years, but really, I'm displacing my own self-loathing. I was jealous because you did the things that I wanted to do for Conrad and his family but couldn't."

"And how does Aden fit into all of this?"

"When he found out I killed myself, he went to Thea and begged her to make me into a secundae."

79

"He did?"

"Yeah. We had only met once before, but I guess he felt compelled to help me, and I'm glad he did. The moment my feet left the tower, I regretted my decision. But by then, it was too late."

"Do you mind if I ask what happened after that?"

"To tell you the truth, I don't really know. I remember slamming into the ground, and then I woke up as if it were nothing more than a bad dream. I didn't go to heaven or hell, but I'm glad Aden saved me from the guilt and despair surrounding that decision. He gave me a second chance at life."

"That was very kind of him. And Aden saved Donovan and gave him a second chance as well?"

"Donovan was right when he told you Aden has a habit of collecting broken things. I believe Aden does it because he knows what it's like to do horrible things and feel regret. I'm not saying he's a good person, but he isn't all bad. It'd be difficult to be transformed into something against your will and then try and fight that transformation every day."

"I've never thought about it like that. I know his eating of the apple was my fault, but it never occurred to me that he could be so conflicted."

"Like I said, my opinion of him is a complicated one. I hate him for killing Conrad all those years ago and last night as well, but at the same time, I owe him everything. He's the reason I got to see Conrad again and atone for what I did to myself."

To my own astonishment, I turned to Helen and hugged her. "I'm sorry if I ever did anything to hurt you."

"You can't be blamed for loving the same man I do." She held on to me for a minute before pulling away. "I'm sorry I tried to come between the two of you back in Chicago. I just wanted—"

"To be with him?"

"Yeah."

"I understand completely."

"All I wanted was to keep him safe," she said.

"I would've done the same thing." I paused for a beat. "Well,

I'm sure you're tired, so I'll let you get some rest. Let me know if you need anything."

"Okay."

I stood and made my way to the door. "Helen?"

"Yeah?"

"I'm going to find us a way out of here." I gave her a slight smile before walking out of her room. Donovan was still stationed at his post. He slammed the door behind me and locked it. Then he shoved the key back into the pocket of his pants with a sneer.

"From now on, you will let me in Helen's room whenever I want," I ordered. He may have been stronger than me, but I wasn't so easy to intimidate. "You may be Aden's most loyal servant, but I was his wife for thousands of years. He'd do anything for me, and you know it. So, if you even look at me in a way I don't like, I'll have you thrown out of here faster than you can wipe that smirk off your face."

He took a step in my direction, moving to hover over me. His left hand balled into a fist at his side while his right grabbed my neck. "I don't like to be threatened," he snarled in my ear.

I ripped his hand from my throat. "It's not a threat. It's a fact." I pulled away from him just as Aden came out of his room.

"What's going on?" He looked from Donovan to me and back again.

"Oh, I was just returning the key to Helen's room," I replied innocently. "I wanted to check on her and see how she was doing since she hurt her hands this morning."

"And how are Helen's hands?"

"Much better."

"That's good to hear," he replied. "Donovan, would you go downstairs and bring up the dinner tray for Evey and me? The two of us will be dining in her room this evening." Donovan bowed to Aden and stalked downstairs without saying a word. As soon as he was gone, Aden moved to stand next to me. My hand massaged the flesh where Donovan had grabbed me. "What's wrong?"

My lungs filled with a deep breath. "He frightens me."

"Donovan won't harm you." He took my hand in his. "I won't let anyone harm you."

"I know. Helen told me what you did for her and Donovan."

"It only seemed right to turn them into my secundae."

"Would you tell me about it?"

"Yes, but first you must eat. You haven't eaten all day." I nodded and allowed Aden to lead me to my room. Pulling the desk from the wall, he placed a chair on either side of it to make a table of sorts. "After you," he said, gesturing toward the nearest chair.

"Thanks." The sky outside my window was slowly darkening. At this time yesterday, I never would have suspected I'd be sitting across from Aden right now instead of Conrad. My life had changed in the blink of an eye, just like it had when Conrad showed up at Tulson.

"What are you thinking about?"

I set my hands in my lap and straightened my spine. "Not much. Just letting my mind wander."

"I apologize if I make you uncomfortable. I'm having trouble figuring out how I should act around you," he confessed. "I mean, we were friends, lovers, and spouses. It's kind of hard to erase the history lingering between us."

"I'd like to say I have an answer for you, but I'm afraid I don't."

A soft knock sounded at the door, drawing Aden's attention away from our conversation. "Come in, Donovan." Donovan opened the door and wheeled in a small metal cart that carried a tray. Two plates of food sat on top of the tray and a bottle of wine and two wine glasses sat on the bottom shelf of the cart. Donovan placed the plates and wine glasses in front of us before offering the bottle of wine to Aden. After his task was complete, Donovan exited the room as quietly as he'd entered. Aden filled a glass with wine before handing it to me. I took the offered glass and drank from it. I had only drunk wine one other time in my life and that was a glass my mother had given me at Christmas dinner last year. Taking another sip of wine, I focused on everything but the man sitting in front of me. I could sense him watching while I ate, scrutinizing each movement.

"Just say whatever it is that you're holding back."

"How could you tell I wanted to say something?"

"Lucky guess, I suppose. What do you want to tell me?"

"I'm not sure how you'll react to it," he said.

"As if that has stopped you before." I released a heavy sigh. "Look, I'm sick and tired of your games, so tell me or don't. Either way, I couldn't care less."

"Please, know I mean you no harm when I tell you this," he replied, pausing to take a long drink of wine. "When we were in Eden and you took the apple, God wanted to curse you with the knowledge of everything evil. Since you were the one who took the apple, he wanted you to have the more severe punishment."

"Then how is it you were cursed with it instead?"

"I asked him to. You're better than I am and you always have been. You're innately good and I couldn't stand the thought of that being corrupted. I thought I'd be able to fight the evil seed planted in my body, but as it turned out, that proved to be harder than I ever could've imagined."

His revelation stunned me into silence, and it took a while before I found the strength to speak again. "So, all of this is even more my fault?"

"All of what?"

Guilt spread throughout my body like a wildfire. "All the horrible things you've done. You only did them because of something I made you do."

"No." He moved to kneel at my side. "This is how I wanted it. I knew I could lose myself, but I didn't care if it meant I could save you." Taking my hands in his, he forced me to look at him.

"Why would you take that risk?"

"Because I love you," he whispered.

8

DEATH AND DESTRUCTION

"Noah! *Noah!*"

I awoke in a panic. Screams echoed throughout the house, thrusting me from the fog of sleep. Rolling to the side of the bed, I flung the box open and grabbed the sickle. I jumped to the floor, my right hand brandishing the weapon.

Another scream pierced my ears and I lunged for the door. But before I could reach it, two souls burst inside, ripping the door from its hinges. One stumbled toward me with its hands outstretched. I stepped back, forcing the soul to come further into the room. Behind it stood the other soul. Grabbing a book from the dresser, I threw it at the soul's face to serve as a distraction. Then I ran forward and kicked the side of its knee. My blow broke the joint and the soul crumpled to the floor. I raised the sickle, and its head quickly followed the rest of the body. The corpse disintegrated as I leapt over it to plunge the tip of the sickle through the abdomen of the other soul. Metal sliced through its charred flesh as if it were no more than a sack of flour. Hurrying over to my bag, I retrieved a holster and filled it with a couple knives. Once I was armed, I made my way to the door.

"Conrad!" Caroline shouted, her voice sounding from across the hall.

"Caroline?"

"Conrad, please hurry!" she yelled. "I can't keep them away from me much longer."

"I'm coming!" I called out. Adrenaline pumped through my veins with fury as I ran to the room opposite of mine and saw Caroline pinned against the back wall while two souls charged for her. A large four-poster bed stood between us, blocking my path to her. She hurled a lamp at one of them, but it did nothing to slow the soul down. "Caroline, jump!" Without another word, I stepped to the bed and kicked it with all my strength. It skidded across the floor, slamming into the backs of the two souls. Caroline jumped on top of the mattress just as the bed crashed into the wall. She stumbled forward and I held out my hand to catch her. "You okay? Hurt?"

"I'm fine. They didn't get a chance to touch me."

I made sure she was steady on her feet before removing a small knife from my holster. Climbing on top of the bed, I stabbed each soul through their temple before jumping down and heading for the door. "Where's Noah?"

"I don't know," she answered, her voice shaking. "He heard Iola calling out for him and ran to her room. I got up to follow him but was stopped by the souls."

"Let's head to Iola's room, then." Glancing in each direction, I made sure there were no immediate threats. I felt Caroline grab two knives from the belt strung across my chest. "Stay close."

"I will. Hey, Conrad?"

"Yeah?"

"Thanks for coming to get me."

"No problem." I stepped carefully to avoid the shards of glass littering the floor.

"I know it's weird timing to be making this observation, but none of the other secundae fight like you do."

"What do you mean?"

"I watched Milton and the twins spar a bit, but none of them move like you do. It's almost as if you were born to destroy things."

"Thanks, I think."

"I mean it as a compliment. Most of them have centuries of experience on you, and yet, you're the one they all revere. Maybe that's another reason why Everest despises you so much."

"What do you mean?"

"He isn't the warrior you are. He'd never be able to lead an army of secundae in a war against demons, but you could. They would blindly follow you into battle. Do you think Everest could make the same claim?"

"He doesn't think like a soldier, but I'm beginning to see your point."

"Even Noah respects your skills; he told me as much himself."

We approached the door to Iola's room with caution. "Stay behind me," I whispered before pushing the door open and sliding inside. A scan of the room informed me that it was empty. The melting form of a soul lay across the bed. Black sludge poured from its orifices, coating the white quilt. "The souls must have taken Iola downstairs and I'm sure Noah followed." Shattering glass sounded from below us. "Let's go." I crept down the stairs with Caroline in tow. Muffled noises grew louder with each step we took. In ten feet, we'd be just outside the parlor. Suddenly, a screech sounded from behind us. I spun to find a soul charging in our direction. Whipping my arms on either side of Caroline, I guided a knife and the sickle through the soul's abdomen before it could touch her. Her back pressed into my chest, and I noticed her weapon was embedded in the creature's heart. "Get down!" When she was out of the way, I heaved the soul over our heads, watching as it burst into a puddle of sludge on the last step. As we crept over the liquefied body, a lone sanguis demon stumbled from the parlor. I only had a second to react before a stream of demon blood aimed at Caroline and me shot through the air. Instinctively, my hand slammed against Caroline's stomach, shoving her into the wall behind us. The yellow acid missed her but clipped my left shoulder as I attempted to shield her.

My flesh sizzled as the acid slid down my skin. "Shit," I spat through gritted teeth.

She pointed at the burn. "Oh my God. Your shoulder."

"I'm fine, but stay here," I ordered, flying over the river of yellow. The sanguis was already pushing on its distended stomach, preparing to vomit more blood. Slipping behind the sanguis, I kicked it in the back as hard as I could. The demon hurtled into a banister, and before it could move, I lunged forward and sliced its spine in half with my weapons. I slid its corpse out of the way to clear a path to the parlor.

The sensation of a hand touching my skin caused me to jump. "I'm just trying to keep it clean," Caroline explained, holding the bottom of her dress to my shoulder.

"It looks worse than it feels."

"Thanks. If you hadn't been standing in front of me——"

"Don't worry about it. Get behind me and follow my lead." Her hands trembled as she held on to my waist. "Nothing will happen to you, I promise."

"Thanks."

Before I could take a step, a body soared through the air and collided into the wall across from the parlor. Rising to his feet, I watched as Noah spit out a mouthful of blood.

"Noah!" Caroline lunged forward.

"No! Get back!" he yelled.

Grabbing her hand, I swung her behind me as fast as possible. A gold chair shot from the room, slamming into the wall beside Noah. "What's in there?"

"Farine was fighting two sanguis demons and I was up against an involos," he answered. Long tears marred the front of his T-shirt, drops of blood spilling from the wounds on his chest.

"Where's Iola?"

"I don't know. When I got to her room, I was attacked by a couple souls and fought my way downstairs. But she's nowhere in sight."

"You and Caroline search the rest of the house and I'll help Farine," I said. Noah nodded and reached his hand out to Caroline.

She ran to him and flung her arms around his neck. He gave her a swift kiss and readjusted his grip on the hilt of his sword. "If you don't find her, come back here."

I sprinted for the parlor and found Farine fighting the sanguis demons on the far side of the room. Both had their mouths open, their jowls sagging to the middle of their chest. "Farine, watch out!" She dodged left as a stream of yellow acid sprayed from their mouths.

"Thanks," she shouted.

"You take the one on the left and I'll take the other one. Where is the involos?"

"I don't know. It's moving too fast to be seen," she replied. "Here, take this." She held a sword in her outstretched hand. "It'll work better than that sickle on the sanguis."

"Thanks," I answered, taking the sword she offered. Readjusting the belt over my body, I attached the sickle and secured it above my right hip. Rage welled in my chest as I raised the sword and prepared myself to cut the demon down. In unison, the sanguis demons began pressing on their grossly rounded abdomens. Their brown flesh wrinkled as they continued to pound on their stomachs. In a few seconds, more blood would spew from their mouths. I stared into black eyes and swung the sword, severing the bottom half of the demon's jaw from the rest of its body. It reeled back in agony, but I wasn't finished. My sword carved through the rounded gut, dividing the sanguis in two. Farine was across from me, fighting near the window. She'd cut off the curtains and thrown them over the head of the demon. Her machete thrust through the face of the sanguis, killing it.

"Have you seen the involos?" she asked, wiping the yellow demon blood off her blade.

"Not yet. Keep your eyes open and stay in the light."

"Right."

A gust of wind blew by one of the bookcases, knocking several books to the floor. "Behind you!" I shouted. As soon as the words left my mouth, the demon appeared. Farine spun around, but she was too late. The demon's claws stabbed through her chest. Lunging forward, I hacked off the demon's arm. Farine collapsed, the claws still embedded in her flesh. Yellow blood pumped from the creature's mutilated appendage. The involos reared and swung its other arm at my head, but I ducked beneath its claws, shoving my sword into its chest. I stared at the demon as its body began to convulse. A pair of curved ram's horns protruded from the eye sockets while large, gray ears protruded from the sides of its face. Acid seeped out of the wound I'd made, slowly devouring the demon's body.

"What happened?"

Noah and Caroline rushed toward me. "The involos got Farine before I could stop it," I answered. "Did you find Iola?"

"No," he answered. "We searched everywhere, but she isn't in the house."

"She was t—taken," Farine replied, blood spewing from her lips. Yanking the arm from her body, she tossed it to the floor.

I knelt beside her and held pressure to her wound while Noah and Caroline loomed just behind me. "By whom?"

"Furia demons. They took Iola and Christopher. I tried to stop them, but they jumped through the window and flew away." Tears pooled in the corners of her eyes. "I failed her," she choked.

"No, you didn't." I tried my best to soothe her. I knew how it felt to fail at protecting the one you served. "We weren't expecting an ambush; we'll get her back."

"Promise?"

Noah bent beside me, taking Farine's hand in his. "I swear to you, I'll do everything within my power to get my sister back."

"I promise to do everything I can as well."

"Good. Will you bury me? So I can come back?"

"Of course," I answered. "We'll let the Concilium know where you are so that when the time comes, you can return."

Blood flowed from her body despite my best attempts to put pressure on her wounds. Her breathing began to slow and her skin paled. "Thank you," she whispered, releasing her last breath.

Noah stood and stomped toward the involos. "That's five. Five of the servi satanam."

I turned to face him. "I know."

"The servi satanam, Conrad!"

"I know what it is!" I yelled.

"Let's be realistic here. That son of a bitch is working with the devil and he took my sister," he shouted. He began to stomp on the demon's face, causing the carcass to crunch beneath his feet. "He'll kill her. He'll rip her heart out of her chest while it's still beating and consume it like the damn monster he is." He continued to crush the demon's body until he became dissatisfied with his work and picked up a picture frame and hurled it into a nearby wall.

"Noah, stop!" Tears poured from Caroline's eyes as she watched him in horror. "Please, stop."

I closed Farine's eyelids and faced Noah. "We have to bury her," I said.

He glared at me. "I know."

"Noah, can I clean the cuts on your chest before the two of you start burying Farine? Your shirt is soaked in blood."

"Yeah, sure," he answered, collapsing onto the couch.

"I'll go look for a first aid kit."

"Try searching the kitchen, I think that's where Iola would keep it," Noah said.

I ripped another curtain off a second window, laying it on the floor beside Farine's body. Gently, I placed her in the middle of it. Blood seeped through the gold fabric. To my left, the remnants of the involos demon continued to disintegrate. Caroline walked back into the room a minute later, and using another curtain as a barrier to protect my skin, I piled the demon's body on top of the two sanguis. Easing the belt from my shoulder, I laid it on the couch by Noah's feet. Caroline pulled out a pair of scissors and cut the front of Noah's shirt open. Four long gashes extended from his collarbone to his abdomen, one running through the handprint that had been set into the skin above his heart.

"What are those things?" Caroline asked, pointing at the mound of demon bodies.

"The two on the bottom are sanguis demons and the one on top is an involos demon," I answered.

"And they are part of the servi?"

"Yeah. The involos demon is very fast and invisible when it's in the shadows. You can only see it in direct light. See the horns sticking out of its eye sockets?" I glanced at her and saw that she was nodding her head in answer to my question. "It can't see, but it compensates by having exceptional hearing. The sanguis, on the other hand, kill by vomiting demon blood, which is how they get their name. They press on their bellies in order to spray blood from their mouths."

"That—that's disgusting," she replied, cleaning blood from Noah's chest. He grimaced as she disinfected his shredded flesh. "You mentioned the servi satanam back in Chicago. What are the rest of the servi like?"

"Well, you've seen tortured souls already," Noah started, "but dissimulo demons can look like people. They tend to take on the most innocent disguises, such as children and the elderly."

"Just like the demon that stabbed Conrad at the auction house?"

"Exactly like that," I answered.

"The other two are furia demons and verto demons. Furia take the form of women, but they have giant wings and talons instead of feet. They also have really long teeth, which they use to their advantage. Verto demons, on the other hand, simply look deformed because their limbs are inverted. Their sallow skin stretches over bone, making them appear emaciated. But don't be fooled by their frail appearance, because they feed on flesh."

Caroline shuddered. "I'm almost sorry I asked. How do you all know about the servi? Have you had to fight them in the past?"

"Every now and then, Satan releases some of his minions from hell to roam the earth," I answered, watching as she applied ointment to Noah's wounds.

"You've heard of the black death?" Noah asked.

"Everyone knows about that. What of it?"

"Well, it spread over the known world in the fourteenth century, killing thousands and thousands of people. That's why Satan saw it as an opportune time to add to the devastation. He released hundreds of souls from hell, letting them devour cities and villages in mere hours. It was pure chaos, and it's also why the death count spiraled into the millions," he said.

"And no one suspected the souls weren't exactly human?"

"There were so many bodies everywhere that people didn't think about it too much. You also have to think about the time period we're discussing. Frequent communication didn't take place between people, families, or towns," Noah responded. "Not to mention, most people who died from the black plague were burned afterward. Souls kill by burning, so any deaths they caused would've appeared to be the result of the plague."

"Plus, only souls were released that time. One time after we put Evey into hiding, we were living in a small village in Italy in the early seventeenth century. We were attacked by a few dissimulo demons, but that was it. Usually, you don't see more than one type of servi at a time. That's why seeing so many makes us suspect Aden is working with the devil, or at least he's using the devil's resources to carry out his own plans," I said.

"So, you think Aden's plan goes beyond completing the Comedere Cor?"

"Honestly, yes, I do," I replied.

"I have one more question."

"And what might that be?"

"If you're the one person Aden seems to fear, then why weren't you permitted to lead an army of secundae after him when he killed Evey?"

"I was angry and reckless when they sent me after Aden. I didn't care what I had to do or how long it took as long as I got to kill him. I wasn't in any shape to lead an army. All I craved was revenge."

"Everest also said that Thea originally wanted to bring Aden back as a way of trying to fix everything," Noah said. "She thought he could be changed, that he could be good again."

"Then why not reincarnate Aden, erase Evey's memory, and force Conrad to abandon his role as a secundae? I mean, if you truly wanted to regain Aden's trust, why not get rid of Conrad?"

"That's actually something I've been wondering for years," I replied.

"It's not that we haven't entertained your idea, but we simply couldn't bring ourselves to force Evey to marry a man who murdered her. We love Evey. As you've noticed, she has an undeniable effect on all of us—secundae and members of the Concilium alike. In the decades leading up to meeting Conrad, her presence, her light had started to wither. Now, I'm not sure if she would've eventually faded away, never to return, or if she would've continued living a miserable existence for an eternity. Either way, when she met Conrad, she was full of hope again. We couldn't deny her that kind of happiness, and we couldn't deny ours either."

"Sounds like the Concilium needs Conrad just as much as they need Evey."

"We do," Noah replied. "Whether Everest wants to admit it or not."

9

AN END IN
ASHES

S leep, it seemed, was beyond my reach as I rolled over for the umpteenth time. My mind longed to drift away from this world into one of my own. A world where I didn't live in constant fear and where I didn't need to pray against all odds that I'd see my loved ones again.

But this wasn't a dream, it was reality. One that became darker and more unbearable with each passing moment. I was the cause of all the pain and suffering that surrounded me. A fire burns. It can scald the earth and leave nothing but ash in its wake, but where would that fire be without an initial spark? I now knew I was that spark. I was the match and Aden the flame. He may be the one destroying everything in his path, but wasn't I just as guilty? Wasn't I just as responsible for his actions as he was? Even though she'd been speaking out of spite, Helen had been right about me. She knew I was the one who had destroyed Aden and she knew I was capable of doing the same thing to Conrad. I'd endure anything to prevent Conrad from becoming like Aden. Conrad was the embodiment of love and compassion. I'd rather have him taken away from me to wait in heaven than be polluted by evil. He need not sacrifice his soul for me as Aden had.

A flutter of pain washed over me as I thought about Aden's confession again. He traded fates with me, knowing he could lose himself in the process. He acted out of love, and yet, I hated him for changing. On one hand, I was angry he had accepted a punishment that should have been mine, but on the other hand, I was grateful. I owed all my sorrows to Aden, but didn't I owe all my happiness to him as well? Turning away from him landed me in the arms of the one man I'd never stop loving. A simple bite from an apple caused me to be reborn. If I hadn't taken that bite, I never would've met Conrad. To say I was conflicted about Aden was an understatement. While part of me despised him with every fiber of my being, the other part felt accountable for his fate and the terrible things he had done as a result of it.

"Evey!"

The shout of my name propelled me from my bed. I scrambled for the door, gathering a handful of my green nightgown as I threw it open.

"Evey, help me!"

Immediately, I turned for Helen's room, but the voice wasn't hers.

It was Aden's.

My feet thudded against the wooden floor as I ran toward the white double doors. He screamed again, the sound of pain evident in his voice. The doors flung open as I entered his room. To my left, Aden was sound asleep. His body writhed back and forth underneath the sheets. Pools of sweat soaked through the green cotton, soiling the fabric. He looked as if he were being tortured. Another loud wail escaped his mouth, and for a moment, I contemplated going back to my room. But when push came to shove, I was unable to turn away from him. Slowly, I approached his bed, careful not to make a sound as I sat beside him. Before I knew what I was doing, my fingers brushed against his forehead, pushing damp curls away from his eyes. "Aden, I'm here."

"No, no!" he shouted.

"Aden," I said, shaking him. His eyes opened, staring at me in surprise. "What happened?"

He flung himself into my arms and held on to me tight. "I was burning."

"What do you mean?" I lifted his chin upward to meet his gaze.

"I was paying for my sins," he answered, his voice shaking with fear. A single tear spilled from the corner of his eye. "It's always the same dream. I'm in hell, lying at the devil's feet, and he touches a finger to my forehead. As soon as he does, my entire body bursts into flame. The smell of my burning flesh overwhelms my senses as my skin melts over my bones. And the pain—" He inhaled sharply and set his palm against my cheek. "The pain is more than I can bear."

"I'm sorry," I replied, averting my gaze.

"Why are you sorry? This is what I deserve."

"You're only burning because of me."

"No, my love, you didn't realize what you were doing."

"Did you truly believe the apple seeds would change me? That I would become evil from consuming them?"

"I don't believe anything in this world could ever corrupt a heart as pure as yours, but I also couldn't take that risk." Drawing his hand away, he allowed the tips of his fingers to caress my neck.

"Why?"

"You know why."

"But you poisoned me," I answered, trying to hold back tears. "You killed me."

"Of all the terrible things I've done, that is the one I'm most sorry for. I know you don't believe me, but please know I've never stopped loving you."

"Aden . . . I—"

"Saving you from being like I am now is the only good thing I've done in my life. All I ask is that you try to do the same for me. Please save me from myself."

"I don't know if I can."

"Then at least sleep by my side tonight. The nightmares won't come back if you stay."

"And what makes you think that?"

"Because I didn't have them yesterday and I was sleeping next to you. It's the only time I haven't had them."

I stood from the bed without speaking and closed the double doors. Glancing at him over my shoulder, I whispered, "I'll stay with you this one time, but only because you accepted a punishment that should've been mine." The bed dipped as I lay down in front of him, covering myself with the sheet.

"Evey?"

"Yeah?"

"May I put my arm around you?"

Apprehension swirled in the recesses of my mind. "Sure." His arm slid around my waist and pressed our bodies together.

"Evey?"

"What is it?"

"Thank you."

"You're welcome." His lips pressed against my cheek. Aden's steady breathing warmed the back of my neck and only a few minutes passed before I was fast asleep.

I dreamed that the earth was springy underneath my feet and that my hair whipped behind me as I ran between rows of tall oak trees. I knew he would be waiting for me by the pond—it was our special place. Quickening my pace, I could just make out the edge of the pond ahead of me. I sprinted faster, closing in on my destination with each step. Once I reached the edge of the water, I dove beneath its pristine surface.

I ascended from the depths of the pond, bursting into the air. Beads of water trickled down my face and neck. I looked around, but there was no sign of him. "Adam," I called out. "Where are you?" Swimming to the far bank, I hoped to find some trace of him, but my search came up empty. As I reached the grass, a bundle of white daisies lay before me. My hand closed around the flowers and I brought them to my nose to savor their sweet fragrance. "I know you're here."

"What makes you say that?" he asked, his voice sounding from behind me.

"You left me these." I jumped onto the grass by the water and watched as he swam toward me.

"You could've plucked those."

"There's no need to do so when you keep leaving bundles of them for me," I replied with a smirk.

He lifted his shoulders in a shrug. "What can I say? Someone as beautiful as you deserves beautiful things." The rate of my breathing increased with every moment that I waited for him to come sit next to me. His hands tugged on my feet, which were still submerged. "What would you do if I pulled you in here with me?"

"Probably kiss you," I whispered, smiling at him. "But you're welcome to try it and see what happens."

Grinning at me, he jerked on my feet. I plummeted into his arms as a wave of water surged around us. My daisies dotted the pond, making it look as if we were standing in the center of a moving garden. "Now what?"

"Now, I kiss you." My arms folded around his neck and I pressed my mouth to his, sealing our bodies together.

His hands slid down my back, skating delicately over my skin. "I love you."

"And I love you," I said, gazing into his warm eyes.

"You are my wife, and you always will be."

"I know."

"Sometimes I think about what this place was like before you found me."

My brow wrinkled in confusion. "Why is that?"

"To remind myself of what you've done for me."

"I haven't done anything."

"You've done more than you know, and for that, I'll always be grateful to you."

"Haven't you done the same for me, then?"

He grinned at me. "I hope so." He led me to the shore, setting me on the grass as he moved closer. "Lie down beside me."

"Why?"

"Because I want to look at you," he answered.

"You're already looking at me."

"I know, but I want to see you up close." His hands slid around my arms to ensure our close proximity. "You're too beautiful not to stare at, my love."

I awoke with a start, shoving Aden away from me as my memories dissipated into nothingness. I didn't want to see these memories, these moments of happiness that had occurred between me and the person I couldn't escape from.

"What's wrong? Are you hurt?" Aden's hand found my chin, studying my features as he waited for me to reply. "What did you remember?"

"Things I don't want to see."

"You saw bad things?"

"I saw things that only make my opinion of you more complicated by the second. What am I supposed to think when I see you condemn Conrad to death in one dream, but the next time I close my eyes, I'm kissing you in a pond surrounded by white daisies?" I collapsed on the bed, unable to make myself leave. "Every fiber in my being is screaming that you're a monster, but then I remember when we were in the Garden. I can recall the way I felt about you, and all these feelings are swirling inside my brain, confusing me in more ways than I ever thought possible."

"I'm many things," he replied, positioning himself next to me. "I only hope I get to show you that."

I rolled over so I could look into his eyes. "If you see your own end in fire, then tell me one thing."

"And what might that be?" He leaned in, nearly eliminating the space between our mouths. His fingertips skimmed along my side as he stroked my body.

"Do I burn with you?"

"No. You'll never burn."

"How do you know for sure?"

"I'm certain you will never burn, just as I'm certain I'll be condemned to hell if I ever stop living." His voice filled with despair as he spoke. I couldn't imagine what a burden it must be to know your own end.

"Is it awful to know what's in store for you?"

"The worst part isn't knowing I will burn."

I studied his features. "Then what is the worst part?" I asked, unsure if I really wanted to know the truth.

"Hope," he replied. "I hope you'll be able to save me."

"Why is hope worse than anything else?"

"It allows me to think I can regain the life I once had, the life I had with you," he answered, lying on top of me.

I swept a stray curl from his forehead. "So, if I fail, you still burn." I stared at him, hoping he had an answer to my predicament.

"No, my love, if you never try, I burn." Before I could say anything else, his mouth was on mine, pressing our lips together. I wanted to break free from him, but my body was incapable of following any of my brain's commands. His arms circled around my back, tightening our embrace.

But his hold was too tight. Slamming my hands against his chest, I pushed until I was free. "Please stop. I can't do this," I said, sliding away from him as I wiped my mouth.

"I'm sorry. I said earlier I wouldn't touch you unless you wanted me to, and I've already gone back on my word." My heart was beating at a mile a minute. The fact that we were bonded to each other made something about kissing him feel comforting. As the first man and woman ever created, we were linked to one another—and perhaps we always would be. "Evey, are you all right?"

"Yes," I snapped. "I just need a minute to think."

"Take as much time as you need. I'm not going anywhere."

"If I ask something of you, will you do it?"

He brushed my fingers with his own. "That depends on what it is."

"I want you to tell me what it was like when you watched me fall out of love with you. I want to know what happened," I replied.

"Well, it wasn't a particular event or occurrence. You fell out of love with me over a period of time. At first, it was small things. You'd pull away when I tried to kiss you or you wouldn't take my hand when we walked side by side." The expression on his face changed, sagging his features. "I do remember one night when I knew without a doubt that you didn't love me anymore."

"What night was that?"

"It was the night of our wedding celebration as Frederic and Isabella. It wasn't anything you said or did, but your eyes . . ." His voice faltered as he spoke. "Your eyes were so empty, so devoid of any emotion when you looked at me. I knew when I looked into them that you didn't love me, that you didn't feel anything for me."

I heard Aden's voice as he spoke, but we weren't in his room anymore. Instead, we were in a grand hall. Tables lined the stone walls while an imposing throne loomed on top of a raised platform at the end of the room. It was the same throne I'd seen before. It was a throne I knew all too well.

"And how are you this evening, my love?"

"Very happy, my king," I answered, placing my hand on top of Adam's as he led me to the center of the floor. An endless sea of faces surrounded us as we started to dance. The gentle sounds of a flute floated around the room like a string of soft clouds.

"I do hope you're enjoying your wedding celebration."

"I enjoy all of our wedding celebrations."

"Good."

My crimson gown trailed behind me as we twirled in circles, causing the scenery of the party to blur into the background. "Do you ever get tired of marrying me?"

"What do you mean?"

"We're always reborn together, and you're never free to be with anyone but me. I was simply wondering if you ever wanted to know another as you know me."

"I've only wanted to be with you ever since I first saw you," he replied. "And I see us having many more wedding celebrations in the future."

I glanced away from him. "As do I."

"May I ask you one thing?"

"What is that?" I asked, returning my attention to him.

"Why did you insist on inviting everyone to our wedding celebration? Surely, we need not invite every subject in the surrounding village."

"Why wouldn't we invite them?"

"Because they're paupers and beggars." His voice was full of contempt. "They don't know how to behave at an event like this, and I daresay they're not accustomed to such finery."

"We are the king and queen. I find it's necessary for us to show the people of our province that we care for their well-being. We're just the same as them. The only difference is we were born into our positions. We've done nothing to deserve such privileged lives," I replied, unable to meet his gaze.

His grasp tightened on my hand as we made another pass around the hall. "You must think I'm horrible."

"I think it's easy to forget why we're here." I smiled at the faces watching us to my right, scanning each of them as we danced past the crowd. When my gaze fixed on a pair of brilliant blue eyes, I stopped. The bright color was like something from a dream, and I found myself unable to stop admiring it. I surveyed the face of the man those eyes belonged to. My chest expanded as I sucked in a deep breath. I was incapable of turning away from this mystery man. His hair was the color of chestnuts, and he was almost a foot taller than everyone standing around him. I must have seen him somewhere before, because the expression in his eyes was all too familiar to me. Adam tugged on my hand, but I had no desire to continue dancing with him; instead, I longed to watch the man with the bright blue eyes.

Sensibility drew me from my daze, forcing me to acknowledge my husband. My feet fell into step with his as we finished our dance. Adam bowed before me, and I curtseyed in return. The troubadours began to play a more jovial song, but Adam held on to me, leading me into another dance. I glanced over my shoulder, hoping to catch another glimpse of the stranger, but he was gone. I frantically surveyed the crowded hall, but there was no trace of him.

Perhaps he was a figment of my imagination. I wouldn't be surprised since I spent most of my time wishing for another life. It was wrong to entertain such thoughts, but I couldn't help it. With each day that passed, I felt less like Adam's wife and more like his prisoner. A harsh voice shook me from my thoughts. Donovan stood at Adam's shoulder, whispering in his ear.

"You're sure they were caught?" Adam asked Donovan.

"Yes, I discovered their meeting place. They were plotting something from the looks of it," Donovan answered.

"I'll be there at once. Send Guy over here to take my place. We must keep up appearances."

Donovan bowed and disappeared into the crowd.

"What's going on?"

"Nothing, there are a few urgent matters I must attend to," he answered. "I'm sorry to leave you during our wedding celebration, but I'll see you later. I have a gift for you."

"There is no need to apologize. I daresay we'll have another ceremony."

He kissed my hand and slunk off the floor, hurrying after Donovan. Guy emerged from the crowd of guests to stand in front of me. "Your Grace," he said with a bow. He took my hand and we began to dance. A few minutes of silence elapsed between us before he opened his mouth to speak. "You seem troubled this evening. Is something bothering you?"

"Yes," I whispered, looking into his familiar brown eyes.

"What is it?" The expression on his face changed instantly, transforming into one of concern.

"I've been sensing a change in Adam as of late. I don't know what it is, but something is different about him. I know I shouldn't think such things, but he's hiding something from me."

"I think you're right in that assumption. I followed him and Donovan into the dungeons under the castle a few days ago. They've been secretly meeting in the middle of the night."

"Do you know why?"

"No, but I promise to find out for you."

"Do you think it could be dangerous? I can't bear the thought of putting you in harm's way."

"It's my duty to protect you in any way I can," he answered with an air of finality.

"But, Guy—"

"But nothing. By now, you surely must know I think of you as my own daughter. Guarding you is what I was born to do, and I have you to thank for the life I have now," he said. "If you hadn't found me and led me to Marie, I would have nothing."

"You're my oldest secundae, and although I do know the testament of your dedication to me, I don't want to see any harm come to you." I followed his lead, twirling in a wide circle as we passed the other guests. "You don't trust him anymore, do you?"

He dropped his head to whisper in my ear. "I haven't trusted him since he begged the Concilium to make Donovan into one of his secundae."

"Me either. Every time we are born again, he is different. His eyes possess less warmth, and I fear the day that light extinguishes completely."

"As do I."

"I don't know what I'd do without you, Marie, Kit, or Mickey."

"You will never be without us," he replied. "You can count on the four of us to be prepared for anything, even if it means protecting you from your own husband."

"You're too good to me," I said, smiling at him.

He squeezed my hands and bent to kiss my forehead. "Family is always good to each other."

Aden was still talking when the visions of our past faded from my mind's eye. We sat on his bed facing one another. How many times had we done this? And how many times would this scene play out in our future? If Aden achieved his goals, the answer to that question would be *indefinitely*.

"You knew I didn't love you, but you still married me that night. Why?" I asked.

His stare fell to his hand beside mine. "Because I believed I could fix things between us. After everything I've experienced, you'd think I wouldn't be so foolish, but that wasn't the case."

"You were already conducting trials of the Inquisition that night, weren't you?"

He cleared his throat. "Yes."

"You tortured and killed all those innocent people. Why?"

He laughed, but the sound was depraved and unnatural. "I guess in my own sick, twisted mind, I thought what I was doing was right. I thought I was doing what He wanted."

"But you weren't."

"I know," he whispered. "But if we're going to have a conversation about all the horrible things I've done—I hate to admit it—we'll be here all night."

I ran my fingers through my hair and sighed. "I don't think I can handle that tonight. But I do have one more question."

"And what's that?"

"When did you know I was in love with Conrad?"

"The day you brought him to live in the castle."

"How did you know?"

"You looked at him in a way that was so similar to how you used to look at me. When you were around him, it was like you'd come alive again."

"Then why did you let him become one of my guards?"

He exhaled deeply and slumped onto the bed. "I could tell being around him made you happy and I didn't want to deny you any happiness. I thought I could handle it. Hell, I thought he would die eventually and that would be the end of it."

"You thought he would die and I'd move on afterward? You claim I looked at him like I used to look at you. You knew how much I loved him, and I'm supposed to believe that you assumed I'd move on like nothing ever happened after he died?"

"Yes."

"That's bullshit," I replied. "What aren't you telling me?"

"I've told you everything. I allowed you to have your fling because I thought we could move on once you got it out of your system."

"You had Conrad executed because you assumed him to be a fling? How naïve do you think I am?"

"What do you want me to tell you?"

"I want you to tell me the truth!"

"Fine," he shouted. "The truth is I never expected him to

become a secundae because I ordered Donovan to burn his corpse after you buried him."

"You did what?"

"Once he was dead, I watched you grieve. I'm not an idiot. I knew you wouldn't be able to carry on as the female primum, and in order to persuade you to do so, the Concilium would have to bring him back."

"If you burned him, how was he able to be healed?"

"I'm not sure, but if I had to guess, I'd say Guy and Marie stole his body and left it with a consiliarius for safekeeping. They found another corpse to fill his grave and they never told a soul about what they did. Not even you."

"That's why you were filled with so much rage when you found out he'd been brought back."

"I didn't want to lose you. I knew you wouldn't hesitate to choose him over me, and the thought enraged me."

"You frightened me more than I could ever express." A lone tear streaked down my face. "I felt your wrath when you assumed Conrad had been made into a secundae. You wanted to break me, like a wild creature you longed to tame."

"Evey—"

"I've relived your reaction. I felt my bones give as you slammed me against a wall made of stone. You didn't love me in that moment; you simply wanted to conquer me."

"Do you know how often I've wished I could go back in time and change the past?" he asked. "Not a day passes by in which I don't wish I could erase some painful aspect of our history together. I know I'm a monster, believe me, I do."

"Your anger, your jealousy, will destroy everything you hold dear." I focused my attention on the green sheets, convinced that if I met his dark eyes, my body would be riddled with sickness. "You murdered my unborn child. You killed an innocent baby before he even had a chance to take his first breath."

"So it was a boy?"

"Yes, he was."

"I'm sorry," he whispered. "I'm so sorry I deprived you of a son."

"Your apologies won't eradicate the pain you've inflicted."

"I'm not blind, I do realize Conrad is the better man for you, but if I don't belong with you, then who do I belong with?"

10

SIX FEET
UNDER

Dry wood cut into my palms as I forced a shovel into the ground. The mound of crumbling dirt beside Farine's grave was something I was becoming all too familiar with. Glancing up from the pit I was standing in, I watched as Noah wiped the sweat from his forehead. Blood from the gashes on his chest dotted the front of his shirt.

"I'm getting sick of doing this."

"Me too," I said, taking a break from my work. "Every time we stop somewhere, the bodies keep piling up."

"Can I ask a favor of you?"

"Sure. What is it?"

"When you kill Aden, will you make sure he suffers down to the very last second?"

"You can count on it," I answered, throwing more earth out of the grave.

"When we sent you to kill him before, what happened?"

I tightened my grip, squeezing the handle as hard as I could. "What do you mean?"

"The Concilium sent you to kill Aden, and you succeeded. You killed him, but what happened?"

"Nothing," I replied, climbing out of the hole and tossing my shovel aside. "I tracked him down and killed him, just like I was ordered."

He flung his shovel on the ground and chuckled. "Seriously, Conrad?"

My jaw clenched, grinding my teeth together. He was bringing up things I'd forced myself to forget. Thinking about what I had turned into that night was something I didn't—something I *couldn't* —dwell on. "I fought him and won. Then I brought his body to Thea. End of story."

"Bullshit," he replied. "The Concilium begged you to come back after Evey died; their sole purpose was to have you kill Aden. I overheard Balen and Everest talking about it once. They said he was left in pieces—"

I shifted my gaze upward and glared at him. "I don't want to talk about it."

"Does Evey know what happened?"

"No. Her memories were taken away the next time she was reborn, and I don't want her finding out about what I did."

"Why not? Aden killed her. She would be happy to see him suffer."

"Because I became like him! I lost myself to everything that consumes Aden and makes him evil."

"You aren't Aden," he said in an even tone.

"You really want to know what I did to him?" I shouted, stepping around the grave to stand in front of him. "I tortured him for hours. I tortured him until his voice gave out and he couldn't scream anymore. I put him in brodequins and drove eight wedges into the boards strapped to his legs, causing the bones to burst. I cut him limb from limb while he was still alive, all the while dangling the rotting remnants of his body above him so he would know what I had in store for him." Farine lay at my feet and I knelt next to her body, tucking the edge of the curtain underneath it. "Whatever happened to you when you got your scars, I can assure you that Aden got it a thousand times worse."

"I—I," he rambled, staring at his feet as he spoke. "Sorry I asked." He bent in front of Farine's feet, helping me lift and lower her body into its resting place.

"Never mention it again," I said, picking up the shovel. "It's not something I like to think about."

"We've all done things in our past that haunt us. It's one of the drawbacks to living as long as we do."

I was too angry to reply, so I nodded instead. We covered the body quickly, not taking a second longer than we needed to. As we were patting down the top layer of dirt, Caroline approached us.

"I finished cleaning inside. The souls disintegrated, so I just had to clean up the leftover sludge, but the demons were a little trickier to dispose of."

"Thanks for helping," I replied, making my way to the house. "After we all get cleaned up, we can get in the car and leave."

"Conrad?" Caroline asked as we walked across the patio and left the shovels by the door as we went inside.

"Yeah?"

"I was thinking about the job of a secundae and the oath they make to the Concilium. But one thing doesn't make sense to me. If you are brought back with Evey, and each time you're brought back you're the same age as when you died but she is brought back as a baby, why aren't you older than she is right now?"

"We don't start aging until Evey reaches her eighteenth birthday. As soon as she turns eighteen, we age just like everyone else," I answered.

"Why eighteen?"

"Because that was Evey's age when she was first put in the Garden of Eden."

"Oh, okay. That makes more sense. If you actually sit down and think about everything we've seen, it's crazy to think we know Eve from the Garden of Eden."

"It's a pretty incredulous notion," I agreed.

"When did you discover her true identity?"

I followed Noah to where she stood on the staircase, trailing behind them as they walked. "She told me when I was one of her guards. I knew she wasn't just Isabella—I knew there was more to her story, that there were secrets. I confronted her about it, and she only told me who she really was after I threatened to leave the castle."

"And when she told you, did you automatically believe her?" she asked, glancing over her shoulder.

"Yeah. I don't know how or why, but I never questioned it. I knew she was Eve."

"Iola was right. You and Evey were fated to be together. After all, you saved her and she saved you."

I set my hand against my bedroom door handle, squeezing the metal knob. "I guess we did." I watched as she and Noah entered their room and closed the door behind them. I trudged into my own with a heavy heart. Evey had saved me in so many ways. She saved me from starving to death in the dead of winter and she saved me from the life my parents had planned for me. They wanted me to marry Helen. I always knew how she felt about me, but I could never love her, no matter how hard I tried. How many centuries had I spent consumed with guilt about what I did to her? I had allowed her to believe I loved her, but when I couldn't keep up the charade anymore, I had confessed the truth. I'd wanted more . . . I wanted Evey. Perhaps I'd always known I was meant to be with another. Any life I would have spent with Helen wouldn't have been what I wanted, what I craved.

I crossed the room, grabbing the box for the sickle. I had returned the ancient weapon to its container before Noah and I began digging Farine's grave, and I checked to make sure the box was still full. Every time I examined the curved blade, the reality Aden could be killed once and for all cemented itself in my mind. Thea couldn't bring him back a second time and his powers as a primum wouldn't overpower Cain's sickle. Aden would finally burn for his crimes. Placing the wooden box in the bottom of my bag, I piled clothes and knives on top of it. Then I quickly made the bed before leaving to take a shower.

Streams of red, black, and brown swirled toward the drain as I stood beneath the blistering water. I tried to scrub the scent of death from my body, but after all the corpses I'd been exposed to in the last few days, the stench seemed to permeate my flesh. A day had to come when all this would be over, when we wouldn't be hunting Aden and burying our fallen friends. This war couldn't continue much longer, because if it did, there would be no one left to fight it. I finished showering and dried off. After pulling on a pair of jeans and a T-shirt, I walked back to my room to collect my bag. I knocked on Noah and Caroline's door on my way out. "I'm heading out to the car. I'll be waiting outside whenever the two of you are ready," I shouted through the door.

"Okay. We'll be down in a minute. We're just packing our stuff," Noah replied. "I'll drive first. I'm not tired and I don't think I'll be able to sleep either way."

"Okay." I followed the stairs to the first floor of the house and exited through the back door, heading toward the car. There was a slight chill in the air. Maybe it was because of the impending doom surrounding us. We were in a race against time now. Aden had Evey and a consiliarius in his grasp. If we didn't find him before it was too late, life as we knew it would cease to exist. Aden would be able to destroy anyone and anything in his path once he absorbed Iola's powers. Climbing into the car, I threw my bag over the back of the seat. I tried to still the thoughts plaguing my mind, but the task proved impossible. Aden had Evey and Helen. It sickened me to think about what he could be doing to either of them. I may not have loved Helen like I did Evey, but even after everything she did in New York, I still didn't want any harm to come to her. The only thing I could do now was lie across the seat and pray sleep would quiet my mind.

"I'll drive after Noah," Caroline said as she and Noah sat in the front two seats. "That way you can get some sleep."

"Thanks," I replied. "If you start getting tired, just wake me up and I'll take over."

"I will." The engine grumbled to life as Noah turned the ignition. The car vibrated beneath me as it lurched down Iola's driveway.

"I know Aden has the most important person in both of your lives, but we'll get Iola and Evey back. I won't let him take either of them away from you," Caroline declared. I watched as she leaned over the center console to kiss Noah on the cheek, before twisting to look at me. "He won't keep them away from us."

"I know," I agreed, meeting her stare. "We won't let him."

She offered a stiff smile and turned back to face the windshield. I rolled to my side and closed my eyes. Helen had betrayed us to Aden and the cost was Evey. A small part of me couldn't blame Helen for her betrayal, especially considering the pain I'd caused her. It hurt me to recall the day I forbade her from coming to see me at the castle. I'm sure she had felt just as deceived that afternoon as I felt in the warehouse. She knew by then I didn't love her, that I never had, but she wouldn't move on. The emptiness in her eyes had mirrored my own when Evey ordered me not to be one of her *secundae* while we were in Chicago. Even though my suffering barely lasted a day, I understood how Helen felt.

She came to see me at the castle every day for months after I moved until I asked her to stop. The day I did so was also the day she realized I was in love with the queen I so diligently protected. The differences between the two women were never more profound than when Evey stumbled upon Helen and me fighting outside the kitchen. I couldn't help but think back to that afternoon. The memory of it and the suffering I inflicted upon Helen were as fresh in my mind today as they were when they occurred all those centuries ago.

"What are you doing here?" I asked Helen, taking her hand and pulling her away from the kitchen door.

"I came to see you," she replied. "I come to see you every day. Why do you sound upset?"

"Helen." My tone was grave; I needed her to listen to me. "I don't want you coming here anymore."

"Why?" she asked, backing away from me.

"I don't want you to have any misconceptions about our relationship."

Her hands grasped the skirt of her dress. "What kind of misconceptions could I have about us? We're supposed to get married. Our fathers arranged it when we were children."

"I know, and I'm sorry, but I can't marry you. I don't love you like you love me."

"But we've been together. You kissed me and held me. Are you telling me it was all a lie?"

"No. I do care for you, Helen, and I always will. I'm just not in love with you. I tried to be with you. I wanted so badly to love you, but it would be wrong of me to let you think something that isn't true." I took a deep breath and stepped toward her. "There are so many men who could love you better than me. They can give you what I can't."

"No, they can't," she cried, wiping away her tears. "Only you can give me what I want."

"I have nothing to give you."

"You love another—" Her hand rose to her mouth, cutting off her voice. "Don't you?"

"Yes, I do." I wanted to tell her that I didn't mean to fall in love with someone else, that it was uncontrollable, but I didn't have time because I heard another person's voice calling for me.

"Good morning, Conrad." I turned to see the queen walking toward us. A lavender gown hung off her shoulders, exposing the fair skin beneath. Gold flower pins dotted with pearls held her red hair away from her face. Even in the dim light of the castle, she glowed. My breathing quickened at the sight of her. It didn't matter how many times I saw her or how many times I stood by her side as her guard, she always had this effect on me. The fragrant smell of flowers fanned from her as she took another step toward me. She couldn't have been more different than Helen if she tried. Helen had a strong-willed, almost harsh countenance while the queen possessed a warm and delicate disposition.

"My lady," I replied with a low bow. As I glanced up from my bent position, we stared at one another, unable to look away. "Were you going somewhere?"

"Yes," she replied, smiling. "I thought I'd take a walk through the village."

"Without any guards?"

"I'll be fine. No need to worry."

"A guard must escort you. If something were to happen——"

"And who is this?" she inquired, stepping toward Helen. Helen had been so silent I'd forgotten she was there.

She curtseyed before the queen, surveying her appearance, and then her focus shifted to me. "You're a fool, Conrad," she spat with a glare. "I just don't understand why it couldn't be me." Before I could say anything in reply, she turned and ran away. I watched her leave, but not even for a moment did I consider or desire chasing after her.

"I hope I wasn't intruding." The queen neared me and took my hand in hers. "You would've told me if I was?"

"You weren't intruding at all," I answered with a smile. "Shall we continue with our walk?"

She squeezed my hand. "Our walk?"

"I'm not letting you go by yourself."

"I could have Guy go with me if you are otherwise occupied." She released her hold, backing away from me.

Helen knew within half a breath that I was in love with the queen. Maybe I was a fool to love someone I could never have, but the way I felt couldn't be replicated with another. "What I meant to say is I'm not letting you go on your walk without me."

"Very well." I offered my arm and she took it without hesitation. Being this close to her allowed me to smell the sweet, floral scent radiating off her.

"You always smell like flowers." The words poured from my mouth too quickly for me to stop.

"You've taken note of how I smell on several occasions," she teased. "Perhaps it's because I was born in a garden." Her smile made my chest tighten, and I couldn't fight the urge to stare at her.

We exited the castle through the doors by the kitchen and

headed through the courtyard, making our way to the surrounding village. The sun shone through the thick clouds hanging in the sky, illuminating the world around us. The queen's hair glowed like a jewel, and I fought the desire to run my fingers through it. Once we were walking amongst the small cottages, she increased her hold on me and whispered, "I want you to know that your friendship means more to me than I can put into words."

"I feel the same way about you."

"I'm glad to hear it."

"And I'm forever grateful for the opportunity you've given me," I replied, guiding her through a narrow passageway between two houses.

"I'm the one who should be grateful," she whispered. As we walked past another house, two small children stood before us, blocking our path. A boy no more than seven years old held the hand of a girl not much younger than him. He held a handful of flowers out to the queen. I watched the two children curiously. "Thank you, Gaspar," the queen said, bending to take the flowers. "Is your mother feeling better?"

The little boy nodded. "She isn't sick anymore."

"That's wonderful news." She grinned at the boy and he wrapped his arms around her neck, hugging her tight. "And is there still enough to eat?"

"We have a good supper every night," the girl answered.

The queen touched the girl's cheek. "Little Francina, you grow a foot in size every time I see you."

The little girl beamed at her, squeezing her brother's hand. "Your hair is pretty." She reached her free hand forward to touch the queen's hair.

"Only because I have pretty things in it." The queen removed one of the floral pins from her hair. Then she took the adornment and fastened it into the girl's blonde curls. "But you have beautiful hair, Francina." Both of the children grinned at the queen. "Now, both of you run back to your mother, she'll be looking for you." Francina stepped to the queen and kissed her cheek before taking off after her brother, running to catch up with him.

"Is there anyone around here you haven't saved in some way?" I questioned.

"Oh," she said, her cheeks blushing. "There are so many I have done nothing for, and I seek to change that."

"You saved my family and me."

"I consider myself lucky to have been robbed by you." Her face was so close to mine I wanted nothing more than to grab her and kiss her, but sensibility kept me from doing so.

"It seems Donovan has finally caught up with us," I said. I watched as he made his way through the streets, heading toward us. "He's been trailing us since we left the castle."

"Then let's make his job harder," she replied, grabbing my hand. She sprinted through the streets, weaving around groups of people. A quick look informed me that Donovan was attempting to catch up with us. He burst through the crowds, knocking people aside. Our feet moved at a rapid pace, widening the distance between us and our assailant. When we rounded the corner of an abandoned shop, I pulled the queen into the empty building behind me. We hid inside the dark room, staying out of sight behind the dusty windows. She burst into a fit of laughter, shaking uncontrollably.

"You have to be quiet or he'll hear us," I replied, unable to suppress my smile. I watched Donovan through the window. He looked about, trying to catch us. I knew without a doubt he would hear us if she didn't stop laughing. I grabbed her and held her against the wall adjacent to the window. Then I set my hand over her mouth, pressing my body against hers in an attempt to quiet her. "I'm sorry, but he is just outside. He'll hear us," I whispered. Her laughter ceased at once as she stared at me. Uncovering her mouth, I slid my fingers down the skin of her neck until my hand came to a stop on her chest. Her heart pounded wildly against my palm.

"Conrad," she whispered, tracing the edge of my lips with her finger.

The realization of our close proximity dawned on me. My queen stood before me, pinned in place by my body. If she felt even the slightest discomfort, I could be punished for being so informal with her. "Please forgive me, my lady. It wasn't my intention to be so forceful with you." I took a step away from her, bending into a low bow.

"You've done nothing for which you need to seek forgiveness, my knight." Her hand caressed my cheek, demanding my attention. "But I'm afraid I must beg for yours."

"Why?"

"Because you saved my life two weeks ago and I've yet to thank you. You protected me from those men and it's taken me so long to express my gratitude."

"You don't need to thank me. I was just doing my duty as one of your guards."

"You did so much more than that."

"I thought I frightened you."

"I only feared those men would injure you." She inched closer to me, taking my hands in hers. "Would you allow me to thank you?"

"Only if you insist."

"I absolutely insist," she replied, wrapping my arms around her waist. Her lips pressed against my cheek. "Thank you for saving my life, Conrad." Her breath warmed my ear as she spoke. She had a crown, a title to uphold, and I had no right to touch her. I attempted to disentangle myself, but her grasp prevented it. "Am I so horrible that you don't even want to touch me?"

"How could you possibly think that?" I asked.

"Every time I get close to you, you pull away from me."

"I—"

"You told me once any man alive would gladly give me whatever I desire. Were you excluding yourself from that list?"

"My lady, I'm not worthy of you."

"You are always kind and you're courageous when others would fall prey to fear," she whispered. "You've protected me, bled for me, and provided me with comfort when I needed it most. What part of that seems unworthy to you?"

I pressed my forehead against hers, staring into her eyes as her fingers danced along the curve of my neck. "You are the queen of Spain."

"Am I not a woman, a human being, in need of love? Am I not as lonely as you are?" she asked. I backed away from her quickly, afraid I would lose all sense of propriety at any second. "Please don't pull away from me. Don't deprive me of your presence." Silent tears dripped from her chin, causing my body to ache at the sight of her pain.

I tugged her into my arms, holding her as close as possible. "As long as I'm breathing, you'll never be without me." In that moment, I needed to tell her how I felt about her. I was seconds away from confessing my love when Donovan burst through the door, forcing us away from one another.

Since the first time we met, I knew Evey was the person I was meant to love. She was the only one I ever pictured myself being with. I sat up from the back seat of the car and stretched. The sky was dark. Miles of road disappeared behind us as the car sped down the interstate.

"If the two of you don't care, there is somewhere we need to go before we head back to New York," Caroline said, breaking the silence.

"Where might that be?" Noah asked.

"We need to stop by my parents' house so I can get some more clothes and tell them I won't be home for a while. They think I'm with Evey and her mom, but I need to give them a more solid story of why I can't come home yet."

"If you want to stay in Tennessee, Conrad and I will understand. There would be no risk to your safety if you stayed behind."

"I can't stay behind. I'm too involved in this now."

"But you don't have to be," he countered.

"You can't expect me to abandon the search for Evey. She's my sister."

"She would want you to be safe."

"She also entrusted me with the apple seeds, or have you forgotten that?"

"I haven't forgotten anything. I simply want you to know you have a choice."

"I appreciate your concern, but I belong with the two of you. I want Aden to pay as much as both of you want him to."

"In that case, know I will do everything within my power to protect you."

"As will I," I said. "And if you're going to stay with us, then we need a believable story to tell your parents so they don't become suspicious."

"Do you have any ideas what your story is going to be?" Noah asked. "If we're going to persuade your parents, we're going to need a heck of an explanation."

"How about I explain that the two of you are distant family members of Evey?"

"There is no way I'm pretending to be a member of Evey's family. Sorry, but I'll just pose as her boyfriend," I answered.

"Okay, fine. What about Noah, then?"

"Just say Noah is your boyfriend," I suggested. "I mean, he pretty much is."

At my reply, Caroline whipped around in her seat to glare at me. "First of all, my parents know me. They would never believe I have some secret boyfriend. And second, Noah's not my boyfriend," she said. I knew she was ticked at me, but I couldn't hold back the grin spreading across my face. "Wow, hearing that out loud makes my life sound so depressing. I really need to get back to high school and get elected for prom queen or something. I need some semblance of normalcy! I mean, all I do lately is hang out with ancient dead people."

"I'm not dead," Noah interjected. "Nor have I ever been."

"Yeah, but you are ancient," I added. Catching Caroline's attention, I winked at her.

"Now that you mention it, he does have some crow's feet just at the edge of his eye," Caroline said, pointing at Noah's face.

"I do not. I'm twenty-five years old. Well, I still look like I did when I was twenty-five, anyway."

"I believe you give *robbing the cradle* a whole new meaning."

"You really are a dick sometimes, Conrad. You realize that, right?" Noah asked.

Caroline smiled at our exchange. "I wonder how my parents would feel about me dating an older guy."

"Oh, sure," Noah spat. "Laugh it up, you two. Anyway, why don't you think of me as your boyfriend?"

"Do you want me to?" she asked.

"I don't hate the idea of it."

"I don't know, Noah," I said. "Didn't you see the way Terrick was looking at her when we were at Everest's apartment? I think he has a thing for Caroline."

"You think so? I'm definitely a sucker for muscles," she added, her voice dripping with sarcasm.

The car came to an abrupt halt. Noah pulled up the emergency brake and shifted to look at her. "Terrick wouldn't know what to do with a woman, much less know how to date one."

"Oh, and you do?"

"I know a couple things," he replied. Before Caroline had a chance to say anything in response, Noah pulled her into a kiss. Within seconds, their arms were wrapped around each other. Looking out the window, I tried to give them some privacy, but when a few minutes passed and their lips were still locked, I decided to interrupt.

"I can drive for a while if the two of you want to make out in the back seat," I piped up. "I mean, it's not like we have anything important to do."

"I can drive for a while," Caroline replied breathlessly. "I just need to get a cup of coffee before I take over."

"I can help you with that," Noah said with a smile. He released the brake and pressed his foot on the gas pedal. Once again, the car shot down the black asphalt, taking the nearest exit. When we stopped at a gas station, I stayed in the back seat while Noah and Caroline went inside the store. They returned with a bag of food and three cups of coffee. I accepted a steaming cup from Caroline and took a large gulp, letting the liquid warm me from the inside out. Then I jumped out of the car to stretch. Noah looked exhausted. The rims of his eyes were lined with red, and he kept running a hand through his hair absentmindedly.

"You look terrible."

"Thanks. You look rather remarkable yourself," Noah answered in an icy tone.

"Seriously, you look beat. Why don't you sleep in the back while Caroline and I take turns driving?"

He glanced between Caroline and me before answering. "I don't know."

"I'll be fine driving, and when I start feeling tired, I'll have Conrad take over," Caroline promised, pushing him to the door behind the driver's seat.

"Are you sure?" he asked, scrutinizing her closely.

"Yes. The cuts on your chest are still all right?"

His eyes dropped to the green T-shirt he wore. "Yeah. They're fine."

"Good. I'll put some more medicine on them later. Now, get some rest," she ordered, giving him a peck on the cheek.

Noah settled himself across the back seat, passing out as soon as his head hit the soft leather. I rounded the car to the passenger side and took my place beside Caroline, fastening the seatbelt over me. A few minutes later, we were back on the interstate, heading for Estill Springs. I sighed as I thought about the last time I'd been there. It was when Evey, Caroline, and I had gone to retrieve the painting. As soon as I appeared in her life again, I'd brought trouble with me. She had a quiet, normal existence until the day I showed up and caused it all to come crashing down around her.

"Whatever you're thinking about doesn't look good," Caroline said, obliterating the silence around us.

I focused my attention out the window. "I was thinking about how much trouble I've caused Evey since I've been back."

"Conrad, believe me when I tell you this, because it is the honest truth. On the first day of class, something changed within Evey. She didn't become a different person or anything, but it was like something clicked into place and made her come alive."

"What do you mean?"

"It was like she became more vivid. Everything about her intensified, and you were the cause of that. Evey and I have been like sisters for almost ten years. She loves you, and even though things have happened and Aden has her now, she'd never go back to her life before she remembered you."

"That still doesn't change the fact that I failed her. I couldn't uphold the oath I made as one of her secundae. Aden has her because of me, because I couldn't protect her," I replied.

"You died trying to protect her, and I know it isn't the first time you have either."

Light from the moon shined through the glass, casting shadows across Caroline's face. "That's part of the job."

"Oh, shut it," she ordered. "Evey is much more than a job to you. She's more like a divine calling and you know it."

I rubbed my chin while I thought about what she said. The rough stubble grated against the skin of my hand. "You're right."

"Of course I am. Can I ask you something?"

"Sure."

"How did you know Evey was the person you're meant to be with?"

"Noah asked me the exact same question earlier," I replied with a laugh.

"He did? Why?"

I zoned in on the bracelet dangling from her wrist as I spoke. "I think he's trying to figure out what to do with his feelings for you."

She glanced behind her, making sure Noah was still sound asleep before answering. "But he said all that stuff about not liking someone unless they can live as long as he can."

"He said that because he's scared. Before he was made into a consiliarius, he lost his family. I think he's afraid to love someone he knows he'll lose."

"I know I shouldn't fall for him, that it'll only bring me heartbreak, but screw it. I might as well do something foolish while I'm young and can use that as my excuse."

"Trust me, it's better to go along with how you feel in the long run. Things might not work out, but at least you'll have no regrets."

"You're right." She paused. "And if he breaks my heart?"

"I'll break his arms and legs."

She returned my smile with one of her own. "Thanks. If I ever had a brother, I'd want him to be like you."

"Sometimes you remind me of Cecily."

"I know you must miss her so much."

"I do, but it's nice."

"What is?"

"Being reminded of her. It keeps her memory fresh inside my mind."

"You know she would be happy you're with Evey, right?"

Surprised by what she said, I asked, "What makes you say that?"

"Because you love Evey and she loves you. Because she's who you belong with."

"I hope you're right about that."

"If I were your sister, I'd just want you to be happy. Even if it meant you were taken away."

I I

1492

The sound of our breath was the only noise for the last few minutes. *If I don't belong with you, then who do I belong with?* His question kept circling around and around in my brain. I didn't have an answer for him, but I needed to say something.

"I don't know how to answer that exactly," I replied. "All we do is hurt one another. Let's face it, that's what we're good at. There's no kind of damage control that can undo the things we've done to each other." I watched Aden as he stared at me. My hand instinctively moved to my chest to clutch the pendant hovering between my collarbones.

"That's why we start over. We make a new life together with a clean slate." His eyes widened, begging me to accept his proposal.

My throat parched. "And what about the past? It can't be swept aside like a worthless afterthought."

"I'm not suggesting we forget everything that's happened. I'm suggesting we move past it. We live as it is written in our combined destiny. We bond ourselves to one another and reform the perfect union we were created in."

"It wouldn't work, too much has happened."

He slid off the bed, rounding the front of it. His arms slid beneath me, carrying me to the empty expanse of floor beside his bed. "I can make it up to you. Give me a few centuries and I'll spend every waking breath rectifying all the wrong I've done to you."

My legs slipped out of his arms as he set me on the ground in front of him. His shoulders hardened beneath my touch, his hands knotting at the base of my spine. A lone tear tumbled from the corner of his eye. "Things aren't always that simple. It's not like a broken object you can repair. Some things should stay broken," I whispered. Agony distorted the lines of his face, displaying the raw emotion he felt. No matter what I did, I'd feel terrible in some way. I wanted Conrad to be the one staring in my eyes, but I couldn't help him now and a part of me didn't want to admit that I needed to help Aden. After everything he did to hurt the people I loved, I still felt the need to comfort him in some way. It was as if I were being pulled in two different directions. Why would I want to help the one responsible for all the pain I felt? It was as if some unbreakable tie existed between the two of us. I was made from Aden, so maybe both of us would always possess a part of the other.

"I know you're in love with Conrad and that I'd be your last choice, but since you can't be with who you really want to be with, couldn't you try to love me instead?" His words were begging, pleading with me to bend to his will.

My voice shook as I spoke. "I don't know what to say."

"Then at least say you'll give me a chance." His hands were at my waist, sliding up my body until they came to a stop on either side of my face. "You're the only one who can save me, Evey." His palms warmed my cheeks as he held my gaze. What was I supposed to do? If I didn't help him, I'd be sentencing him to hell, and if I did, wouldn't I be condemning myself? My eyelids clasped shut. Staring into his warm brown eyes made it that much harder to say no.

"You need to save yourself." I backed away from him, disentangling myself from his touch.

At my response, he chuckled. "Believe me, I've tried."

"It didn't work?"

"What do you think? How can I try to change and be good when the only good part of me is standing before my eyes?"

Sweat lined my palms. "What are you saying?"

"I'm saying you're the only piece of me in existence that wasn't corrupted by the apple," he answered, his voice sliding over my skin like a soft caress.

"Because I was made from you?"

"Yes." He dropped to his knees before me. "Please, you're the only one who can help me." More tears dripped down his cheeks.

As I stared at him, a flutter of emotions coursed through my bloodstream. I bent forward to touch his face. "I was afraid this would happen," I choked out.

"What were you afraid of?"

"That I would feel anything for you but absolute hatred."

"And what do you feel for me?"

"Sympathy."

He gave me a half-hearted smile. "I can live with that."

"But that's not the real question you should be thinking about."

"What question should I be thinking about?" he asked.

"Whether or not you can live without it." Grabbing his hands, I helped him stand from the floor. "Let's lie back down," I said, walking back to his bed. We resumed our places, side by side. He inched closer to me, his hand clutching my waist. I knew at one point in time this had been normal for us. We spent innumerable nights curled together, sleeping as one. If I was made for Aden, then why was it that I fell so deeply in love with Conrad? It couldn't just be the fact that Aden had been corrupted—there was more to it than that. It wasn't a coincidence I noticed Conrad's eyes out of all the guests at my wedding celebration. There were hundreds of faces, but only one forced me to stop dead in my tracks. One look was all it took. I knew he didn't see me as Isabella or Adam's wife. He saw me. I may have been born as Adam's wife, but I'd been made to love Conrad.

"No matter what happens between us, I'll always love you, Evey," Aden whispered, his arms tightening around me.

"I know you will." I descended into the darkness of sleep cradled in Aden's arms. My mind drifted through obscurity, never settling into a dream or memory for the remainder of the night.

Maybe the same sense of peace that filled Aden as he slept beside me had affected me as well.

Maybe, for this one night, I was where I belonged.

I awoke the next morning to an empty bed. I looked around the room for Aden, but the only glimpse I caught of him was from the paintings decorating his walls. Rolling off his mattress, I made my way over to his desk. I shuffled around a few papers and found a watch. It was just before noon. I wasn't sure what I was supposed to do, but instead of waiting for him to return, I decided to go to my room to get dressed. When I opened the double doors, I expected Donovan to be camped in the hallway, but to my surprise, it was completely empty. After entering my room, I headed for the closet to find something to wear. My fingers sifted through countless dresses before settling on a light blue one covered in flowers. I set the garment on the bed while I went to the bathroom to finish getting ready. I curled my hair and finished my makeup, applying a deep shade of plum lipstick. Once dressed, I peered out into the hallway. There were still no signs of life, and my heart leapt at the thought of being able to escape. I sprinted for Helen's door and grasped the handle. But to my disappointment, her room was locked.

Just as I was about to admit defeat, I heard voices downstairs. I crept down the steps, listening to the conversation unfolding between two men. One voice I knew to be Aden's, but the other was unfamiliar to me. As I continued on my path, my feet slid over the wood with great care. I descended the final step and walked toward the voices. Passing through an empty dining room, I was barely able to make out the back of Aden's guest. A shadow hid all of the man's features except his black suit.

"I should have Christopher soon," Aden said. "He is on his way here as we speak."

"And the girl?" the man asked.

"She has been recovered as well." I took another step, desperate to hear more. However, as my foot made contact with the floor, a loud creak announced my presence. Aden's features contorted in surprise. "Evey?"

My mouth parched as he stared at me. The stranger he was talking to slowly turned. Hope filled my heart, the organ ready to combust as the man's face came into view. His tan skin was offset by the most wonderful blue eyes I'd ever seen. "Conrad!" I cried, running forward. I jumped into his arms, hugging my body to his with all my strength. His muscles tensed as he increased his hold on me. Before he could say anything, I pressed my mouth to his, kissing him like my life depended on it. "I—never—thought—I'd see you again," I said between kisses. My lips moved over his face and neck in a ravenous manner, leaving prints of my lipstick on his skin. "Oh, Conrad," I whispered into his ear.

"Evey!" Aden shouted. The tone of his voice abruptly ended the daze I'd surrendered to. "That's not Conrad. Conrad is dead."

I stared at the man still holding me. My hands flung over my mouth as I gasped in horror. A pair of hazel eyes stared back at me. "But you looked like him." My fingertips trailed down his cheeks. The man's dark blond hair was combed away from his handsome face. I'd never seen him before, but at the same time, I had the strange feeling that I knew him.

"I did look like him," he whispered, lowering me to the floor.

"How?" His hands gripped my waist to steady me.

"I can make myself resemble anyone I want," the man said. "You're still as beautiful as the first day I saw you."

"Luke," Aden warned

"Not now," Luke ordered with an air of superiority.

"What do you mean the first day you saw me?"

"I mean exactly that. The first time I saw you, you took my breath away." He took my chin in his hand, lifting my face toward his.

"How do I know you?"

"We were well acquainted at one point in time."

Who was this man and how did I know him? I thought frantically, trying to recall where I'd seen him before, but my mind drew a blank. "Why did you make yourself look like Conrad?" Every fiber of my being screamed at me, begged me to fear the man who stood before me. I tried to heed the warning, but something about him

129

was oddly invigorating—as if his very presence was terrifying and beautiful at the same time.

"Like most men in your presence, it's impossible not to give you what you most desire," he replied. He took a step away from me and pulled a white handkerchief from the pocket of his black slacks. He dabbed at the lip prints covering his face. "I do believe this is my new favorite shade of lipstick," he teased, holding the fabric up to me.

"What are you?"

"A mass of contradictions." He stuffed the handkerchief back in his pocket. "You may speak now, Aden."

"Luke, she isn't part of our agreement," Aden said.

Luke altered his focus, regarding Aden with a wicked smile. "As always, Adam seeks to protect his Eve. Actually, allow me to correct myself," he continued, clearing his throat. "Aden and Evey, the quintessential yin-yang. Now that I look at the two of you and note the vast differences from the first time we met, it's even easier to discern your blatant juxtaposition—Evey, the stunning pillar of light, and Aden, the opposing swirl of shadows." I scanned each man, sensing an air of discord rapidly enveloping the room. "And I believe that is my cue to bid you both adieu." He nodded his head in Aden's direction before turning to me. Taking my hand in his, he bowed before me. Just as he was ready to plant a kiss on my knuckles, he turned his head to the side to glance at Aden. Luke jerked me forward as he placed his mouth on top of mine. The touch was the equivalent of an injection of ice water straight into my veins.

Our kiss was brief, but it rattled my composure. An impish grin slithered across Luke's face. Aden blanched, reeling from the kiss. "It's been an absolute pleasure, my queen," Luke said. I nodded, too baffled to form a reply as I watched him exit the room. "No need to call on formalities. I'll show myself out."

When we were alone, I rounded on Aden like an expert interrogator of the FBI. "Who on earth was that?"

"He's a business partner."

"A business partner?" I scowled at him. "Just how stupid do you think I am?"

"Apparently, I'm not the only man who wants you," he answered more to himself than to me. "And I don't think you're stupid. I was trying to protect you."

"What on earth do you think you need to protect me from?"

"Now is not the time for that discussion."

"I have a right to know."

"I happen to agree with you; however, as I've already said, it's not the appropriate time for such a discussion."

"Why?" I asked.

"Before you know it, there will be too many things vying for your attention, and I want you to be fully aware of my intentions concerning you." He approached me, intertwining his fingers in my hair. "Such a wave of happiness brightened your features when you thought he was Conrad. I only wish you could look at me like that."

"I believed Conrad to be dead, and when I thought he was alive again, I wanted nothing more than to be with him."

"You would never hesitate to choose him, would you?"

"Not for a second," I replied.

"I see." He stepped around me, moving toward the antique dining table in the next room. "In that case, how about we eat some breakfast?" Pulling out a chair, he beckoned for me to sit. I accepted the seat he offered and waited for him to join me. But instead of seating himself at the table, he disappeared and returned a few moments later with two plates of food. "I was making us crepes for breakfast when our guest arrived," he said, placing my breakfast in front of me.

I stared at the food, my mouth watering at the sweet scent of strawberries and fresh cream. I picked up my fork, diving into the food with haste. Aden watched me devour my meal in silence. He poured me a mug of coffee, pushing the steaming liquid toward me. "Thanks," I whispered, taking the offered drink.

"Do you take cream?"

"Yes, please." Out of nowhere, Donovan swooped into the room, carrying a white pitcher of cream and a jar of sugar. He set them beside my plate, leaving without uttering a single word. "Aren't you going to eat?"

"Yes, though I was enjoying watching you."

"Well, you can eat without watching me," I replied nervously. "I doubt I'll evaporate into thin air if you take your eyes off me for more than a minute."

He smiled, digging into the food in front of him. "I just don't want to let you go again."

I shifted my attention back to my plate, savoring in the silence as we ate our breakfast. Even as Aden ate, I sensed him watching my every move. I caught his eye for a second, but the expression in it was unreadable. Whatever thoughts were circling his mind were privy to him and only him.

"I want you to do something with me today," he began, shattering the stillness of the room.

"And what might that be?" There was no telling what his request would be, and I wanted to make sure I knew what I was getting myself into before I agreed.

"I thought we could bake cookies together. You know, something fun we would both enjoy."

"Cookies?" I inquired, dumbfounded. "You want us to bake cookies together?"

"Well, when you say it out loud, it sounds rather ridiculous." He combed a hand through his thick hair, tossing the curls astray. He was nervous. He was actually worried I would refuse his invitation.

"No, it's not that. I was just surprised by it."

"I thought everyone liked cookies," he countered nonchalantly.

"It's true," I agreed. "Most people do."

"Shall we start after we've finished breakfast?"

"Sure." I opened my mouth to say something else but thought better of it.

"What were you going to say?"

"I was just thinking that either you are really genuine about wanting to change for the better or you're the most cunning person in the world and asking me to bake cookies with you is your latest ploy."

He reached over the table, taking my hand in his. "I can assure you that I want to change."

"Forgive me, but I'll believe it when I see it."

He released me, backing away from the table as he stood. "I'd be more than happy to show you." He walked toward a swinging white door. "You can follow me if you want."

I rose and followed his lead, stepping into the kitchen. All the cabinets were white with glass fronts, showcasing intricate pieces of china. Steel appliances broke up the dark marble countertops. "May I ask you something?"

"What would you like to know, my love?"

"Did you decorate this house as you thought I would've done it myself?"

"Yes."

"Why would you do that?"

"Because I want you to feel at ease around me," he answered. "I thought if I surrounded you with lovely possessions, it would be easier for you to feel at home here."

"I assumed as much." Black bowls filled with sugar, flour, chocolate chips, and eggs lined a long stretch of counter next to the stove. "It seems you were confident I would agree to your request," I noted, pointing to the ingredients sitting before us.

"I wanted to be prepared just in case," he answered. "Allow me." He took a red gingham apron and slid it over my head, covering my dress. With the ties in either hand, he fastened it around my waist. His lips skimmed over my bare shoulder, eliciting a chill to blanket my skin. Not wanting to prompt more affection from him, I stepped to the counter and began pouring flour into a large mixing bowl. "It's always been a dream of mine to see you like this."

I quirked an eyebrow. "And why might that be?"

He walked to the fridge to remove a carton of milk and handed it to me before answering my question. "I've imagined millions of different endings for us over the years. I've thought of us getting to start over, having a clean slate. Every time, we would live normal lives where you weren't Eve and I wasn't Adam. And in every single thought I've had, we were happily married, just like we used to be all those years ago." I listened to him, stirring together the ingredients. "I would come home from work and you'd be here in the kitchen, making dinner for us. Then we would sit down to a nice meal and laugh about trivial things we did that day."

"That's a pretty vivid fantasy," I replied, watching as he added chocolate chips to the batter.

"It could be a reality." He slipped his finger inside the bowl, stealing a sampling of dough.

"Don't do that!" I swatted at his hand, but it was too late. He'd already licked his finger clean.

"What?" he asked, his voice full of innocence. "I couldn't resist. It looked too delicious."

"Resisting isn't exactly one of your strong suits."

"You try it." He dipped his finger in the batter again, offering it to me for a taste. I glanced at him uneasily, contemplating whether I should accept the morsel he presented. "Oh, come on, Evey. I'm not going to hurt you."

After a long minute, my lips parted. The dough was sweet on my tongue. "Thanks," I whispered. Our eyes locked for a fleeting moment before I returned to the task at hand. What the hell was I doing? I should be trying to slam his head in the oven, not fraternizing with the enemy. But there was something between us, something I couldn't quite define—and it felt right.

"You seem conflicted." I stared at him, hoping the answers I sought would appear to me through divine intervention, but no such luck. I was on my own. He pulled a cookie sheet from a cabinet in front of him, coating the gray surface with a layer of non-stick spray.

"Somehow, conflicted doesn't seem to be a good enough descriptor."

"I'm not all bad."

To my surprise, I took his face between my palms. "You aren't all good either."

He pulled away from me, hurt evident in his dark eyes. "And Conrad is?"

A jolt of panic coursed down my spine. "What do you mean?"

"Conrad isn't the savior you believe him to be."

"And why do you say that?"

"He's done things that would shock you."

"What kinds of things?" I demanded.

He shook his head. "You wouldn't believe me even if I told you. Just forget I said anything at all," he said, storming out of the room.

I stood there at a loss for words. What was he talking about? Conrad was one of the best men I'd ever known. He wasn't dark and sinister like Aden. Conrad had too much of a conscience. He'd never be able to inflict pain as Aden did. Tearing off the apron, I tossed it on the counter next to the cookie dough and darted after Aden. I had to know what he was hiding from me. "Aden! Get your ass back here right now and talk to me!" I stomped through the first floor of the house, searching for him. "Aden!" I wove around the dining table, eyeing the parlor where he had spoken to Luke earlier, but Aden wasn't there. I set off in the other direction, heading for the stairs. Just to the right of the staircase was a door. I threw it open and burst into an office. Dark floor-to-ceiling shelves lined the three walls in front of me. A black leather chair was turned away from me on the far side of a glass desk. I could see Aden's feet through the clear surface. Apparently, he was avoiding me. "Aden," I said in a softer tone, expecting him to reply as soon as he heard my voice.

"Not now, Evey," he spat. "I'm not in the mood to argue, and I don't want to talk to you."

I tiptoed around the desk without making a sound. "Aden—"

"Please just go." His face was buried in his hands. Something had affected him so much that he was hiding. I couldn't believe it. After everything he went through to find me and bring me back here, he was avoiding me.

"Adam," I whispered, moving closer to him.

His head lifted, stunned by my words. "Did you—"

"Yes," I said, my voice almost a whisper. I reached out to him, feeling the need to comfort him in some way.

He stood, allowing me to wrap my arms around him. "Please say it again."

"Adam." I uttered the name into his ear, touching my lips to his skin. I was being drawn to him against my will. I wanted to release him, and yet, I couldn't let go. I knew what he was capable of. I knew he would undoubtedly inflict more pain, but I stood my ground. "We've all lived for so long that we're bound to hurt one another."

"I know I don't deserve you, but hearing you say my name—" He swallowed, struggling to find his voice.

"I think my anger with you before prevented me from seeing all the hurt in your eyes. You feel remorse, don't you?"

"For every wrong thing I've ever done. I want to be good so badly, but something within me has been polluted right down to the core. I'm being drawn in two different directions and it's unbearable."

His body trembled beneath my touch. Pain dominated the expression on his face, tugging at my emotions. I knew what it felt like to be pulled by opposing forces. While my heart demanded kindness and compassion, my head was yelling at me to run away and never look back. "I know," I whispered. I tossed all sense of reason out the window and leaned toward my former husband. Finding his mouth with my own, I planted a modest kiss on his lips.

He inhaled deeply. "Do you even realize what kind of an effect you have on people? Even someone like Luke falls prey to your touch."

"I think you might be imagining things."

"You think so?" he asked. His hold on me increased, locking our embrace. "I've seen men lie at your feet just to catch a glimpse of you, watched them pledge their lives to fight for your cause." His breath fanned over the side of my neck as he spoke. "You can't see it, but trust me, everyone else can." His lips moved along my flesh as he pressed soft kisses onto my skin. Heat bubbled to the surface with each contact.

"Adam, if you hadn't—"

"Don't even think of the word *if*. It will keep you up at night and haunt your every waking thought. Trust me, my love," he replied with a bleak smile. "There's no way to fix the past, but we can change the future."

"I don't know what to do." I studied his dark eyes, hoping to see what was in store for me. If I could heal Aden and save him from himself, then he wouldn't be a threat anymore. There would be no need to run from him. He could find some way to prove to the Concilium that he sought to rectify the sins of his past. He could make amends. And maybe he could change his fate of judgment and persecution. But before I could ponder the situation any further, a knock sounded at the door. My arms dropped, breaking our embrace.

"Yes?" he asked, his attention settling on the door.

"Christopher is here to see you," Donovan announced, his voice booming through the polished wood.

"Send him in," Aden replied casually.

Stepping back, I watched as a lanky man with shoulder-length, brown hair entered the room. His eyes widened as he saw me.

"Eve?" The man uttered my name with surprise and uncertainty. Gathering his senses, he faced Aden. "I wondered when you would come for me."

"Good things come to those who wait, Christopher. And I've been waiting for a very long time."

I observed the exchange with curiosity. So, this was the Christopher who Aden had mentioned when he was talking to Luke. I wondered why Aden needed him. This day had been filled with mysterious men, and something in my gut told me things would only get stranger. "We all expected this day to come eventually," Christopher replied.

"Forgive my rudeness, my love," Aden said. "Allow me to reintroduce you to Christopher Columbus."

"Christopher Columbus?" I gaped at my former husband. "'In 1492, he sailed the ocean blue.' That Christopher Columbus?"

"That would be me," Christopher answered, his voice completely devoid of emotion.

"And what do you want with a notorious Spanish explorer?" I inquired.

"He wants me to show him the way to Eden," Christopher replied. "Searching for a faster route to India was a good cover for what you really ordered me to search for."

"I sent you on a voyage to find the Garden of Eden?" I asked, unable to contain my astonishment. "Why?"

"You sent me because you knew Aden was changing for the worse. You knew he was planning something, and you wanted to know the location of the Garden so you could have the upper hand. Although you never confirmed it, I always suspected you intended to flee there." He cleared his throat, running a hand through his long brown hair. "It's the one place Aden would never be able to find you."

"How do you know that?"

"Because I'm the only person alive who knows where it is," Christopher answered.

It felt like my feet were knocked out from under me. With every passing second, a new revelation was being thrown in my direction. "And why do you need to know where the Garden is now?" I directed my question at Aden. Did he still intend to complete the Comedere Cor? Had he really been sincere in his proclamations to change or was it just bait on the hook he'd been setting for me?

"So we can be with one another forever," he answered, smiling at me. "To regain what we once had, we have to go back to the start of it all." A knot began to form in the pit of my stomach. Aden only thought of me in one way and that was as his wife. Anything he wanted to regain would have the two of us bound to one another forever—just as we were originally intended to be.

12

OLD WOUNDS

I stole a quick glance at Noah as we stood on the front porch of Caroline's house. He appeared out of sorts, which was especially unusual for him. "Feeling nervous, Noah?" I tried to hide the humor in my voice, but it was impossible. It was too entertaining to watch him squirm.

"Shut it, Bourdet," he snapped. His fists twitched as we waited for Caroline to unlock the door with her key.

"Oh, both of you just calm down," she replied, annoyed. "It's just my parents. They're a little off-kilter, but they're good people. It's not like they're going to make you pledge your undying love for me or pick out china patterns for our wedding." Noah blanched at her words and she burst out laughing. "It's way too easy to tease him," she said to me.

A few moments later, an older version of Caroline was on the other side of the doorway, inviting us into her home. Caroline's mother was tall and slender with a mass of blonde curls intricately pinned to her head. She beamed and pulled her daughter into a tight hug. "My sweet baby girl is finally home!" she squealed. "And who have you brought with you?" I shut the white door behind me, catching a glimpse of the sun setting behind the trees on the other side of the street.

"Mom, this is Conrad, Evey's boyfriend, and this is Noah. He's Evey's cousin. They came to help me pack another bag to take to Indiana," she explained, introducing us.

"Mrs. Brewer, it's nice to meet you," I said, taking her outstretched hand. She smiled at me before accepting Noah's.

"Mrs. Brewer, lovely to meet you," he added with a curt nod.

"Oh, please, call me Denise. You can set your bags by the door." She walked through a tidy living room with red walls and beige carpeting. "The three of you are just in time for dinner! Good thing I made a pot roast tonight."

I followed Denise, catching a whiff of the delicious food. Noticing I was by myself, I stopped and turned to observe Noah and Caroline. "Come on," she ordered with a smile. "It's just dinner. It's not like I'm going to strip down to my underwear and sneak into your room in the same house as my parents."

"Your dad is here!"

"Oh, Noah, when will you learn?" She grabbed his hand, practically dragging him to the dining room. Denise led us to a small round table with five chairs seated around it. The oak wood gleamed underneath the place settings. Caroline's father sat at the table, drinking a beer. Noah and I stood by Caroline as we awaited our next introduction. "Noah, Conrad, this is my father. Daddy, this is Conrad, Evey's boyfriend."

"Mr. Brewer," I said, extending my hand to him. His expression softened a bit when he heard I was attached to Evey. But I wasn't so sure Noah would elicit the same response.

"Nice to meet you." He responded to me, but his eyes stayed on Noah, raking over him and surveying him intently.

"And this is Noah. He is Evey's cousin."

Noah offered his hand to the man standing before him. "Nice to meet you, Mr. Brewer."

"Of course," he replied.

"Well, you all must be exhausted. Please seat yourselves while Caroline and I bring out dinner." Denise and Caroline stepped into the kitchen and loaded their arms with dishes of food while the rest of us fell into an awkward silence as we waited for dinner to be served.

"What line of work are you in, Mr. Brewer?" I asked, trying to start a conversation.

"I'm a cop," he answered, taking another swig of his beer.

Caroline and Denise walked into the room, setting food on the table. Caroline took the seat to Noah's left, closest to her father, and Denise sat to my right. The scrumptious aroma of beef and potatoes filled the air around us. Once we loaded our plates with pot roast, rolls, salad, and potatoes, the faint air of tension began to dissipate.

"So, Noah," Denise began. "What kind of work do you do? Or are you in school?"

"I'm out of school actually. I own an art gallery in Chicago that procures special pieces."

"That's fascinating. How long have you been doing that?"

"Just a couple years."

"What kind of clients do you sell to?"

"All different kinds. I sell some pieces to larger museums all across the country, but I also work with individuals. Last month, I was able to get my hands on a Picasso for the mayor of Chicago."

"That sounds exciting!"

"It is. You never know what you might stumble upon," he answered. "I've always had a deep love of art, so owning my own gallery is the perfect fit for me."

"That's so wonderful. What's the name of your gallery?" she asked.

"It's called Vulnera," he replied, taking a drink of water.

"And what does that mean? If you don't mind me asking."

"It's Latin for *the wounds*," Noah answered, his voice somber. He stared off into space, absentmindedly raising his glass of water to take another drink. Caroline shot me a questioning glance, and I nodded in confirmation of her suspicions.

"And, Conrad?" Denise asked, switching her attention to me. It seemed Caroline had inherited her perceptiveness from her mother, because Denise switched the focus away from Noah rather quickly. "You're dating Evey?"

"I am," I answered, swallowing a mouthful of pot roast.

"She is such a lovely young girl and so beautiful."

"That she is."

"I can just picture the two of you side by side. What a handsome couple y'all would make!"

"That's kind of you to say. Evey is very special to me," I responded.

"And are you in school with the girls?" she asked. Mr. Brewer was obviously a silent man. He just sat at the table, observing Noah and me with an astute gaze as his wife carried the conversation.

"Yes, I just started at Tulson this year. After I graduate, the plan is to go to college. Ideally, I'd like to work for the FBI or a private security company."

"Well, the two of you seem like very ambitious men," she said. "It's so nice both of you are helping Evey and Marie through this difficult time. John and I were shocked and devastated by everything that happened with Guy. The whole town is just beside themselves. Guy and Marie are such wonderful people."

"It's surprising what some people are capable of," Noah replied. "It's a difficult time for our family right now." Caroline's hand slipped under the table to squeeze Noah's. This conversation was challenging for him for many reasons.

Denise nodded her head in agreement. "That's so true. What matters most is that you have good people surrounding you, offering their support." She glanced at Caroline and me.

"Caroline, has Officer Zimmerman gotten in touch with you?" Mr. Brewer asked. "He told me he tried to call Evey several times but wasn't able to get ahold of her."

"Oh," Caroline replied.

"Evey's phone is broken. I believe she and Marie will be taking it to get fixed soon," I lied. "Do you know what Officer Zimmerman wanted to talk to Evey about?" So much had happened since last week that I'd forgotten about Evey's conversation with the police officer. After Evey was taken from us, Caroline had given me her bag, so, I was the one currently in possession of her phone.

"It was about a disturbance at the auction house last week. One of the neighboring businesses reported that the house was vandalized. When we went to search the premises, nothing seemed to be missing," he replied. "Zimmerman suspects some kids poured oil around the building and broke a few windows."

"He doesn't believe it was related to the break-in at Evey's house?" I asked.

"No, not after we searched the house."

"Did anyone try calling Marie?" Noah asked.

"Zimmerman wanted to, but I talked him out of it. When Marie came in to identify Guy's body, she was so distraught, almost to the point of being in a catatonic state," he said. "At least, that's the only way I can think to describe it. How would you put it, Denise?"

"I tried to comfort her as best as I could when she came to the station, but I don't think it did much good. She was in shock."

"Losing Guy has been very hard on her," Noah said. "On both of them."

"And Caroline told us Evey was very upset, but she sounded more stable than Marie, so I figured it'd be best to notify Evey of the disturbance at the auction house rather than her mom."

"I think that was the right decision. And as soon as Evey's phone is fixed, we'll have her call Officer Zimmerman," Noah replied.

"I'd appreciate that. I know the last thing Marie and Evey want to do is answer questions, especially about something so painful, but we just need to make sure all loose ends are tied up at the station," Mr. Brewer explained.

The rest of dinner went by without much conversation, which proved to be a relief. The three of us were exhausted from everything that had transpired in the last few days, so our minds seemed to be functioning on autopilot. Not to mention, having to lie in order to maintain a normal façade was quite tedious. When it was time to clear off the table, Noah and I jumped up to do the dishes.

"Noah, Conrad, y'all are guests here. You don't have to do that," Caroline said, watching us gather the dinner plates.

"Well, your parents were gracious enough to host us for the evening, so it's the least we can do," Noah replied. Denise beamed at his response, glancing between him and Caroline. She seemed to already know something was unfolding between the two of them.

"Yes," I added. "Thank you again for the wonderful meal."

"Oh, it was nothing." Denise smiled. "I hope the two of you like blackberry cobbler, because that's what I fixed for dessert. Maybe we can all look through some of Caroline's old baby pictures while we eat."

"What?" An expression of utter panic settled on Caroline's face. "Mom, you promised you wouldn't pull those out again. Daddy, please make her stop!"

"I quit thinking I could talk your mother out of anything years ago. Once she's made up her mind, it's best to stay out of her way," Mr. Brewer replied, pulling Caroline into a hug. As he held on to his daughter, the faint trace of a smile broke his rigid expression.

"Funny, that sounds exactly like you, Caroline." Noah grinned.

"Oh, Noah, you should've seen her as a little girl. She had a pair of hot pink cowboy boots and she wore those suckers everywhere. She even wore them to church on Easter Sunday."

Noah's eyebrows rose as his gaze settled on Caroline. "Pink cowboy boots?"

"You're only jealous because you know you can't pull them off like I can," she snapped back.

"You're right, I'm completely jealous," Noah replied, winking. I followed him to the kitchen, setting the dirty dishes in the sink. He washed the food off the white china while I dried and set it to the side. Caroline and her parents remained at the table, and as we worked, I watched the three of them. You could see the adoration in her parents' eyes when they spoke to her. It was obvious they loved her with every fiber of their beings. I remembered my own mother's eyes when she looked at me. It was almost like I could do no wrong to her, and even if I did, she'd do anything in her power to help me. "I envy them too," Noah mumbled, handing me a clean plate to dry.

"You can almost feel the love and happiness in this home, as if it's embedded into the walls."

"We both come from broken homes," I said, my attention never leaving Caroline and her parents.

"Somehow, that seems like a vast understatement."

I stacked the dried plates on the counter by the sink. "That's because it is."

Before I could say anything else, Denise burst into the kitchen, laughter trailing behind her. She walked over to the fridge and pulled out a blackberry cobbler before turning toward us. "That girl is a whole mess of trouble, Noah, so consider yourself warned," she said, pointing at Caroline. Caroline must've been telling her father a wild story because the two of them erupted with laughter.

"Believe me when I say I've noticed," he replied. "And if you don't mind me being frank, I wouldn't want her any other way."

"I had a feeling you'd say that. Now, let's all have some dessert!" Noah and I followed her to the table, carrying the plates we'd just finished washing. Noah appeared to be more relaxed as the five of us ate dessert. I wasn't sure if he was starting to feel more at ease in Caroline's home or if simply being near Caroline was enough to settle his nerves. My guess was the latter. Caroline affected him the same way Evey affected me. It was strange how one person could do that to another. One day, you're going about your life, continuing with the same things you've always done, and then suddenly, everything changes. You meet the one person who has the ability to turn your world upside down, but you realize you never want things to go back to the way they were.

Resuming the same seat I'd occupied during dinner, I accepted the mound of blackberry cobbler Caroline offered me. "Thanks." When Caroline finished serving dessert to everyone at the table, she tried to take the seat between Noah and me, but Denise shooed her away.

"You go sit by your dad," she ordered, pointing to her empty seat. "I have something to show Noah." Without waiting for Caroline to reply, Denise plopped down between Noah and me and set an old photo album on the table.

"But, Mom—"

Denise shot Caroline a look that instantly silenced her. "See, these are the boots I was talking about." She turned the album toward Noah. I glanced at the pictures from across the table, and sure enough, the picture showed a tiny Caroline wearing a ruffled, white Sunday dress with a large white bow sitting on the top of her head. Blonde curls fell past her shoulders and she clutched a blue Easter basket filled with eggs in her gloved hands. On her feet, a pair of bright pink cowboy boots clashed with her clothing.

Noah erupted in laughter as he examined the photograph. He pointed between the picture and Caroline several times as Denise and I joined in his amusement. Even Caroline's father broke a smile. The only person not laughing was Caroline. She stared at the four of us, horrified. "You weren't kidding when you said she wore them on Easter Sunday," Noah finally said, trying to catch his breath. His face was flushed red from laughing so hard.

"Caroline wore those damn boots everywhere! When we finally had to throw them out, she pouted for at least a month. She isn't used to not getting her way." Denise chuckled.

"That sounds like the Caroline we all know and love," Noah replied, catching Caroline's eye. He stared at her, no doubt wishing they were the only two people in the room. I watched as she opened her mouth to speak, but after a fleeting second, decided against it. If I had to guess, she probably didn't want her parents to hear whatever she was about to say.

"Alright, Denise, it's time to leave Caroline alone," Caroline's father teased. He winked at his daughter, wrapping her up in his arms.

"It's good to know at least one person at this table is on my side!"

"It's a great picture, Caroline," Noah replied. "There's no need to be embarrassed by it."

"Noah's right, sweetie," Denise added. "Besides, I have the whole photo album saved on my computer. I could always email it to him."

"I don't think I like the two of you being in cahoots with one another," Caroline muttered, shaking her head. "And now, I think it's time for all of us to go to bed and get some sleep. The two of you can finish harassing Noah and Conrad in the morning." Caroline stood from the table and grabbed on to my and Noah's shirts, leading us from the dining room to a narrow hallway. "We have to leave early tomorrow and we could all use the rest," she added with a glance back to her parents. Just like that, we were out of the room before Denise or Mr. Brewer could say anything in reply. "The two of you can sleep in here," Caroline said, opening a door for us. "This is the guest room. Mine is just across the hallway."

"Thanks for having us for dinner," I answered. I walked into the room. It was small with only one bed and a dresser.

Noah grinned at her. "Yes, thank you."

Caroline rolled her eyes. "I'll get both of your bags and bring them here. I don't trust you around my parents," she replied, glaring at Noah.

A few minutes later, she returned, shoving our bags at us. "What time should we leave in the morning?" I asked.

"I was thinking we could leave around ten," Noah said. "That gives us a good amount of time to rest."

"That sounds good. The bathroom is down the hall on the right. There are fresh towels in the linen closet. If you need anything else, just let me know." Caroline left abruptly, almost sprinting from the room.

I sifted through my bag, pulling out a pair of shorts to wear. "Caroline seems pretty embarrassed."

"Which seems fairly strange for her," Noah said.

"As far as I know, it is. Also, I think I'll sleep on the floor. I'm not sharing that tiny-ass bed with you."

"Fine with me." He stretched across the mattress. I stared out the window beside the bed. The sky was completely dark now. I stripped off my jeans and shirt, replacing them with a pair of loose-fitting black shorts. Then I grabbed an extra blanket and pillow to make myself a pallet on the floor. Noah changed as well, lying down for the night. "I think I'm falling for her," he said out of nowhere.

"Yeah, no shit, Sherlock," I replied with a snicker. Rolling over, I faced the wall as I readjusted the pillow beneath my head.

"No, I'm being serious. I really think I'm falling for her." That was when I heard it. It was there, ever present in his voice as he spoke. The pain he had suffered so many lifetimes ago lingered around him like a dense fog.

"They were killed in front of you, weren't they?" I paused for a moment, hoping my question wouldn't anger him. "Your family?"

"Yes," he answered, his voice hoarse. "I don't know what to do. I know if I allow myself to fall in love with her, I'll eventually have to watch her die too."

"But wouldn't that be better than not having her at all?"

"Sometimes I think so, but other times, I'm not so sure. I'm not like Caroline, Evey, and you. I can't fling myself headfirst into something and not worry about the consequences."

"Having those feelings for someone isn't something that comes around every lifetime. Shouldn't you know that better than anyone?"

"I'd like to think so."

"Let me put it to you this way: I had nine days with Evey before Aden killed me in that warehouse, and holding her, kissing her was worth every second I bled out on the floor. When I was one of her castle guards all those years ago, I would have gladly given my life just to touch her for one night, and I'd still make the same sacrifice without a second thought." I recalled the last night I saw her. It had been worth it; whatever punishment or agony I had suffered was forgotten as soon as I laid eyes on her. She had always been worth it, and she always would be. "You also didn't seem to like the idea of Terrick getting with Caroline," I added, testing his emotions.

"Never mention that again," he growled.

"I'll try my best not to."

"Seriously, though, you'd die for one night with Evey? One night seems like minutes in the span of my lifetime."

"I would. The first night I was ever with her? I was executed by Aden the next day."

"What did you do?"

"What do you think?"

"I'm not an idiot, I know what the two of you did," he answered. "What I was trying to ask is how could you enjoy your last night knowing you would undoubtedly meet your end the next day?"

"Evey and I were locked in her bedroom for an entire night before I was executed. The fact that I was scheduled to die the following day hardly crossed my mind. You'd be surprised how much time you can make up for in a single evening," I said, unable to stop the smile spreading across my face. "If you knew you were going to die tomorrow, how would you want to spend your last night?"

He went silent. For a second, I wasn't sure if I'd overstepped my bounds with him or not. "I'd want to spend it with her," he whispered.

"Then, I think that's your answer on what you should do."

As he was about to say something else, our conversation was interrupted. "Noah? Conrad?" Caroline asked from the other side of the door. "Is it okay if I come in?"

Noah walked over to the door and opened it for her. "Come on in, Boots," he teased.

"Shut up," she groaned, holding a coffee cup in each hand.

I sat up from my pallet on the floor. "Hi."

"Hey! I brought y'all some hot chocolate." She handed both of us a steaming mug and sat on the bed beside Noah.

"Thanks," I replied, taking a drink.

"So, tomorrow we'll be back in New York?" she asked.

"I guess so." I glanced at Noah for confirmation.

Noah grasped his mug. "It's really the only place to go."

"I'm sure Everest will want to get Iola and Evey back at any cost." She crossed her legs and tugged on the bottom edge of her oversized orange T-shirt. Noah stared at her bare legs, his eyes widening at the sight. "I can't wait for all this to be over, but then again, it sure beats physics class," she said. "Anyway, I'm going to head to bed. I'll see the two of you in the morning."

Noah's gaze followed her to the door as she reached out to open it. "Are you not wearing any shorts?" The tone of his voice was drenched with shock as if he couldn't believe what he was seeing.

She turned, a knowing smile already covering her face. "Nope, no shorts. And I also don't believe in wearing underwear either." At that, she hurried out of the room, leaving Noah in a frazzled state.

"Maybe you shouldn't go after her. She'd eat you alive."

"Ha ha. You think it's funny now, but I'm sure Evey had the same effect on you," he countered.

"I never claimed she didn't, but maybe you should try doing the same thing to Caroline," I said, taking a drink before setting the mug beside me. "She'd probably like it if you gave back what she dished out every now and then."

He took a long gulp from his mug before setting it on the table beside the bed and switching off the lamp. "That's not a bad idea. Got any ideas on how I'm supposed to do that?"

"You're on your own with that." I laughed. When he didn't say anything in reply, I interpreted his silence as the all clear for me to fall asleep. Even though I'd gotten a little sleep in the car, I was still exhausted. Sleep was something I couldn't seem to catch up on in the past few days. We'd been all over the country and still had to drive back to New York tomorrow. It was like we were on a never-ending journey with the treasure always just out of reach. My thoughts, as usual, wandered to when I first met Evey—the beautiful Queen Isabella. I was an empty shell before she came along, completely obsessed with trying to provide for my mother and Cecily in my father's absence. Life was difficult after he died, and I didn't know how to fill the void he left behind. I'd been so consumed with my family's survival that I'd forgotten to live. It didn't matter how many times I held Helen or tried to feel something when I was with her. I was empty on the inside until the first time I laid eyes on Evey. That was the day I began to want more, the day I realized I wanted to live.

Our eyes only met for a brief moment during her wedding cele- bration, but hers were different from every other pair in the room. In an instant, I knew she felt as empty as I did. I couldn't fathom why a queen—someone so beautiful with everything provided for her—would seem so hollow. It wasn't until I met Evey that I understood. She'd been forced into a marriage and life she didn't want. Guy, Marie, Mickey, and Kit all helped her as much as they could. The four of them protected and cared for her, but none of them offered her the same thing I did. A way out. By falling in love with me, she had a reason to leave behind her life as Adam's wife. It had been a miracle we were even able to meet, but once we did, we both sparked to life. We savored in the beauty love had to offer.

It didn't matter where Aden took her or what lies he spewed, I was determined to find a way to be with her again. Because not even death could stop me.

I pulled the blanket tighter around me and gripped the strap of my bag with my left hand. I wanted to make sure I could get to the sickle in case anything happened during the night. That weapon was the only shot we had at killing Aden, and I wasn't going to let it out of my sight. My eyelids grew heavier by the second, and it wasn't much later that my body finally succumbed to exhaustion, sending me into a dreamless sleep. For once, I didn't wake to the screams of my friends and loved ones or souls trying to kill me. Instead, I didn't stir until Noah shook me the following morning.

"Conrad, it's time to get up."

Noah's voice sounded like a distant echo as he roused me from the depths of sleep.

"What time is it?" I asked, rubbing my face.

"Six minutes after nine."

My head was already throbbing and I hadn't even tried to stand yet. Something in my gut told me it was going to be a long day. I glanced at Noah. He was already dressed in jeans and a white button-up shirt. I slipped out of the room, heading toward the bathroom. After I'd shut the door behind me, I turned the faucet to cold and splashed water over my face and hair. The freezing temperature shocked me awake. Any remnants of sleep had been effectively purged from my body. When I made my way back to the room, I removed a pair of jeans and a blue flannel shirt from my bag. Once I was dressed, Noah and I packed up our bags and walked down the hall to meet Caroline in the kitchen.

"Good morning!" Caroline rang out as soon as we stepped inside the kitchen. "What would y'all like for breakfast?"

"Anything," I mumbled, still wishing I was asleep.

"Yeah, I'm not really picky either," Noah added.

"Okay, I'll bring you both something in a minute."

Noah and I sat at the table just as Caroline's mother walked into the room.

"Good morning. Did you both sleep all right?"

"Yes, thank you for letting us be guests in your home," Noah replied.

"Oh, it's no trouble at all. John wanted me to tell you that he enjoyed meeting the two of you. He left early this morning for the station." She took a long drink of coffee. "I'll be going in after the three of you leave. I wanted to make sure I got to say goodbye."

"Here you go," Caroline said, setting a bowl of steaming oats and a small plate of scrambled eggs in front of each of us. "Can I get either of you some coffee or juice?"

"I'd like a cup of coffee," Noah answered.

"Just water for me." I dove into the food, eating most of the oatmeal before Caroline returned with my drink. Within a few minutes, I finished every bite of food in front of me. When I got up to wash the dishes, Noah scooped them up from me. "Thanks," I said, watching him stack the bowls and plates on top of each other.

He nodded before heading over to the sink with Caroline following close behind him. I watched as they whispered to one another.

"She's quite smitten with him." Denise was observing the two of them just as I was.

"And he with her. Although, Caroline definitely has the upper hand of the two."

"Knowing my daughter, that doesn't surprise me one bit," she replied with a laugh. "Just be sure to keep an eye on her. She can be quite the wild card sometimes."

At her words, I instantly pictured Caroline knocking out Noah with a wooden beam in the warehouse. I would've paid a large sum of money just to witness it. "Don't worry, I'll watch out for her as if she were my own sister."

"I'm glad to hear it. Do you have any siblings?"

I pulled in a deep breath, forcing the air into my lungs. "I did," I replied, not meeting her gaze.

"Sometimes life has a funny way of returning things once thought to be lost." Her hand squeezed mine for a second before she stood from the table, leaving me with my thoughts.

When Noah and Caroline finished, we filed out of the kitchen, heading for the front door. I picked up my bag along the way, throwing it over my shoulder as I walked. The sun was already high overhead and the black SUV loomed in the driveway, serving as a reminder of the journey ahead of us. I took all the bags and loaded them in the back of the car. When I finished, Denise was still hugging Caroline goodbye.

"I'll be fine, Mom. It's only for a little while and then I'll be home," Caroline soothed.

"I know, but still. You've never been away from home for this long."

"I'll be home before you know it."

"You're right," Denise replied, brushing away her tears. "Oh, I'm sorry to be a mess in front of you boys. I'm so glad I got to meet the two of you."

"Thank you for welcoming us into your home so graciously," Noah answered, offering his hand to her.

"You put that hand away and give me a proper hug," Denise chided. Much to Noah's surprise, she pulled him into a tight hug. "And feel free to come back and visit anytime."

"Thank you, I will," he answered.

"Now your turn, Conrad," Denise added, turning to me.

I returned her hug. "Thank you again for letting us stay here."

"It was my pleasure. Y'all be safe driving back to Indiana. Please call me when you get there, Caroline, so I know you made it safely."

"I will, Momma," Caroline answered, kissing her mother on the cheek.

The three of us piled into the car and Noah threw it into

reverse, backing down the driveway. Denise stood outside, waving to us until we disappeared from sight. We were back on the road, headed to Everest's and then to Evey. We had the weapon we needed, and now, the only thing missing was someone to use it on. I studied my reflection in the window beside me. I seemed years older than the day I'd come back for Evey. Then again, losing someone you care about does that to you, doesn't it? Didn't I age ten years the night my father died? And how could I forget the night Aden poisoned Evey and our unborn child? I didn't simply age ten years overnight; I broke. It was my worst fear come true, and no matter how hard I tried, I couldn't forget it.

As the car barreled down an abandoned country road, I gazed past my reflection to observe the world around me. It continued on without a care for the things we'd done or still had to do. That was one thing that never changed in all the years I've lived. Life goes on. It had to or we wouldn't survive. Bright white clouds swirled about the blue sky, and as we drove away from town, civilization grew less dense. Suburban homes were replaced by rural farms, and the asphalt curved through the countryside. Up ahead, I could see an old barn, which looked as if it might collapse at any second, and an abandoned gas station. There were no other buildings around—the area seemed completely deserted. Just as we were about to pass the gas station, I noticed a gaunt figure rounding the back of it.

"Stop," I shouted, my eyes still fixated on the vacant building.

"What's wrong?" Caroline asked, worry creeping into her voice as she spoke.

"I saw something unusual."

Noah pulled on the brake, immediately halting the car. "What did you see? What was it?"

"It's going to sound crazy, but I swear to you, I saw a verto demon walking around the side of that gas station." Peeling my gaze away from the window, I reached for my bag in the back. I grabbed it and pulled a short sword and some knives from it. I handed one to Caroline and another to Noah.

"Mine is in my bag," Noah said, looking at the weapon in my hand. "Will you get it for me?"

I turned in my seat again and retrieved the sword for Noah. He took it from me and crept down the road that led to the gas station. I scanned our surroundings, trying to find some sign that there were more demons lying in wait. But I noticed nothing out of the ordinary. We all exited the SUV, cautiously approaching the building. I motioned for the other two to get behind me and stalked toward the front entrance.

A layer of dust coated the outside windows and door, preventing us from scoping out the interior. I pushed on the metal handle, causing the bell at the top of the door to ring. At the sound, six verto demons who had been feeding on an animal carcass turned. Blood dripped from their mouths, and their eyes were already hungry for more flesh. "Oh, shit. Six verto," I shouted, warning Noah and Caroline of what was ahead.

"What is this?" A voice cackled. "A brother of the secundae come to stop our fun?"

I followed the voice. A man, no older than forty, stood there also coated in blood. "And a dissimulo," I added, never breaking my glare. "Aden's leash around you proves to be quite extensive if he allows you to stay here." I stepped toward the dissimulo, never losing the group of verto from my line of sight.

"We only take orders from Aden for the time being." The demon laughed again, spraying blood into the air around him.

My fist clenched around the hilt of my sword, bonding metal with my own skin. "Caroline?"

"I'm right behind you," she whispered.

"Stay in my and Noah's line of sight. Don't go anywhere by yourself."

"Okay."

I didn't hesitate for another second as I ran toward the verto. Drawing closer, I dropped to the floor, sliding along the soiled tile. From the ground, I cut off the legs of a verto to my left. The creature howled, spewing a waterfall of blood. Once incapacitated, I jumped on top of it, thrusting my knife into the gaunt flesh of its face. Before I could even remove my blade from the demon's flesh, another one began to rush in my direction. It clawed at my face, but

I blocked its attack. After shoving my sword and knife through the beast's stomach, I withdrew my weapons. Then I spun out of the way as the demon melted, the remnants of its body collapsing to the floor.

Out of the corner of my eye, I observed Noah taking on two at a time. His blade glinted in the air, its shining surface tainted with demon blood. Just behind him, I saw Caroline dodging the teeth of another verto, her knife slashing its face as it lunged forward. The two of them were making quick work of the demons, so I began to search for the dissimulo, but it was nowhere to be seen.

A cry of pain demanded my attention. One of the remaining verto demons had jumped on top of Noah, biting his shoulder. The sleeve of his shirt was instantly soaked with crimson. When it recoiled from him, preparing itself to take another bite, I slipped behind the verto, guiding my sword through its neck. The head tumbled to the side, splashing into a pile of acidic blood. The demons had no sooner fallen than their bodies began to disintegrate.

"Where's Caroline?" I asked, extending my hand to Noah and helping him from the floor.

"I just saw her a second ago," he replied, searching the area around him. "Caroline?"

"Noah!" she cried from across the room. Immediately, we spun to face her.

"So, that's what you call this beautiful creature? Caroline?" The dissimulo stood behind Caroline. One hand jerked her hair, exposing her throat to the knife brandished by the other.

"Let her go!" Noah ordered.

"I'd rather not," the demon spat.

"I'll take her place. A consiliarius for her."

"A consiliarius? You must be very special," the dissimulo taunted in Caroline's ear.

"Let her go and I'll make your death quick," I shouted.

He cackled at my words, pressing his knife to Caroline's throat with more force. "You threaten me when I hold the power to take her life?"

156

"It's no threat," I answered.

"Perhaps I should have some fun with her first." He smiled, before slowly sliding his tongue over her cheek, relishing in the feel of her skin.

"Touch her again and it will be the last thing you ever do," Noah shouted.

"You forget your place, consiliarius!"

"And you forget yours—it's in hell!" Before I realized what was happening, Noah sprang forward to tackle the dissimulo. I ran after him, dragging Caroline away from the fight.

"Are you okay?" I asked, helping her stand.

"I think so."

I turned on my heel to help Noah, but the fight was already over. He rose from the ground, rivulets of blood pouring from the wound on his shoulder. The dissimulo lay motionless at his feet. Noah had knocked him unconscious. "Did he hurt you?"

"No, I'm fine," Caroline answered, walking over to Noah. "Just a little shaken up." A thin line of blood marred the side of her neck.

"You've been hurt—" Noah whispered, wiping away the blood.

"It's just a scratch."

A sad smile broke over his face as he pressed his lips to Caroline's hand. "Conrad, do you think you can get some information out of him? He might know something about Iola or Evey."

"You realize what you're asking me to do?"

He hesitated for a moment before answering my question. "I do."

"I'll see what I can do," I replied. "If he knows anything about what Aden has planned or where he is, I'll get it out of him."

13

WAKE

I left Aden's office feeling more confounded than when I'd first entered it. Had I actually found comfort in his embrace? The only thing that concerned me more was that I called him by his true name. For a brief moment, I hadn't seen him as Aden anymore. He was the Adam I first saw sleeping underneath the shade of a large tree. He was the first man I fell in love with. I needed to clear my head and escape everything trying to pull me into the past. How would I ever be able to outrun thousands of years together? The thought of breaking away from Aden became more difficult with each passing second.

I stumbled around the staircase, making my way back to the kitchen. Along the way, I saw Donovan posted at the entrance to the dining room. His hands were balled into fists at his side. I stared at them, wondering how many lives they had extinguished. Those hands, which killed my mother, now sought to injure me at every turn. Donovan hated me almost as much as I despised him. How could I not when he was responsible for ripping so many people away from me. He helped take Conrad, my mother, Milton, Mickey,

Kit, and my father. Although, the same could be said of Aden. How could I be forgiving when his hands were soiled with the same blood?

"You and Aden took my dad's body from the morgue?" I turned on Donovan, demanding an answer.

"We did."

"And where is he now?"

"That's privileged information," he sneered.

"And I'm a primum. If you don't tell me, you'll have to explain to Aden why you denied me such information," I countered.

I returned his glare with one of my own as I waited for him to speak. After a long moment of silence, I finally had my answer. "There is a row of trees marking the entrance of the woods behind the house; his grave lies at the foot of a tree. There's a fresh mound of dirt marking the site."

I headed for the door. "Follow me. I'm going to see my dad."

"I have orders to stay here."

"And now you have new ones!" I shouted, all my hatred for him seeping into my voice. "I'm going to see my father whether you like it or not. You can either follow or stay here. I think you forget I can have you removed as one of Aden's secundae. Because he would never hesitate to do something that would keep me by his side." I spun on my heel, resuming my path to the door.

Donovan's feet fell in line behind my own as I stepped outside. Dark clouds blotted the direct rays of the sun, casting a shadow over the ground. I meandered to the back of the house and stopped in front of a hydrangea. The soft white and purple flowers seemed out of place in the gloomy light. I plucked a few flowers, bundling them together until I had a large bouquet.

The grass was damp beneath my feet as I approached my dad's grave. A lump caught in my throat and tears threatened to burst from my eyes as I stared at the freshly turned dirt. His body had been tossed into the ground with no marker or headstone. Placing the flowers upon his grave, I knelt beside him. This was the price he paid in order to protect me. It wasn't fair. I didn't choose this. I didn't want to be a primum or the first woman. And I was so tired of watching my loved ones die at my expense. I stared at the flowers, wishing I could talk to him and my mom one last time. An hour or two passed as I sat there. My mind flitted through memories of my childhood. The field of poppies, riding on his shoulders as we walked along the beach, the sound of his and my mom's voices reading a bedtime story to me. All these moments flashed before my eyes, never lasting longer than a second or two. There was nothing I wouldn't give to live in those memories again. A cold chill crept over my body as the wind picked up speed. The air around me grew heavy and it started to rain. But as the drops fell, I made no effort to move. I wanted to stay by his side.

"He was the first secundae."

My head tilted in the direction of Aden's voice. "Really?" I asked, glancing back at the fresh grave. I placed my hand on the soil, wishing I had the power to heal his body and bring him back to life. "Would you tell me about it?"

"Well, we were traveling through Germany, stopping from village to village as we made our way back to France. We were riding through the woods when a band of thieves attacked us." He placed a thick coat over my shoulders before kneeling beside me. "When they attacked, you were knocked off your horse. I couldn't find you anywhere and assumed you'd gotten away, but I was wrong. I fled into the trees, hoping to find you on my way to the next village. Everyone left behind had been killed. A couple guards and I were the only ones who managed to escape, except you."

"And how did I get away?" I clutched the coat, pulling it tighter around me.

"Guy was one of the thieves who attacked us, and he was also the one who saved you. He told me about it when he was first turned into a secundae. He said he had his knife drawn and was about to kill you, but when he looked into your eyes, he couldn't do it. He knew he had to protect you and lead you to safety. The thieves followed after you, but Guy found a hiding place in the woods. When night fell, he took you to the small town where I'd taken shelter with my guards. He returned you to me and asked to remain by your side. He protected you for fifteen years or so before he died saving your life."

"He died protecting me?" I repeated, dazed by the notion of his words.

"Yes, and it wasn't the last time either. Because of his devotion to you and because the Concilium recognized the constant danger we were in, they decided to create the secundae to serve as our protectors."

"Conrad died for me and then was made into a secundae. Is that how it works?"

"For you, yes." Aden grabbed a handful of dirt, rubbing it between his fingers, clearly avoiding my gaze.

"What do you mean?"

"Your secundae were all brought back by the Concilium because of their sacrifices. Who better to protect you than people willing to sacrifice their own lives for you?"

"I'd never want that kind of sacrifice to be made on my behalf," I said, guilt overwhelming my already burdened conscience.

"And that is why they gave up their lives so willingly. You are a just cause; you're worth dying for."

"But I've done nothing to deserve such loyalty."

He laughed at me. "You showed each of them a kindness that, before meeting you, had been unknown to them. You cared for Conrad's family, provided them with a home and food. You saved Marie from being stoned to death by her village. And those are just a few of the things you've done."

"Then how are your secundae chosen?"

"I got to choose mine because no one gave up their life to protect me. I've never inspired the same sense of devotion in people as you have." He wiped dirt from his hands, cleaning the pale skin. "I choose my secundae based on one thing," he added.

"And what might that be?" I asked, my curiosity piqued past the point of no return.

"I choose people who are as lost and broken as I am."

"Why?"

"Because it makes me feel like I'm helping someone. Like I'm doing something you would do."

"I can't help but find so much irony in your statement, because you say something like that, but you took my father and mother from me. You ripped away everything I hold dear and justify your actions by proclaiming to do it in the name of love."

"I know."

"Why do it, then?"

"It's the only way to be with you, and I know you'll forgive me."

"I wouldn't be too sure of that if I were you," I snapped.

"You can't help but forgive me, it's your nature. You always do the right thing."

"And is such a quality a blessing or a curse?" I jumped to my feet and threw the jacket beside him, not wanting to seek comfort in anything he provided. Before he could reply, I headed back to the house, back to my prison. Bursting through the back door, I left a trail of wet footprints in my wake. The house was silent. From the looks of it, you'd think a happy family lived here instead of captives locked away inside the rooms. I was halfway up the stairs when Aden flung the back door open. Our eyes connected for a brief second before he lunged toward me. A sense of panic forced my body to react to the situation. I pushed forward, taking the stairs two at a time until I reached the landing. I could hear Aden behind me, his speed increasing with each step. The harder I tried to push him away, the more determined he seemed to join us together. "I don't want to see you!" I shouted, rounding the corner and shooting down the hallway to my room.

"Please don't push me away." He was out of breath, but he never slowed down.

I slammed the door to my room behind me and pressed my weight against it. It didn't matter, though, Aden was too strong. He shoved the door open, sliding me across the wooden floor. I quickly stood. We faced one another, staring at the person we were once bound to in marriage. How could I ever outrun the man I was created for? "I don't want you." I panted, breaking the silence that threatened to smother me. "Not like that."

"Just let me tell you one thing, and I'll leave." Every inch of ground he gained caused me to shiver more and more. My dress was drenched, sticking to my skin with each movement.

"What is it?" I was too exhausted to fight or argue with him. My resilience was cracking one small piece at a time. What would happen when nothing remained?

"It kills me to look at you and remember every moment we've shared, knowing you can't recall any of it. I look at you and see my wife. I see the woman who came to me in the Garden, but you don't know me. I'm just some person you can't really remember and don't want to."

"I didn't choose to have my memories taken away," I whispered.

"After everything we've shared, I'm nothing to you. I just want you to see me for who I am now—or at least who I'm trying to be."

"I—this—isn't easy for me either. To see and hear about the horrible things you've done and then to remember kissing you or how much I used to love you . . . It's exhausting and confusing." I rubbed my arms vigorously to return some semblance of warmth to my icy flesh. I watched as Aden walked to my bed and retrieved the comforter. He moved behind me, holding the blanket in one hand. With the other, he snapped the clasp on my dress. The garment slid down my body, crashing to the floor around my feet. I couldn't move. The weight of the comforter pressed against my shoulders. He walked a slow circle around me, wrapping the ends of the blanket to cover my front.

"I can't let you freeze to death." His teeth chattered together as he uttered the words.

I observed the man standing before me, studied every part of him visible to my eyes. He was as lost as I was. The only difference was that he'd felt this way for centuries. I tried to fathom what that would feel like. "And what about you?" I stared at the soaked clothing clinging to his body. "Can we let you freeze to death?" Opening my arms, I tugged the blanket around him. His body was flush with mine, and wet fabric was the only thing remaining between us. It intensified the bitter cold, causing both of us to shiver. He gripped the bottom of his shirt and lifted it over his head before throwing it to the floor. My heart seized inside my chest as his pants followed his shirt.

Grabbing my waist, he pulled me closer to him. "I just want to feel something again," he whispered.

"And what will it take to make you feel again?"

"You."

I opened my mouth to speak, but his lips silenced my words. In an instant, my hands were on his neck, driving us closer together. I didn't want to kiss him, but it was as if an unseen force was governing my body. My will wasn't my own. Instead, it was being controlled by something else, some tiny part of me that I thought to be extinct. His mouth increased its hold on my own, extending our kiss while his fingers dug into my waist. Part of me was shocked by the prospect of kissing him so intimately, but another part of me felt comforted, as if the need for human contact was greater than my revulsion. I held on to the blanket tighter, wrapping it around us to eliminate the chill of wet skin. Aden's lips moved away from my own to make contact with my shoulder. The lace edge of my underwear was tugged away from my body. He kissed me again, returning my gaze with one of his own. "Is this how you seduced Thea?" My voice was barely above a whisper, but he flinched at my words as if they were shouted.

"Why would you even ask me that?"

"There had to be a reason she would go against the Concilium to bring you back. Sheer pity isn't enough to sacrifice one's loyalty to their family."

"I didn't seduce her."

"Then what did you do?"

"Over time, Thea and I became very close, just as you and Everest did. Although, you were Everest's shining glory—much like any daughter is to their father."

"Guy is my father."

"Yes, but Everest accepted a similar role in your life. He was assigned to reincarnate you every time we were slated to live again, and Thea did the same for me."

"Wouldn't that make her more like you mother, then?"

"She was my companion, my confidant. When you rescinded from my touch, Thea ran to me with open arms. She loved me and sought to deliver me from the apple's curse."

"Did you love her?"

"Yes."

"Then why weren't you able to find happiness with her?"

"Because my love for you is deeper," he answered, his hands greedily slipping along the curves of my waist. "Her attempts to keep away the darkness failed."

"If she couldn't save you, then why do you believe I'm your salvation?"

"We were designed for one another. Your love delivered me from isolation in Eden, and it will deliver me from the darkness coursing through my veins."

"And if I fail, will you claim my heart as well?"

"In the time you've been here, have I raised a hand against you? Have I treated you with even a miniscule amount of violence?"

"Not yet, but I'm simply wondering what will happen to me if I get too close to you. Will I suffer the same fate she did?"

"I would never harm you," he replied, his hands still around me.

"Did you believe that sentiment before you poisoned me too, or did you only start saying it afterward?"

He released me, taking a step back. "You were pregnant with another man's baby. What was I supposed to do? What would you have done in my shoes?"

"Not that. I could never murder an innocent child."

"It wasn't me! It was this thing, this disease inside me. It eats away at me with each passing day. I'm compelled to do things against my will. Thea betrayed me to the Concilium. I was butchered like an animal for what I did to you. I was tortured until I died!" he shouted. "Is that merciful? Is that something you would do? Because that was done on orders of the Concilium."

"Was it merciful to kill a woman who no longer loved you?" I stared back, daring him to counter my argument, daring him to defend his actions. "My only crime against you was that I stopped loving you and fell for another. Conrad loved me without seeking anything from me in return." I paused for a moment to catch my breath, never allowing my courage to falter. "And what have your crimes been against me?"

He choked on his words, the sound hitching in his throat as he tried to answer me. "There have been too many to count." His gaze dropped to the floor. "I need you to teach me how to be Adam again."

"And if I refuse?"

"More people could die. I can't control what's happening to me. I've tried to change back into the man you used to love, but every attempt has ended in disaster. But you're the key to helping me— that much I'm certain of."

"And what if I help you and it doesn't work. Then what?"

"I don't know."

"Would you take your life to prevent yourself from harming anyone else?" The question slipped from my mouth before I could really consider what I was asking him to do.

"You can change me; I know you can."

"But if I can't, I want to know how far you're willing to go to do the right thing. I need to know if you would sacrifice yourself in order to protect others."

"I—I," he stammered. "Is that really what you would have me do?"

"Yes."

"And you know where I would go—" His eyes shone with tears.

"I do." Aden had been born in the light of a beautiful garden and the thought of suffering an eternity of persecution in the depths of hell frightened him. But I was incapable of comprehending how he felt. I hadn't done any of the things he had. "You were executed by Conrad after you poisoned me?"

The line of his jaw stiffened. "Calling it an execution is putting it mildly."

"Well, you were dead, and then you were brought back. But when you died, were you in hell?"

He swallowed hard. "Yes."

"And it scared you to the point you would do anything, hurt anyone, to keep from going back?"

"You can't even begin to imagine what it was like," he said, his voice faltering. "The pain was so unbearable that I can't describe it. The only constant was that I would endure it for an eternity, like an incessantly ticking clock counting down to nothing. You can't see—darkness envelops everything. All you hear are screams. You know you aren't alone, but you also know no one is coming to save you."

I closed my eyes, not wanting to see his memories darken the lines of his face. The things he had suffered were inconceivable. But at the same time, his actions demanded some type of reparation. "I'm sorry," I breathed. It was the only thing I could manage to say. He was recounting the time he'd spent in hell, and there wasn't anything I could say or do to make him forget.

"You don't think you can help me change, do you?"

"I don't see how I can. I couldn't stop you from changing in the first place."

"You can," he replied, bending to his knees in front of me. "I have faith in you." He guided his mouth to my stomach, running his lips over my skin as his fingertips slid down my thighs. "Please help me, Evey."

"I need some time to think about it." He instantly stopped kissing me and lifted his gaze to meet mine. "I need to think everything over first. There are so many memories swirling around my head, and I've got to have my bearings if I'm going to help you."

"I'll leave you to your thoughts, then." He retrieved his clothes from the floor and walked back to me, leaning in close. "When you're done thinking, come find me." Then he took my chin in his hand and kissed me.

Once the door was shut behind him, I slumped to my knees and hoped to erase the sensation of Aden's hands from my mind. The more I tried to fight against him, the more I felt for him. It'd be impossible to erase our history together, but I wanted to cling to my memories of Conrad. I wanted to think of his every touch. But the time we spent together was so brief, and my memories of him from other lives were out of my reach. I racked my brain, trying to recall one moment with him at will. I would have accepted any mundane second of time together. Anything at all to remind me of the man who owned my heart. As if by a miracle, my prayers were answered. Without warning, the room around me began to fade from sight, and I knew without a doubt I was in the past.

The brash knock on my bedroom door startled me. I'd sent everyone away and told them to leave me with my thoughts. I'd come out to the country to get away from the palace and everything reminding me of the existence I was being forced to live. This small house was my sanctuary. I'd sit here for hours on end, remembering Conrad's touch. He'd been taken away from me, never to return. I died as Isabella, wife of Frederic, but I'd been reborn as Gabrielle d'Estrees. Once again, I was meant to marry Adam and continue the excruciating lie I'd been living since the beginning of time.

Because Conrad had been a simple guard, he wasn't mentioned in any records or paintings. It was as if he'd never existed. All I had were my memories and the ruby pendant hanging from my neck. Adam attempted to steal my necklace and burn it with everything else Conrad had owned, but I threatened him with my life. If he took it away, then I'd slit my throat. I'd kill myself in front of him over and over again until the end of time. Getting to keep this part of Conrad was a small victory in a never-ending war.

"Come in," I ordered. All I wanted was to be left alone, but my request, like so many other things, was denied. Standing from my chair by the window, I waited for the guest to enter. "What do you want?" I asked, gazing at the blooming trees outside.

"Only to look upon your face, my lady, and then I'll leave."

I shook my head, knowing I was imagining Conrad's voice. I squeezed my eyelids shut. "He's dead. He can't be here. You'll never see him again," I told myself.

"My lady—"

I turned at hearing his voice again, but my knees were frail and I stumbled to the floor. I was seeing things again. This wasn't the first time I had imagined seeing Conrad and it wouldn't be the last. I'd wandered through the snow for hours on end, following the visage of his ghost. Guy, Marie, Mickey, and Kit had to remind me that he was dead, that he wasn't coming back. And still, my mind played tricks on me. It forced me to hear his voice and catch a glimpse of his eyes when he wasn't there. He was bits of bone and flesh buried deep in the ground. The remnants of his body lay beneath the shade of a withered apple tree hundreds of miles away. "Evey, look at me," the voice begged.

"Leave me alone," I pleaded. The pain of loss gripped my heart and refused to let go. "You aren't real. Please stop torturing me." Hot tears crashed onto the skin of my hands as I cried. I'd already been forced to watch the man I love die. And now, I had to continue to live without him for an eternity. What else was I to endure? What other punishment could I bear? "Your face haunts me everywhere I go. What else am I to suffer to prove how sorry I am for what happened to you?"

"If I'm not real, then why is it I can touch you right now?"

Rough hands grasped my own. I lifted my head to gaze at the man who touched me. Bright rings of blue stared back at me, and I knew in an instant that he was real. "Conrad?" I withdrew my hands, placing them on each side of his face. "It's you."

"It is," he whispered, turning to kiss my palm.

"But how?"

"You stopped living," he answered. "The Concilium brought me back to be one of your secundae because they saw how much you needed me." His fingers gently wiped my tears.

"Whenever I think I can't take anymore, whenever I'm ready to lie down and die, you come and save me."

His arms wrapped around me, providing the most genuine form of comfort I'd ever known. "And I always will."

"You've no idea how I've longed to hear your voice."

"What would you like for me to say?"

"Anything you want."

"No one will ever separate us again, my lady."

I breathed deeply for the first time since he'd been taken away from me. Now that I had him again, I didn't want to merely exist—I wanted to live. "I love you so much. I never stopped, not even for a second."

He shook his head, smiling at me. "I've been in love with you since the first time I laid eyes on you." Before I could answer him, Conrad's mouth claimed mine. A shiver coursed through my body, settling into my bones as he continued to kiss me. My fingers tangled in his hair, grabbing on to the soft brown locks, as he swept me off the floor. He increased his hold on me, compelling our bodies to dissolve into a singular being. This was how I was supposed to feel. His every touch was desired, longed for. I didn't have to submit to the demands of someone who sickened me.

Instead, I could give myself to Conrad in every way imaginable.

"Please don't stop touching me," I whispered, relishing the sensation of his fingertips sliding down my neck. I felt him set me on top of the table by the window. Leaning away from him, my back arched in response to his caresses.

"In that case, I'm afraid you're a little overdressed, Mrs. Bourdet," he teased, ripping apart the ties at the back of my dress.

My brow furrowed in curiosity. "Mrs. Bourdet?"

My question was met with the most sinful grin I'd ever seen. "Well, on the last night I spent with you, your dress was hanging around your ankles and you told me to take you as my wife. I'm just doing as I was ordered."

"Who am I to interfere with such orders?" I grabbed his shirt and tugged until no part of it covered his flesh.

"Thank you," he answered, lowering my gown to the floor in a slow, deliberate movement. My heart threatened to burst from my chest as the fabric slid past my ankles. His fingers gripped the curve of my hip, leading the way for his mouth as he planted soft kisses on my skin. "It would be my absolute pleasure to carry out such orders . . . Or rather, I should say it will be *your* pleasure." His tongue tasted the inside of my thigh, fulfilling his promise. I relished in the feeling of his lips as he worshiped my body. Every fiber of my being ached for him to touch me. Excitement swirled in my blood as he rediscovered the curve of my spine. My hands unfastened his pants with haste and I smiled as they disappeared from sight. When we were both free from our clothes, we stared as if seeing each other for the first time. I marveled at his strong frame, memorizing each muscle that stretched beneath his skin. If a lifetime would have happened to transpire while I stared at him, I wouldn't have cared. After being denied his presence for so long, he was too handsome not to admire. His chest was hard beneath my hand, and my fingers skimmed leisurely over the surface of his skin.

I watched as he appraised my figure. "I almost forgot how beautiful you are," he said. "And now, as I stand here before you, such a statement seems criminal, because you're too lovely to forget."

"I just had the same thought about you."

"It's sometimes difficult to fathom that you would yearn to belong to me."

"I've belonged to you since the moment we met, so please say it again," I begged.

"Say what again?" His breath was hot on my lips as he spoke.

"Say that I'm your wife one more time."

"My lady," he began, trailing kisses along my shoulder. "Would you take me as your husband and allow me to love you, care for you, and protect you until the end of time?"

I smiled, unable to resist the lure of his unbelievable blue eyes. "I would."

"Then, I believe I'm supposed to address you as Evey Bourdet, seeing as how you're my wife now."

I wrapped my arms around his neck, my lips brushing against his ear. "I'll always be yours." At my words, he grasped my hips and completed our union. "Oh, Conrad," I moaned, unable to feel where his body ended and mine began. Time ceased to exist as he rocked into me. With each movement, new sensations flooded my consciousness. I dug my nails into his shoulders as his hips melted into mine. The spark that had vacated my body the moment Conrad died ignited with a renewed fervor. His presence, his touch was intoxicating, driving my deepest desires to the forefront of my mind. The table buckled beneath our weight, but it did nothing to slow us down. Some part of me acknowledged Conrad's strength as he lifted me from the wooden surface and carried me to the bed by the opposite wall. I floated through the air, my back crashing on the soft pillows covering the mattress. I found his lips with my own, deepening the kiss so I could taste him. My legs intertwined with his, sealing our embrace. Conrad's hands delicately stroked my back in response to my sighs. Then, when anticipation threatened to become too unbearable, Conrad pushed inside me, fusing our bodies together once more. He pressed deeper, increasing our pace. Gripping his waist, I pulled him into me as our breathing grew ragged. The bond between us intensified with every touch, every kiss. It didn't matter if we would have years together or just one night. We were together right now—for this one fleeting moment in time—and nothing else mattered. Gasps filled the air as an all-consuming pleasure rained across my flesh. This was the pinnacle of ecstasy, and no one would ever be able to love me the way Conrad did. Once we'd pushed ourselves past the point of exhaustion, we collapsed on the bed. Conrad drew me closer to him and guided my head to rest on his shoulder. "I can't believe you're really here," I whispered. My gaze found his bright sapphire eyes. "Every day, I've woke up never expecting to see you or hold you, but here you are, lying beside me."

"And I always plan on being by your side."

"He frightens me."

"Adam?"

"Yes. He tries so hard to be good, but sometimes, I can't help but picture him in the dungeons torturing people. He started the Inquisition. And what's worse? He liked participating in it. He enjoyed doing those things to people."

"Evey, I promise he'll never hurt you. I won't let him," he said, kissing my forehead. "I'm one of your secundae, and I've sworn to protect you until the end of time. No one will take me away from you again."

"Can I see it?"

"See what?" he asked uncertainly.

"Your sacramentum. I have to look upon it and see that it's real."

A devious grin broke over his face as he released me. Rolling over, he displayed his back for me to see. The sacramentum was there, just below his left shoulder, forever imprinted into the skin.

The wild roots curled into an imaginary ground, mirroring the vast branches covered in leaves stemming out from the trunk of the tree. "What do you think?"

My fingers traced over each line with great care. "I think it's the most beautiful thing I've ever seen." His sacramentum, his oath to stay by my side, couldn't be washed away from his flesh. It was a part of him now. "I can't believe they asked you to join the secundae."

"I didn't think I was that terrible at being your guard," he teased.

"That's not what I meant. I already have four secundae. That's more than anyone else, the Concilium included. I just didn't think they would bless me with another."

"From what I understand, I don't think you gave them much of a choice," he replied, shifting to face me. "You were supposed to keep living."

"I tried to keep my promise, but it was so hard after you were gone. Could you live repeatedly, knowing I was dead and gone, never to return?"

His eyes avoided my gaze. "Such a fate would be worse than death," he whispered.

I took his face in my hands. "I just want to apologize for what happened to you," I began, willing him to look at me. "I'm so sorry your life was taken from you because of me, because of who I am. Please know that I offered my own life in exchange for yours, but Adam wouldn't accept that. I never wanted you to make such a sacrifice on my account."

"I agreed to be one of your guards so I could protect and be near you. I knew the risks involved and gladly gave my life to protect you."

"I wish I were someone else. I wish none of the people I love or care about needed to risk their lives in order to protect me. It's cruel to care about you, Guy, Marie, Mickey, and Kit when I have to watch you die to save me."

Conrad moved to lie on top of me, pressing his body against my own. "Don't wish that. Everything that's happened in your life has made you into the woman I fell in love with. Even if I could change one thing about you, I wouldn't."

I leaned toward him to kiss him on the lips. "I'd give my life to save yours."

"No," he said immediately. "You won't."

"But why?" I asked, surprised by his harsh tone.

"Because I forbid it."

"That isn't fair."

"It's not supposed to be fair. It's my duty to protect you, not the other way around. I love you, but you can't sacrifice your life for mine. I won't allow it."

"You're impossible sometimes. Is this what I'm supposed to put up with as your wife?"

"Not in the least, Mrs. Bourdet," he answered with a broad smile. Before I could reply, his hands swept down my sides to clutch my waist. My head turned, giving his lips more room to discover the curve of my neck. I savored the feel of my husband on top of me. He was the only man I wanted, the one I'd choose to be with above all others.

Almost as soon as it began, I felt the memory of Conrad slipping away. Desperately, I tried to focus on the color of his eyes, the warmth of his flesh, and the way he touched me, but I was no longer in the past. I was the same woman I'd been in my final years as Queen Isabella—broken and only truly alive when dwelling within my memories of Conrad. I collapsed on my back, focusing on the white ceiling of my room. During all the years I'd spent in Estill Springs, I wished for something to happen. I prayed for some exciting adventure to occur, to pull me away from my simple life. Now, I'd discovered my past as a queen, my history as the original woman, and my former husband trying to rekindle the love we once shared . . . But all I wanted was to fade into the background of my simple existence.

14

DISTURBING
BEHAVIOR

I checked the ropes once more, testing their strength. The dissimulo had information I needed and I would obtain it one way or another. Caroline and Noah stood behind me, neither daring to break the silence. The demon was strapped by the arms and feet to an old chair. I couldn't help but think back to a similar scenario that occurred almost four hundred years ago. Aden had received no mercy when I carved him into pieces, and neither would this demon. I'd become something different that day and I hadn't ever been the same since. Maybe when you stared into the eyes of another man and killed him, you couldn't be the same. I would always be tainted, unclean. The Concilium recognized what I was, but they kept me around because Evey needed me. To them, I'd always be another polluted seed.

"Where is Aden hiding?" I asked.

The demon smiled widely and cackled. "Even if I knew, I wouldn't tell you." He sneered at me through decaying teeth.

"If you tell me now, I'll give you a quick death. I'll cut your head clean off with one stroke. It'll be fast, much better than you deserve."

He spat on the ground beside me. "As I said, secundae, I don't know."

I leaned closer, glaring into his eyes. "When you're begging for death, screaming for me to show you mercy, I want you to remember my offer. I want you to spend your final moments choking on your own blood, knowing there's nothing you can do to save yourself." I squeezed the knife in my hand. "Where is Aden hiding?" The demon threw his head back, erupting in laughter. I swung the knife down, stabbing it into the forearm of the demon. The tip pierced his flesh and I dragged the blade through the demon's arm toward his hand. Blood bubbled from the wound, spilling to the floor. It oozed and burned, fueling his screams. Metal carved into bone, reshaping his limb. I watched his body twitch with agony beneath the restraints. The thick rope scoured his unspoiled flesh, leaving indentations. When the knife met the bone in his wrist, I removed it and stepped away from him. "Where is he?"

"I'll see you soon, secundae. You'll rot in hell beside me," he spat.

I wiped the stained blade on his shirt. "But not today." Moving over, I grabbed the index finger on his other hand. "Last chance."

"You know he'll get her."

"Aden already has Evey."

"Not Aden. Luke," he answered between heaving breaths.

"She'd never go with him." I pressed the metal tip into the base of the finger, drawing a drop of blood.

"It doesn't matter. He'll get her one way or another. That soft, sweet skin . . . I wonder how long it'll take to burn off her flesh." He howled.

My composure snapped like a broken bone. I shoved the blade through his skin, carving around the joints in his finger. His flesh split apart. Grabbing a piece of skin, I peeled it from the bone as if it were no more than a ripe piece of fruit. Screams filled the air, multiplying as I fileted each finger on his hand until only bone and yellow blood remained. "If you ever speak Evey's name again, I'll shove whatever flesh I remove down your throat until you choke on it." The sound of liquid splattering against the floor disrupted my focus. I glanced over my shoulder to find Caroline kneeling on the ground. Noah was at her side, steadying her as she retched. "Now look what you've done." I returned the blade to his hand. The knife slid through tendons like they were hot butter. "Where is he?" The demon wailed in agony. "Answer the question now or I'll rip the flesh off every bone in your body until you do." I glared into his dark eyes, waiting for a reply. As the silence elapsed, I took out another knife. Brandishing the two weapons, I made a large slit in his forearm. Slowly, I sliced small chunks from the arm until it showcased the bone beneath.

"Conrad," Noah called out from behind me.

"You might want to get her out of here. She doesn't need to see this."

Noah lifted her from the floor. "We can wait in the car," he said, leading her to the entrance.

"No." She stopped him just short of the door, refusing to go any further. "I'm staying."

"It's going to get a lot worse," I replied. "The two of you don't have to stay and watch this."

"Evey is my best friend, and this is the only way we can find out where Aden is keeping her. I'm staying until it's finished."

"I know I asked you to do this, Conrad, but if you've changed your mind, I understand," Noah said.

"Can you think of any other way to learn where Aden is keeping Evey and Iola?" He was silent for a few moments before shaking his head in reply. "I'll do whatever is necessary to find them. If you're that adamant about staying, you might need this." I slid an empty mop bucket across the floor. "Noah, if you want to leave, I'll watch over her."

He laughed at my words. "Yeah, there's no chance I'm leaving if she's staying."

"Okay then." I turned back to the demon. "Let's try this again. Where is Aden, where's the man you're serving?"

"We don't serve Aden." He spit again, covering the ground

beside me with a spray of demonic blood. "Demons will never be servants to man."

"Then why are you following his orders?"

"Because they come from a greater power. The servi only have one true master, and it is under his orders that we do Aden's bidding."

"What's Luke doing in all this? What's his end game?"

"Like I would tell you," the demon replied, smiling.

I wielded the two knives again, one firmly grasped in each hand. "Doesn't matter, because I won't ask again." I shoved the knives through his skin, stripping it away from the bone and pinning it to the sides of his chair. He howled, staring at his arm that now resembled a demented animal dissection.

"What Luke wants is the same as Aden," the dissimulo gasped, desperate to catch his breath.

"He wants Evey?"

"Doesn't every man seem to?"

"She isn't some trophy to be put on display."

"Not to you," the demon replied.

His body shook, causing the visible muscles to vibrate like the keys of a piano. "Why does he want her?"

"You'd have to ask him that."

"Where is Aden keeping Evey?"

"What makes you think Aden would tell me where he's staying?" he asked with a sneer

"Because you're a dissimulo. Even worthless things like demons have their own class system. Dissimulo demons can hide in plain sight and live amongst people without detection. It makes you the most useful and dangerous. Plus, you're in Evey's hometown and that isn't a coincidence. Aden may be many things, but he isn't stupid. He ordered you to stay here to see if anyone from the Concilium comes back."

"You've studied demons," he replied, clearly amused with my knowledge of the servi.

"Helps to know how you think and act. It makes you easier to kill." I removed one of the knives pinning his flesh to the chair and held the tip of it to his bicep. "Where is Aden?"

His smile widened. "I don't know."

I thrust my hand forward, continuing the gash on his arm all the way up to his shoulder. Then I removed the blade, allowing him a moment to scream. "Did Aden ever tell you about a similar occurrence between him and me?" I asked. "I was sent by the Concilium to dispose of him. He poisoned Evey and she died as a result." I cleaned the knife by wiping it against his tattered jeans. "After I tracked Aden down, I locked him inside a barn. At first, I went slow, testing his limits. I put brodequins on him and tightened them until the bones in his legs burst. He screamed a lot at first . . . but eventually, his voice died out." I put the tip of my knife against the demon's knee and began to twist it as I continued talking. "I sawed off his feet first and then his legs up to his knees. They were the easiest to cut through since the bones had already been destroyed. I started with his hands after that. First the left, then the right. I hung the limbs from the ceiling so that he could watch as I cut him apart. I added more and more body parts, hanging them like trophies. When all that remained of him was his torso and head, he was barely alive. But before he died, I made sure to decapitate him. I cut his head off just like he took mine." The end of the knife continued twisting into his flesh like a drill in wood. It bored into his leg, tearing through the fabric of his jeans. "The worst part of it was the smell," I said, turning the knife harder. "Pieces of his body hung from the roof of that barn for days. When bugs and maggots infested the rotting limbs, it got even worse. But it bothered him more than it did me. Lying there, staring at the decaying body parts hanging above his head made him quite sick. His vomit mixed with the blood and putrefying pieces of his body. The smell only went away when I threw him in a sack and got rid of him." Blood pooled from the hole in the demon's leg, spilling over his knee and shin. He bent forward, wincing as his mutilated arms tugged at the ropes tying him to the chair. He was panting, wheezing for air. It wouldn't take much more for him to break.

"He's in New York," the dissimulo croaked. "He's got a house in the country, outside the city. That's where he's keeping her."

"I need an address," I replied, still holding the knife to his leg.

He stared at his knee in horror. "I don't know."

"I find that hard to believe." I shoved the metal deeper. "What's the address?"

"It's 510 Willow Lane. It's near Lake George. He's got a house up there on some land he owns. There's no one around for miles."

"You better not be lying to me," I warned, not moving my hand from the knife.

"I'm not! It's the truth. If you want to find Aden, that's where he'll be."

"Noah!" I shouted. I stared into the demon's eyes, searching for any sign he might be providing us with a fake address.

"I'm looking it up. It's a real address. He's not lying."

"How long?"

"It's going to take sixteen hours to get there," he answered.

"We better get going, then. Get the car ready." My hand was steady on the handle as I pressed it down, deepening the wound. There was one more question I wanted to ask the demon, and I needed to make sure he had the right motivation to answer it. I jerked my hand toward his hip, slicing him open. "One last question. What's Aden's plan? What does he want with Evey and a consiliarius?"

"He's going to where it all started," the demon panted.

"To where what all started?"

"To the start of it. To the beginning."

I shook him once more, but he was barely conscious. I wouldn't be getting any more information out of him.

"Conrad, it's time to go," Caroline said, heading for the door. "Noah is starting the car. We've got to go get Evey."

"Okay. I'll clean up this mess and meet you outside." I turned back to the demon, scanning the filleted flesh that hung in pieces from his hand. Scouring the overturned shelves to my left, I searched for anything that would catch fire. I grabbed a couple cans of gas and poured them on the floor around the demon. I coated the shelves with the liquid so a fire would spread through the room, dousing the dead verto bodies as well. Nothing could be left behind for anyone to discover. The last can of gas was poured over the demon, soaking every inch of him.

"To the beginning," the demon muttered. Running to the store's entrance, I snagged a rock from outside and swiped the blade of my knife against it a few times. Sparks fanned from the rock, landing on the demon's clothes. "Please finish me," he moaned, staring as his shirt caught fire.

"You already had your chance for mercy," I replied. A wave of yellow flames started at his chest, spreading over his arms and legs. He screamed as the fire consumed everything around him. I ran to the door, only looking back to make sure the fire would cover the whole building. The gas I had poured over the shelves ignited, and everything in sight was quickly set ablaze. Running to the car, I jumped in the passenger seat. Noah peeled out of the parking lot, speeding down the empty road in front of us. If someone witnessed us leaving as the fire started, we'd have even more problems to deal with. The faster we could get out of town, the better. We hurried down the highway, careful to use back roads where we were less likely to run into other cars.

"I feel like we should all talk about what just happened," Caroline said. Her hands worked methodically, cleaning and applying a fresh bandage to the wound on Noah's shoulder as he drove. If this war continued much longer, she'd be as adept at sewing up our wounds as Evey was.

"There isn't anything to talk about," I replied.

"Really?" she asked, looking between Noah and me. "Because Dr. Phil would have a field day talking to the two of you and discussing all your baggage."

"I don't have any baggage. What about you, Noah?"

"I'm not answering that," he replied, keeping his focus on the road.

"No baggage, my ass! Kidnapping, torture, arson . . . Let's see what other felonies we can add to our repertoire on the drive to New York," she replied sarcastically.

"I did what I had to do to find out where Evey is, remember? Aden still has her, and we have no idea what he's planning next."

"I know we need to get her back, but you're a little too good at that."

"At what?" I asked, turning in my seat to face her. "Torturing things?" She nodded, returning my stare. "Tell me something I don't already know."

"Is that really what you did to Aden?" Even though she posed the question, I knew she knew the answer.

"If you had to watch the person you love most die in your arms, you wouldn't have been able to stop yourself. I couldn't, and I didn't want to."

"She was about to give birth to your child, wasn't she?"

My eyes closed for a minute as I inhaled. For a second, my mind flashed to an image of Evey lying beside me. Her belly was rounded from the presence of our son living inside her. "He's kicking, Conrad. Can you feel him?" She held my hand to her stomach, smiling as she waited for me to feel. Just as I set my palm to her skin, he kicked. "He already knows his father," she added, softly touching my lips. In that moment, I was so happy, so overjoyed at the thought of starting a family with her.

I sucked in another deep breath. When my eyes opened, Evey was gone and so was our son. I'd never get to hold him, never get to see him. That's why I did it. To remind Aden of what he took from me. "She was," I finally whispered.

"You did the right thing, then," Caroline replied. "Aden murders and kills for sport. You had a justifiable reason to take his life. You shouldn't let it haunt you so much."

"Yeah, I should."

"And why is that?"

"Because I enjoyed it. I enjoyed every second of torturing him, and when he died, I didn't want it to be over."

"That doesn't make you a monster," Noah added, staring at me from behind the steering wheel.

"Yes, it does. And what about your life before you joined the Concilium? Didn't you want retribution for what happened to you?

If given the chance, what would you have done to the men who killed them?"

"We're not talking about my past," he replied.

"You never talk about your past. So why the hell do I have to keep talking about mine?" Anger welled within me and I raised my voice as I spoke. "You're just like me. Just as haunted by the things you've seen. Maybe you're better at hiding it than me, but don't tell me that I'm a good man like you. Don't tell me I'm honorable and virtuous, because we both know you'd be lying."

"Sometimes you have to do things that are wrong in order to do good," Noah said.

"That's because you've never done anything wrong," I replied under my breath.

I looked out the window, not wanting to talk to either of them. If we rode the entire sixteen hours in silence, that would be fine by me. Neither of them knew what it was like to kill for enjoyment, but I did. I seemed to have a taste for it, just like Aden.

"Conrad? What are brodequins?"

I sighed heavily. I didn't want to answer her question, but I knew I had to. "They're a set of wooden boards secured to both sides of each leg. You drive wedges into the top of the boards with a mallet and it causes them to squeeze the legs. Eventually, after all the wedges are inserted, it causes the bones in the legs to burst. It was a popular form of torture in the Middle Ages."

She grimaced at my explanation. "Sounds excruciating."

"It is."

"In Mr. Rieder's class, he said the Spanish Inquisition happened during Ferdinand and Isabella's reign. That was also when you met Evey. Did you ever see what they did to the people they held tribunals for?"

"Yes, though the documentation of the Inquisition occurred after I died. Aden had already started holding secret trials in the dungeons of the castle. I discovered what he was up to one night when I followed him and Donovan down there. They tortured prisoners to the point of death. It was terrible. I knew it would only be a matter of time before his lust for blood spread to the other men of his advisory council. He used brodequins quite frequently. They seemed to be his favorite method of torture."

"And that's why you used them on him?"

"It seemed fitting."

"Then it sounds like you didn't only avenge the wrongful deaths of Evey and your unborn child, but you also brought retribution to all the people he murdered during the Inquisition," she replied.

"I've never thought of it like that before."

"Maybe you should. Then you might be able to see that what you did wasn't all that terrible."

"I wish it were that easy."

"Despite whatever thoughts are filling your head, you're still a good person, Conrad. I've seen you sacrifice your safety to protect Evey and me more times than I can count."

"Thanks."

"Don't mention it," Caroline said. "I hope Evey is at that address, but at the same time, I don't. Everywhere we go, we leave a trail of bodies behind us."

"He won't hurt Evey," I said. "She's too important."

"I know, it's just hard not to worry." She paused for a minute to clear her throat. "So, what's our plan for when we get to New York?"

"Sneak in, kill Aden, and get Evey back. That's all I've come up with so far."

"And Iola," Noah added. "I'm not letting him have my sister."

I nodded my head. "Of course."

"Okay, I have one more question," Caroline started. "Why don't we go in with guns or something? Burst in with a blaze of gunfire."

I chuckled. "Guns are nice, but they're not without faults. Guns are loud, much louder than knives, and they don't do as much damage to demons. I'm not sure why, but you can shoot a demon ten times and do minimal damage. Blades are more efficient. You can hack off an appendage just as quickly and cause more damage."

"Oh."

"Plus, all the weapons we use are blessed. It makes them more deadly against the servi."

"But what about the sickle?"

"I have no idea whether or not it has been blessed, but it's very powerful. More powerful than any other weapon I've been around."

"You really have studied demons, weapons, and all this secundae stuff, haven't you?" she asked.

"It's my job. I'm good at stuff like this. It comes easy to me."

Miles of road continued to stretch behind us, making our journey seem never-ending. An hour passed by with nothing but anticipation forcing time to move forward. Noah sat behind the steering wheel, staring at the road ahead.

"How old were you when you met Evey?" Caroline asked.

"I was twenty-five."

"A few years older than you're pretending to be right now?"

"Yeah."

"Over the centuries, has it been hard to keep up with the world as it changes?"

"I don't think it's been that bad, but I've mainly been Evey's secundae since she was placed into hiding, so we were brought back without any extensive gaps in time. But I've heard Guy and Marie talk about times when fifty or sixty years would pass before they were reborn. They said it was quite startling to see how the world changed sometimes."

"What an adventure it must be to have such a life," she said. "I mean, I know it's not without its downsides, but if they had the choice, do you think Evey's parents would ever choose not to be her secundae?"

I mulled over her question as I thought about Guy and Marie. "They think of Evey as their daughter. Even if given the chance, they'd never leave her or abandon their oath to the Concilium. And besides, if they hadn't agreed to be made into secundae, they never would've met or married each other."

"It's crazy to think of everyone who has found love outside of their own lifetime," she said. "It's almost like it was supposed to happen. What do you think, Noah?"

I glanced at Noah, trying to gauge his reaction. "I believe everything happens for a reason," he answered, focusing on the road.

"Does that mean you believe there's a reason you're in this exact car with Conrad and me?"

"Yes. I'm here to get Iola back. She needs me—us—to save her."

"We'll get her back. We'll get both of them back," I said.

"When you've lived for hundreds of years, does everything still seem so urgent?" Caroline asked.

"What do you mean?" Noah questioned.

"Well, last week, what I was going to wear on the first day of school was my biggest concern, and who I was going to prom with seemed like a matter of life-and-death. Does that feeling ever go away?"

Noah chuckled, obviously amused by her question. "It does with some things, not so much with others. What we're doing right now is urgent, very urgent. But I think that's just your personality," he teased.

She socked him on the arm. "Hey! I'm not that bad!"

"Yeah, okay."

"You know, if we weren't committing felonies left and right or hunting down a homicidal maniac, this would almost be a fun road trip."

"You need to get out more, Caroline," Noah said.

She shrugged. "I'm from a small town where nothing ever happens. What did you expect?"

"You need to spend more time in Chicago. There are so many restaurants, museums, and clubs. You'd almost be overwhelmed."

"You go to clubs?" she asked, the doubt apparent in her voice.

"I've been known to party with the best of them," he countered. "I own an upscale art gallery. The job sometimes requires me to wine and dine the customers."

"And how do you get into that kind of job?" she asked.

"In my life before I joined the Concilium, my father was an apprentice to an artist who lived in our village. He painted all the nobles of the nearby cities. He taught me to paint when I was a boy. From there, my love for art grew. Like everyone else in the Concilium, I've made good investments with my money, and it's allowed me to maintain a certain lifestyle for myself."

"But aren't you supposed to be helping Evey lead all of mankind toward God or something like that?"

"Yes, we aid her in that journey, but since she's been in hiding for the last few centuries, we haven't been as active. We've had to find other things to help pass the time."

"So, you're rich?" Caroline asked.

"If that's how you want to phrase it. I still spend a lot of my time working with charities and homeless shelters. All members of the Concilium have an innate need to help others."

"That's very kind of you. What about you, Conrad?" she asked, turning to meet my eyes. "When you save Evey and whisk her away to marry you, will the two of you be living comfortably?"

"I suppose so," I answered.

"How did you make your millions? Same way as Richie Rich over here?" She nodded her head toward Noah.

"Not at all," I replied. "I've had many lifetimes to save money, and I've also sold some medieval weapons to a couple of museums. I've made a habit of collecting things, because someone will always find value in antiquities. Look at Guy and Marie. They owned an auction house because they had extensive knowledge of ancient artifacts."

"Basically, you're saying it's best to play to your strengths?"

"Exactly."

"I'm passing another exit in a few miles. Do either of you need me to make a stop?" Noah asked.

"I'm good for a few hours. I can take over driving whenever you need a break though," I answered.

"Same with me. There's one more thing I want to ask you, Conrad."

I rubbed my fists over my eyes, fighting the urge to yawn. "What's that?"

"Will you tell me the best way to kill each type of demon?"

"You really want to know all this stuff? Most eighteen-year-old girls would run away screaming."

"I already told you, I want to learn to fight like you."

"All right. Decapitation is always going to be the best method, but each demon has specific weaknesses. Souls aren't very intelligent, so you can use your surroundings to outsmart them. Sanguis spray demonic blood, so if you can hack off their jaw or cut through their stomachs, they won't be able to spray as well. Verto are very vulnerable at their legs, especially at their knees. Take their legs out and the rest will follow. Furia can fly, so if you damage their wings, it lessens the ways they can attack you. Personally, I go for their claws first, then the wings. But that's only because I caught a talon across my face one time. It almost ripped my eye out."

"Ouch," she winced.

"Yeah, that wasn't too fun. Involos demons are the ones you have to fight in light. Don't get caught in a dark alley with one because it'll kill you before you can even lay eyes on it. Surround yourself with light and never let your guard down. Farine was a skilled fighter with centuries of training, but that didn't matter once an involos crept up on her."

"And what about dissimulo demons?"

"They don't really have weaknesses. They're the trickiest to find and kill because they can hide in plain sight," I answered. "Trust your instincts. They won't betray you."

"Have you ever been asked to train any of the other secundae?" she asked.

"What do you mean?"

"Since you're the most skilled fighter, I figured they would have you train the other secundae or something like that."

"No, I haven't trained anyone. In my first life, I learned my father's trade—blacksmithing—but fighting always came naturally to me. I was a horrible blacksmith."

"Somehow, I don't find that too surprising."

"My father was very skilled at forging armor and weapons, but I was always better at using them."

"Why didn't you become a soldier after your father died?" she asked.

"Because I had to take care of my mother and Cecily. I couldn't leave them to fend for themselves."

"You keep claiming you're not a good person, but from the things you've told me, you seem to be contradicting yourself quite a bit."

"Love and loyalty for one's family aren't indicators of a decent human being," I replied, countering Caroline's argument. "Even a monster can love his family."

"What about your love and loyalty for Evey?"

"That's different."

"Is it?" she asked. "Because you demonstrated love and loyalty for her before you knew she was the original woman."

"Anyone in the Concilium and any secundae would do the same for her."

"Yes, but how many of them are loved by her the way you are?"

"I suppose you have a point there."

"Do you think she would love you so deeply if she didn't feel you were worthy of it? When Aden changed, didn't her affections also change?"

I pondered her statement. Aden changed over the course of many years, but Evey noticed his transformation. Her love for him died with his kind nature. "Her affections for him did change."

I shifted my focus to the blurring countryside outside. A hand grasped my shoulder, demanding my attention. "You should believe in your own goodness, Conrad," Caroline whispered.

"Why?"

"Because we all believe it. Noah, Guy, Marie, Mickey, Kit, Evey, and me. We all know it to be true."

I smiled at her words of encouragement. "I promise to try."

She nodded at my response, shifting in her seat. "How does the Concilium decide who to make into a secundae?"

Noah released a deep sigh. "It's a long process. Evey's were chosen because they each sacrificed their own lives to save her. But for everyone else, it's different. I went centuries without any secundae until I accepted Helen and Milton as mine. Helen had been one of Aden's secundae and Milton had been with Thea. Both of them only came to me after Thea died. Helen didn't want to serve Aden anymore and Milton was without someone to protect."

"Why didn't you have any before them?"

"I refused to make any for myself," he replied. "I didn't want to force someone into this life or force them to protect me. It's not the type of existence I would wish on anyone."

"Then why did you choose it for yourself?" I asked.

"Because of Iola," Caroline answered for him, a knowing look in her eye.

"When she met Everest, he was quite enamored with her. He asked her to join the Concilium and she consented, but she wanted a place for me as well. Everest was reluctant at first, but after he met me, he decided I should be made into a consiliarius. He also thought the bond Iola and I have as siblings would strengthen our bond to the Concilium. Since I had no reason to continue my human life, I agreed."

"Do you regret your decision?" she asked.

"Sometimes I wonder what my life would've been like if I'd chosen to grow old and die, but it's rare. I'm happy with my choice. It's allowed me to have more time with Iola and it's allowed me to meet people I never would've had the chance to meet before," he replied with a smile.

"I think the opportunity to help other people is a wonderful thing," Caroline said. "Could you ever make yourself more secundae?"

"I don't believe the Concilium would let me. They're pretty strict on our numbers. Anytime someone is brought up for consideration, they hold a meeting to decide if the person in question should be made into a secundae, but the entire Concilium must agree. Conrad, however, is the one exception to that rule. I don't think Everest wanted to bring him back as a secundae, but Evey didn't really give us a choice."

"That sounds about right," I said. "She can be a pain in the ass sometimes."

"You better be glad too, otherwise Everest never would've allowed it. Although, I suspect Iola persuaded him to agree as well."

"Well, weren't you one of Conrad's biggest supporters?" Caroline asked. "It makes sense that Iola would support you and your judgment."

"Yeah, I suppose so. He's saved my life many times, so it'd be very difficult for me not to believe I made the right choice. And what's more important, he's saved Evey's life countless times as well."

"She's the central pivot everything seems to move around. The Concilium, secundae, you're all dependent on her, aren't you?"

"She's the link between humanity and the divine," I answered. "In a sense, the Concilium is as well, but they don't live and die as she does. She experiences life the way it was originally intended: birth, love, loss, death."

"It almost sounds as if she is some sort of vessel."

"In a way, she is. I'm more biased than most, but the first time I saw her, she made me want to be better, kinder. And she has that effect on the people surrounding her," I answered. "When she was Queen Isabella, she touched people's lives in a way that inspired admiration and devotion. It's unlike anything I've ever seen."

"In their own way, everyone seems to need her, but the one person she needs is you."

I returned her smile and closed my eyes, focusing on what would happen once we reached Aden's house in New York. I wasn't sure what he was up to, but I wanted to be prepared for any situation. He wouldn't catch me off guard this time.

I would never fall before him again.

15

SECRETS
AND
SERVITUDE

I slid away from the door with just enough time to miss running into it as someone on the other side pushed it open. Aden had told me to find him after taking enough time to myself, but all I'd managed to do was stand with my hand on the knob, deliberating my next move. I could still taste Conrad on my lips and I didn't want the memory of our reunion to fade away. We'd only just found one another when he'd been taken away from me. How long must we exist like this? Would I always be drifting from death to birth, birth to death, waiting for another chance to see him? The thought was as daunting as it was exhausting. I couldn't go on like this for eternity. I knew Aden was trying to be good, or at least I hoped he was, but Conrad wouldn't give up on me and something in my gut told me I would see him again.

I had to see him again.

"Did I startle you?" Aden's voice wrenched me back to the present situation.

"I was lost in thought," I whispered.

"Do you need me to come back later?"

"It's fine, the moment passed. Do you need something?"

His grin widened. "Am I that obvious?"

"Only sometimes. What do you need?"

"I'm sorry if things moved too fast for you earlier. I don't want you to feel uncomfortable around me. I know that's not something you want to do just yet, but if you ever change your mind, I'm always here."

"Okay," I replied hesitantly.

"I'm sorry. I'm forcing this too much, aren't I?"

"You think?" I stepped back again, trying to distance myself from him. "That has to be the understatement of the century."

"I know what I'm asking of you is a lot but——"

"Do you? Because if you know that, then why are you still asking it of me?"

"If I were him, would you do it?" he asked. His fingers tugged at his gray sweater and his gaze dropped.

"If you were Conrad?"

"Yes," he whispered.

"Yes, but only because he'd never ask me to do it."

"So, if I stopped asking you to, you'd do it?"

I shook my head. "That's not really how it works."

"Then how does it work? How do I get you to trust me?"

"I'm not sure you can," I replied. I pulled a thin cardigan around myself, closing it in the front. Why did I always feel so exposed in front of him despite wearing layers of clothes? Perhaps it was because he'd known me before clothes existed, when I had nothing to hide from his eyes. And I wondered if that was still how he saw me. Was I forever the innocent woman kneeling beside him beneath the shade of a tree? Or was I the queen who drew away from him and found comfort in the arms of another man? Or was I me, someone who couldn't—and didn't want to—remember the time we'd spent together?

"Are you still cold?"

"I'll be all right," I replied. He moved closer, setting his hands on both my arms.

"There's food downstairs if you're hungry. I thought we could eat together."

"What about Helen?"

"I brought her a tray of food. She's eating in her room. Don't worry, she isn't being harmed or neglected in any way."

"You care for her?" I asked.

He bent closer, moving so that his mouth was just a breath from my ear. "Always so surprised."

"Can you really blame me?"

"I guess not, but then again, I could never blame you for anything." He shrugged nonchalantly. "Most think of me as a monster, but what they don't realize is that I still have feelings. I care for Helen. She was once one of my secundae, and just because she left doesn't mean I hate her."

"You understand why she broke her oath to you?"

"How can I hold it against her when I'm just as guilty of breaking an oath?"

"And what oath are you guilty of breaking?"

He pulled away from me, staring into my eyes. "I broke my oath to love and honor you until the day I die." I opened my mouth to speak, but he pressed a finger to my lips, not wanting to be interrupted. "I've murdered, maimed, and tortured countless people. I've hurt you in so many different ways that I can't name them all. I've been with other women, even when we were still married."

"I've done that too," I replied. "I was with Conrad when we were Isabella and Ferdinand."

"Yeah, but I pushed you to that. I drove you away, Evey. And I was with Thea when I was Ferdinand. I felt you slipping away, so I held on to her even though I knew it was wrong."

"Why did you do it?" I asked, shocked by his confession.

"Because I was a king. I thought I was entitled to anything and everything I wanted."

"What does it matter if you were a king or not?"

"It doesn't now, but life was different back then. We were wealthy, powerful, respected, and admired. We lived continuously. It was easy to be seduced by that kind of life."

"So what? That makes it okay?"

"No! That's not what I'm saying. Being a primum didn't come as naturally to me as it did to you. You've always been so grounded and good-natured; you'd never be corrupted by the same things as me."

"You almost sound like an addict."

"In a way, I suppose I am."

"I'm sorry this is how things turned out."

"Me too. Should we go eat?" he asked.

"Sure." I stepped around him, making my way toward the door. His footsteps sounded from behind me as we descended the stairs.

It was funny how quickly the world could be turned upside down. After all the secrets kept in order to protect my identity, after placing me in hiding far away from Aden, he still found me. It couldn't be a coincidence. We fought, we ran to the other side of the world, but it didn't matter. Blood was spilled, sacrifices were made, and yet, none of it made a difference. What was the point? I thought through the list of people I'd lost. They each laid down their lives for me, and for what? For me to help Aden, the man who had condemned each of them? The more I considered the true nature of my situation, the more hopeless I felt. Maybe this was supposed to be my fate. I'd caused others pain and I deserved to be punished for it.

The wooden floor chilled the soles of my feet as I walked through the dining room. My green dress rustled against my legs as I pushed through the door leading into the kitchen. The thin material wasn't made to keep me warm, and a slight shiver trickled down my spine. Aden brushed past me, heading for the stove. He pulled out two plates loaded with some kind of casserole and pot roast. Steam wafted into the air and fanned out from the warm food. I watched as he pulled out two forks and set them on each plate. Then he carried them over to a small table on the other side of the room. It was surrounded with windows, providing us with a broad view of the darkening sky. I sat across from him, accepted the plate he held out to me, and slid a piece of roast onto the fork as I gazed outside.

"I'm sorry," he said, breaking the silence.

"For what?" I asked, startled by his apology.

"That I can't make you love me."

A pang of guilt pulled at my insides. "That would make two of us." My mouth felt dry as I swallowed the bite of roast. It burned in my throat, almost choking me. "I need a glass of milk. Would you like one too?"

"Sure."

Standing from the table, I retrieved a carton from the refrigerator. After pouring the milk into two glasses, I picked up a glass in each hand and stepped away from the counter.

"Dinner for two? How quaint," a voice said from behind me.

The sound startled me, causing me to drop the glasses of milk. They fell to the tile floor and shattered upon impact. Shards of glass sprayed across my feet. Looking over my shoulder, my gaze was met by a pair of hazel eyes. Luke stood behind me, leaning against the doorway. His dark suit from earlier still glistened as if it had just been pressed.

"Luke," Aden said, standing from his chair. "What are you doing here?"

"Oh, I acquired some interesting information from one of my sources this afternoon and thought I'd come over to relay it to you in person," he replied. Even though he was addressing Aden, Luke's gaze never left my face. "I had no intentions of startling you, my queen." He moved toward me. I tried to turn around, but my body was incapable of moving. Pieces of glass embedded themselves into my skin. When I stared at my feet, I saw red swirls in the white milk.

"I'm not a queen anymore," I whispered. "You don't have to refer to me as such."

"Not yet. But you will be."

"What kind of information?" Aden asked.

"Not now," Luke answered. Without warning, Luke grabbed my waist and set me on top of the kitchen counter. He then picked up a small towel, kneeling before me. "Pull your dress up," he ordered. "We wouldn't want to get blood on it." I obeyed his command, bunching the light fabric in my hands. My head pounded and the room began to spin. I struggled to fill my lungs with oxygen; my chest heaved with labored breaths. Luke laid his hand on my leg, holding it up as he cleaned my feet. I winced as the cloth snagged on a piece of glass stuck in my foot. Carefully, he removed the shard. "You know, you could make yourself useful by cleaning up the floor," he said to Aden.

Aden nodded. My eyes darted back and forth between the two men, unable to decide who I trusted less. They worked in silence, neither wanting to acknowledge the other. Aden finished cleaning the floor just as Luke pulled the last piece of glass from my flesh. His touch was light, delicately skating over my skin. Placing my fingertips underneath his chin, I lifted his face upward. "Why do you want me?" I asked. I knew this man wanted me. I could see his desires swimming in the depths of his eyes and I needed to know what they were.

The corners of his mouth curled into a smile as he looked at me. "Because you're you," he replied. As he stood to his full height, his hands slid up my leg and onto my thigh. "Beauty and goodness radiate through every inch of your skin. It's intoxicating, especially to me."

"And who are you?" I asked.

"Fate."

"Luke, get your hands off her," Aden shouted. He stood at my elbow, hovering over us.

"Are you raising your voice against me?" Luke's voice startled me. He glared at Aden, animosity rolling off him in waves. In an instant, his seductive and mysterious demeanor turned dark. Aden flinched at his words, too afraid to challenge the man standing in front of him.

"She isn't yours to touch," Aden replied.

"Apparently, she isn't yours either. The only man she wants is dead," Luke countered in a matter-of-fact tone.

"How do you know about Conrad?" I asked. This man was foreign to me in every way imaginable, and yet, he seemed knowledgeable about the intimate details of my life.

"Because he was sent to protect you."

"Protect me from what?" I asked.

"Not from what, from whom," he replied.

My eyes darted to Aden. "Conrad was sent to protect me from Aden?"

"You seem surprised," Luke answered. "You never once wondered why he came into your life when you needed him most?"

"I—"

"Everything happens for a reason."

I braced my hands on the counter. I was becoming more light-headed by the second. Too many forces were pulling at me. I felt trapped. I was suffocating beneath the unyielding gazes of the men standing before me. "I suppose it does," I whispered. "Do you envy him?" I asked Luke.

"Envy is one of the most unappreciated sins; however, it's always been my favorite," he answered with a devious smile. "But you're asking if I envy Conrad?" I nodded, waiting for him to reply. "Yes, but not in the way you think."

"What do you mean?" I asked. This mysterious man had piqued my curiosity in more ways than one. Excitement and terror seemed to naturally exude from him. He scared Aden—that much I knew—but what concerned me more was the fact that he didn't have that effect on me. Maybe, since I was aware Luke wanted me for some reason, I wasn't as cautious as I should be. But until I knew exactly what his motives were, I wouldn't allow myself to be afraid. Fear bombarded me at every turn, and I couldn't continue to submit to it. I would fight back.

"Well, Aden is envious Conrad has taken his place in your heart. In a sense, that is something I can identify with, but since I've never experienced your love, I can't say it's what I envy most."

"Then what do you envy most?" I could see Aden's body twitching out of the corner of my eye. This conversation was rapidly unraveling his composure.

"What I envy most is that he lives in the light with you."

I shook my head. "I'm not sure I understand."

"Conrad was made into a secundae even though he shouldn't have been. He's lived by your side for centuries: he's been showered with your love and admiration. Your love has made him better." He paused for a moment to move closer to me. "He lives in your light."

"My light?"

"It's how you make people feel when they're around you. You make them want to be better, much like an aura," Luke replied.

"That's ridiculous." I stared at Aden and Luke, unable to contain my laughter. "Living in my light? That's nothing to be envious of."

"Tell that to those who live in shadow," he countered, holding my gaze. My smile faded. Both of these men had darkness within them. They knew what it meant to be loved and adored, only to fall from grace. I was their last chance at redemption—their futures rested in my hands.

"Let me see if I understand you. I'm basically your one shot at redemption?"

"In a sense," Luke replied. "Although, some of my intentions differ from Aden's."

"And what might those be?" I asked.

"You'll have to wait and see."

Aden stared at the floor, his fingers fidgeting with the collar of his shirt. "And if I wanted to know now?" I asked, sliding off the counter. I took a step toward Luke, taking in the features of his handsome face. Like Aden, he seemed to be a mixture of death and deception hidden beneath a beautiful disguise.

"For someone so demure, you do always seem to get what you want."

"It's quite amusing you think that since I don't ever remember wanting to see my loved ones murdered right in front of me."

"They can still be reborn," Luke said.

"Not unless I die. And then I'd have to start over again as an infant."

"There are worse things."

"Speaking from experience?" I inched closer to him. His gaze dropped to my lips as I leaned forward.

"Yes," he whispered.

"You won't be able to change me."

"What makes you think I want to?"

"Just a hunch."

"And you don't think I'm up for the challenge?"

"I do, but you won't succeed."

His eyes sparkled with excitement as he examined the lines of my face. "It will be a difficult task, but that's what makes it so stimulating. No other woman in the world is like you."

"You make it sound like a game."

"Life is a game, my queen."

"If you consider me your queen, then do you consider yourself a king?"

He flashed an impish grin. "Sometimes."

"Evey," Aden whispered. He had been so silent throughout the exchange that I'd momentarily forgotten Luke and I were not alone. In unison, Luke and I crooked our heads to acknowledge him. As he stood just a foot away from me, he didn't resemble the defiant man from the abandoned warehouse in New York. He looked more like a frightened child, turning more wan and helpless with each passing second. Only Luke's presence affected him this way. To every other soul walking this earth, Aden was a proud, almost haughty man, but to Luke, he was a quivering infant. "Stop."

"I can think for myself," I replied.

Luke studied us. He was taking in everything, watching our interaction like a movie. "I think I'm in agreement with her on this one, Aden."

The men looked like they were having a staring contest. If it came down to it, Luke would win, but Aden seemed determined to mark his territory. I was beginning to feel more and more like a piece of property and less like the original woman. "We had an arrangement," Aden said. "She isn't part of it."

"If there is one thing I know, it's that arrangements are always negotiable. Don't forget who you serve," Luke countered. His voice was smooth and even—as if he'd had hundreds of years to perfect his speech. A wide grin unfurled across his face as his hazel eyes once again focused on me. "What do you think, my queen?"

I crossed my arms over my chest and leaned against the granite countertop. "Honestly, I couldn't care less. The two of you are just standing there, belittling each other in the hopes that I'll find myself undeniably attracted to one of you," I spat, sucking in a deep breath to steady my voice. "When I was little, I used to hunt fireflies in the summer. I thought they were magical, the way they could light up at night, and I wanted their light for myself. So, I trapped a couple in a glass jar and poked a few holes in the lid. I kept them beside my bed for a couple days, but when I accidentally knocked the jar off my nightstand, it broke. All my fireflies flew away, free of their cage. No matter how hard you try, you can't tame them."

"I'm not trying to tame you," Aden replied, setting his hand on my shoulder.

"Aren't you though? Isn't that what both of you really want?"

"I'd rather unleash you," Luke answered.

"Don't listen to him. He's lying to you," Aden countered. "He'd tell you anything to get you. He's already disguised himself as Conrad, and you played right into his hands."

"And how do I know you aren't doing the same thing? You're the one who killed the only man I've ever truly loved. Luke didn't run him through with a sword and hover over me as I watched him die." The image of Aden's sword piercing through Conrad flashed before my eyes. Blood had poured from the wound, devouring his shirt like shadows devour the remaining sunlight at dusk. I fought back the tears building inside me. That moment, that brief second when my mind was able to comprehend what my eyes were seeing, was when I knew I was dying too. It didn't matter if my chest rose and fell and forced oxygen into my body; I was dead. If my reason to live was gone, then what reason did I have to continue living this excruciating existence?

"Tell yourself whatever you want, but you did love me. Whether you want to admit it or not, you did," Aden replied.

"The keyword there is *did*. I did love you." My gaze faltered and dropped. Tiny nicks in my skin dotted the tops of my feet.

"And you will again."

"Let me ask you one thing," I began. "Do captives often become enamored with their abductors?" I shifted my gaze from Aden to

Luke. "Because it doesn't seem like they do." Pushing myself through the space between their arms, I came to a stop in front of Luke. "Could you do something for me?"

"Whatever your request, I'll see it done," he replied. His eyes studied my face, waiting for me to speak. He was completely serious now; any lingering traces of mischief had been purged from his features.

I licked my lips and swallowed hard, trying to push my nervousness to the pit of my stomach. My hand rested on his chest, and I prayed the contact would provide me with courage. As soon as he felt me touch him, he set his hand over mine. "Please, will you show him to me just one more time?" The words spilled from my mouth sounding more like a plea than a question.

"Evey, don't—" Aden began before I cut him off.

"If you truly know what you're asking of me, then you'll keep your mouth shut," I spat. "You think only of yourself and not of what I'll be sacrificing if I help you. You're always so concerned with your own happiness, but have you ever given mine a second thought?" I stared at him, daring him to speak, daring him to deny the truth. "That's what I thought."

"Is that all you want?" Luke asked, still grasping my hand. He held on to me tight, like his very existence was contingent upon my own.

"Yes." I stood before him, my heart picking up speed with every second that ticked by. I thought of Conrad. I pictured him in my mind with complete accuracy. The curves and lines of his face were etched into my memory. The color of his eyes, the arc of his lips when he grinned at me . . . I thought of all his unique characteristics.

"Evey, open your eyes."

I waited another second, wondering if I should gaze upon his face at all, but something in his voice forced my eyelids open. Bright blue eyes stared back at me. Sure enough, Conrad stood before me, looking the same as the first day I'd met him. The ends of my mouth curled into a smile. I moved my hands over his face and traced the tips of my fingers down his cheeks. As I stared at him, he returned my smile with the devilish one he'd sported the first time we spoke. I moved closer, wanting to savor the few moments we had left. I wanted no part of his face to go undiscovered, especially since this was the last time I would get to see it. My thumb rubbed the soft skin of his bottom lip. Then, as if it were really Conrad standing before me, he turned toward my other hand resting against his cheek and kissed my palm. Closing my eyes for a second, I took in a deep breath. A solitary tear trickled from my eye. But he brushed away the drop before it could fall from my chin. "You may kiss me if you'd like," I whispered. My body hummed with anticipation as I waited for Conrad to kiss me. Just when I thought he'd changed his mind, his lips crashed into my own. He mirrored the movements of my mouth. The tips of my fingers became entwined with the strands of his thick brown hair as he held on to my waist and drew our bodies closer together. For one fleeting moment, my life was bearable again. I could endure any hardship with Conrad standing beside me, but I had to wake up from my dream. Conrad was gone and only one thing could bring him back. I hugged him one last time before stepping away. When I opened my eyes, Conrad had already been replaced with Luke. He stood before me, trying to regain his breath. His cheeks were flushed with color, and for the first time, I noticed a crack in his suave demeanor.

"I don't believe I've ever been so envious of anyone. Now I know why he fights so hard for you."

"Conrad is everything I've ever wanted and everything I've ever needed."

"You have the ability to do it," he replied, smiling softly.

"To do what?"

"Change the world. If ever there were someone who could, it'd be you."

I returned his smile. "There's only one thing I would change." I glanced behind me to Aden. His face was pale, as if a white sheet had been plastered to his features like a mask. He was upset, that much was obvious. I had no doubts I'd encounter his fury concerning my request for Luke. I set my hand on Luke's chest again. "Thank you for giving me that," I said, planting a light kiss on his cheek. He stared at me, watching my every move. "I'll leave the two of you to discuss whatever it is that brought you here."

I left before either man could say another word. I stepped around the antique chairs and looming grandfather clock in the dining room. The hands on the clock moved with every minute, continually counting down to the end of this life. It wasn't fair all my secundae had to sacrifice their lives to save mine. They'd forfeited everything countless times, and I'd never lifted a finger to repay the debt. I stood by, allowing them to do it. All the while, I told myself it was what they wanted. They sought to protect me, to save me from harm, and they were willing to lay down their lives to do so. It wasn't right. Everything that happened was my fault. Aden didn't care who he killed as long as he got me. My only option was to take myself out of the equation. I could deprive Aden of what he most desired and bring my loved ones back. My soul would be in turmoil, but it was a price I was willing to pay. It was a price I owed to them. Even if Aden was able to bring me back, all secundae would live again because of my death.

Like the constant tread up the staircase, my heart beat in a steady, monotonous rhythm. In a few minutes, all my pain and suffering would be over. I wasn't sure where I would go, but anywhere had to be better than this. Only one other person knew exactly how I felt, and that was Helen. She understood the consequence of taking your own life, and in this moment, I needed her council. We were opposite sides of the same coin, and yet, we fell in love with the same man. We both knew how it felt to have the person you loved most taken away from you. Perhaps we would always be at odds with one another, but in some ways, we were bonded. I slid the key to her room out of the pocket of my dress and cautiously turned the lock. After a quick glance in either direction, I opened her door and slipped inside. At the sound of my entrance, Helen stood from a light blue armchair and moved to stand in front of me.

"Is everything okay?" she asked, inspecting my appearance. "Your feet are bleeding."

"It doesn't matter. I wanted to ask you something."

"And what might that be?"

I cleared my throat, willing myself to speak. "When you killed yourself, what happened?"

"I already told you that I don't remember. Why are you asking me about this?"

"I need to know what you can remember. Even the smallest details."

She shook her head and stepped in the direction of her bed. The mattress sank beneath her weight. I watched as she sat down, wishing I knew the thoughts swirling in her head. "There is nothing to tell."

"Please, Helen," I begged.

"I remember falling through the air," she began, glancing away from me. "And then, nothing. When I awoke again, I was one of Aden's secundae." Her voice was the epitome of sorrow, and I wondered if she would ever be able to forgive herself for taking her own life. "I'm lucky I was given a second chance, but the regret I feel will never fade."

"I'm sorry. I understand why you did it, why you thought there was no other choice."

"There's always a choice," she croaked. Her hands brushed the tears from her eyes.

"Not always." I smiled, moving in front of her. "I'm sorry if I ever did anything to hurt you. I know why you told Aden where to find me, and I don't blame you."

"I thought Conrad would be safe. It was the only thing I wanted."

"I know. Please take care of yourself. Aden cares for you, he won't hurt you."

"Why are you telling me this?" she asked.

"I just want you to know that you're safe."

"Okay."

"You have a lot of courage. I admire that about you. I think in another life, we could've been friends." To my own surprise, I took her face in my hands and kissed her forehead. Then I turned away from her, heading back toward the door.

"What's happening? Why did you want to know about what I did?"

"Because death can return all things thought to be lost."

In an instant, Helen's blank expression transformed into one of recognition. She sprinted for the door, but I was too quick for her. I slipped through the doorway and turned the lock. Not a second later, her hands slammed against the wood.

"Evey!" she shouted. "Evey! Don't do it!"

"There's no other way. The ones I love have made too many sacrifices on my behalf. I must repay their debt. It's the only way to bring them back."

"Please don't. The Concilium needs you. We all need you."

"Take care of Conrad for me."

"Don't do what I did. Please, I beg you!" she cried.

"I'm sorry," I whispered, running away from her door. The entrance to Aden's room was just ahead of me, and within its walls was my means of escape. The doors burst apart as I slammed my hands against them. Everywhere I turned, I could see my own image staring back at me. My past with Aden had been transcribed into the pages of history for centuries. I was born, raised to be a ruler, married to Aden, and then I died. That was the cycle of my life—to be repeated over and over again for eternity—but no more. I had the ability to change this fate. I kicked drawings and loose papers out of my way as I ran to his desk. Clearing off its surface, canvases fell through the air, ripping as they collided with the floor. Helen's cries grew louder with each passing second. She would soon be heard downstairs, and Aden would come running. I pushed the heavy desk away from the large window it had been blocking. The latch opened with ease and I pushed against the pane, clearing a place for me to fall.

Closing my eyes, I took a moment to steady my composure. Conrad would understand why I did it, and after some time passed, he would learn to forgive me. More importantly, he'd be alive. He'd have my parents, Mickey, and Kit to take care of him. Their lives were worth any sacrifice to me.

The sound of footsteps echoing down the hallway startled me. I had to act before Aden could stop me.

"Evey!" He shouted my name, but in another step, my troubles in this world would come to an end. "Evey! Stop!" Every inch of my body trembled, but my determination was resolute. I would see this through. I drew my hands off the windowsill, turning to face him one last time.

"I'm sorry," I said as he stepped toward me. Then my head dropped backward and I was lost to the dark night sky.

16

BODIES FOR
BREADCRUMBS

Daylight faded, and darkness ruled the remainder of our drive. The sun rose and set for another day, a signal of time slipping away. No matter how hard we tried, Aden was always a couple steps ahead of us, but something had to give. Something had to fall through for him and give us the opportunity to settle the score. But until then, exhaustion and time were beginning to take their toll.

I sat quietly in the passenger seat, awaiting my turn to drive. It wouldn't be much longer until we were at Aden's, and the thought of meeting him face-to-face had me on edge.

"Ah!" I cried, clutching my chest.

"What's wrong?" Caroline jumped, obviously surprised by my sudden outburst.

"I don't know." I rubbed the muscle under my collarbone. "It felt like someone stabbed me with a spike."

"What do you mean?" Noah asked, leaning toward me from the back seat.

"I had a sharp pain in my chest. It lasted for a second and then it was gone."

"Oh my gosh! Doesn't that mean you're having a heart attack?" Caroline asked. "I clearly remember my health class during freshman year, and my teacher said that's one of the classic symptoms of a heart attack."

"I'm in perfect health," I replied. "There's no way I could be having a heart attack."

"If you die again, I swear I'm not bringing you back a second time," Noah said.

"Glad to know you're on my side," I said at the same time Caroline shouted, "Oh, yes, you will, Noah!"

"If Conrad dies before we get Evey and Iola back, you most certainly will bring him back. You'll bring him back so I can kill him!" Caroline continued

"What?"

"You heard me! And then you'll bring him back a third time because we have shit to do."

I shook my head, looking between them. "The two of you are impossible."

"I'm not impossible. He is," Caroline said, nodding her head in Noah's direction.

"Wait, how am I impossible?"

"You have the power to bring Conrad back, but you're so worried about what Everest thinks. Maybe you have amnesia and can't remember how we got Aden's address, but we both know Conrad is the only one of us who can fight Aden and win."

"I don't care what Everest thinks. But I do care about him stripping me of my powers and throwing me out of the Concilium. Like I've said before, there are rules."

"You brought Conrad back for the greater good! Doesn't that carry some weight with you people?"

"Well, it's nice to know I'm only needed for my innovative interrogation techniques," I deadpanned.

"Oh, stop it, Conrad. Evey needs you. We all know she can't live without you," she said.

"Look, all I'm saying is that Everest is in charge of the Concilium. It's within his power to hold me accountable for my actions. No other consiliarius has ever disobeyed an order from the caput. There will be serious repercussions for what I did."

"I understand what you're saying, but don't forget about Everest's love for Iola. He'll want her back at any cost," Caroline replied.

Noah nodded. "I hope you're right." Before he could say anything else, Noah was pulled back into his seat as the car lurched forward. "Slow down, Caroline! You shouldn't be driving a hundred miles per hour. We'll get pulled over, and this car really doesn't need to be searched by a cop."

"Oh, relax," she chuckled.

"I don't think you'll be laughing in jail," he countered.

"We need to get to Evey as soon as possible. Besides, I can easily talk my way out of a speeding ticket."

"Oh, really? And how are you going to do that?" he asked.

"They're called boobs, Noah. Maybe you've heard of them in the thousands of years you've been alive."

"I—I," Noah stammered.

"Geez, you're always such a prude!"

"Well, we can't all be like you!"

"You say that like it's a bad thing," Caroline said. "Conrad? What do you think?"

I shook my head. "I'm honestly trying to decide which is worse: getting decapitated or listening to the two of you bicker for the next six hours."

"Seriously?" he asked.

"What? It's a valid statement, considering I've had to endure both."

Before they could bicker any further, Noah's phone began to ring.

"Oh, shit," Noah said.

"That doesn't sound promising." I shifted in my seat so I could see him. "What's up?"

"It's Everest."

"*Oh, shit* is right." My eyes scanned his face, noticing the traces of panic dominating his features.

"I've got to tell him the truth. If I ignore the call, he'll suspect something is wrong and probably go to Iola's or call her."

"It's not your fault Iola was taken and Farine was killed. Just be rational and talk to him. He'll understand," Caroline said.

"I don't think you know Everest all that well," Noah replied.

"Well, on the bright side, he'll probably just blame me, so you'll be off the hook," I added.

"True. Here goes nothing." He answered the phone, wincing as he pressed it to his ear. "Everest, I'm going to put you on speaker. Caroline and Conrad are in the car with me."

"Caroline, Bourdet," Everest said stiffly. "Were the three of you able to recover the sickle? How is Iola?"

"Everest, I'm not sure what you're doing right now, but you should take a seat," Noah replied.

"What is it?"

Noah let out a deep breath. "When we were at Iola's, we were attacked in the middle of the night. Iola and Christopher were taken by furia demons and Farine was killed."

There was a long pause before Everest spoke again. "What do you mean *taken*?"

"I tried to get her back. I fought to get to her, but she was gone before I could reach her," Noah replied. "You know I'd do anything to protect her."

"And where were you during all this, Bourdet?"

"He was fighting too. He and Farine killed an involos and two sanguis demons. We were all fighting," Noah answered.

"This is what you were brought back for, Bourdet!" he shouted. "Protection against souls and demons is the sole reason you were ever allowed to live again. I don't know how many times I'll have to repeat this sentiment before it sinks in."

"And I'm the one at fault," I mumbled. "Really, I never saw that coming."

"Conrad isn't at fault," Noah said.

"Then, who is?" Everest asked. "Who is responsible for this? Is it not the man who is skilled at fighting? Is it not the man who swore an oath to protect all the members of the Concilium?"

"I swore an oath to protect Evey! I'm not some sword for hire that you can order around any way you see fit!" I shouted.

"You know nothing of your oath!"

"I want the three of you to stop right now!" Caroline shouted. As if controlled by an unseen force, Everest, Noah, and I snapped our mouths shut. "Everest, I know you're devastated Iola is gone, but blaming Conrad won't get her back. You left the sickle with her. You knew doing so could put her in danger, and now, you must deal with the consequences."

"It's all my fault. If something happens to her——"

"Look, I don't mean to be harsh, but we need you to be strong right now. The Concilium needs you to be strong," Caroline said.

"You're right."

"Honestly, I don't know why everyone acts like me being right is such a revelation. Of course I'm right."

"Where are the three of you now?" Everest asked.

"We're tracking down a lead that will hopefully take us to Aden," I replied. "We're pretty sure it will, but there's always a chance we're wrong."

"I've talked to everyone else in the Concilium. They're aware of what's going on, and despite my better judgment, I think it'd be prudent for everyone to meet and discuss our course of action," Everest said.

"I think that's a good idea," Noah agreed. "Now that we know Aden is controlling the servi, we must be proactive."

"Keep me informed on your progress with this lead, and once you're done, I want you back in New York," Everest ordered. "Please be careful."

"We will," Noah replied.

"I'll get both of them back, Everest," I said. "I promise you."

"Please see that you do." With that, the call was disconnected.

"I guess that could've gone worse," Noah said.

I chuckled. "This is true."

"Poor Everest," Caroline said. "I'm sure he feels so guilty about leaving the sickle with Iola."

"I don't know about that. I mean, his main reaction was to blame me."

Caroline flashed me a knowing look. "I'm sure he did that because of how awful he feels. I mean, how did you feel when you found out Aden had Evey?"

"Terrible," I whispered.

"I know he's hard on you, but I think it's because the two of you are actually quite similar."

"Yeah, right," Noah countered.

"Everest is pragmatic, methodical, loyal, intelligent, and caring. He is very kind to your sister, Noah," she said. "Now, tell me what part of that doesn't sound like Conrad?"

"To be honest, it all does," I answered.

"And if I had to guess, I'd bet you anything Everest is jealous of you. You fight better than all the other secundae. You're the only one with the ability to save Evey and now Iola. Imagine how helpless Everest must feel, knowing all he can do is stand by and watch another man rescue the ones he loves."

"I've never thought of it like that before."

"Maybe you should," she replied.

"Thanks for sticking up for me."

"Don't mention it. You've saved my life at least a dozen times this week."

"I have to say, Caroline, you do seem to have a talent for putting Everest in his place," Noah said.

"Well, it's not like I'm a member of the club, so he can't really punish me. Plus, it's just how I am, and I can't change that."

"Nor would we want you to," he replied with a grin.

"What do you think we'll find when we get to the address?" Caroline asked, uncertainty masking her usually light tone.

"I don't know. Hopefully, Evey and Iola, but it's hard to say," I replied. "All we can do is be prepared for anything." I readjusted my seat, leaning it back to stretch out my legs. Anxiety welled inside me. Waiting was one of the worst punishments. It was how I spent the last eighty years of my existence. I was incessantly biding my time until I could see Evey again. How many nights had I spent recalling every curve of her face? My hands twitched with anticipation, aching for the feel of a hilt. When a weapon was in my hand, I had some control over my own fate. I had the opportunity to tip the scales in our favor. The first time I died, Aden took my head. He hadn't even given me a chance to fight because he knew I was a skilled fighter. I may have lost in that warehouse, but we both knew I could beat him. I'd done it before, and this time, history *would* repeat itself. "Wake me up when we get close."

When I closed my eyes, my mind created images of the past—it was early spring, the first one after we'd moved into the castle at the queen's insistence. I decided to go outside the castle walls and venture into the surrounding village. I was going to pay back some of the debts I'd accumulated just after my father died. Now that I was one of the queen's personal guards, my pockets never lacked coins. My feet ambled down the dirt roads, aimlessly kicking at stones while I made my way to the butcher's cottage. Antonio had been kind enough to give us a few cuts of meat on credit while we struggled for money. It only seemed right that I balance the scales as soon as possible. I only needed to round the next cottage to find myself at his place, but when I heard the faint sounds of crying, I turned in the direction of the square. I wasn't the only one to gather at the noise. In fact, a small crowd had begun to form around the cowering figure of a boy and a burly man who I recognized to be a farmer. The man loomed over the boy, shaking his fist in the air. After a minute or two, it was understood that the boy was being punished for taking a handful of vegetables from the man's stand in the market. In an instant, I was filled with pity. I, like many others, knew the pains of hunger. Even the most strong-willed individuals couldn't keep their composure when surviving on a few bites of bread each day. Hunger was one of the strongest motivators. It had compelled me to steal, and I understood the boy's plight better than most. Because of it, I couldn't remain a silent witness any longer.

"You dirty scoundrel!" the farmer bellowed. "What makes you think you can steal from me?"

The boy whimpered, too afraid to speak. Stepping through the crowd, I moved to stand between the boy and his overbearing accuser. "I don't mean to intrude, but perhaps you would allow me to compensate you for the food taken by this boy," I said, squaring my shoulders as I faced the farmer. Even though I stood in his path, the man lunged around me, planting a strong kick to the boy's leg. He cried out in response, scuttling in the dirt behind me. "That's enough!" I shouted, shoving the man back. "I said I would pay you for the vegetables. Now leave the boy alone."

"He needs to be taught some manners. If he thinks he can just take things as he pleases, then let him learn otherwise!"

"He's just a boy. I'm sure he regrets stealing from you. Let me pay you and then the boy can be on his way."

"And what's to stop him from stealing from me again? The penalty for stealing is losing a hand. That seems justifiable for his crime."

I glanced at the mass of people surrounding us. Some nodded their heads in approval of his suggestion, but others simply watched in stunned silence. "I'm one of the queen's personal guards. I can have this matter brought before her, and she can set her own punishment." I knew the queen would never agree to any punishment that allowed a boy to have his hand cut off.

"It's none of your business or hers. This boy stole from me and I'll have my payment." He tried to dive around me again, but this time, I was prepared for an attack and countered with a swift punch to his gut. The man backed away, doubling over as he dropped the vegetables in his hand. They crashed to the road, instantly covered in a layer of dust.

I turned to the boy. "Take this," I said, offering all the coins I had. "I want you to run home and stay there until tomorrow. Do you understand me?" He answered my question with a nod and wrapped his arms around my waist. "Go," I ordered, patting him on the back before urging him to run away from the square. As I turned to watch him, wanting to make sure he got away without further interruption, a crushing blow landed on my left arm. The force of it almost knocked me off my feet. Waves of pain shot through the bones, distracting me. I had just enough time to dodge out of the way when he swung again, aiming for where my head had been a second earlier. Rushing toward the man, I collided into his chest with all my strength. The surprise of my attack disrupted his balance, and he crumbled to the ground with me still on top of him. Drawing my injured arm close, I set to work landing blows with my good arm. The two of us struggled against one another— much to the enjoyment of the crowd. I rose to my feet faster than the farmer and thrust my good fist into his jaw. The strength of my punch twisted his head, and a combination of blood and teeth sprayed from his mouth. "Allow me to cover the boy's debts and let's see an end to this matter." The man struggled to his feet. Picking up the scrap of wood he'd struck me with earlier, he proceeded to attack. I was fast enough to dodge his first three attempts, but on the fourth, he managed to clip my left elbow. The jolt of pain dropped me to my knees. The arm, which was already broken, would surely shatter beneath another attack. I met the man's dark eyes as he lifted his weapon to strike again.

"You will stop what you're doing immediately!" A woman's voice spoke with complete authority. The farmer and I spun at once, wondering who had given the order. To my surprise, I saw the queen standing beside us in the town square. A gray cloak rested beside her feet. She stood before us, glowing in tones of crimson and gold with a ring of pearls fastened neatly in her hair. To everyone else, it was a crown, an indication of who she was and how they were supposed to treat her. But to me, it was a halo of salvation. Upon realizing they were in the presence of royalty, everyone dropped to their knees and bowed before her. "How dare you injure one of my personal guards. I could have your neck for such an offense!"

The farmer cowered at her statement. "I was merely enforcing the law on a small boy who stole food from me."

"I saw. This man also offered you payment for the loss and you refused him. You wanted blood for payment." Her voice was cold and domineering as she spoke. She could order any punishment she desired and there was nothing this man could do to stop it.

"I'm sorry," he cried. "Please show me mercy."

"As you showed the boy? As you showed Conrad?"

"Please."

"You attempted to enact revenge on a child and you injured one of my guards. I hope you realize the seriousness of your offenses."

"Your Highness."

"You will spend a week in the dungeons with nothing but water and a few breadcrumbs. Perhaps a personal struggle with hunger will make you more sympathetic in the future."

"Thank you, Your Highness," he muttered. "Thank you."

"If I ever hear that you've attempted to place yourself above the law again, the cost will be your head." She walked past the man to stand before me. "Come, Conrad. Let's see that your arm is treated properly." She held on to my good hand as I stood and we began our path through the crowd still on their knees. I bent to retrieve her cloak before we parted with the scene behind us. Carrying the gray material on my left arm, it felt as if I were toting a sack of bricks instead of a cloak. "Give me that." She reached for the garment. "You mustn't put any weight on it. It's already broken."

"I appreciate your concern, my lady, but I'll not have you help me back to the castle and carry your own cloak as well."

"I'm perfectly capable of carrying my own clothes. I don't know why everyone must insist on treating me as if I were a piece of glass."

I winced as a burst of pain radiated from my wrist to my shoulder. "Perhaps it's because no one has ever laid eyes upon anything as lovely as you." I shut my mouth, horrified that a little pain could make me forego all notions of sense. I was a guard and she my queen. My back stiffened as I prayed she wouldn't find offense in my compliment.

"You've told me before that you think I'm beautiful. Am I to understand that you think I'm lovely as well?" she asked, smiling.

"I do."

I could smell the fragrant scent of roses as she leaned closer to me. "I think very highly of you too."

At her words, a sudden rush of excitement flowed over my body. Pain gave way to elation as we continued the rest of our journey back to the castle in silence. Although we didn't continue talking, her hands tightened around my arm. The effect was intoxicating. She was kinder and more beautiful than any woman I'd ever met.

A dainty servant stood by the door, allowing us entrance into the castle. "Fetch the healer," the queen ordered. "And send him to Conrad Bourdet's chambers." With a quick curtsy, the small woman disappeared. The queen led me to the opposite side of the castle, disregarding the looks and stares of others as she continued her hold on me. Within a few minutes, we were in the confines of my room. She arranged two chairs near the fireplace, pushing me into one. "You need to take off your shirt so the healer can see your arm." She took the cloak from my bad arm and laid it on a small table a few feet away. The pain in my arm made it too hard to try to bend, and I struggled to free myself from the thick linen of my shirt. "Let me help you," she said after watching my failure. Stooping in front of me, she slid the material off my right arm and then the left. Her face was so close to mine, and I caught myself staring at her lips, unable to avert my eyes. "Oh, Conrad," she whispered, examining my left arm. Bruises blanketed the skin from shoulder to wrist. She set her hand against my cheek. "Does it pain you terribly?"

"I'm sure it looks worse than it feels," I answered with a stiff smile. Truth be told, the arm ached like hell, but I forced myself not to utter those words.

Knowing I wasn't being truthful with her, she stared into my eyes. "Is there anything I can do to help you forget it?"

My gaze dropped to her lips. They were plump and rosy, and I suddenly felt the need to touch them. A lump caught in my throat as she noticed how intently I had begun to stare. "I'm not sure there's anything you can do, my lady."

"Are you quite certain?" After posing her question, she took my hand in between hers and rubbed my skin. Then she leaned close enough to press her cheek against my own. "I'm touched by the kindness you showed that boy today."

"I couldn't let that man harm him. I've been guilty of stealing before as well. You bestowed kindness upon me, and I felt obligated to do the same for the boy."

"Even still," she added. "Thank you for doing it." She kissed my cheek, holding her lips against my skin for a long moment. As she pulled away from the embrace, our faces slid past one another. Unable to control myself, I turned toward her, allowing my lips to graze the line of her jaw. She sighed at the touch. It was a soft noise teeming with contentment and pleasure. Emboldened by the sound, I drew my hand from hers and trailed it down the slope of her neck. Her head rolled back in response. I could feel the rhythmic beating of her heart beneath my hand as she raised her hand to cup my cheek. As if acting out of habit, I moved to kiss her palm. Even though I'd never done the gesture before, the familiarity of it was undeniable—like I'd done it thousands of times instead of just once. "Do you believe in fate?"

"I'm afraid I do," I answered.

"And do you think a person's destiny can be changed?"

I assumed she was speaking of her own plight, but I was forced to apply the situation to myself. With her help, I'd managed to raise my family from destitution. My path, laid before me by chance and circumstance, had been forever altered. Everything changed within the blink of an eye, and if such things could happen for a blacksmith, then the same could no doubt be said for a queen. "For you, I believe anything is possible."

"I pray you're right," she whispered. "Conrad?"

"Yes, my lady?"

"How is your arm?"

Reluctantly, I withdrew my eyes away from hers to study my arm. "That's right. It's broken, isn't it?"

"I'm afraid it is."

"I'm not going to be dismissed because I have a broken arm and can't guard you to the best of my abilities, am I?" I was trying to make light of the situation, because every time her eyes surveyed my bruised skin, it seemed like she was about to cry.

"Do you really think I could do that to you?"

"I hope not," I replied. I found my attention drawn to her lips once more as she smiled at me. Each second that passed made it harder not to admit my true feelings for her. But luckily, I was spared from confession by the entrance of the healer.

He was a man of short stature with a thin frame. His balding head and face were covered in wrinkles, but his expression hinted at a kind nature. "Well, I believe it's safe to say your arm is broken," he declared, walking over to where I sat. He took my bruised appendage in his hands, surveying the damage. His fingers felt each joint, making an assessment of what needed to be done. "I'll need to set it and splint it in order for the bones to heal correctly."

"Do what you must," I replied.

"It's going to be quite painful. You'll need this." Without warning, he shoved a thick strap of leather in my mouth.

I readjusted the strap and dug my teeth into it. The queen moved the other chair closer to mine and sat, taking my right hand in hers and leaning close. "I'll try to distract you as much as I can," she whispered in my ear.

"That might be easier than you think." At my words, her cheeks flushed.

"The strap goes in your mouth," the man chided. "I'll have to reset the bone in your arm and then your shoulder. Let me know when you're ready."

The queen bent closer, squeezing my hand tight. "Think of something that makes you happy."

I stared into her gray eyes. They were the color of fog after a heavy rainstorm. "I'm ready," I said, replacing the strap in my mouth. There was a loud crack before a sudden rush of pain seared the muscles of my arm. I bit on the strip of leather hard, grinding my teeth back and forth to flush the pain from my body.

And then . . . I noticed her hand combing my hair and her breath warming the flesh of my ear as she whispered into it. Her voice was hushed, and the words she spoke spilled from her lips with urgency. It sounded like some sort of prayer, but the language was of a different tongue. It took me a minute to decipher what it was, but then I recognized it as Latin.

Strips of cloth were being tied around my arm as the man splinted it to lie straight, but the sensation was dull. The pain was a distant humming, like the murmurings of a small crowd. The gentle rubbing didn't subside, even when the physician excused himself to leave. It was only after the door shut behind him that I noticed we were alone once more. "What were you saying?"

"Why?" she asked. "Did it work?" I watched as her mouth broke into a soft smile as she waited for me to answer.

"It did."

"I prayed to be given your pain so that you may be free from it."

"And who will take your pain?" I asked.

"I'm not sure."

"I'll take it away from you."

"Why would you do that?"

"Because you shouldn't have to carry that burden alone."

"That's very kind of you to say."

I squeezed her hand with my good one. "It's the truth." Her lips spread into a wide smile at my reply. The more moments I spend with her, the more I love her.

I leaned closer but felt myself slipping away. My body lunged forward, propelling me through the air. A single strap across my chest stopped me from going too far and slammed me back into my seat. I forced my eyes open, surveying my surroundings.

"Sorry!" Caroline yelled. "Are y'all okay?"

"What the hell?" I asked. "What's going on?"

"I thought I passed the house. There isn't a lot of light or other buildings out this way, so it's kind of hard to see the street signs."

"We're here? You let me sleep that long?"

"You needed the rest. We didn't want to wake you," Noah replied.

"Well, now we're here and I don't feel prepared."

"You really believe you aren't prepared?" Caroline asked. "Look at your hand."

My hand was grasping a knife, ready to strike. "That's just a reflex."

"So, you always sleep with a knife?" she asked.

"Only on Wednesdays."

"Cute," she answered, sighing. "Anyways, I don't know why you're panicking about not having time to prepare. You can go from dead asleep to DEFCON 1 in a matter of seconds."

I rubbed my hands along the scruff covering my chin. The friction warmed my skin, invigorating my senses. I could do this. Aden was just a man. He could be killed, and I was about to do just that. "I'm glad one of us thinks we're ready to do this."

"Either way, we're here and we can't go back now," Noah said.

Slowly, the car crept down a long gravel driveway. The clock on the dashboard read three o'clock. It would be dawn soon and we needed to attack underneath the cloak of darkness. As we approached the end of the driveway, we couldn't see any light coming from the house. A large cloud passed over the moon, and all of a sudden, everything around us was drenched in shadow.

"Stop the car here," I ordered. "Noah, can you hand me my bag?" I took my bag from his hand and removed a sword and the sickle from it. I stuck a knife in the back of my jeans and stepped out of the car. Noah and Caroline followed my lead, quietly closing their doors behind them. "We stay together at all times. Follow my lead through the house. We'll clear one room at a time until we find Evey and Iola. Once we have both of them, we'll head back to the car and leave."

"Got it," Noah whispered.

"I left the car unlocked and the keys are in the ignition. That way, we can just jump in and drive," Caroline added.

I nodded my head, gripping the sickle. "Follow me."

The three of us moved to the front entrance of the house. We snuck along the outside wall up to the front door, barely making a sound as our feet moved through the flower beds. The house was a two-story brick colonial, which is all I could make out in the darkness. Once we reached the front door, I pulled a pin from my pocket and inserted it into the lock of the house. After a few twists of my fingers, the lock clicked and I eased the door open. We quietly stepped inside, turning left into a dining room. My eyes scanned the room, adjusting to the darker interior and searching for any signs of life. Two of the chairs surrounding an impressive dining table were overturned. Moving around the furniture, I cleared the area. The next room appeared to be some sort of den, but it was also empty.

Random books and objects were scattered about the floor between the adjoining spaces.

"It doesn't seem like anyone is here," Caroline whispered.

"We've got to keep searching. We can't know for sure until we check the entire house," I replied.

Methodically, we maneuvered through the rooms on the bottom floor of the house. The steady rhythm of my heart kept me focused on the task at hand. But the longer we searched without discovering any signs of life, the more desperate I became to find them. We picked apart closets, cabinets, and a small office at the base of a staircase before moving on. Small creaks sounded from the wooden steps as our feet climbed to the second floor. A short hall lay before us. Two doors stood to our right, and at the end of the hall, double doors marked the entrance to a third room. I sucked in a quick breath and moved right. The first room was a small yellow bedroom. The three of us cleared the area in less than a minute, stepping to the second door. This room was completely white. Its extravagance was unsettled by an overturned chair and lamp, but those were the only indicators that anyone had ever occupied the room. Finally, we turned our attention to the end of the hallway. As the doors spread apart to reveal the room's interior, I prayed Evey would be standing before me. But once again, we found nothing.

"I really thought we'd find something," Caroline whispered, picking up a few sheets of paper lying on the floor. She was the only one brave enough to break the silence hovering around us. "Conrad?"

"What?"

"It's her."

Caroline's hands trembled as she held the papers out to me. I thought they'd been blank, but I'd been wrong. Evey stared up at me from each piece of paper. Her face had been drawn with exact detail, and the sight made me long to see her even more.

"I mean, this is the right house. They were here at some point, and it looks as though they packed up and left in a hurry," she said.

"Aden knew we were coming."

I turned on my heel, storming out of the bedroom and back down the stairs. I didn't know if Caroline and Noah were in tow or not, and quite frankly, I didn't care. We'd been on a wild goose chase for days now, and our only solid lead turned up empty. Anger raged like an uncontrollable inferno within me. Aden always seemed to be a step ahead of us. I paced through the dining room and into the kitchen. Somewhere, there had to be a clue telling us where to go or what to do. I refused to admit defeat, especially when we were this close to finding them. I stepped toward the small table in the kitchen and kicked it as hard as I could. It skidded across the floor, slamming against the wall. The sound resonated through the house, drawing Noah and Caroline from upstairs. Unsatisfied with the disruption, I balled my fist and threw it through the window in front of me. The glass shattered beneath the force and sliced the skin along my knuckles. Fresh drops of blood oozed from the joints, dotting the floor. "I'm so sick of this. This was a damn waste of time!" I yelled, staring out the window.

"Conrad, you're bleeding. You better let me check it," Caroline said, taking my hand in hers. I felt her pull a chunk of glass from my index finger. The sensation was dull, not even worth acknowledging. "You don't know it was a waste of time. There still might be something here."

"Like what? A map detailing exactly where they're hiding?" I asked.

"You can't get discouraged now. We just need to regroup."

"She's right. We need to keep our heads straight. What did the demon say again?"

"He said that we needed to go back to the start of it," I replied. I'd barely finished speaking when something in the backyard caught my eye. The cloud had passed from in front of the moon, and I was able to just make out a single mound of dirt. A bundle of flowers lay on the center of it. I burst through the small door beside the smashed window and ran into the yard. Beneath those clumps of mud lay a body, and I knew whose it would be. Falling to my knees, I thrust my hands into the soft earth. I worked frantically, spraying everything around me with soil. After a few short minutes of digging, I reached the sallow sheen of burned flesh. I cleared the dirt from Guy's face and brushed a few worms from his eye sockets. The large welts where his skin had been burned were highlighted by the bleak contrasting colors surrounding him. By the time the three of us finished digging, we had excavated his body.

"We can't leave him here," Noah said, brushing hair from his eyes. "We at least have to take him to Everest's to be buried. That way, he can rise again."

Noah and I lifted Guy from his grave and wrapped him in some spare linen Caroline had recovered from the house. As we tied the fabric around his body, I couldn't help but replay the demon's instructions in my mind again. "Back to the beginning," I muttered. "The beginning of what?"

"It's hard to say," Noah answered.

I grabbed Guy's shoulders, lifting him up from the ground as Noah carried his legs. "Did he mean back to Estill Springs? Where the souls first came for Evey?"

"It could be anywhere or anything," Noah said. "And the demon wasn't in the right state of mind. He may not have known what he was saying."

"True."

"No." Caroline walked beside us as we headed toward the car, staring at Guy's lifeless body. "Not Estill Springs."

"Well, what do you think he was talking about?" Noah asked.

"There's only one thing it could be."

"And that is?" I asked.

"He's talking about the Garden of Eden. It's the beginning of everything, of life. It's where Evey and Aden's story started. It's the only place he could be talking about."

"Yeah. The only problem is no one alive knows where to find the Garden. Its location has been hidden for millennia," I countered.

"Even Everest isn't sure where to find it," Noah added.

"That's because the only person who does is dead."

"And who might that be?" I asked.

"Milton. He told Evey and me that Thea wrote the Book of Adam and Eve. She knew things about the primums that no one else did. Milton was also Thea's closest confidant and he was madly in love with her. If she revealed the secrets of that book to anyone, it would've been him."

"And you're sure he'd know where to find that book?" Noah asked.

"I'm positive. If anyone knows, it's Milton," she answered.

I glanced at Noah. "You ready to raise the dead again?"

"I thought you'd never ask."

17

FRAGMENTS

Somewhere in the darkness, I heard voices screaming my name. When I awoke, my eyes opened to the roof of a moving car. Aden was there. He held me in his lap, cradling me like a small child.

"Why?" he asked, tears streaking the skin on his cheeks. "Why would you do it?"

"I'm so tired of this endless game," I whispered. I held my eyes shut, not wanting to accept that I was still alive. "I have this unimaginable burden weighing on me every second of the day. I think of everyone I've loved getting murdered in cold blood so you can retain your claim on me—as if I am a piece of property. I'm sick of being bound to someone who whispers promises of love in one ear and orders the execution of innocent people in another."

"I'm trying to be better."

"I don't want to hear it." I held my hand in the air, commanding his silence. "For once in your life, can't you just leave me be? Secrets and deception haunt me at every turn, and I can't bear it any longer. Can't you see what you've done to me?" I stared at him, awaiting his answer, but Aden didn't speak. "You've broken me, and I'll never be the same again. I'm not your wife anymore."

"You were made to be my partner."

"Because I stopped loving you, is that why you started the Spanish Inquisition? Is that why you poisoned me?"

"Those are both past events. I've done horrible things in the past. I've never tried to cover that up."

"And what about things you've done recently?" I pushed away, sliding until my back made contact with the door opposite him. "You killed Conrad. You had Donovan slit my mother's throat. Mickey and Kit died on your orders too. And my father—" I seethed. "My father was burned beyond recognition. You sit on a throne of corpses, and yet, you proclaim your innocence."

"I did all of that for you!" he shouted. "I did those things so we could be together."

"I don't think you truly realize the sacrifice you're asking me to make. If I stay with you, if I change you, I'll never be able to see my family again. My parents, Mickey, Kit, Caroline, and Conrad are all I've ever known, but you want me to forget about them like they mean nothing to me."

"I don't want you to forget them. I know how much you care for your family. All I ask is for your help. You've had centuries with them. Don't I deserve a chance to be with you, to become the man I once was? You were given to me."

"I never asked to be yours. I was created and you claimed me for yourself. At what point will you realize I don't want to be with you?" Disgust swirled in my veins as I stared at my captor. "I never have and I never will."

"You don't mean that," he whispered.

"You don't know anything about me."

"Is that what you think?" His cold glare stared through me, still moist with fresh tears. "I know you can't live without this." He held his hand out between us, and a gold chain dangled from his fingers. My attention dropped to the bright ruby pendant swinging through the air.

I lunged forward, desperately reaching for my necklace. "Give that back!"

"Why?" His free hand caught my own, holding me at arm's length. "All this thing does is serve as a reminder for the life we've left behind. This meaningless trinket is our past. Just let it go, my love."

"It's the only thing I have left that's mine."

"Have I not given myself to you? Am I not yours?" he asked.

My gaze swayed back and forth, not daring to lose sight of my necklace. "Forcing yourself on me doesn't make you mine. I didn't choose to be with you."

"That isn't how it used to be."

"Why do you keep talking about the past as if it were relevant to our current situation? It's the past. Things change, people change, and not everything is meant to last forever." I watched his countenance change as he pondered my words. After a few moments, his hand stretched toward me. I swiped the necklace from it before he had a chance to change his mind. Quickly, I fastened it around my neck, pressing the pendant into my skin. For a brief second, tranquility overtook anger. This piece of jewelry was a palpable source of strength for me. It reminded me of why I needed to continue fighting for not only my future but the Concilium's as well.

"When you've lived as long as we have, it gives you the chance to notice trends or, really, patterns in human behavior. Trust me when I tell you this: history always repeats itself."

I glared at him. "Well, you should trust that I know who I want right now and who I'll want in the future." I turned toward the window, studying the scenery outside in an attempt to discern my surroundings. "And that man will never be you." Out of the corner of my eye, I noticed a black Corvette had pulled up next to us, matching our pace as we tore down the interstate. "Where are we going?"

"Somewhere safe," Aden replied. "How much longer, Donovan?"

"Three more hours," Donovan answered from behind the steering wheel.

"Who's in the car beside us?"

"Luke."

"Why is he following us?"

"The place we're headed to is his house," Aden replied in exasperation.

"Stop the car," I demanded.

"What's wrong?"

"If I'm going to be carted around everywhere you go like some captive, at least let me choose who I spend the next three hours with," I spat. "If I have to stay another minute in this car with you, I'll lose my mind."

"I don't know what else I can do to demonstrate how much I want to make you happy."

"You could start with letting me have a few hours away from your overbearing and obsessive infatuation with a relationship that doesn't exist anymore."

He was silent for a moment, no doubt contemplating my words. "As you wish," he replied. "Donovan, pull the car over. I won't subject my former wife to the torture of my company."

To my relief, Donovan pulled the vehicle to the shoulder of the interstate and switched off the ignition. Behind us, the black Corvette followed suit. Before Aden could change his mind, I jumped out of the car and ran to the passenger seat of Luke's. He opened the door from inside the car just as I reached the handle.

"Is something wrong?" he asked.

"May I continue the rest of our trip in your car? I refuse to sit beside Aden for the next three hours."

A glimmer of satisfaction shined through Luke's eyes. Maybe I was throwing myself into a worse situation by being alone with him, but I couldn't care less. I had to get away from Aden at any cost. His presence was overwhelming. I was sure to suffocate at any moment from the undesired attention he showered upon me. I needed reprieve from his dark gaze, no matter how short-lived. As I bent to the passenger seat, Luke held out his hand to assist me inside. "I'd be honored to have the privilege of your company." Nestling into the low seat, I shut the door behind me. "Allow me," he said, pulling the seatbelt across my chest.

"Thanks," I replied. "There's no chance you could tell me why we're on our way to your house, is there?" I wasn't expecting Luke to be upfront with me, but at the same time, it couldn't hurt to ask.

"I'm afraid I can't, my queen," he answered. "However, I can assure you every measure will be taken to ensure your comfort."

I released a soft sigh upon hearing his reply. "I appreciate your honesty and hospitality. My only need will be to have a room to myself."

"I'll see your request done," he said with a nod.

"You may call me Evey if you'd like," I said, turning to face him. As per usual, he was wearing a crisp black suit with silver cufflinks. "At the moment, I don't feel like anything remotely close to a queen and I don't know you well enough to be considered yours."

"Evey it is, then," he agreed, laughing. "Would you like to have the opportunity to get to know me?"

"I'm not sure I know how to answer that question."

"It's a simple yes or no."

"Is it really?" I asked. For a brief moment, our eyes met. In the depths of his existed a subversive undercurrent of seduction. I may not have known exactly who Luke was, but his end game was so much more than a simple yes or no answer. Darkness enveloped the front of Luke's car as we barreled down the interstate. His foot pressed harder on the gas pedal, shooting us past the car Aden was in and another just like it.

"I suppose you'll just have to wait and see," he replied.

Aden had the ability to lead mankind toward darkness, and yet, he was afraid of Luke. That meant the man sitting beside me couldn't be a mere demon. He was powerful, but too tainted to be a servant of God.

"You said before that you've never experienced my love, so there is no way you could be a past romance, but did you ever act as my confidant?"

"I've been known to whisper in your ear from time to time."

And with that confession, recognition dawned on me. I'd been oblivious to the answer staring me in the face. He was the one who orchestrated the Fall of Man.

The devil. Satan. Lucifer.

Luke.

I should've been consumed with fear, but instead, peace flowed through every muscle in my body. Luke wouldn't hurt me because there was something he wanted from me, and he might liberate me from Aden's grasp.

"May I ask you something?"

"Of course."

"Am I in danger?"

Intrigued by my question, Luke tilted his head to appraise me. It seemed he wanted to gauge my expression to determine whether or not I was serious. "What do you mean?"

"Aden believes I can help reconstitute his humanity. He wants me to help him become the man he once was. I told him I would try, but I can't help thinking that if I'm unsuccessful or if by some miracle I am successful and still deny his advances, he'll enact some sort of punishment on me."

"Why do you think he'd seek to hurt you after you try to help him?"

"He's killed me before. I'm sure you're aware of that fact."

"I am."

"It's in his nature to hurt people. He's been slowly descending into the depths of savagery for centuries, and when things don't go the way he wants, he can become quite vindictive," I said. "I don't fear death. I'm afraid that, over the course of time, he'll bend my will. I'm scared he'll exploit the link connecting us as the original man and woman and find some way to force me into being like him, into committing unspeakable acts against other people."

"I know for the most part I'm a stranger to you, but I've watched you from afar for quite some time now. Your heart is pure, and it'd take something much stronger and darker than Aden to corrupt it." To my surprise, Luke's hand reached across the center console and grasped mine. "And if it is bodily harm you fear from Aden, then know I'll do everything within my power to protect you."

"Thank you. I appreciate it." It may have been foolish to place any kind of trust in Luke, but he wasn't the one who murdered my family. Aden was. So until Luke proved himself to be an enemy, I would treat him as an ally.

"How about some music?" Luke reached forward, switching on the radio. "Do you have a preference?"

"Whatever you want to listen to is fine with me," I replied. I watched Luke press a button on the dashboard, illuminating everything with blue light. As soon as he touched it, sounds of a lone violin flooded the car. The somber tones filled my ears, transporting my mind into a temporary state of reprieve. The musician played on, intertwining note after note into a single beautiful melody. It seemed so familiar, but I'd never heard it before. It was intriguing, forcing me to wait in agonizing anticipation for the next sound to fill my ears. "I don't believe I've heard this before. What is the name of this song?"

"Do you like it?"

"It's breathtaking. I'm not quite sure how to describe it. It's so somber, but there is such serenity to it as well. As if the musician was destined to an insufferable fate, but at the same time, they embraced it."

"It's called *Et Consommer Désir.*"

"What does that mean?"

"It translates to *a consuming desire.*"

"Was the violinist a woman?"

"She was," Luke replied.

"Did she have a consuming desire for you?" The words poured from my mouth before I could stop myself. I didn't know what possessed me to ask the question, but something in my gut was screaming that he had some connection to this woman. He'd already made it known that he was privy to intimate details about me, so the more things I knew about Luke, the easier it would be to figure out his end game.

"She had many desires. I merely helped her recognize them."

"And is your goal to do the same with me?"

"Could you blame me if it was?" The lines of his mouth

unfurled into a devious grin. Whatever his goal, the intentions behind it weren't entirely innocent.

No matter where I turned, I was never alone. If I escaped Aden, would I be made into a captive again by Luke? "Sometimes I feel like being the original woman is more of a curse than a blessing."

"Everything comes with a price."

"Believe me when I say I know that better than anyone."

"I wish I could remedy that for you, Evey." To my surprise, he took my hand in his and kissed it.

"Why are you working with Aden?"

"Let's just say he and I have several interests coinciding with one another."

"But you're aware of what his plan is?"

"Essentially, yes," he replied. "Although, I don't bother myself with memorizing every detail."

"So, you don't care he's killed people I love to get what he wants?"

"I never said that. All I did was supply him with the means to execute his plan. Everything else is his doing."

"I don't understand how you can be so ambivalent about the whole situation."

"It's not my battle."

"And what would it take to make it your battle?"

"Are you trying to recruit me in your opposition to Aden?"

"You know what he is up to, even if you won't admit to it. You know what he plans to do with me. You respect me more than you do Aden—that much is obvious—but all I'm asking for is your help." I took his hand in mine, demanding his complete attention. Luke could help me out of my current predicament, and once I was free, I could return to the Concilium and Caroline.

"And you claim you aren't a queen."

"I'm just a girl," I countered.

"It's surprising how little you believe in yourself." His hands returned to the wheel and silence filled the car for a moment. "May I ask you something?"

"Why not? You already know more about me than I know myself."

"Why did you jump?"

"Technically, I fell."

"You tried to take your own life," he whispered. "I know you comprehend the weight of such a decision."

"I was hoping to reset things. I wanted to offer my life in exchange for my loved ones. You said it yourself: when I die, they get brought back and I'm reborn. It was a gamble, sure, but it was one I had to make."

"I don't understand why. What if you sacrificed your life and they still weren't brought back? You'd embrace that kind of uncertainty for the chance to rectify things?"

"I would. Maybe I can help you understand. Pull over for a second." Luke acquiesced and halted his car on the side of the road. Once stalled, I took his hands in mine and set one over my heart and the other over his own. "Close your eyes and focus on my heartbeat." A few seconds passed before I continued. "Now, I want you to focus on yours. Feel it fall into pace with my own."

"This is touching but—"

"Open your eyes and look at me." Our eyes met, locking on one another. "Imagine the very rhythm of your heart is dependent upon my own. Your greatest fear is to have that bond severed. You've forgotten what your own heartbeat feels like because all you can remember is the pace of mine." My hand rose to his face, stroking his cheek. "I'd risk everything because so many things that make up my loved ones are wrapped up in my own being, and it's impossible to remember who I am without them." Luke's hand trembled against my skin. "The loss of my family—knowing they felt pain and fear in their final moments—torments me more than whatever fate or punishment awaited me."

"I believe I finally understand."

Before I could reply, Luke transformed before my eyes. Instead, a smiling Mickey sat before me. "Mickey." I studied the lines down his cheeks and his thick mustache, but no sooner than he appeared, Mickey was replaced by Kit. "Oh, how I miss you, Kit." Pools of water formed underneath my eyelids, waiting to be released. As Kit's curly hair faded from sight, my mother's green eyes stared back at me. "Mom!" I flung my arms around her neck, praying she wouldn't leave me. "Please don't go." When I ended the embrace, my father's face was only inches from mine. "I need you here with me, Daddy." A knowing smiled brightened his features. "I'm so sorry I left you there." Tears dripped from my chin. I didn't want to lose them again.

"Evey." The sound of my name was barely more than a hum, but it was more than enough to gain my attention.

"I knew I'd see you last."

"You could never get rid of me so easily, my lady." Conrad's bright gaze flickered with mischief.

"In this moment, I feel like I don't know what is or isn't real anymore and I don't care." I took his face in my hands, pulling him closer. "All I want is to kiss you." Our kiss was soft, tentative at first, but as my need intensified, I melted into him. Rough hands caressed my shoulders, solidifying our hold on one another. My lips grew desperate, making contact with any part of his skin I could find. I knew the man before me wasn't Conrad. It was a fabricated face, a false set of eyes, but I needed to feel him.

I felt the lines of Conrad's face shifting beneath my fingertips, and when I came up for air, Luke was staring back at me.

"You don't have to stop," he teased.

Heat engulfed my cheeks. "I'm so sorry I keep doing that to you."

"You'll never hear me complain."

"Sometimes, I feel as if I've lost my grip on reality."

"Maybe you feel that way because you know Aden is beneath you. In your heart, you don't want to be here. You can leave him and come with me if you'd like. I'll take you out of here right now."

I considered Luke's offer for a second. Part of me wanted to go with him, but the other part thought of Helen and Christopher. If I ran off, there was no telling what Aden would do to them. I couldn't allow anyone else to get hurt because of me. "And trade the frying pan for the fire?"

"Not all fires burn with the intent to maim. Some just provide warmth and comfort."

"And that's all you're trying to offer me? Warmth and comfort?"

"Maybe . . . then again, maybe not."

"I'll take your offer under consideration. Even though I want to get as far away from him as possible, I still have an obligation to the Concilium."

"Evey, ever the thoughtful diplomat."

"I'm just trying to be a decent human being," I countered.

"If you can't leave, does that mean you're still going to help Aden regain his humanity?"

I shifted my attention toward the window, staring into the endless night. "I agreed to help Aden because I can't sit by and watch him suffer. I know he is capable of kindness, and it's the least I can do for being the cause of his fall from grace. If I hadn't persuaded him to take a bite of that apple, he wouldn't be cursed with darkness."

"It seems you're faced with quite the predicament."

"I just don't want to make the wrong decision. I know what he's done is terrible and unfair, but at the same time, isn't it just as unfair to leave him to fend for himself? More people could suffer as a result of my own selfishness. If there is something I can do to prevent him from killing and torturing, then shouldn't I take that course of action?"

"Which do you want more? Vindication for your loved ones or deliverance for Aden into the hands of salvation?"

"How can I be expected to choose between those things?"

"Simply decide which is easier for you to live with."

Before either of us could utter another word, Luke pulled back on to the road, and we were once again speeding down the interstate. I pondered Luke's statement. What did I desire more, vindication or salvation? The whole time I'd been under Aden's lock and key, I'd believed myself to be helpless, but after contemplating Luke's question, I realized I possessed more power than I originally thought. I had the ability to decide Aden's fate—and my own as well. What would my fallen *secundae* want me to do? Though the burden was mine alone to bear, would they understand if I decided to aid their murderer? "If you were my family, what would you want me to do?"

"I'm afraid I'm not the best person to answer that question."

"And why is that?"

"I'm not an advocate of forgiveness."

"Because you'd rather deal out punishment instead?"

"That's an interesting way to phrase it."

"How would you phrase it?" I asked.

"I'd retaliate against those who were guilty of committing crimes against me by any means necessary."

"Meaning you're no one's savior?"

"It depends."

"On what?"

"On what you consider saving."

"What do you mean?"

"In some cases, punishment is the only way to save."

"I've committed horrible acts against Aden. I fell in love with another man, gave my body to him while I was still bound to Aden in marriage. Is that not an act deserving of punishment?"

"I doubt there is a man alive who could bring himself to punish you."

"Is that what you think?" I studied Luke, feeling as if I were a fish on a hook slowly being reeled to shore. If he wanted, he could be even more dangerous than Aden.

"Men have lain at your feet in order to find themselves in your presence. There is no war they wouldn't fight for you, no task they wouldn't fulfill at your request. Your allure as the original woman can be a weapon more powerful than you realize."

"You think it's time I use my so-called power, my body, to my own advantage?"

"I think you do yourself a disservice by not wielding the most influential weapon known to man."

18

REVOCATION

I held Milton's head, observing the rest of Noah's ritual. Sweat trickled down my back as the sun continued its cycle in the sky. Raising a secundae without explicit permission from the Concilium was idiotic at best, but then again, there was no other conceivable alternative. The lead I tortured out of the dissimulo was a dead end. This was our only other option. I trusted Caroline and her hunch about Milton. She was quite adept at reading people, and if she believed he could help us get Evey back, I was all in.

"I'll tell Everest this was my idea and take full responsibility for it."

"You don't have to do that," I whispered.

"I want to," she replied. "Besides, you'd do it for me."

"In case the two of you haven't noticed, I'm in the middle of a sacred ceremony here, and as I explicitly said before, I need absolute silence or I'll have to start over. So, stop gossiping like a couple of teenage girls."

"Maybe it's slipped your mind, Noah, but I happen to be a teenage girl."

"The fate of humanity is doomed," Noah replied with a heavy sigh.

I suppressed a laugh and readjusted my hold on Milton's head. "Since we're short on time, I promise we'll shut up. Just do your part and bring Milton back."

Noah hovered over the body and murmured incantations under his breath. He worked diligently, rocking back and forth as he pressed his hand over Milton's heart. It was only a few days ago Noah was praying over my corpse, and now, I was here helping him do the same for another secundae. I waited, focusing on the wound separating Milton's head from his body. The laceration began to fade. It wouldn't be much longer now.

Suddenly, Milton sprang upright, ripping his head from my grasp. He coughed and expelled a cloud of dust from his lips. "What happened? Where am I?"

"We're at Everest's airstrip," Noah informed him.

"What happened in the warehouse? The last thing I remember seeing is Donovan." He accepted the bottle of water I handed him, draining it within a few seconds.

"Well, Aden killed me and took Evey and Helen with him. We don't know where they are, and we've been all over the country trying to track him down."

"Wait, if Evey isn't dead, why were we brought back?"

"You should ask her that," Noah said, pointing at Caroline.

"First of all, I'm glad you're alive again, Milton," she started. "Second, I made Noah bring Conrad back because he's the only one who can defeat Aden and we all know it. Why beat around the bush about it?"

"Because it's forbidden to heal a secundae without the caput's permission," Milton answered. "Especially after Thea decided to revive Aden on her own."

"I tried explaining that to her, but you can see how well it went," Noah said.

"And how did you and Caroline make it out of the warehouse without being taken or killed?"

"Caroline hit me over the head with a piece of wood. Once I was unconscious, she hid in a closet with me until the fighting was over."

"Smart thinking. It would've been a disaster if Aden got his hands on the heart of another consiliarius." Noah and I stood, helping Milton to his feet.

"Actually, Aden does have a consiliarius," Caroline whispered.

"But how? Who?"

"Iola."

Milton turned to Noah, pulling him into a hug. "I know what she means to you. I promise we'll get her back."

"Thanks."

"That's the reason we came for you," I said. "We think Aden is taking Evey and Iola to the Garden of Eden."

"Because it's the only place he can correctly perform the Comedere Cor," Milton finished.

"Exactly."

Milton's knees buckled, disrupting his balance. Noah and I moved around him and supported his weight with ours. "Thanks. It always takes a bit for me to adjust after being brought back."

"I know what you mean," I replied.

"We'll need to retrieve the Book of Adam and Eve," Milton said. "Thea wrote detailed instructions on how to find Eden in there."

Caroline smiled smugly. "I knew Milton would know where to get the book!"

"If Aden has Evey and Iola, then we don't have much time. Noah, call your pilot. We need to leave as soon as possible because the book is in England."

"The book is in England? Like the *country* on the other side of the ocean?" she asked, unable to contain her surprise.

"That's what I said," Milton replied.

"Are you freaking kidding me?" she shouted. Milton, Noah, and I exchanged looks of confusion. "We've been all over the continental

US, and now, you're telling me we have to fly to merry old England?"

"The book was hidden at Balen's estate. I left it there on Thea's orders for safekeeping. He doesn't even know I put it there, no one does."

"You people and your ancient artifacts hidden all over the world are really starting to tick me off. Oh, wait! Here is a biblical weapon we must obtain, but it's on the other side of the country! Oh, and this book, we must have it too, but it's in stinking England!"

"It makes sense to spread everything out," I added. "It makes it harder to find."

"I mean, haven't you people heard of a scanner? In a couple minutes, you could have a copy of the book on your computer. You could take it with you wherever you want and protect it with lots of encryptions and passwords."

"You want us to scan the second most important book in the history of the world, a book detailing the history of the Concilium and the primums, on to a laptop?" Noah asked.

"Yeah, I do. This is the age of technology. My grandma is on Twitter, so get with the program. As the world changes, the Concilium must adapt as well."

"We aren't formatting a sacred book into a Microsoft Word document. I won't agree with that," Noah countered.

"She might have a point though," I said.

"You're going to take her side?"

"Hell yes, I am. Caroline is perfectly capable of kicking your ass, and the Concilium does need to change on some matters. A little modernization would be good."

"You know, I'm starting to regret ever recommending that you be made into a secundae," Noah countered.

"Don't forget I can kick your ass too."

"Yeah, yeah," Noah replied, rolling his eyes. "We should get to Everest's before he sends a search party for us. I'm sure he'll be less than thrilled to see what we've done."

"It's not like we *have* to tell him what we did," Caroline

suggested. "We could just keep him in the dark about Milton's newly revived state."

"As much as I'd like to do that, Everest isn't a fool. He'll demand an explanation on how we know where to find the book when it's been missing for the last four centuries, and he'll want to know our plan for rescuing Evey and Iola. He won't approve our mission without being well informed," I added.

"Conrad's right," Milton agreed.

"Let's hope Everest's desire to rescue Iola will outweigh any anger he'll feel over having his orders disobeyed," Caroline said.

"It's not like he'll have some unexpected reaction," I replied. "We all know he's just going to blame me anyway."

"This is true."

"Wait, what about the seeds?" Caroline asked. "Aden can't properly perform the ritual without them."

"At this point, it doesn't really matter. He still has my sister. He can cut out her heart and consume her powers whenever he feels like it. That'll give him more time to find the seeds."

"Plus, he has Evey too. I'd bet my life he'll use her to find out where they are."

"But how does he know how to find Eden?" Caroline asked.

As soon as she formed her question, I realized the answer. Aden didn't just take Iola, he kidnapped Christopher as well. He didn't do it because of Christopher's role as a secundae. He did it because Christopher was one of the world's most prominent explorers. "Christopher," I mumbled.

"Iola's secundae? But why would he be privy to that kind of information?"

"Because Christopher's last name is Columbus," Noah replied.

"Like discoverer-of-America Christopher Columbus?"

"That'd be the one," he confirmed.

"You've got to be shitting me."

"I almost wish we were," I said.

"Aden's a step ahead of us, but that doesn't matter. We know what his plan is and we can stop him," Milton began. "I'll lay Guy to rest beside Marie while Noah talks to the pilot."

"Caroline and I can do a quick inventory of all our weapons. That way, once the plane arrives, we can be ready to go."

Caroline and I headed to the car to help Milton lower Guy's body from the vehicle. Carefully, we laid his corpse inside the hole Milton had just occupied. I moved to help shift the mound of dirt over Guy's body, but Milton stopped me. "I can finish this now. See to the weapons."

I nodded, leading Caroline to sort through our things. A quick search informed us that we had five hunting knifes of varying sizes, two swords, an axe, the sickle, and a large machete. It wasn't the best arsenal I'd ever fought with, but at least each of us would have a proper weapon to wield. I took the sickle, attaching it to my belt. Until all of this was over, I would not be letting it out of my sight.

"What's the damage?" Noah asked.

"Not too bad. There's enough to arm each of us with a larger weapon and a small knife as a backup. I've had worse."

"We'll also have the element of surprise, so that'll give us a slight advantage," he replied. "The pilot will be ready within the hour and Everest is on his way. I figured having him meet us out here would be better. It'll level the playing field so to speak."

"That's not a bad idea."

"And if you need me to wrangle him in line for you, I'd be happy to do so," Caroline offered.

"This is true," I agreed. "Whatever happens, we're all in agreement about the course of action we've taken, and if we make a stand to support those decisions, he'll have to agree with what we've done."

"I hope you're right," Noah replied.

"I do too."

"What part of England will we be headed to?" Caroline asked.

"Balen's estate is south of Manchester and on the outskirts of a national park. The last time I visited it, the manor was surrounded by forest. The nearest cities were pretty far off, though that's likely changed," Milton said.

"And you remember exactly where the book is hidden?" I asked.

"We need to retrieve it as fast as possible so we can intercept Aden in Eden."

"I hid it in one of the foundation blocks of the manor. It shouldn't take us long to remove it."

"Good." I tossed Milton a fresh set of clothes that I'd taken out of my bag in the car. "Here, I figured you'd want to change out of your suit."

"I appreciate it. This thing is stifling."

Within half an hour, our plane arrived. The pilot let down the stairs, jogging over to Noah.

"Where will we be headed today, Mr. Ragnavaldr?"

"Thanks for coming on such short notice, Bill." Noah rushed forward to shake the pilot's hand. "It looks like we'll be headed to Manchester, England. There's a piece I need to buy from Lyme Park. The client I'm procuring it for will be here within a few minutes. Once I've spoken with him, we can leave."

"Of course," Bill replied, nodding. "I'll radio over to Arclid Airfield in Manchester and let them know we'll be arriving tonight. Would you like me to have a car waiting when we land?"

"That would be fantastic. Thank you again. I appreciate you making the time to help me out today."

"Anytime." Bill smiled before returning to the plane.

Bill had just disappeared when Everest's black Cadillac pulled up. I watched as Everest marched toward us, the twins flanking him on either side. His eyes narrowed on Milton, and in an instant, I could tell he was infuriated. "I'm not ready to deal with his shit," I mumbled.

"If it makes you feel better, I've got a bottle of scotch on the plane," Noah muttered.

"Just the one?" I asked.

"I'm down for a drink," Caroline whispered. The three of us stared at her in surprise. "Why not round out our list of felonies by adding *contributing to the delinquency of a minor?*"

I suppressed a snicker, straightening my back as Everest stood before us. "We're definitely doomed," Noah added.

"What in God's name is going on here?" Everest asked. He glared at us, trying to instill fear with his hawk-like gaze.

"Well, we brought Milton back to the land of the living," I answered.

"I can see that, Bourdet," he seethed. "What I want to know is why."

"I brought him back because our lead turned out to be a dead end. Aden left the house in a hurry and all we were able to find was Guy's remains." Noah paused for a moment, no doubt wanting to keep his cool while speaking to Everest. "When Conrad interrogated the dissimulo, the demon told us Aden's plan was to go back to the start of things. At first, we weren't quite certain what he meant, but then Caroline was able to figure it out. The demon meant back to the Garden of Eden. Aden is headed there so he can finally perform the Comedere Cor."

"Yes, but that still doesn't explain why you brought back Milton."

"We brought him back because he knows how to find Eden," Caroline began. "A few days ago, Evey and I were talking to Milton about how he used to be one of Thea's secundae. He told us that she wrote the Book of Adam and Eve and that he was her most trusted confidant. I put two and two together and had a hunch he would know where to find the book."

"I see. But why resurrect him without my consent, Noah? Why not tell me all this and get everything approved through the appropriate channels?"

"Because there isn't time for us to go through the appropriate channels! That madman has your wife, my sister, and her days are numbered. I don't know about you, but I'm tired of putting people I love in the ground to rot."

"You think I want Iola to die by Aden's hands?" he shouted. "I've been in love with her since the moment I laid eyes on her."

"Then, let's not stall anymore," Noah yelled. "We need to get to England and retrieve the Book of Adam and Eve as soon as possible."

"You broke our laws, Noah! Did you think I'd slap your wrist before sending you on your merry way? We make decisions as a single unit, not individually. Thea made a rash decision four hundred years ago and she paid the price with her life! I swore then I'd never bury another consiliarius," Everest said.

"Noah isn't like Thea. He brought back Milton to help the Concilium, not jeopardize it," I countered. "Every decision he's made has been to save us all!"

"How did I not see it before?" Everest asked, pacing back and forth. "You were killed in the warehouse, weren't you?"

I took a moment to collect my thoughts. If I allowed my anger to get the best of me, it would only make things worse. "I was."

"Of course you were," he replied. "How else would Aden have been able to take Evey? Even with more souls, you'd rather die than stop fighting for her."

"It's my job. At least that's what you keep telling me."

"After thousands of years, you've finally decided to relinquish your loyalty to the Concilium in pursuit of your own goals." Everest shifted his hatred from me to Noah.

"My choice to bring back Conrad and Milton without your permission was made because of my love for the Concilium. Our very survival rests in their hands. Milton is the only one who can lead us to the Garden of Eden. Conrad is the best warrior any of us have ever seen, and given the time we've spent on this earth, that's saying something."

"Our powers are seductive, Noah. We can't use them any way we see fit. We're meant to serve a higher power, not carry out our own desires."

"By doing everything I can to stop Aden, I'm serving that higher power!"

"Really? Because bringing back the dead whenever you feel like it seems like you're trying to play God, and if you continue down this self-serving path, you'll fall prey to darkness and corruption, just as Aden did."

"I've protected Noah for years and he's never been seduced by power. His heart and desire to protect the Concilium are pure," Milton said.

"I appreciate your sentiment, Milton, but Noah's actions suggest otherwise. As the caput, I'm tasked with ensuring the safety of everyone around us. Every consiliarius and secundae depends on me to make the hard decisions, decisions no one else wants to make."

"What are you getting at?" Noah asked.

Without saying a word, Everest stepped toward Noah. He thrust his hand against Noah's heart, muttering with fury. In an instant, Noah was on his knees. His body shook violently as the rest of us watched in shock. When Everest backed away, I knew the damage was done.

"What the hell just happened?" Caroline asked. Noah lifted his shirt in response. The red handprint he'd carried on his chest for thousands of years was gone. His powers had been revoked. Her hand flung over her mouth in horror as she bent closer to him. "I'm so sorry, Noah. If I hadn't persuaded you to act against your better judgement . . ."

"It's not your fault."

She stormed at Everest, slapping him across the face. "You asshole! Don't you realize what you've just done?"

Terrick shoved Caroline to the ground, hovering over her with Warrin at his side. Each of them flaunted a small knife, indicating their readiness to strike. I slid in front of her, brandishing the sickle in my right hand. Adrenaline pumped through my body, the sensation more potent than any drug known to man. "Touch her again and I'll slit your throats in front of your precious caput."

"I've been waiting for this fight for a long time, Bourdet," Terrick replied.

"And here I thought you got your fill when I beat you at Everest's apartment." I smiled at the twins, twirling the sickle in my hand. "As if both of you would even be a match for me."

"Stop this!" Everest shouted. "How dare you threaten my secundae? You've overstepped your bounds, Bourdet!"

"I know you regard me as a piece of trash, Everest, but have you even stopped to think about all the lines you've crossed tonight?"

"What are you talking about?"

"If anyone here is guilty of being seduced by power, it's you!" I shouted. "You revoked Noah's powers without blinking an eye. Where was the rest of the Concilium when that decision was made?"

"Such a statement could be considered an act of treason," Warrin said.

"Then why don't we gather the rest of the Concilium and see what their opinion on the matter is? Because I for one am sick and tired of serving that idiotic dictator." I pointed an accusing finger at Everest.

"I knew making you into a secundae was a mistake. Everyone else was blinded by Evey's love for you, but I knew it was a reckless decision. You're too brash with your actions. We'll never be able to control you."

"I didn't know I was supposed to be your puppet."

"You're supposed to protect Evey. Protecting her is the service you provide to the Concilium, but all you ever manage to do is put her in constant danger."

"I've done everything within my power to protect her. If anything, she's been safer since I was brought back."

"Has she? She'd sacrifice her own life to protect you! How does that make her safer?"

"You know I'd never allow that! My commitment to Evey has never wavered."

"And what of your commitment to us, the Concilium? You've disobeyed our orders more times than I can count. We can't lose her to Aden. All our fates are tied to your ability to bring her back to us. How do I know I can trust you with something of this magnitude?" Everest asked. "Loyalty is the foundation on which the Concilium and its secundae were built. Your oath to us is just as important as the one you made to Evey."

"Have I not been loyal?" I asked Everest. "I've honored my oath to the Concilium for over four hundred years. I've been decapitated, stabbed, burned, beaten, and shot. I've paid my debt to you with my own flesh and blood." My fists balled as I stared him down. "Let's face it, Everest, you've never had the stomach for killing and you'll never be able to get Evey and Iola back without me. I'm the only one strong enough to kill Aden." I increased my hold on the sickle and turned to leave. "Just stay here where it's nice and safe. I'll go do what needs to be done."

"Bourdet." I glared at Everest over my shoulder. "Do whatever you must to bring them back."

"Don't I always?" I hustled for the plane, wanting to put as much distance between Everest and myself as possible. I couldn't believe he had the gall to deprive Noah of his powers. After thousands of years of devotion, Noah's faith had been doubted in an instant. The Concilium was still operating like they did in the old days. It was infuriating. If we continued with this kind of ignorant existence, there wouldn't be anything left to save. We had to adapt in order to survive. I paced the length of the plane, waiting for the others to board.

"Did that really just happen?" Caroline asked. "I thought he'd react badly, but that was borderline insanity."

Noah slumped into a seat. "Milton, would you tell Bill we're ready for takeoff?"

"Of course," he replied, bowing before Noah.

"I'm not a consiliarius anymore, so you don't have to treat me with so much reverence."

"I treat you with reverence because I respect you for the man you are, not the consiliarius you were."

"Thanks," Noah replied with a stiff smile.

"Did Everest say anything after I left?"

"Not really. The Concilium is going to hold a trial to decide my fate as a consiliarius. Their ruling will determine whether or not I'll ever get my powers back."

"This is my fault." Caroline sat in the seat beside Noah, draping her arm across his shoulders. "If I hadn't been so stubborn in trying to get you to bring back Conrad, none of this would've happened."

"You were right though. We need Conrad and Milton. There's no way we can get Iola or Evey back without them. Ultimately, I performed the ceremony of my own accord."

"But still, I'm so sorry," she replied, brushing away a stray tear.

"There's nothing you need to apologize for." Noah returned her embrace.

"Bill said we'll be in England by nightfall."

"That's good. Thank you for checking for me."

"Let's get some rest," Caroline suggested. "We'll need all the energy we can get once we land in Manchester."

"But first, there's a bottle of scotch with all our names on it," I said.

"The bottle is in there." Noah pointed at the cabinet I was leaning against. "There should be enough glasses as well. Ice is in the freezer."

I poured each of us a glass and buckled myself into an empty seat to prepare for our ascent into the sky. In less than an hour, all cities and land would fade from view, only to be replaced by an endless expanse of blue. After draining the amber liquid from my glass, I settled in my seat. It was going to be a long night.

19

A LONE
VIOLIN

Night was still in full bloom as the car rolled through a pair of intimidating iron gates. Metal lions formed the barriers, serving as silent protectors for Luke's home. The curving driveway extended well past the gates before coming to a stop in front of a grand mansion. Massive white columns supported the front of the house. It resembled a traditional Southern plantation home.

"So, whatever happened to the gifted violinist?"

"She proved to have an addictive personality."

"What is that supposed to mean?"

"She was innately drawn to things she shouldn't have been."

"Are you referring to yourself?"

"Why so interested in the musician?"

He wouldn't willingly give me more information than he had to, but if I ever wanted to return to the Concilium and Caroline, I needed to learn everything I could about him. "You seem to be privy to the most intimate details of my life. I think it's only fair I be privy to yours."

"Touché."

"Besides, showing you're capable of complex emotions and displaying your humanity would only serve you in your cause."

His car rounded a final loop in the driveway before halting just outside his front door. "And what cause might that be?"

"The one that involves you basking in my light."

"You make my intentions sound terribly selfish."

"Did the violinist provide you with light as well?"

Luke's hands slid down the black material of my seatbelt, releasing the buckle. "She provided what she could," he confessed. "She was beautiful, kind, and passionate. Her love of music was intoxicating as well."

"What was her name?"

"Delphine."

Shifting in my seat, I opened the door. By the time I was ready to stand, Luke was already there, assisting me to my feet. "You've made yourself look like Conrad several times now. Do you enjoy pretending to be him?"

"Pretending to be Conrad is rather enjoyable, and judging by the way you react when presented with his visage, I'd say Aden wishes he could make himself look like Conrad as well," he whispered in my ear. Luke's close proximity caused the hairs on the back of my neck to stand. "He may yet prove to be your new apple."

"That's how you plan to test my resolve?"

"If you give yourself to me right now, I can make all of this go away." As he spoke, his lips caressed the length of my neck before finally coming to a stop at my collarbone.

"You know I can't do that."

"Is everything okay, Evey?" Aden's hands wrapped around my waist, tugging me from Luke's grasp.

"I'm fine."

"I'll have Donovan retrieve our luggage and bring it to our rooms," Aden announced, pressing my back into his chest. "Luke, would you show us to our living arrangements?"

"It would be my pleasure," he replied, planting a soft kiss on the back of my hand.

The malicious tone of their voices informed me that the long drive to Luke's house had done nothing to stop their continuous battle for my affections. "You have a beautiful home," I said, hoping to ease some of the tension surrounding us.

"Thank you, and if there is anything you need during your stay here, please don't hesitate to ask," Luke replied.

"We appreciate your hospitality," Aden said.

The three of us made our way through a set of mahogany double doors only to find ourselves in a grand foyer. A pristine chandelier dangled above us. Light danced off the fragile crystals, illuminating the room. To our right, the foyer opened into a large salon. Delicate sofas littered the room, each facing a central focal point. A single violin stood on a pedestal in the center of the room. When I turned to face Luke, I noticed he was watching me intently.

"Delphine?" I asked.

"She gave it to me as a gift."

"Why?"

"Because we were very much in love."

"Are you capable of love?"

"You'll just have to wait and see." At Luke's words, Aden tightened his hold on me, his hand never leaving my waist as we made our way through Luke's house. "The dining room and kitchen are in the back left area of the main floor. There is also a library and office past the main salon. All of the bedrooms are upstairs." Luke led us through the salon, past Delphine's violin, and up an ornate staircase. "This first room on the right will be yours, Aden," Luke announced, opening the door for him. "Mine is the last door on the right, and you will be staying in this room, Evey."

Luke crossed the hall to show me my bedroom. Deep plum walls surrounded me as I followed him into my room. It seemed Donovan had already brought up my suitcase as it lay open on the bed. I moved to touch the belongings Aden had packed for me. Though this bag was considered to be mine, I owned nothing inside it. "Thank you so much. It's a beautiful room."

"Please make yourselves at home. Would you like something to eat or drink?"

"No, thank you. I'd just like to take a bath and get some rest."

Luke bowed before me. "Of course."

"Are you sure you want to stay by yourself?" Aden asked.

"I'll be fine." I trailed both men to the door, wanting nothing more than to lock them out of my room. "What about Helen and Christopher? They have rooms as well, right?"

"They're in capable hands," Luke answered. "You have nothing to worry about."

He had no idea how much I wished that sentiment were true. "Good night." I shut the door and unpacked my clothes and toiletries before clearing off the bed. My body craved sleep, but my brain needed to unwind. I wandered over to the bathroom and found an impressive tub. Filling it with steaming water, I added a generous amount of bath oil. A basket of fresh rose petals sat on the side of the tub. I grabbed a handful, sprinkling them over the surface. Water warmed my muscles as I submerged myself. The combination of petals and oil made the whole room smell divine, like I was swimming in a sea of flowers. Finally, I was able to enjoy a little solitude. With Aden and Luke engaged in a constant struggle to win my favor, it was nice to have some time to myself. "This is heaven," I whispered, relaxing into the bath.

"I couldn't agree more."

I sat up quickly, hugging my knees to my chest in an attempt to cover myself. "What do you think you're doing in here?" My voice was on the verge of being a scream.

"I must say no one has ever talked to me in such a tone before."

"You will look away, Luke," I demanded. "Don't have me make my request a second time!"

A fire lit behind his hazel eyes. "There she is, there's the queen I've been waiting for."

"Luke!"

"Of course, my queen," he acquiesced. His hand covered his eyes, blocking his sight. "You have my sincerest apologies for startling you."

"I couldn't care less about your apologies. Right now, I'd like you to exit my room in the exact way you came in."

"There's nothing your body possesses I haven't already seen."

"Yes, you've seen a naked woman before, color me not at all surprised."

"I've also seen you," he replied. "You weren't wearing clothes the day you were first created."

"I get it. I was born naked, who isn't? But that doesn't mean my body is an all-you-can-eat buffet."

"If only it were." He uncovered his eyes and proceeded to stare at me.

"Well, it's not. It's my body. I'll choose who can see it and who can't. Guess which category you fall into."

"For now," he replied with a wink.

I grabbed the nearest towel I could find, hastily wrapping it around my naked form, and charged in his direction. "Why are you spying on me while I bathe?"

"What man wouldn't?"

"I demand an answer." I shoved him into the wall, pressing my hands into his chest to keep him in place.

"I wanted to make sure you were comfortable."

"And has what you've seen not satisfied you enough?"

"There is much satisfaction to be had where you're concerned."

"I'm not Delphine," I whispered.

"You're something better." He grabbed my waist and spun me around until I was the one plastered against the wall. "Say the word and I'll get rid of Aden for you. One command from your lips and he could be a distant memory."

"You would do that for me?"

"I'd do anything for you."

"And when you've taken care of Aden, would you allow me to return to the Concilium?" My voice was barely discernable as I breathed my question into Luke's ear. His advice from the car was too valuable to be ignored. If I was in possession of the most influential weapon known to man, why not wield it?

"Probably not," he answered. "But only because I'd want to keep you for myself."

"Evey, are you okay? I thought I heard shouting." Aden rounded the door of the bathroom and halted. He glanced between Luke and me, taking note of my obvious state of undress and our intimate embrace. "What the hell is going on in here?"

"I was just seeing if there was anything I could do to make Evey more comfortable," Luke answered.

"You could start by not interrupting me while I'm taking a bath," I said. "You could also leave."

"In due time, my queen."

"She said to leave," Aden replied. He crossed the tile floors, prying me from Luke's grasp. Then Aden ushered me behind him, blocking my body with his own as we stared at Luke.

"Are you picking a fight?" Luke asked with a wicked smile.

"I'm trying to protect Evey's modesty."

"We both know she has nothing to be modest about."

In an instant, Aden's hand was around Luke's throat. "Make another comment like that about my wife and you will know the meaning of pain!" Aden's grip tightened with each word, but Luke didn't even grimace.

"I was wondering when your darkness would resurface."

"You want to see my darkness?" Aden asked.

"Stop!" I shouted. Hatred harshened the lines of Aden's face, his free hand shaking uncontrollably at his side. If I didn't act fast, a war was sure to ensue. "Would both of you just stop? I'm neither a trophy nor a prize, so both of you can quit these games you're playing." I forced myself between the men, hoping my presence would dissipate their discord. "Luke, thank you for hosting us so graciously, but it has been a long night and I need to rest." Both men relaxed beneath my touch. The last thing I wanted was to be a mediator, but if it would ease the mounting tension between Luke and Aden, I had no other choice. I remembered how Aden had acted subservient to Luke in his own home. If Luke had the ability to instill that kind of fear through a casual conversation, I would hate to witness the extent of his wrath when angered.

"I will let you rest, then," Luke said. He kissed my cheek before slipping out of the bathroom. When I heard the door to my room close, I breathed in a sigh of relief.

"Are you all right?"

"Of course."

"Why was Luke in your room while you were naked?"

"Are you accusing me of something?"

"I want to be sure I can trust you."

His implications were obvious. He foolishly suspected that some kind of romantic or passionate entanglement was developing between Luke and me. "I understand what you're implying, but do you believe I would slip into bed with Luke?"

"You found comfort with another man before."

I grabbed a red nightgown from the closet, sliding it over my head before removing the towel I still had on. "You found comfort in another's arms too," I spat. "I'm not the only guilty party in this room."

"You're right," Aden agreed. He grabbed my waist and forced me to face him. "I'm sorry, but the thought of you and Luke together makes my blood boil." I stared into his eyes. The once brown irises were eclipsed by shadows. Whatever maliciousness had originally conquered Aden was returning, just as Luke had said.

"And have I ever betrayed you as you have me?" When he had taken me, I'd only focused on the warmth radiating from his gaze. But the tortured undercurrent had always been present, whether I wanted to acknowledge it or not. Despite my hopes, Aden wasn't strong enough to defeat the darkness threatening to claim his soul. No matter what I did, he was fighting a losing battle. But didn't I owe it to him to at least try and guide him toward redemption?

"No, but you did give me reason to hope . . ." His words stung like an open wound. I'd sworn to help restore his humanity, but what action had I taken to fulfill my promise? Turning my back to him, I pulled the covers off my bed. I was being a coward. I'd eventually have to take responsibility for my actions, but when I opened my mouth to speak, no sound flowed from my lips. Aden collapsed on the bed beside me. I watched as he rolled over and stared at the ceiling. "I'm exhausted." He yawned.

I laid my hand over his, praying the gesture would comfort him. "I assume you'll be staying in here tonight?"

"Yes," he replied. "I know this kind of sleeping arrangement isn't your preference, but I don't trust Luke around you."

"If you don't trust him, then why did you let me ride in his car?"

"Because it's what you wanted," he answered. The warmth of his skin against my shoulder startled me. "I'm sorry I tried to destroy your necklace. That was wrong of me. I was so upset at the thought of losing you and I snapped. I know that's no excuse, but controlling this terrible thing growing inside me becomes harder with each passing day. I'll never try to take your necklace away again, you have my word."

I twisted on the bed to face him. "Thank you. You can't know what that means to me."

"I believe I may have a vague inclination."

"I have an apology of my own to make," I said, cupping his cheek. "I'm sorry for trying to take my own life."

"Evey, you don't—"

"I do," I replied, cutting him off. "I vowed to help save your soul and then ran away from that promise the first chance I got."

"You were trying to save your family. I understand your love for them; they were my family once too. If anything, your willingness to sacrifice yourself for the ones you love makes me more enamored with you."

My fingertips skimmed along his jawline and down his neck. "It's so peculiar."

"What is?"

"Hundreds of years have passed without us seeing one another, my memory of you was erased, and despite everything, this famil-iarity still exists between us," I whispered. "Part of me is afraid of you, afraid of the things I know you're capable of, and the other part wants nothing more than to remember what we had together."

His breath warmed my lips. "I can show you if you want."

Trepidation and excitement churned together inside my chest. "Am I losing my mind?"

"Maybe you're just regaining it." My mouth opened to his as he kissed me tenderly. The way his arms held my body against his was soothing, and I relaxed into the embrace. "I know I'm only your second choice, but I'll gladly spend my life making up the difference."

I was struck with a pang of guilt upon hearing his words. He knew I would always love Conrad more and there was nothing he could do to change it. "I know," I said, kissing his forehead. "I'll spend mine trying to fix what I've done to you."

"The only thing you've done is give me something worth fighting for."

"Aden—"

"Please don't call me that," he begged. "I don't want to be that man anymore."

"Adam." He was so desperate to become Adam again. How could I deny him this idealistic notion?

"That's who I want to be. I want to be the first man you fell in love with."

"You can be."

He hugged me tighter, burying his face in my hair. "Whenever I have you in my arms, I believe I can be him again."

"Do you want to be good more than anything or do you want me?"

"Aren't the two things one and the same?"

"No," I whispered. "If you had to choose, which would you desire more?"

"You."

I had my answer. He'd always choose me over restoring his humanity. "Why don't we get some sleep?" I tugged the covers over us, adjusting myself as I curled up next to Aden. Dawn was beginning to break through a window on the opposite side of the room.

"Good night, my love."

"Good night, Adam."

Just before surrendering to the lull of sleep, I thought of

Conrad. Aden slept at my side, where he could retain his hold on me, but Conrad only slept beside me when he knew it was what I wanted. We'd spent centuries with one another, and time and again, he sacrificed his own comfort to provide me with mine. At Noah's apartment, Conrad had made his bed on the floor because he didn't want to force things between us. Though I was spending this night in the arms of another man, I couldn't stop myself from silently praying a time would come when I would know his comfort once more.

By the time I woke up, the sun had set for the day. My room was vacant, but someone had draped a black velvet dress across my legs. I slid the garment to the end of the bed before making my way to the bathroom. I showered quickly and had just finished drying my hair when Aden walked in my room.

"Luke has asked us to dine with him this evening. I took the liberty of selecting a dress for you to wear."

"I should've figured Luke would do something like this."

"He isn't used to being around people who aren't under his control."

"The two of you have quite a few things in common to be at odds with one another."

"That seems to be an accurate assessment."

I clutched the towel around my chest. "Would you care to turn around while I change?" He nodded once and turned his back to me. "Does Luke always require formal attire for his dinner parties?"

"I've never dined with him before, but if I had to guess, I'd say it has everything to do with you."

I slid the fabric over my legs, pulling the straps over my arms as I adjusted the gown into place. It hung off my shoulders and fit tight through my waist and thighs. "I was afraid you'd say that." I snuck around Aden to complete the finishing touches on my makeup before heading to dinner. I felt him watching me as I applied a fresh layer of lipstick.

"You're beautiful."

"Doesn't it seem a little ridiculous we're so dressed up for dinner?" Aden was practically wearing a suit and I knew Luke had to be sporting his usual attire.

"It's just how Luke is."

"You'd know better than I would," I replied, sighing. "Do you really expect to have me all to yourself?"

"I'm well aware there are those who seek to whisk you away from me."

"You mean Luke?"

"Of course."

"And what about the Concilium? They won't stop searching for me."

"They fear for their own lives. Who is to say they'll search for you at all?"

"Caroline will. She won't give up, not ever."

"She was your friend in this life?"

"She is my sister." When I emerged from the bathroom, Aden wrapped my hand around his arm, escorting me from my room. "She will come for me."

"For her sake, I hope not."

His comment shook my composure. What will he do to Caroline when she finally finds me? "If you harm her, you'll need another savior," I spat, ripping my arm from his grasp and descending the elaborate staircase.

"Fight me all you want, but we belong together," he replied, following me through the parlor and to the dining room on the other side of Luke's mansion.

"I know you believe that to still be true, but after everything that's happened—"

"We do."

"How do you know?"

"Because of the way you kissed me last night." My feet stopped just short of the dining room. When I turned to regard Aden, he inched closer to me, easing his hands around my waist. "Luke must see us together. If he knows you want to be with me, he'll leave you alone."

"You're sure?"

"There's always a chance I'm wrong, but I promised to protect you and that's exactly what I intend to do."

"Okay," I replied, nodding. Aden's grasp on my waist tightened before we walked down the remainder of the hallway as one. Luke greeted our arrival with a humbling bow and ushered us in the direction of an ornately decorated table. White orchids cascaded from oversized vases while another chandelier dangled above our heads with crystals dripping from its arms like drops of rain. There was no doubt Luke maintained an extravagant lifestyle, even more so than Aden. But what was the point? Was all this opulence meant to impress me?

The two men positioned themselves at each end of the table, engaged in an unending opposition toward one another. Both sets of eyes watched my every move as I took my place to the side. I was the sacrificial lamb, preparing to dine amongst wolves and lions. The black velvet of my gown hung low around my shoulders, making me feel as bare as the day I was born. A warm hand pressed against the base of my spine, stealing my breath away.

"Allow me," Aden said, pulling out my chair to help me sit.

"Thank you," I whispered. He kissed my cheek before returning to his own seat. Although not unexpected, the small gesture of affection was disquietingly reassuring. Would Luke even believe this illusion we had adopted? The sensible portion of my brain ordered me to be wary of him. Was he a friend? Foe? Or some convoluted creation hovering in between? I knew he was powerful, manipulative, seductive, and would only wait so long before taking what he wanted from me. At this point in time, who did I consider to be the lesser of two evils?

"May I offer the two of you some champagne?" Luke asked.

"Are we celebrating something I'm not aware of?"

Luke maneuvered around the room with ease, filling champagne flutes with amber liquid. Bubbles floated to the rim of my glass. "I thought we could toast to the honor of your presence."

"You mean the honor of my captivity." The words slipped from my mouth before I could stop them. So much for keeping up the charade with Aden. I wanted to steal a glance at him but decided to down the contents of my glass instead. A heavy silence presided over the room.

"All that matters is that you're here," Luke replied, smiling.

"To Evey," Aden agreed, finishing his champagne.

"What kind of dinner have you prepared for us this evening?"

"Duck confit with sautéed mushrooms and risotto."

"Sounds delicious," I replied.

"It is, my queen."

Luke placed a silver plate in front of each of us. Our food had been meticulously prepared and presented, and I felt a twinge of guilt at the thought of ruining its beauty by eating it. However, hunger overpowered guilt, and for a few minutes, we were engulfed with silence as the three of us ate.

"This is a superb meal," Aden said. "Thank you for inviting us to dinner."

"It's my pleasure. I rarely have guests, so it's nice to entertain when the opportunity arises."

"Why don't you have more guests?"

Luke fixed his hot gaze on me. Every infinitesimal cell in my body felt as if it were on fire. I reached for my champagne flute, forgetting I'd already emptied its contents. "Allow me," he intoned, refilling my glass. "It's hard to find someone whose company I enjoy. I tend to tire of people rather quickly."

"Oh," I whispered, taking a drink of champagne. I knew Luke's attention was still on me, but the more I focused on that fact, the more unnerved I became. Despite my desires, my mind was over-powered by a vision, and it wasn't one from my past. Luke and I were alone in his dining room. I glanced around, expecting to see Aden, but he was nowhere in sight. Luke approached me like a beast stalking its prey, and before I could utter a single word, he grabbed me by the waist, fixing his mouth on mine. The hard table bit into my spine as he pinned me to it. I wanted to object, wanted to shove him away, but my body wasn't under my control. I was a silent observer in this twisted fantasy.

My hands slipped beneath the jacket of his suit, easing the fabric off his shoulders. He kissed me frantically, his fingers playing with the zipper at the back of my dress. After another minute, I removed his shirt, dropping the crisp garment to the floor. His hands spun me around, finally unfastening my gown. His breath warmed my neck each time his lips met my skin. Velvet slid down my thighs, forming a puddle around my feet. My lips parted, wanting, expecting to speak, but as Luke's mouth found my own once more, I was unable to resist him.

"Evey . . . Evey." The voice uttering my name sounded a million miles away. It was a vague annoyance, much like a bumblebee buzzing in my ear. "Evey!"

This time the voice was loud enough to snap me out of my daze "What?" I asked, panting.

"Are you okay?" Aden asked.

"I'm fine." Heat radiated through my skin as I blushed. "I think I just drank a little too much champagne."

"You do look a little flushed," Luke replied.

When I finally found the nerve to meet his stare, his smile widened. What was his end game? Was the vision meant to entice me, or did he simply want me to taste the true extent of his power? "Well, it does feel warm in here." I pushed my dinner plate away from me, unable to eat another bite.

"I could get you some ice if you'd like to cool down."

I smiled, a witty retort on the tip of my tongue, but my reply never made it past my lips. An ear-piercing scream reverberated throughout the walls of Luke's house. Instinct drove me into action. I grabbed the sharp dinner knife resting on top of my plate and sprinted past Luke and Aden, nearly knocking them over. I skidded out of the dining room just as I heard another shriek. My feet turned left, following the sound. Forcing my way down a short hallway, I made another right. A third scream set my teeth on edge. It was a sound filled with terror and pain, one you could feel in your bones. Flinging open a door, I took the steps two at a time. When I reached the bottom, I was in a dimly lit room.

A young woman lay bound to a table. Her strawberry-blonde hair hung over the edge, dangling in long waves. Donovan loomed above her, a serrated blade pressed to her chest. He pulled the dagger over her flesh with astonishing ease. Blood spilled from the wound, soaking her dress. I collided into his side, knocking him off-balance. We scrambled for a few moments, but when we stood, I was wielding both knives. Dazed, Donovan stepped backward and collided with the wall behind him.

"Help me," the girl cried. She pulled at her restraints, desperate to free herself.

"I won't let them hurt you."

"Evey?"

The woman's gaze met mine for a brief second. She had the most vivid green eyes I'd ever seen. Something about them seemed eerily familiar. *Noah*, I thought, shocked by the striking similarity. She had the exact same eyes as Noah. "I'm here." I sensed Conrad's training rushing back to me, and because of it, I was prepared for Donovan's attack. My foot shoved against his sternum, kicking him square in the chest. He reeled away from me and I took the opportunity to strike again. Stabbing his hand to the wall, I pinned him in place with his own knife. He howled in agony as red liquid coated his arm. When he tried to move, I added the second blade, piercing through his flesh a second time. Aden and Luke rushed down the stairs before I had time to free the woman. "What the hell is going on?"

Luke silently slid into the background, removing himself from the situation. His reaction was the only answer I needed. The bleeding, frightened woman in front of me was being tortured at Aden's request, and if Donovan was slicing open her chest, she had to be a consiliarius.

"I could ask you the same question," Aden replied.

"You will hand her over to me right now!" I shouted. I turned the knife, twisting through the meat of Donovan's hand. His body shuddered with pain. I watched him suffer for a few more seconds before ripping the blades from his palm. He cowered at my feet, cradling his mangled arm.

"And why should I do that?" Aden asked.

"You promised to be better. This is not upholding your promise!"

"My life on this earth is rapidly coming to an end! I'm trying to be better, but I need more time, Evey! I can't change myself overnight."

"This isn't the way."

"How do you know?"

"Because you're better than this! I know there is good in you, and sometimes, doing the right thing requires a sacrifice."

"You want me to risk eternal damnation in the hopes that when I die, I'll be forgiven by God because I spared this woman's life?"

"You told me you'd take yourself out of the equation if need be. I'm just holding you to your word."

"What I need is to get back my life, my wife, and everything else I held dear when I was still a man."

"I'm begging you."

"Why should I release the only chance I have to save my soul?"

"Because I'll give you what you want."

"Is that so?"

"If you let her go and promise not to harm her or another member of the Concilium, I'll stay with you. I won't leave, I won't push you away, and I'll try my very best to love you just like I did all those years ago."

Aden considered my proposal for a minute. "And you'll help me become good again?"

I nodded. "I'll try my best."

"There's one other thing I want before I accept."

"What might that be?"

"I need the seeds."

"Why?" I asked. "I won't allow you to complete the Comedere Cor."

"Those seeds are from the very fruit that instigated the dissolving of our union. The sin that separated us can also join us together once more."

"You seek to bind us to one another?"

He nodded once. "I will leave the Concilium alone, but you must partake in the linking ritual."

"What about my love for Conrad?"

"It will cease to exist once our bond has been unified."

The knives slipped from my hands, the metal clanging against the tile floor. I braced myself against the wall, desperate to stay on my feet. "You can't ask that of me." My lungs burned, demanding air, but I couldn't breathe, couldn't think. Aden wanted me to relinquish the only remaining vestiges of my soulmate. "You've no right to make that demand." Tears began to spill from my eyes.

"Then I cannot agree to your terms."

"Please," I whispered. "Do whatever you want to me, but let me keep my memories of Conrad."

"You'll still have your memories of him."

"It won't be the same. Not if I don't love him anymore."

"You know what I want. You have the power to choose our fates."

"I won't give him up."

"Then you've ordered her death."

"No! Please, Evey! Don't let him do to me what he did to Thea!" the woman cried.

"Donovan, please continue with our harvest."

Guilt surrounded my heart, tightening its grasp like a vise. What was I to do? Do I forfeit innocent lives or renounce my love for Conrad? Either way, I lose. There is no right choice. There is only shame and remorse. "Stop!" I clasped my hands together to keep them from shaking. "You win."

"What?"

"You win," I repeated. "You've stolen everyone I love and everything I have to live for. So please, help yourself to whatever is left of me."

Before I could stop him, Aden took my face in his hands, willing me to look at him. "One day, you will realize everything turned out for the best."

"Whatever you have to tell yourself so you can sleep at night." I jerked out of his embrace, incapable of tolerating his touch for another second.

"The seeds."

"I don't know where they are," I countered.

"Don't toy with me, my love."

"I'm being serious. I don't have them and I can't tell you where they are."

"You always carried them with you. I know you, Evey. I'm not a fool."

20

TIES THAT
BIND

We touched ground in Manchester under a cloak of darkness. We seemed to be functioning in a constant state of exhaustion, but there was still more work to do, and I would see it done. I was the first off the plane, leading our ragtag procession down the narrow set of steps. Bill waited by a black car, conversing with its driver.

"It seems a Mr. Balen has sent his personal chauffeur to drive you to his estate," Bill said, gesturing to the man. The stranger stepped out of the shadows, coming forward to meet us. At first, I thought it was odd an introduction hadn't been made, but as soon as I set eyes on him, I realized one wasn't necessary—Balen had sent Zachariah.

"Thank you, Bill," Noah said, shaking his hand. "I appreciate you flying us out here on such short notice."

"No trouble at all, Mr. Ragnavaldr."

"Would you care to stay nearby? We shouldn't be long."

"Of course. I'll have the plane on standby for whenever you're ready to leave."

"Thank you."

Milton and I each shook Bill's hand, watching as he headed toward a hangar on the opposite side of the tarmac. "It's good to see you, Zachariah," I said, taking his hand.

"You too, Conrad. It's been a long time."

I nodded. "That it has."

Zachariah shook hands with Noah and Milton before setting his sights on Caroline. He stood in front of her, inspecting her like she was a work of art on display at a museum. "Who is this?" Zachariah asked.

"This is Caroline. She is a very close friend of Evey's," Noah explained.

"It's nice to meet you," Caroline said.

Zachariah bowed before her, graciously accepting her hand-shake. "The pleasure is mine," he replied with a smile.

"She's with me." Noah moved behind Caroline, placing his hand on the small of her back.

"Of course." Zachariah smoothed his hand over his blond hair, tying it into a bun at the base of his neck. "We should get going. Balen's waiting for you."

"Have you and Stephen been briefed on the situation?" Milton asked.

"Yes. Everest called Balen. From what I was able to hear, they had quite a heated conversation."

After rounding the trunk, I settled into the passenger seat beside Zachariah while Caroline, Noah, and Milton sat in the back. "Everest is quite talented at heated conversations."

Zachariah laughed. "You'd know better than anyone. In nearly 1200 years, I've never seen him take a shine to anyone like he does you, Conrad."

"What can I say?" I asked. "Everyone just loves me."

"Good thing Balen likes you more than Everest does." Zachariah clapped my shoulder, winking at me from behind the steering wheel. "Balen said you were brought back before the appointed time, Milton."

"That was all my doing," Caroline confessed.

The sleek black car sped through deserted roads, winding through the countryside. I hadn't been to Balen's estate in years, but despite this, I still remembered the bold extravagance of his home. It reminded me of living in the castle with Evey. "How so?" Zachariah asked.

"I convinced Noah to bring Milton back so he could take us to the Book of Adam and Eve. It's the only lead we have to find Evey and Iola."

"That's pretty revolutionary thinking considering it's a matter involving the Concilium."

"We're well aware," Noah spat. "Trust me."

"It's been a long day," I said, trying to ease some of the tension.

"I'm sure it has," Zachariah agreed. "I'm sorry, I didn't mean to cause offense."

"If anyone has caused offense, it's me. Technically speaking, I was the one who got all of us into this mess," Caroline said. "And I can't wait to get back to New York and give Everest a piece of my mind. Believe me, that smug asshole won't know what hit him."

Zachariah gaped at me. Like everyone else, he wasn't used to Caroline's spirit. "Does she speak to Everest like that?"

"Honey, I speak to everyone like this. Everest may be the pretentious man in charge when it comes to the Concilium and its secundae, but his rules don't apply to me. I'm a free agent, so to speak."

"What I want to know is how the combination of you and Conrad didn't cause our caput to drop dead?"

"God only knows the answer to that," Noah answered, unable to keep himself from laughing. "Caroline is certainly revolutionary."

"I think her spirit is exactly what we need," Milton said. "Thea would've liked you a lot."

"I appreciate you saying that."

We arrived at the gate before we could even see the manor. Tall walls of iron barred our entrance. These barricades served one purpose: to ensure security and privacy—something every member of the Concilium valued in spades. Zachariah swiftly typed in the security code and the gates parted, permitting our entrance.

My hands trembled with anticipation. We would soon have the

book in hand and, with it, the location of the Garden of Eden. Somehow, I knew within the very fibers of my being that Evey would be there. Every step we've taken, every battle we've had to fight had led us to this. When we were at Noah's apartment, I'd told Evey I believed above all else Aden wanted to win her back. And what better way to do that than to take her to the first place they met, the first place they fell in love. "We won't be staying long," I said. "We have business to take care of, and as you no doubt know, we're pressed for time."

"I understand," Zachariah replied, pulling the car into a dim garage.

Once he killed the engine, we shuffled into the dark room that housed at least five pristine cars almost identical to the one we'd just climbed out of. The only positive aspect of this part of our journey would be the fact that it was Balen's home we were about to enter. Somehow, I'd managed to earn Balen's respect, much to Everest's chagrin. We followed Zachariah as he led us through a small pantry into an expansive kitchen. Granite and marble seemed to cover every surface of the room, adding to the home's blatant richness. We rounded the oversized island and passed a dining room before finding ourselves in the main hall. The ceiling was at least twenty feet over our heads, suspended in midair by rows of ornately carved columns. I scanned my surroundings, soaking in the beauty of the manor. It was a pristine exemplification of the regency era—a period when beauty and refinement had dominated English society.

The sound of footsteps echoing throughout the hall disrupted my train of thought. Balen and Stephen stood at the entrance to a large study. I rushed forward, accepting Balen's outstretched hand.

"Conrad!" He clapped my shoulder with his free hand. "It's good to see you. Although, I do wish it were under happier circumstances."

"I know just what you mean."

Balen combed through his dark beard, thoughtfully nodding at my reply. "You're here now and will see our light returned to us."

"Upon my life," I agreed, because that's exactly what Evey was to me, to all of us. She was our light. He smiled at me, though the gesture didn't reach his eyes.

Stephen stepped forward, and I returned his hug, thankful to be reunited with another fellow secundae. "It's been too long, Conrad."

"That it has."

"I've been practicing," he said. "And when things return to normal, we will finish our duel."

"You'll never be that good," Zachariah countered.

Stephen shot him a glare. "We shall see." His brown eyes bored into the other man. Though his sharp countenance and shaved head made him appear severe, I knew him to be the exact opposite.

"I'm sure you'll have a thing or two to teach me," I replied, drawing a grin from Stephen.

Once Stephen had greeted the others, Balen stepped forward to shake hands with Noah and Milton before placing his focus on the newest member of our party. "And you must be Caroline."

"That's what they call me." She leaned forward to accept his handshake.

"It's a pleasure to make your acquaintance. I've already heard quite a bit about you."

Zachariah attempted and failed to conceal his amusement, but Caroline took Balen's remark in stride. "You know how Everest is," she said. "Half the time, you gotta spell everything out for him, and the other half, you need to graciously bow like he's the queen of England."

"Evey always did have remarkable taste in people," Balen said, winking at me. "I know you've had a long journey and are pressed for time, but please come in and eat. We'll retrieve the book once you've had a bit of rest."

"Thank you, Balen," Noah replied, following his fellow consiliarius into the open room behind us.

A fire crackled quietly on the far wall, and light from the flames illuminated the gilded carvings adorning the mantle. The etching displayed a lion and a stag locked in a battle of epic proportions. I stopped just inside the interior, my feet unexpectedly feeling as heavy as a pair of cement blocks. The others filtered in around me,

Noah and Caroline sitting on a couch near the hearth and the others claiming armchairs surrounding a circular wooden table. Balen had already taken the time to cover its surface with all different kinds of food and drinks. Noah and Milton dug in, but Caroline took note of my absence. She approached me in a careful manner, gauging my apprehension.

"What's wrong?" she asked after a few moments of silence.

"I don't know," I answered. "Evey is out there somewhere and it feels wrong to rest, especially when we're so close to getting her back."

"I had the same thought when we first arrived, but we need our strength if we're going to defeat Aden. We have to have our wits about us so we can finish this once and for all."

I nodded, knowing she was right.

"I'm not just Evey's friend, I'm yours too." She took my hand in hers, squeezing tight. "Now, let's go work on getting our girl back."

I trailed behind her as she led me to the couch and sat beside me. Balen was right, Evey did have remarkable taste in people, and Caroline was living proof. The affirmation of her sentiment reignited my fervor to complete our mission. I graciously accepted the plate of food she handed me, not recognizing how famished I was until the scent of baked chicken filled my nose.

"I was going over some documents I've kept over the years, and the Book of Adam and Eve is only mentioned in one of the scrolls I acquired after collecting Thea's remaining possessions." Balen unrolled a small piece of papyrus with great care, his fingers nimbly sliding over the document's ancient text.

"No one but the caput was supposed to know of its existence," Milton replied.

"That's what Everest always said as well," Balen said with a nod. "When Thea left us, we thought the book was lost forever, but Everest said you'd hidden it at my estate centuries ago." He looked at all of us before settling his intense gaze on Milton.

"I hid the book on Thea's orders," Milton confessed. "She told me what it contained and how important it was to her, to all of us. The night before she healed Aden, she gave me the book, made me promise to keep it safe, and told me to never reveal its location to anyone."

"Why would she do that?" Stephen asked.

"I'm not sure," Milton replied.

"You don't think she knew what was going to happen, do you?" Though Balen's voice never faltered, I still heard the smallest inkling of despair.

"At first, I didn't want to believe such a thing was possible, but over the years, I've changed my mind. She wasn't frightened the last time I spoke to her . . . She was determined, resolute. Almost like she understood her own destiny and was preparing herself to face it head-on."

Caroline covered her mouth in horror. "She went to Aden knowing what he would do once she healed him? But why?"

"Because she was very much in love with him," I answered.

"Things just got a hell of a lot more interesting," Caroline said.

Noah nodded his head in agreement. "You can say that again."

"What I am curious about is how Christopher knows the location of Eden," Zachariah said.

I washed down the rest of my chicken with a glass of water before answering his question. "My only guess is that Evey was somehow able to remember the right direction to send him in. We know neither she nor Aden can recall the Garden's true location, but when she was Isabella, she sent him in search of Eden. We can only assume he somehow found it."

"At least he doesn't have the seeds," Stephen added.

"Yes, but he can still steal Iola's powers and use that time to find them," Noah whispered.

"Then, let's not stall for another moment," Balen announced. "If the four of you have eaten enough and feel up to it, I think it's time for Milton to lead us to the book."

Noah, Caroline, and Milton looked to me for instruction. I motioned for Milton to stand. "Lead the way."

Milton stood and headed for the hallway. "I hope you have some tools handy, because I stored the book in one of the stone columns in the courtyard surrounding the main entrance."

We tailed him in earnest, bursting through the grand mahogany doors at the end of the hall.

"How did you manage that?" Caroline asked.

"Balen's sprawling estate used to be our home at one point in time." Noah took her hand, leading her down the steps and into the courtyard. "The Concilium used to live here before we were forced to separate."

The moon glowed above our heads like a round disc, slicing through the black sky. Milton rounded the fountain in the center of the courtyard and headed to the right. We passed six arched columns before he came to a stop. "After I learned what Aden did to Thea, I came here to hide the book. Balen, you were conducting renovations at that time, so while everyone else was engrossed in the aftershock of her death, I snuck out here and stored the book. I even sealed it in, making the entire structure appear untouched."

My fingers traced the grooves of the rectangular stone. "This is where the book is hidden?"

Milton nodded. "Upon my honor as a secundae."

"Zachariah, Stephen, run to the gardener's cottage and retrieve everything we'll need to remove that stone," Balen ordered. His secundae shot across the grounds, sprinting through the grass as they continued down the south end of the estate. As we hovered around the column, waiting for the others to return, Balen shifted to stand next to Noah. "Everest informed me of the revocation. I'm sorry."

Noah's shoulders buckled beneath an invisible weight. "I appreciate your sentiment."

"When all of this is over, I'll petition on your behalf to have your powers restored. Your rightful place is alongside your family."

"Do you think he'll return them?" Caroline asked, increasing her hold on Noah's hand.

"With the support of the rest of the Concilium, I believe so."

"Thank you," Noah replied, his voice adopting the faint sound of hope.

Milton and I each placed a hand on Noah's shoulders. "You have our unwavering support," I stated.

"What did I do to deserve such loyalty?" he asked.

"You helped make me into a secundae, and for that, you'll always have my devotion."

Before he could utter a reply, Stephen and Zachariah returned, toting an armful of tools. "Here." Stephen handed Milton a sledge-hammer and chisel. "Let's get that book."

The seven of us worked in a crazed frenzy, chipping away the ancient mortar protecting the book. Chunks of cement flew through the air, spinning to the ground in a cloud of dust. I'd feared tearing out the stone would consume the majority of the night, but less than an hour after the work began, we managed to loosen it. Stephen, Zachariah, and I lifted the enormous block out of its resting place. Milton reached into the gaping hole, pulling out a wooden box identical to the one in which Noah and I had found the sickle.

Once our work was complete, we raced back to the study. I cleared off a section of the table, anxiously waiting for the book to be opened. The cover was comprised of thin stone littered with carved symbols.

"What kind of language is that?" Caroline asked.

"Aramaic," Noah and I answered in unison.

"And do any of us know how to read Aramaic?"

"Balen and I do," Noah replied. His hands slowly ran along the white shale. "The Book of Adam and Eve."

Each consiliarius held one end of the book. "So far, it's mentioned the primums' punishment following the Fall of Man," Balen said. After flipping a few more pages, they found what we'd been looking for. "The Garden of Eden is located on a small island off the coast of Cyprus."

"Now we're off to another part of the world. Really, I never saw that coming," Caroline mumbled under her breath.

I chuckled at her remark and gave her a wink when I caught her eye. "Does the book say anything about reaching the island or finding the Garden's entrance?" I asked.

"There should be a map somewhere in there," Milton replied. "I was never able to decipher the inscription on it, but from what Thea told me, it'll lead us right to the Garden."

"The map shows Maluma, an island off the coast of Cyprus," Noah said.

"That's excellent," I replied. "Call Bill and have the plane readied. We'll fly to Cyprus tonight and purchase a boat to make the rest of the journey."

Caroline, Milton, and I started for the hallway. "Wait!" Noah shouted. "There's more."

"What else could there be?" I asked.

"The bond," Balen whispered.

"What bond?"

"If you wield the sickle in the Garden of Eden and Aden falls to your blade, it will kill him," Balen answered.

"We already knew that."

"But Evey was made from Aden and they are bound to one another," Noah began. "If you kill Aden, Evey will die too —permanently."

A knot formed in the pit of my stomach, eating away at my insides like acid. I felt Caroline's hand grasp my arm as she struggled to stay on her feet. "No, it can't be," she whispered.

I hugged her to my chest, supporting her weight with my own. "That can't be how this ends," I yelled, anger consuming my voice. "Find me another answer."

"I'm telling you what the book says. If you kill Aden with the sickle, then Evey dies too!"

"Then we kill him with something else," Stephen suggested.

Noah shook his head. "It won't matter. He won't stay dead. The primums are meant to be reincarnated. Their revival is cyclical. He'd come back no matter how we killed him."

"We could hold him prisoner," Zachariah countered.

"We'd only be putting the safety of the Concilium at risk. Aden has the power to influence humanity, to lead the masses on a path to darkness," I replied.

"There may be another way!" Balen shouted. "There is no way to sever the bond linking their souls, but it can be transferred."

"How?" I asked.

"To transfer the bond, one must consume the seeds of the first sin and merge their blood with Aden's. Only then will the sacrifice be complete and the link transferred."

I made sure Caroline had a stable footing before I let go of her. "Consider it done."

"Conrad!" she cried. "You can't!"

"It's our only option."

"You aren't thinking clearly," Noah reasoned. "The first time you died, it almost killed Evey. She won't survive without you."

"Then erase her memory of me. You've done it before, you can do it again."

"How can you even suggest that?" Caroline asked. "Is that what you would want if you were her?"

"What I want doesn't matter."

"What about what Evey wants? You can't expect us to deny her true happiness," Balen added. "I promised myself after last time that I would never do that to her again."

"We can't let Aden live," I countered.

"I'll do it." Milton placed his hand on my shoulder. "I'll transfer the bond."

I shook my head. "I won't let you do that. Aden's rage only spiraled out of control when Evey brought me and my family to live in their castle. I'm the reason she was poisoned, the reason she was stolen away from us, and it's time for me to make amends now."

"Conrad," Balen began.

"I already gave my word. I will return our light, upon my life."

21

PENANCE

When I heard a knock at the door, I walked over and opened it slightly to reveal Luke toting a first aid kit. I snagged the box from his hands.

"What?" he asked. "You're not going to invite me to come inside and stay?" The grin twisting the corners of his lips was unmistakable, and his underlying implications were unavoidable.

"My room is pretty full as it is," I replied. "But thank you for this."

"Is there anything else I can assist you with?"

I shook my head. "Not at the moment, but if something should arise, I'll call for you."

To my surprise, he innocently kissed my cheek before disappearing down the hall. I locked the door behind me and turned around, only to be greeted by three sets of eyes.

"I don't think you being so informal with Luke is a good idea," Helen said.

She stood before me with her arms crossed over her chest. This was the first time I'd seen her since I tried to take my life at Aden's house, and her demeanor informed me she wasn't very pleased with me at the moment. Then again, when was she ever?

"Yes, you said as much when I called him to my room earlier and asked him to bring me the first aid kit." I sighed and moved around her, making my way toward Iola.

"Luke is more powerful than any of us can even comprehend," Christopher chimed in. "You're playing with fire."

"When I'm in the mood for commentary from the peanut gallery, I'll ask for it," I spat. "Besides, we're all in the same boat here."

"That doesn't mean I have to agree with you."

"You're the one leading Aden to the one place he's been dying to find for thousands of years. He'd never be able to find the Garden without you."

"He promised not to hurt Iola if I told him where the garden was."

"And you believed him?" I asked, stunned by Christopher's optimism. "Look, we're all Aden's prisoners. I'm just trying to find us an ally."

"And you think Luke is that ally?" Helen asked on the verge of laughter.

"Do you have any better ideas?" I asked. Her lips pursed in frustration and she slumped against the far wall to sit next to Christopher. The beautiful, frightened woman I'd saved in the basement now sat before me on the bed. Blood still oozed from her chest where Donovan had attempted to slice her open. Since then, I'd learned that she was Noah's sister and the consiliarius under Christopher's protection. My heart ached at the sight of her in pain. She rocked back and forth, muttering under her breath. It didn't matter what any of us said, we seemed incapable of breaking her trance. I pressed a peroxide-soaked cotton ball to her chest, cleaning the long gash across her chest. "Iola?" I whispered her name, not wanting to frighten her. I waited, hopeful that I'd be able to break through to her at any minute now. However, despite my efforts, she continued rocking.

"She isn't going to snap out of it," Helen said.

"How do you know that?"

"Iola hasn't been the same since Thea died," Christopher replied, sweeping his long hair from his face. "She was there, you know. Iola saw everything. Thea had hidden her in a closet."

"What?" My eyes grew wide with shock. "Iola watched Aden cut out Thea's heart?"

"She knows better than anyone what Aden has planned for each consiliarius," Christopher said with a nod. "And after what she's been through tonight, I doubt she will ever be able to talk again. Aden frightens her more than anything."

A pang of guilt swallowed my insides as I listened to him. "I'm so sorry," I whispered to her. I finished cleaning the wound, applying small Steri-Strips to help seal the wound. Once I'd placed a gauze bandage over it, I was struck by something Conrad had told me a lifetime ago. He'd said I had the ability to make any secundae or consiliarius feel happier, more joyful. They considered me to be their light. If they all thought as he did, then I was the only one who could eliminate the damage Aden had done.

"What are you doing?" Helen asked as I knelt before Iola.

"Eliminating the darkness." I took Iola's face in my hands, concentrating all my focus on the contact made between her skin and mine. I didn't know what I was doing, but then again, I did. Somehow, I knew I loved this woman and that she was a dear friend. I began to pour all my energy into helping her. If Conrad believed in me, then didn't I owe it to him to believe in myself? Luke had been absolutely correct when he'd referred to Aden and me as the quintessential yin-yang. Aden was a destroyer, a bringer of darkness, and I was light. I was the one able to repair all the damage he left in his wake.

Warmth flooded Iola's skin, flushing her cheeks with color. I knew I was getting through to her, I could feel it deep in my bones. I recalled the love I had for my parents and Conrad and focused on it, realizing I cared deeply for every single member of the Concilium and its secundae. Because when all was said and done, they were my family. Channeling all that love, I pushed it through my hands and into Iola. Slowly, the glazed look in her eyes dissipated, as if her entire being was shifting into focus.

"Evey?" she asked, settling her green eyes on me.

"It's me," I replied, smiling.

Christopher stood from the floor, moving to kneel in front of Iola. "I don't believe it," he mumbled, turning to stare at me in amazement.

"Where am I?" Iola asked.

"Somewhere safe," I answered. "But more specifically, at Luke's house."

"How did we get here?" she asked, directing her question to Christopher.

"I'm not sure," he replied. "The last thing I remember is being at home with you and Farine."

"Where is Farine?"

"I don't know. When I woke up, Donovan took me to Aden's study."

"Aden," she whispered, her eyes wide and full of fear. "What does he want with you?"

Christopher took her hand in his, rubbing her knuckles with his thumbs. We all approached her like she was a wounded doe, like the slightest disturbance would send her bounding for the hills.

"Aden wants me because I know where the Garden of Eden is."

Tears dripped from the corners of her eyes. "Then that means he plans to complete the Comedere Cor."

I moved to sit beside her, wrapping my arm around her shoulder. "Aden has no desire to complete the Comedere Cor. I've made sure of it."

"What do you mean?" Helen asked.

"Originally, he wanted to, but I offered an exchange."

"What kind?" Iola asked.

"Aden won't harm you as long as I promise to let him perform the relinking ceremony, binding us together once more."

"So, when complete, you'll be in love with Aden again?" Christopher asked.

A lump caught in my throat upon hearing his question, and it took me a minute to regain my composure before I could speak. "That's what he told me."

"And what about your love for Conrad?" Helen asked.

"It will cease to exist," I answered, unable to meet her gaze.

To my surprise, Helen was the first one to speak up. "You can't let that happen!"

"What other choice do I have?" I asked, brushing away a stray tear. "I'd rather die than give him up, but Aden isn't giving me much of a choice. If I don't allow him to unify the bond between us, he'll kill Iola."

Iola's body quivered as her tears fell and carved miniscule rivers down her cheeks.

"I'm sorry, Evey," Helen said after a long pause.

"Me too," I whispered. "But it's what I have to do. I won't allow him to hurt any of you—you must know that." I took Helen's hand as she knelt in front of me, and with my other, I held on to Christopher. "Besides, it's what Conrad would do," I added with a weak smile.

The four of us sat that way for a while. Their presence was comforting, and it made my heart ache as I thought of all the ones I'd lost along the way. A small strip of light spilled across the floor as someone opened the door to my room.

"I need Helen and Christopher to come with me. It's time for me to show them back to their rooms," Luke said. I kissed both Helen and Christopher on the cheek, watching as they made their way over to Luke. "I'll make sure they're taken care of."

"Iola stays with me," I ordered.

"Of course."

"You'll make sure he stays in another room tonight?" I asked.

"If that is your heart's desire."

"It is,"

"Then I'll see it done." Luke bowed his head toward me before allowing Helen and Christopher to exit the room.

I helped Iola bathe, watching in silence as the last vestiges of her wound swirled down the drain. I'd seen enough death to last a lifetime. It seemed to follow me everywhere I went, clinging to my heels like a shadow. I tried not to think about the fate awaiting me in the Garden of Eden. I knew what a life without Conrad felt like; I'd known that type of existence for centuries, and it was by no means one I ever wanted to experience again.

A hand brushing my cheek startled me. "You're thinking about him, aren't you?" Iola asked.

"Always."

"I'm so sorry for what my life will cost you."

"It's my sacrifice to make. And your life is more than worth the cost."

My response drew a slight smile from her. "Your heart has always been His greatest gift to this world."

"What do you mean?"

I helped Iola change into one of my nightgowns as I waited for her to answer my question. However, she remained silent until we were both nestled beneath the covers of my bed. "Not all who roam this earth are blessed with the innate ability to love. It's a learned trait," she said. "You were the first woman ever created. You're the embodiment of everything good, something passed to you by the Tree of Knowledge. The only reason we all know what it means to love is because you showed us how."

A huge weight settled across my chest, making it difficult for me to breathe. "I don't know about that."

"I do," she countered. "Thank you, Evey, for all you've done for us and for everything you still are willing to give."

I squeezed her hand in reply, incapable of forming any other response for fear I'd erupt in a fit of tears. She wasn't lying—I still had so much more of myself to give, and Aden would see to it.

With my presence and close proximity, it didn't take long for Iola to drift into a deep slumber. I continued to hold her hand throughout the night, even as sleep eluded me. When the sun finally rose, I hadn't had more than an hour of rest. Dread and despair coiled in the pit of my stomach much like a snake wraps around its prey, squeezing until every sign of life had all but vanished. Aden hadn't confirmed my suspicions, but something in my gut told me I'd soon be on my way to the first home I'd ever known.

I chose a dress made of chiffon in the exact shade of Conrad's eyes. He was the only man to truly possess my heart and soul, and the color would serve as a silent reminder of the one I'd always love above all others. After the bonding ceremony, I would once again be the woman Aden had first met beneath that tree in the Garden. He meant for us to start life anew, to reclaim the relationship we forged in Eden. It probably wasn't his intent, but Aden's plan possessed an undeniable symmetry—The Garden of Eden was the place where my life started and it seemed only fitting it be the place where it ends as well.

The ends of my dress swished against the back of my knees as I paced my room. I wished I had a plan that would allow Helen, Christopher, Iola, and me to escape, but if I didn't give Aden what he wanted, he'd hunt down consiliarius after consiliarius. The sound of my door opening caused me to halt. Luke entered my room, rolling a cart that looked as if it had been swiped from a classy hotel.

"I thought you might want breakfast in your room this morning," he explained, removing the lids from several plates as he presented two stacks of blueberry pancakes and a mound of bacon.

"Thank you," I said, pulling up a seat to the cart. I ate slowly, forcing down bite after bite. Luke leaned against the wall, his gaze drifting to where Iola slept before shifting back to me.

"I didn't just come to bring you breakfast," Luke began. "I also wanted to let you know that you'll be leaving within the hour."

"Leaving for the Garden?" I asked, taking a long drink of water.

"It would seem that way."

"I figured as much."

"You don't have to agree to his terms."

I adjusted my hair to hang over my left shoulder, nervously twisting the long locks out of my way. Helen and Christopher had made a similar argument just last night. "I have no other choice."

"And you don't believe I can provide you with another one?"

"At what cost?" I asked, trying to keep my voice as low as possible. "I have no doubts you would grant me any favor I desire, but what would you ask of me in return?"

"Who says I'd ask for anything in return?"

"Luke, I appreciate the kindness you've shown me, but all this started with Aden and me, and that's the way it'll end. I'm done running and I won't hide from him any longer. There will be no more violence or bloodshed. All I seek now is peace."

"I must say no one has ever thanked me for being kind."

"Perhaps it's time for you to let more people see that side of you."

"Wouldn't that be a sight?" he asked with a wicked grin. "I'll leave the two of you to eat and prepare for your trip. When it's time to leave, I'll be here to collect you." He bowed to me and nodded in Iola's direction before slipping out of my room.

"We're leaving soon?" she asked around a yawn.

I turned to Iola, my focus settling on her emerald eyes. "Yes."

The two of us finished off the remaining food in silence, neither brave enough to bridge the conversational gap. I helped Iola dress and brushed her hair, grateful for such a simple distraction, but almost as soon as I felt the slightest bit of comfort, Luke was knocking at my door. No one spoke a word as Iola and I trailed behind him. His mansion was desolate, almost like it had never been lived in, and as we passed Delphine's violin, I brushed my fingertips over the delicate strings. I knew Luke was watching me, but before his gaze could slide over another inch of my flesh, I spun on my heel and followed Iola outside. Donovan seized her, placing her in the back of one of the black sedans we'd ridden here in. When I passed Luke, he reached for my hand. Across from me, Aden stood just outside the driver's seat of another car. Helen and Christopher were already locked within.

"I wish I could accompany you, but my presence is unwelcome where you're headed."

"I can't say I'm surprised, but thank you for everything you've done for me."

"You are most welcome." He took my hand in his. "If you should ever need me, don't hesitate to call," he said, grinning against my skin as he kissed my knuckles.

"All I have to do is call for you?"

"Yes, and I'll come." I nodded, unsure of what to say. "When this is over, I'll see you again," Luke promised, sliding his fingers up and down the length of my arm.

"I suppose that means you're still intent on making me your queen."

"You and I are bound to one another in deeper and more intimate ways than you could possibly imagine. I know your strengths and your weaknesses, and I can't wait for us to explore every last one of them together." I tried to pull from his grasp, but his hands tightened around me like a vise. "Our time together is far from over, and one day soon, I'll unleash you upon this world."

He led me to the car, assisting me into the back seat. "Is that a promise?" I asked, trying to swallow the unease creeping up my throat.

"It is . . . And I always keep my word."

A breath I didn't even realize I'd been holding spewed from my lips as I absorbed the gravity of his promise. We held each other's stare until he slammed the car door and Donovan stomped on the gas pedal. I turned in my seat, shocked to the core by his ominous declaration. Pressing my hands against the back windshield, I watched Luke until he was nothing more than a speck in the distance.

My heart and head pounded to the beat of an internal drum. I'd barely spoken since we'd left Luke's mansion. My mouth was dry like I'd swallowed a wad of cotton. We boarded a small plane and hurtled toward the sky before I could even comprehend what was happening. Helen, Christopher, and Iola exchanged nervous glances as they stared at me. Perhaps I should've spoken, should've attempted to alleviate the growing tension, but words turned to ash in my mouth. Luke was the one who had exploited my naivety, and it seemed he intended for history to repeat itself.

The sky shifted from bright blue to dusky rose as we crossed a vast ocean. The others slept during our flight, but my mind was incapable of rest. My eyes grew weary as I continued to stare out the window, but this was to be my life now. I was to do whatever Aden wanted, and the sooner I accepted that fact, the easier it would be to let my old life go. Our plane touched ground beneath a shroud of darkness, and Aden and Donovan quickly herded the four of us into another car. I was placed in the front next to Aden as the others settled in behind me.

"Where are we?" I asked.

"Cyprus," Aden replied, his hands maneuvering the steering wheel as we rounded a steep curve in the road.

"Cyprus?"

"Yes."

"And we'll be staying here?"

"No," he replied.

"Our final destination is Maluma," Christopher said from the back seat. "That's where we'll be stopping."

"Maluma?"

"It's an island off the coast of Cyprus. It's where the Garden is hidden," he replied.

"I'm no geography aficionado, but I've never heard of it."

Christopher chuckled. "That's because it's not on any map known to man. I'm not sure if it's cloaked somehow, but you can only find it if you know where it is. Otherwise, it's virtually invisible."

"Then how did you discover it all those years ago?"

"I searched for what I couldn't see," he answered. "Even though I couldn't see the island, I could see changes in the waters around it, discrepancies in the currents of the ocean."

I glanced at him in awe. "That's ingenious."

"You thought so back then too."

"So, we'll be taking a boat to get there?" I asked Aden, switching my attention to him.

"Yes, there is one waiting for us as we speak."

"And what will happen to Helen, Iola, and Christopher once we've finished the bonding ceremony in the Garden?"

"I have three plane tickets ready to fly them to New York. From there, they can each return to their homes. As I promised, I won't hurt any of them."

Iola's face paled as Aden spoke, but her body no longer shook as it had last night. I couldn't imagine the fear flowing through her, to be so close to the person who'd written her nightmares. I reached behind me to give her hand a slight squeeze and met Helen's eye. Fortunately for them, this would all be over soon. Silence saturated the interior of the car as it had the plane. Once again, what was there to say? The six of us pressed onward, continuing our journey like a band of soldiers preparing for an inevitable battle as we drove through the winding streets of Cyprus.

My stomach leapt into my throat as we approached the yacht Aden had reserved. Its white exterior glowed in the breaking dawn. Ironically, the name of the boat was *Penance,* and I couldn't help but wonder if Aden had chosen this particular boat just for that reason. Brushing the ominous sign to the back of my mind, I grabbed both Iola's and Helen's hands. The three of us crossed the ramp together and stepped onto the boat with Christopher behind us.

That was when my tears started. Drops trickled from my eyes like rain. Every limb of my body quivered and I dropped to my knees. Their arms tightened around me as they tried to soothe me, but the attempt was useless. I'd never be the same person I was now. There was no way I'd walk away from this unmarred. The continuous cycle of life and death that Aden and I had been engaged in for thousands of years would end with the surrender of my soul.

"It's okay, Evey. You'll be fine," Helen whispered in my ear. "You're strong, you can overcome anything."

"Not this." I cried. "I'll never be the same. I'll never see my family again."

"You don't know that."

I held her tighter, hoping to glean even a fragment of the strength she possessed. "Yes, I do."

"We love you," Iola added. "All of us."

I buried my face between them, still shaking as my tears dried out. I refused to watch for the end, refused to watch as I walked my own last mile to the Garden of Eden. Helen, Iola, and Christopher surrounded me in a protective cocoon, shielding me from everything. Aden came to my side, but in a true act of compassion, Helen screamed at him until he slunk back into the cabin to steer the vessel. Wind and water sprayed our faces. Salt clutched to the edges of my lips and the heat from the sun caressed my spine as I held on to my family.

Even though my face remained buried in Helen's chest, I could feel the island as we approached. It called out to me, drawing me from her protective embrace. A colossal rock formation rested before us. At first, I thought it was a mountain, but the dipped rim at its pinnacle gave it the appearance of a dormant volcano. I stared at the structure—it was my home, it was the birth of life, and yet, it seemed to be nothing more than a lonely mountain surrounded by an endless sea.

We left the yacht on the beach and I cringed as my feet met the hot sand.

"After all this time, we're finally home," Aden said, taking my hand in his.

I didn't resist as he pulled me up the beach to a worn stone path at the base of the volcano. "I suppose we are," I mumbled, stepping onto the first smooth step as he led our group into the heart of the mountain. Rock surrounded us on all sides as we navigated through the narrow corridor. The sun faded away as we pushed onward. We were submerged in complete darkness for a few steps before spilling out of the passage and into the most glorious light I'd ever known.

"Oh my God," I whispered, awestruck.

"It's just as I remember," Aden breathed in my ear as he planted a soft kiss against my neck. "And I get to see it again with you at my side."

Two gates loomed before us, showcasing our entrance to the Garden. Thick vines swirled and wove together to form a living doorway. The greenery was as intricately formed as the most ornate iron gates. It was the most beautiful thing I'd ever seen. Without saying a word, Aden and I approached the vines together, placing a hand on each side of the Garden's entryway. Dust billowed from the opening between the doors as each side flung open.

Gasps sounded from behind me as we took in the first sight of Eden. Floating through the tall grass, I spun in a circle as I tried to take in every detail all at once. The air smelled of honey, the scent more intoxicating that anything I'd ever known. Roses, lavender, and hibiscus flowers blended together in a harmonious orchestration, each flower like a single note in a grand symphony. To our left, a herd of deer flocked toward a row of towering oak trees.

I wanted to stay and admire the beauty of my home, but when Aden jerked me forward, I had no choice but to follow. I dared a quick glance over my shoulder to make sure Helen and Iola were still behind me. Dread settled in the pit of my stomach. I'd assumed the gasps I'd heard at the opening of the gates were in awe and wonder, but I'd been wrong. My friends were being held in place by souls. Steam rose from their shackled wrists as their flesh sizzled beneath the touch. Iola had tears pouring from her eyes as she winced in pain.

"You promised you wouldn't hurt them!" I shouted, ripping my hand from his grasp.

"They won't be! I'll heal their burns as soon as the ritual is complete."

"I'm doing exactly what you want! There is no need for this!"

"I'm not taking any chances. You will be mine again," he spat. "Come. Now!" The tone of his voice sent a shudder down my spine, so I dared not test his leniency any more than I already had. He was a murderer, and he wouldn't hesitate to kill any one of them if he felt so inclined.

He dragged me over rolling hills and past a small pond I'd seen before in one of my memories until we reached the Tree of Knowledge. The thick trunk was at least half the length of my body. The lush branches twisting together toward the sky were an exact replica of Conrad's sacramentum. For the second time in a matter of days, I felt like the solitary lamb preparing for sacrifice. Blood pounded in my head and my vision blurred as Aden began chanting in a foreign tongue. The faster he spoke, the more my consciousness waned. I wobbled somewhat, fighting to remain upright. The others watched with bated breath as the air around us stilled. Aden was practically convulsing now, reciting his ancient prayer over and over again. My heartbeat raced in time with his words. I continued swaying in place, preparing myself to feel the sting of earth as I collapsed to the ground. But my fall never came. Pain seared across my left palm. Red dripped from my skin as Aden drew the blade over his own hand.

His lips crashed into me, greedily kissing me as his mouth devoured mine. "Remember, everything I've done has been for us, my love." He joined our bloody palms for a moment before turning to slam them against the tree.

I felt nothing at first. The realization was a welcome relief, and a small part of me dared to state what I hoped to be true—that the love I had for Conrad could never be erased, it was unbreakable— but even as I had the thought, something shifted. The pain started in the middle of my spine, radiating outward as it shot down my arm connected to Aden. My body begged for oxygen. I hadn't even realized I'd been holding my breath until my lungs began to burn. Gasping in agony, hot air filled my nostrils as I struggled to breathe. I forced myself to look at Aden, the man who had finally stolen everything away from me.

I'd learned about phantom limb pain from a medical documentary I watched last year. It was a real condition experienced by patients who underwent amputations. Though their limbs were gone, they still felt the presence of the missing arm or leg. I was just like those patients. Their pain and grief were my reality now. I'd loved Conrad for centuries and the loss of something so sacred could never be undone. I would never see Conrad again, and the one thing I still had left of him was now gone. I could recall every moment of time we'd spent together, but it was nothing more than a scar upon my soul.

For the first time since we met on that frigid, snowy night, I was no longer in love with Conrad.

22

BRIEF
CONFESSIONS

Balen sighed, his hand resting on my shoulder. "You know I'd try to talk you out of it if I thought I could change your mind." Deep lines extended from the corners of his eyes, disappearing into his thick black beard.

I nodded. "This is what I have to do. For all of you, for her."

"Despite what you believe, you're more than just a soldier."

"Fighting is all I've ever been good at." I clenched my jaw and my spine straightened even further, solidifying my resolve.

"As much as you wish that were true, it isn't." His hand gave my shoulder another reassuring pat. Balen had been like a father to me ever since I'd been made into a secundae. He was the first consiliarius to support Noah's suggestion of bringing me back, and I'd always be grateful for his unwavering support. I never had many opportunities to make my own father proud, but this was one instance where I could atone for that. I had the chance to make Balen proud of me and I wouldn't waste it.

Milton's approach ended our conversation on the matter. He walked to the corner of the library, head bowed, obviously lost in thought. The sickle rested in his right hand and he twisted it, cutting through the air in a graceful arc.

"Did you want to speak with us?" I asked.

He nodded once, still turning the sickle over. "There's something I neglected to mention earlier when we were discussing the book."

"And what might that be?" Balen asked.

"Thea didn't order me to hide it," Milton confessed, his gaze meeting mine and Balen's for the first time.

I took a step toward him. "What do you mean?"

"She didn't order me to hide the book. I did that all on my own."

"But why?" Balen asked, his hand now on Milton's shoulder.

"Thea did love Aden. Over the years they spent together, she fell for him, but as she did so, she began to change," he said. "Her heart was pure, we all know that, but she wasn't strong enough to resist the temptation."

"The temptation?"

"Aden was slowly driving her toward darkness," I whispered, answering Balen's question.

"It was just small things at first. Something she would say or do that could easily be overlooked or brushed aside, but I knew for sure when she learned Aden had been killed by Conrad," Milton said. "She wanted me to keep the book safe for her and Aden. Thea was aware I loved her, that I would do anything for her, and she thought I'd hide the book for her and Aden to use once she'd resurrected him."

"No," Balen replied, shaking his head. "I don't believe it."

I looked at both men, stunned by Milton's confession. "And what about Iola? She was there when everything happened. She saw what Aden did to Thea."

"I've been analyzing that scenario for the past few centuries. I believe Thea brought her there to help Aden complete the Comedere Cor. I think they planned to use Iola's heart to secure Aden's powers so the two of them could rule together."

"Dear God," Balen muttered.

"But Thea must have had a moment of clarity in her madness,

because we all know she forced Iola to hide herself, which in turn, ended up saving her life."

"She was the best of us. We all looked up to her, admired her."

"But Aden was cursed with the knowledge of everything evil," I added. "And only one of us has ever been able to withstand that type of influence."

"Evey," Balen and Milton whispered in unison.

"Why didn't you tell Everest about Thea's change?"

"I wanted to, but she was good, despite everything that happened at the end. Losing her almost broke the Concilium; I didn't want to add fuel to the fire."

"And why are you telling us now?" Balen asked.

"This weapon is the only thing that can truly kill Aden." Milton held out the sickle, balancing the ancient weapon on the tips of his fingers. "He killed the woman I loved. I took an oath to protect Thea, but I abandoned her when she needed me most. Let me atone for my mistake by being the one bound to Aden."

I exhaled deeply, feeling the rush of air as it passed through my lips. Milton's offer would give me what I wanted most, and the desire to agree to it was more enticing than I could've ever imagined. Every fiber of my being begged me to accept, to take the easy solution, but then I was bombarded with thoughts of what Evey would do if she were in my situation, and I knew what my decision would be. "I'd be lying if I said I didn't want to accept your offer," I began, meeting Milton's eyes. "I'd love nothing more than to be with Evey, but I wouldn't hesitate to sacrifice everyone's safety in order to protect her. You demonstrated true loyalty to the Concilium when you disobeyed Thea's orders and hid the Book of Adam and Eve. By doing so, you've probably saved us all. You have the ability to lead others by example. You're the type of secundae we need surrounding Evey, not me." Milton nodded once, his gaze falling to the floor. When I looked at Balen, his features were masked once again by a grim expression. "Will you take care of her for me when I'm gone?" I held out my hand to Milton, awaiting his answer.

He laid the sickle in my palm, clasping his hands around mine. "It would be my honor."

"In that case, we should gather our things and head to the plane," I replied. "We don't know how much of a lead Aden has on us, but he can't slip through our fingers again."

I stepped past Milton, still clutching the sickle as I made my way back toward the couches on the other side of the library.

"Is everything okay?" Caroline asked as she stood from her perch on the sofa.

"Yeah, but it's time for us to go."

Her fingers twisted the bracelet around her wrist, playing with the silver charm hanging from its center. "We're right behind you."

Milton, Caroline, Noah, and I made our way through the hall and kitchen, heading in the direction of the garage. I could hear Balen, Zachariah, and Stephen close behind us, their steps echoing off the vast ceilings. The insides of my palms were slick with sweat, but I increased my grip on the sickle anyway, my body already preparing to fight for the only woman I'd ever loved.

Our goodbyes with Balen and Stephen were rushed. Quick hugs and well-wishes of luck were uttered in a hurry because we all knew the importance of getting to Maluma as soon as possible. Zachariah drove us back to the airstrip. His sleek car curved around the country roads that led away from Balen's estate. No one was brave enough to break the silence filling the car. Tension built slowly, the palpability of it rising as we neared the plane.

Bill was waiting by the stairs leading up to the plane's cabin by the time we reached the tarmac. Noah shook Zachariah's hand and rushed forward to meet with his pilot. Milton followed behind him, carrying a bag.

"It was nice to meet you," Caroline said when she hugged Zachariah, much to his surprise.

"Likewise."

"And be sure to thank Balen again for his hospitality." She took off after Milton and Noah, only pausing briefly to wave over her shoulder.

"She fits in with us," Zachariah said.

"That she does."

"As secundae, we are driven by our need to protect others."

Zachariah held out his hand for me to shake. "We may not be assigned to her, but all of us would gladly forfeit our lives to ensure Evey's safety."

I shook his hand, smiling. "Aden will be dead soon. It shouldn't have to come to that, but I appreciate your promise. She'll need all of you now more than ever."

His head bowed in response and I spun on my heel, running for the plane. Once the door was fastened shut behind me, I moved to sit next to Milton and buckled my seatbelt with haste. Within a few minutes, we were in the air again.

The sky was still black, but dawn would be breaking in a few hours. Dark circles marred the skin beneath Noah's eyes. Each of us appeared battered and worse for wear. Sleep beckoned as we traveled through the sky, but our bodies only seemed capable of resting in short increments. We each took turns napping and questioning Bill on the amount of time until our arrival in Cyprus. I wondered what Bill's thoughts were on the events of the last day. He'd flown across an ocean on short notice, and he would be navigating over the Mediterranean Sea before long. Whatever Noah was paying him needed to be doubled. Though he didn't realize it, Bill was helping us ensure the protection and preservation of the entire human race.

After more than two hours in the air, stiffness began to seep through my bones. My muscles itched for activity, for a distraction. If I was going to spend a few more hours in here, I needed to do something to keep me from destroying the interior of Noah's plane. Dropping to the floor, I began to hammer out push-ups at a rapid pace.

"What are you doing?" Caroline asked.

"I can't stand to be cooped up for another second when we're this close to finding her."

"And push-ups are going to help you with that?"

"It beats pacing up and down the aisle."

"What about meditation?"

I chuckled. "Meditation?"

"Yeah. Why not?"

"There is only one other activity that could distract me and since my wife isn't here . . ."

At my words, Caroline's cheeks flushed. I didn't believe she could be embarrassed about anything, but to my surprise, she sat before me and turned a very deep shade of red. "Push-ups it is, then," she agreed. She stood, the apples of her cheeks still tinged with pink, and wandered over to where Noah sat. Their heads bent close together, deep in conversation as I heaved my body weight up and down in a steady rhythm. Across from them, Milton poured his nervous energy into sharpening and polishing the blade of every weapon in our arsenal. Metal glinted beneath his grasp, the blade shaking as his hands worked. Whether the movement was from anger or nerves, I couldn't tell. However, I did understand the thoughts plaguing his mind. He sought revenge for the woman he loved. Hadn't I wanted the same thing when I hunted Aden like a wild animal all those centuries ago? I succumbed to every malicious and barbaric inclination that had entered my mind. I felt his dark influence just as Thea had, and like her, I hadn't fought it.

The sound of Caroline's laughter pulled me from my own thoughts. She knew what we could be facing once we arrived in Maluma, and yet, she had this innate ability to lighten everyone's moods. Zachariah had been right; she did fit in with this strange, unconventional family of sorts, and I wondered how she would fare against Aden's power. She was ostentatious—that was obvious—and it was hard to believe anyone could distort her blunt, carefree nature. Noticing my attention, she immediately plucked herself from the seat next to Noah and plopped in front of me.

For a moment her smile faltered, but as soon as I was about to comment on it, she began to count. "Fifty-one, fifty-two, fifty-three," she said, slapping the floor in front of me as I continued my exercises.

"You don't think I can do this and count at the same time?"

Over her shoulder, I noticed Noah stand with a grim expression plastered over every inch of his face and disappear into the cockpit. "I thought you might need some help," she replied with a shrug.

"What's wrong with him?"

"He doesn't want me to go to Maluma." Her eyes turned upward as she clearly avoided my gaze. "He ordered me to stay behind in Cyprus with Bill, as if that were even an option for me."

I stopped, moving to a crouch in front of her. "He does have a point."

"Not you too!"

"Look, I'm not your father, so I won't tell you what to do, but there are people at home who love you and are depending on you to return to them."

"I'm a good fighter! I want to kill him just as much as you do," she countered. "Evil will only triumph if we do nothing to stop it."

"If you're sure you want to fight, then you know I'll support whatever decision you make, but there is something you must do for me once . . . once I'm gone."

"Okay."

I seized Caroline's hand, willing her to comprehend the seriousness of my request. "You must make her understand why I chose this."

"How?" she asked, her voice cracking as she spoke. "What can I possibly say to make her be at peace with the fact she'll never see you again?"

A single tear trickled down the side of my cheek. "Simply tell her that I couldn't live in a world where she didn't exist."

Caroline helped me to my feet, her fingers brushing away my lone tear. "I will," she promised, giving me a quick hug.

The four of us elapsed into a heavy quiet as the plane landed in Cyprus. We traded one mode of transportation for another, dawn coming and going by the time we reached a small marina on the edge of the island. Milton and I carried two bags of weapons to the dock with Caroline in tow. Noah had gone ahead to commandeer us a boat. I prayed he would be successful, though the stack of cash he carried with him would surely work. The sky was a crystal blue and white clouds drifted across the bright sun. Caroline studied the map Noah had copied before we'd left Balen's estate.

"According to this map, Maluma is about seven miles off the coast heading toward Egypt," Caroline announced. "Seven miles isn't that far. If it's that close, I wonder why more people don't know about its existence."

"Eden hides in plain sight," Milton replied. "Thea told me once that you can only find it if you've been there before."

"Then how are we supposed to find it?"

"Look for what we can't see," I answered.

"Right, because that makes complete sense!"

"Actually, it does," Noah said, dangling a set of keys in his hand. "I've procured the yacht at the far end of the dock for our use."

I nodded once and took off for the boat at a run. It only took us a few minutes to load our gear and set off for Maluma. Milton assumed the captain's position while Noah stood beside him with the map. On the front deck, Caroline and I stared into the sea, watching as the sapphire tone morphed into an inky black.

"Friggin' Maluma," she mumbled with a sigh.

"What does that mean?"

"It means that for the first time in my entire life, I'd actually like to go back to Estill Springs." She turned to face me, her back leaning against the rail. "Which seems like utter insanity since all I've ever wanted was to leave it behind, but traveling around the world at this pace is exhausting."

"It is. But this is our last stop and everything will soon come to an end."

"Yeah, I suppose so."

"It will, I promise."

"When my mother gave birth to me, she experienced some complications that prevented her from being able to have another child. I always wanted a sibling, more specifically a brother, so when she told me I was destined to be an only child, I was devastated," she said. "But meeting you and going on this crazy adventure made me realize that maybe I got my wish after all. Maybe that wish just came in the form of an almost six-hundred-year-old soldier of God."

I laughed, shaking my head at her description. "I'm glad I got to know you too. I wish you could've met Cecily; she would've loved you."

"Me too."

I stepped away from the railing, beckoning for Caroline to follow. "Come on, let's get the weapons ready so we can get you back home."

We arranged four stacks of weapons, one for each of us. Caroline was to carry an axe as her main weapon and two knife holsters fitted to each of her legs. I outfitted myself with the sickle across my back and a long dagger down my left thigh. We left two short swords with onyx-engraved handles for Milton to wield and a curved Arabian blade with several smaller knives for Noah. As we worked, the boat glided through the rough waves with grace, but the water became more and more tumultuous the closer we came to reaching the end of our journey.

"Okay, we're at seven miles," Noah shouted from the cabin.

"There's nothing here!" Caroline called back. We scanned the empty sea in front of us, searching in each direction as far as the eye could see. "Maybe we're in the wrong area. I mean, seven miles out can cover a huge amount of water."

"You're sure we're heading in the right direction?" I asked.

"Positive!" Noah slid out of the cabin, joining Caroline and me on the deck. With the map still clutched in his hands, he moved to the bow. "Nothing," he mumbled, switching his focus back to the map.

I stared at the exact spot he had just been studying, my gaze narrowing on the water several yards in front of us. "Wait!" I shouted. "I think I see something."

"What is it?" Noah asked, rushing forward.

"Remember when I said we need to look for what doesn't exist? Look at that spot about fifty yards out," I explained, pointing in the right direction.

"The waves are moving inward, like they're being pulled into an invisible beach!"

"And the current just outside those waves seems to be moving around something quite large," I added.

"Milton, take us about ten yards out from that current and drop the anchor! We'll take the life raft the rest of the way in," Noah ordered.

"Got it!"

Noah folded the map and stuck it inside his waistband. I handed him a holster, so he fastened it and the Arabian blade across his chest. He attached the remaining blades to the underside of each forearm. Then the two of us pulled out the life raft from the yacht's cabin and inflated it. Once we had thrown a couple oars into the interior, Noah and I dropped it into the water. I climbed down into the small dinghy first and turned to help Caroline as Noah and Milton lowered her off the boat. When our two final passengers made it aboard, we each took an oar and paddled furiously toward the mysterious water anomaly.

As we reached the water's changing point, an invisible barrier lifted all around us. Suddenly, a vast mountain of stone loomed before us. Blood coursed through my veins, increasing my heart rate. This was what we'd been looking for, this was Maluma.

"It seems we aren't the only ones here," Noah said, gesturing to a boat that was pulled ashore.

"We need to hurry."

The others nodded at my reply, my words fueling their work. We pulled the raft all the way onto the beach, discarding the paddles inside it.

"What now?" Caroline asked.

"We follow their trail." Footsteps littered the sand, leading to a small stone path at the base of the mountain. I moved through the narrow pathway with ease despite the plunge into darkness. The sun, which had shone overhead as we landed on the shore, was now completely blotted out by the ancient rock surrounding us. With my hands feeling along the jagged crag I moved deeper into the abyss. Labored breathing sounded from behind me as the others matched my pace. The inside of my gut churned with anticipation, and just as the darkness almost became unbearable, the path ended and we were thrust into the brightest light I'd ever seen.

"It's a volcano," Caroline announced, awestruck. "It's a volcano and the Garden of Eden is inside it."

"It's beautiful," Milton whispered.

Two enormous gates made of vines stood ajar. Behind them, rolling hills of green covered everything in sight. Flowers of every shape and color dotted the landscape like a floral sea and birds chirped a joyous melody. The smell of honey filled my senses, a soft breeze driving the glorious scent through the Garden's entrance. Milton was wrong. It wasn't just beautiful—it was a breathtaking blend of every perfect thing ever created.

Withdrawing from our momentary daze, we focused once again on the task at hand and removed our weapons, preparing ourselves for whatever lay behind those gates.

"Wait!" Caroline called out just as I moved to take a step forward.

"What?" I asked.

She ignored my question, rushing to stand in front of Noah. "When Everest took away your powers, he made you completely human, didn't he?"

"Yes."

"That means you can die."

"It does."

"I know we're about to go in there and face who knows what kind of evil, but before we do, there's something I want to tell you," she said.

Noah tightened his hold on his blade. "What is it?"

"In case we die in there, I just want you to know that I love you."

Each of us stared at her, unsure of how to react. I focused my attention on Noah. Fear and shock swirled together, altering his countenance. Whatever he had been expecting her to say, it wasn't a confession of this magnitude. "How can you say something like that to me right before we walk through those gates to face the most important battle of our lives?"

"The fight we are about to face is the whole reason I'm telling you this!" she shouted. "How can you be so enraptured with me one second and pretend like I don't mean a damn thing to you the next? It's bullshit!"

"You wouldn't be saying that if you'd watched someone murder your wife and child before your eyes!" His voice rose to match hers, his face turning red with anger as he spoke.

"You're right," she whispered. "I can't imagine that kind of pain, and I'm so sorry you had to witness such a terrible crime. If there was any way I could change what happened to you, I'd do it in a heartbeat."

"I can't put myself out there like that. We can't all be as brazen as you are."

"You think this is easy for me?" she asked, laughing. "You think I wasn't terrified to confess how much I care about you when I know you don't feel the same way?"

"Then, why tell me? Why say anything at all?"

"Because don't you think it's time you allowed yourself to be happy?"

"I—" Noah began but quickly stopped himself. "What do you want me to say?" I watched as he took a step toward her, reaching out to touch her arm.

"Nothing," she replied. "I just wanted you to know how I feel."

I glanced between the two of them, not sure who I felt sorrier for. I thought Noah had decided not to be influenced by his past, but I was wrong. You'd have to be blind not to see how much he needed Caroline—even Iola had known and she'd only spent a few hours around them. Perhaps some wounds cut too deep to ever heal properly. When Caroline shifted to stand next to me, my arms wrapped around her.

"Are you okay?"

She returned my hug, burying her face in my chest. "I don't know."

"You don't have to go in there and fight. I know you're a part of all this now and you want nothing more than to save Evey, but above everything, she'd want you to be safe."

"She's my sister. Do you think there's anything that could hold her back from fighting to save me?"

"There isn't a force strong enough to prevent her from doing what she wants."

"Then, it's settled, I'm staying to fight."

"Good, but there's still something I must do before we head inside," I replied, turning so I now stood in front of Noah. "Just so you know, I'm only a little sorry about this."

"What are you—" Before he could finish his question, I flung myself forward, punching him in the jaw. The blow knocked him back a few feet, and he cradled his chin gingerly. "What the hell, Conrad?"

I shrugged. "I made her a promise."

"Thanks," Caroline whispered with a weak smile.

"Anytime. Okay, it's time to go in. Caroline and I will take the lead while you and Milton follow." Each of them nodded, confirming that my orders were understood.

"Here goes nothing," Caroline mumbled as the four of us walked through the gigantic gates to face Aden and whatever chaos he might have waiting for us.

23

LOST

Blood dripped from the tips of my fingers as I knelt in the grass. Wave after wave of shock riddled my body.

"You have what you want. It's time to let them go," I cried, the voice sounding foreign and unnatural even to my ears.

"They will be released once we're back on the boat," Aden answered, dropping to his knees in front of me. "Look at me, my love."

He lifted my chin, smiling as my gaze met his dark eyes. He'd wanted to not only reinforce our bond, but also reignite the love we once shared for one another. But no love for him swelled in my heart. The only emotions swirling inside my chest were regret and despair. The revelation that his plan hadn't worked like he wanted would send him over the edge, and I still had Iola, Helen, and Christopher to think about. A satisfied Aden would send them away without a second thought, but an enraged Aden would channel every malevolent and sinister thought into torturing them. My fingertips gently stroked the line of his jaw. "Is this what you wanted?" I asked.

"It is." He held his palm over my own, the cut on his skin already beginning to heal. An indecipherable incantation escaped his lips, and a breath later, my wound was erased.

"Thank you."

His arms slid around my waist, tugging my body to his. "Anything for you." His hands stroked the length of my spine, touching and caressing every inch of me. As he held me, a strangled sob sounded deep in my throat. "What is it?" he asked, yanking me away from him to study my face.

My mind raced, desperate to think of a convincing lie I could feed him. "I just never thought we would be like this again, Adam. After all these years, I finally feel whole," I whispered.

At my words, he beamed, tackling me into the grass as he hovered above me. "I love you."

"I love you too." It was a lie, but Aden responded to it just as I'd hoped. His lips made contact with my face and neck repeatedly before settling on my own. For a long time, he stared at me, content for us to exist in the same space. We lay beneath the tree where I'd committed a simple act that had altered our lives forever. If I hadn't relinquished my reign of self-composure to temptation, we wouldn't be here now. But at the same time, I wouldn't have known Conrad either. Although the all-consuming love I felt for him was gone, I still had my memories of the way he'd made me feel, and that was worth any punishment I may face.

I couldn't tell how long Aden kept me beneath the tree. Whether it was an hour or thirty minutes, it didn't seem to matter much anymore. How could I be concerned with the notion of time when he planned on keeping me by his side for eternity?

"I have to confess that in my darkest times, I had my doubts as to whether or not we could even go back to the way we were before. I knew it was what I wanted, what I needed to defeat this sickness, but it seemed impossible on some days." I accepted Aden's hand and allowed him to pull me to my feet. "After all this time, we're finally as we should be: together."

"I beg to differ." My head snapped in the direction of the voice. It was the voice that had filled the majority of my waking thoughts since Aden had taken me.

Conrad, Caroline, Noah, and Milton stood in front of us,

weapons poised. I wanted to speak, to cry out to them, but my throat closed, sealing my only way to communicate.

"No!" Aden shouted. "You were dead! I saw it."

"Things change."

"But the Concilium, they can't bring you back before it's time. They wouldn't!"

"Well, they can and they did," Conrad spat.

Iola, Helen, and Christopher were still being restrained by the souls to my left, and their flesh burned where they were held in place. I tried to reach for Iola, wanting to clean her cheeks of the fresh tearstains, but Aden's nails dug into my arm, preventing my escape.

"Noah!" Iola shouted.

"Just stay there! I'll get you soon," he ordered.

"You shouldn't make promises you can't keep." Aden dropped to one knee and slammed his hand against the ground hard enough to shatter bone. He muttered another chant, breaking into a sneer as he uttered the last syllable.

I ran to Aden and latched on to his arm, finally able to speak. "Please stop this," I begged.

"If I don't do this, they'll just keep coming for you!"

"You don't have to do anything, you don't have to be like this."

He broke away from my grasp and moved to stand next to Donovan. "Leave Bourdet for me. Kill the rest," Aden commanded.

"As you wish," Donovan replied, pulling out two swords and tossing one to Aden. Donovan pointed the tip of his weapon at Milton before drawing his thumb across his throat. He was singling out his prey, preparing for the kill just as he had done in the warehouse.

I heard their screeches before I could even lay eyes on them. Screams resonated throughout the Garden and grew louder by the second. Twenty souls raced through the grass, singeing the tall blades as it touched their flesh. They moved abnormally fast, wind whipping their charred clothes, and within a few minutes, they surrounded our rescue party.

"That's it?" Conrad asked, a mischievous grin playing across his lips. His eyes roved over each one, counting the newly added bodies. "I would've thought you'd summon more."

"That can be arranged," Aden replied in an even tone.

"Not if you're dead."

For a fraction of a second, I had the strangest sensation of déjà vu. It was almost exactly like the fight in New York; the only difference was that I couldn't allow it to happen this time. I had to do something to stop this carnage before it could even start.

I positioned myself in front of Aden, blocking his path to my friends. "You can stop this!" I shouted. "You can still change."

"Maybe I don't want to!" he yelled.

"Aden, please." I pressed my hand over my mouth, instantly realizing my mistake and wishing I could take back what I'd said.

Shock and then rage distorted his once handsome features. All remaining traces of color leached from his skin as he stared at me. "What did you call me?" His voice was now above a scream. It was a mix of hatred, agony, and pure rage. "Am I Aden now? Am I the man you hate once again?" I tried to slip out of his path, but he grabbed me by the shoulders and shook me so hard I thought my neck would snap in half. "If I can't have you, no one will!" My former husband wanted me to suffer, but I wasn't going to acquiesce to his control anymore. I summoned all my strength and thrust my knee upward. My blow connected with his rib cage just as he was ripped away from me.

In the blink of an eye, Conrad had Aden pinned to the ground. Punches landed on Aden's face in an incessant barrage. A final blow made contact with Aden's nose, snapping the bone. Blood spurted from his face, coating Conrad with crimson spray. Aden tried to throw Conrad off him, but his actions only made it worse. Conrad brandished a deadly-looking sickle in one hand and a long dagger in the other. He plunged the tip of the dagger in Aden's left thigh, eliciting a scream. When he stood, Aden writhed on the earth in agony.

"Are you okay?" he asked, kissing my cheek. "Free the others, I'll take care of him."

I nodded as he shoved the dagger in my hand and motioned toward Aden's captives. The soul restraining Helen saw my approach and jerked on her arms in retaliation. She grimaced at the pressure, struggling against its grasp.

"Duck!" I shouted. At my order, she threw her head back into the soul's face. Black liquid oozed from its mouth, and the soul released her. I tossed the dagger in the air, catching it by the blade. Once she was out of the way, I launched it at the soul. The sharp tip protruded from its eye, more sludge pouring from the wound. The souls that had been guarding Iola and Christopher discarded their charges and sprinted for Helen. She removed the knife from the demon and lunged forward to meet them head-on. I hurried past her, heading toward Iola and Christopher. When I reached them, I grabbed his arm and forced him to face me. "Take Iola and hide somewhere in the Garden. She doesn't need to be around this."

He nodded once and reached for her hand. "Let's go!"

"You'll be okay," I said, smiling at her as the two of them disappeared into the tall grass to my left.

"What now?" Helen asked, cleaning the dagger on her pants.

I scanned the battlefield in front of us, assessing our surroundings. Milton and Donovan circled each other while Noah and Caroline fought through the crowd of souls. Their backs were almost flush together, their weapons glinting in the sunlight as the bodies dropped around them.

"You help Caroline and Noah. I'm going to find Conrad."

"Okay." She gave my arm a quick squeeze before taking off across the grass.

I spun on my heel to face the tree. Aden stood with his back pressed against its trunk. All of his weight rested on his uninjured leg. Conrad was pacing back and forth in front of him.

"Why didn't you just finish me when you had the chance?" Aden panted.

"Because when I kill you, I want you to know it's because I'm better than you. My enemies die on their feet, not by the hands of an executioner!"

"You died in a manner befitting your station!" Aden shouted, spitting on the ground at Conrad's feet.

Conrad twisted the sickle in a circle, beckoning Aden forward.

"After all these years, you're still angry about that?"

"You slept with my wife in our wedding bed!" Aden yelled. "I'm not angry, I'm furious."

"First of all, Evey is my wife," Conrad countered, smiling. "And second, she and I were married for over four hundred years. We've slept in many beds during the last few centuries."

Something in Aden snapped and he lunged at Conrad, sword poised to strike. Their blades met with a deafening crash. All humor had faded from Conrad's face as the two men battled back and forth. I tried to move, but my legs were cemented in place, forcing me to act as a spectator of their fight. Aden's movements began to slow, and it was obvious that Conrad would emerge as the victor. However, in a last-ditch effort, Aden tossed a handful of dirt into Conrad's eyes. He staggered away from his opponent, wiping an arm across his face. Whatever Aden's next move would have been, I'll never know, because my legs sprang into action.

"No!" I screamed, launching myself in front of Conrad. I wouldn't hold him as he died in my arms again. My back pressed into Conrad's chest and I wrapped my arms around him, shielding him with my own body. Aden didn't see me until it was too late. His sword sailed through the air, heading straight for my chest. I braced myself for the inevitable pain, but it never came. Instead, Conrad whipped the sickle past my side and pulled me out of the way. The tip of the sickle pierced Aden's flesh like a knife slicing through hot butter.

His body hit the ground with a sickening thud. Drops of red splattered across Aden's face as he curled protectively around his wound. "Tell her," he wheezed, staring at Conrad.

"Tell me what?"

"She already knows."

Aden laughed at his reply. "No, she doesn't. I'm willing to bet you never told her."

"Told me *what?*" I asked again.

"How he hunted me down and tortured me after I poisoned you," he answered. "You need to realize he's destined to become like me. You'll turn him just as you did me."

"He'll never be like you."

Aden laughed again, but this time, his amusement was cut short by Conrad taking the sickle and embedding it through Aden's left hand, pinning him to the ground. "We've got to help the others," Conrad said. He took my hand and led me to our friends. Noah and Helen fought off the last of the souls as we approached. Caroline tied a bandage to Milton's arm, pieces of Donovan's body lay scattered at their feet.

I ran to Caroline and wrapped my arms around her neck. "I missed you!"

She held on to me so tight it was hard to breathe. "I missed you too."

"Where is Aden?" Milton asked.

"Over there," Conrad replied, pointing to the tree. "He's wounded and has already lost a lot of blood."

"Conrad," Milton began, "just hear me out one last time."

"We've already been through this," Conrad replied. "I'm not changing my mind."

"Changing your mind about what?" Helen asked. She and Noah now stood at my side, staring at Conrad and Milton as their conversation unfolded.

"There isn't much time left. He can bleed out any minute, and I want to say goodbye first," Conrad answered.

"Goodbye?" I asked.

Conrad pulled me into his arms, holding on to me as if for the first and last time. "I know I didn't get a chance to tell you earlier, but hi," he whispered.

"I didn't think I'd ever see you again." I leaned away from him so I could see his beautiful blue eyes. My fingers trembled as I traced the lines of his face.

He grinned. "I came back for you."

"Oh God." I thought my heart couldn't endure any more, but I was wrong. The taste of salt stung my tongue as I cried. "Conrad —" Before I could utter another word, his lips found mine. It was a soft kiss at first, teeming with joy and contentment, but as we continued the embrace, it turned ravenous. Passion pulsed from his mouth to mine, every dream and hope he'd ever had poured into a single demonstration of love.

"You won't agree with what I'm about to do, but it's what has to be done in order to keep you safe." His fingers tangled in my hair as he spoke, the warmth of his body radiating to mine. "Just know that I love you—always have and always will."

He released me and turned to walk away. I glanced at Milton and Noah, hoping for some sort of explanation. "What are you talking about?"

"If I told you, you would try to stop me."

"Wait!" I screamed. "There's something I haven't told you."

I moved to stand in front of him, the others forming a circle around us. I caught Helen's eye. She knew what I needed to say, but how could I possibly tell Conrad that I no longer loved him?

"What is it?" he asked, his palm pressing against my cheek.

I traced the edges of his lips, my confession shattering me from the inside out. "I'm so sorry," I whispered. "There was no other way."

His hands cradled both my cheeks now, concern flooding his crystal blue irises. "What are you trying to tell me?"

"What the hell are you doing?" Aden's shouting broke our focus, and we all spun to look at him. He was still pinned to the ground, but Caroline now loomed over him. Blood seeped from his palm, dotting the earth beneath him. Her hand grasped the sickle, and she shifted her gaze to meet mine.

"The love the two of you share rattles me to my very core. Something that beautiful should be shared with the entire world."

To my right, Conrad began sprinting to where she stood, but he was too late. She shoved the tip of the sickle through her chest, directly above her heart. A scream escaped my lips as I watched her body crumple. Conrad caught her just before she hit the ground, the sickle still sticking grotesquely from her chest. Noah and I ran to them in unison, our hands pressing around her wound.

"Caroline," I cried. I glanced at Noah, his face turning as pale as Caroline's. "Why are you just sitting there? Heal her!"

"I can't!" he shouted.

"Yes, you can!"

"Everest took my powers away."

The entire world was slipping through my fingers and there was nothing I could do about it. "Oh my God." I choked on the words, spewing them from my mouth like they were poison.

Blood gurgled around the blade, coating our hands and drenching her white shirt in crimson. "I still meant what I said earlier," she whispered, staring at Noah. "I do love you, even if you don't love me."

The bright green of her irises faded, death staunching the vibrant color. My best friend and sister died with her eyes wide open, staring at a sky she would never see again.

I ripped the weapon from her flesh and pressed Noah's hand over her wound. Then I furiously began pumping on her chest. I'd never performed CPR in my life, but my body moved of its own accord. I pushed hard, counting all the way to thirty before I blew breath into her lungs. When I finished, my hands resumed their pounding. I worked harder, faster. Like a fool, I believed I could somehow infuse life back into her rapidly cooling corpse. However, the stiff cracking of her ribs stopped my hands and bile rose in my throat at the thought of breaking her body any further.

"No," I screamed. "No, no, no." My body was wracked by hysterical sobs. I tried to catch my breath, tried to pull fresh air into my lungs, but the act was impossible. Strong arms wrapped around me, carrying me away from her. Conrad's voice whispered into my ear. He tried to console me with words of love and comfort as he held me. But his unwavering affection only fueled my cries even more and misery ate away at my soul as I realized my best friend had sacrificed herself for a love that no longer existed.

End Book Two of The Concilium Series

Coming in 2020

THE

FINAL

TEMPTATION

THE *CONCILIUM* SERIES

A.P. WATSON

Book Three of The Concilium Series

ACKNOWLEDGMENTS

I want to start by thanking everyone who took the time to read this book. This series has been such a special part of my life and I am truly grateful so many people have read this series and connected with the characters. I also want to thank my wonderful family who always encourage me to chase after my dreams! Their unwavering support is such a blessing. I also have a fabulous editor, Tamara, who really helped me refine this story and whip it into the best shape possible. Tiffany, this series wouldn't exist without you and I will always be grateful for your love and support. Will, thank you for always celebrating my triumphs with me, I am so thankful to have you cheering for me to succeed. I also want to say a special thank you to my friends and co-workers. Y'all are wonderful and your support truly means the world to me!

OTHER BOOKS BY

A.P. WATSON

Paranormal Romance:

Seeds of Eden (The Concilium Series: Book One)

Contemporary Romance:

I Know Better (By Your Side Series: Book One)

You Deserve Better (By Your Side Series: Book Two)

Not Without You (By Your Side Series: Book Three)

Burning Violet

ABOUT A.P. WATSON

A.P. Watson grew up in the small town of Estill Springs, Tennessee. Living in a rural area allowed her imagination to run wild, and she began making up stories in her head at a young age. Being an avid reader furthered her love for storytelling. Her favorite books to read have almost always been heavily doused in romance, but she continues to enjoy a variety of authors—from Jane Austen and Charlaine Harris to Ayn Rand and Edgar Allan Poe. Finding herself immersed in unfamiliar worlds only inspired her to put pen to paper, and eventually, her love for reading transformed her into a writer.

While her reading preferences have no limits, she tends to write stories in the realms of contemporary and paranormal romance. Her stories are the culmination of her passions, combining her love for art, history, dance, and medicine. As she grows as a writer, A.P. would like to branch out into other genres while maintaining a central romantic theme.

When she isn't reading or writing, A.P. spends the majority of her time dancing. She has been an avid pole dancer for several years and has performed in major cities all over the South. She is constantly enraptured by the athleticism, grace, and beauty of the sport and always looks forward to choreographing her next routine. A.P. has a Bachelor of Science in Nursing from East Tennessee State University, and in 2019, she obtained a Master of Science in Nursing with a Family Nurse Practitioner concentration from the same university. She has worked as a critical care nurse for over eight years and loves to incorporate her medical knowledge and experience into her writing. Her goal as an FNP is to combine her love for aesthetics and skincare by becoming certified to administer Botox and dermal fillers. She currently resides in Johnson City, Tennessee, with her adorable rescue pup, Elle.

FOLLOW ME:

www.apwatsonauthor.com

Facebook: A.P. Watson Author

For giveaways, sneak peeks of cover reveals, and new book material, join my Facebook reader group: Elementary My Dear Watsons

Instagram: @apwatsonauthor
Twitter: @APwatsonauthor

www.ingramcontent.com/pod-product-compliance
Lightning Source LLC
Chambersburg PA
CBHW021304250626
47155CB00002B/373